GATEFATHER

BY ORSON SCOTT CARD
FROM TOM DOHERTY ASSOCIATES

ENDER UNIVERSE

Ender Series
Ender's Game
Ender in Exile
Speaker for the Dead
Xenocide
Children of the Mind

Ender's Shadow Series
Ender's Shadow
Shadow of the Hegemon
Shadow Puppets
Shadow of the Giant
Shadows in Flight

The First Formic War
(with Aaron Johnston)
Earth Unaware
Earth Afire
Earth Awakens

Ender Novellas
A War of Gifts
First Meetings

THE MITHERMAGES
The Lost Gate
The Gate Thief
Gatefather

THE TALES OF ALVIN MAKER
Seventh Son
Red Prophet
Prentice Alvin
Alvin Journeyman
Heartfire
The Crystal City

HOMECOMING
The Memory of Earth
The Call of Earth
The Ships of Earth
Earthfall
Earthborn

WOMEN OF GENESIS
Sarah
Rebekah
Rachel & Leah

THE COLLECTED SHORT FICTION
OF ORSON SCOTT CARD
Maps in a Mirror:
The Short Fiction of Orson Scott Card
Keeper of Dreams

STAND-ALONE FICTION
Invasive Procedures
(with Aaron Johnston)
Empire
Hidden Empire
The Folk of the Fringe
Hart's Hope
Pastwatch: The Redemption of
Christopher Columbus
Saints
Songmaster
Treason
The Worthing Saga
Wyrms
Zanna's Gift

GATEFATHER

A Novel of the Mithermages

ORSON SCOTT CARD

A Tom Doherty Associates Book
NEW YORK

GATEFATHER

A Tor Book
Published by Tom Doherty Associates, LLC
175 Fifth Avenue
New York, NY 10010

www.tor-forge.com

Tor® is a registered trademark of Tom Doherty Associates, LLC.

Library of Congress Cataloging-in-Publication Data

Card, Orson Scott.
    Gatefather : a novel / Orson Scott Card. — First edition.
        p. cm.
    "A Tom Doherty Associates book."
    ISBN 978-0-7653-2659-1 (hardcover)
    ISBN 978-1-4299-5208-8 (e-book)
    1. Magi—Fiction. 2. Families—Fiction. 3. Good and evil—Fiction. I. Title.
    PS3553.A655G39 2015
    813'.54—dc23

                                                                    2015028838

Our books may be purchased in bulk for promotional, educational, or business use.
Please contact your local bookseller or the Macmillan Corporate and Premium
Sales Department at (800) 221-7945, extension 5442, or by e-mail at
MacmillanSpecialMarkets@macmillan.com.

First Edition: October 2015

Printed in the United States of America

0 9 8 7 6 5 4 3 2 1

To Kyle Rankin:
a fellow dreamer
of the greatest dreams,
devoting your life to making them all
come true

GATEFATHER

It was Pat who called the meeting of Danny's friends. "Right after school, in the place," she said to each of them. Then she immediately changed the subject, to forestall questions. Parry McCluer High School was not the place to have this discussion. They couldn't afford to be overheard.

Pat cut her last class of the day, so she was already in the small clearing in the woods overlooking the high school when the others began to arrive. As she expected, they each popped into existence in their regular spot. First Laurette and Sin, because they had last period together. Then Xena, who arrived talking, as if she had used her gate in mid-conversation with somebody else.

Xena caught Pat's glare and glared back. "I was talking to Wheeler," she said, "behind the school with nobody else around. I'm not an idiot."

"Wheeler is," said Laurette.

"Wheeler is what?" asked Wheeler, who arrived wiping his hands on the back of his pants. Pat wondered idly if he had come a few moments after Xena so he'd have a chance to pick his nose and wipe his finger on his clothes. Well, give the boy credit for wanting to do it when nobody was looking.

"Drop it," said Xena. "You're here *now*."

"What about Hal?" asked Pat.

"He's doing some kind of computer experiment thing," said Wheeler. "Might as well start without him."

"Might as well not," said Pat.

"What's this about?" asked Laurette.

"When Hal is here," said Pat.

"So mysterious," said Sin.

"You like mystery," said Xena. "It's like we're living inside *The X-Files*."

"Is this another intervention?" asked Wheeler.

"Do you see a sign?" asked Laurette.

Pat thought back to the time when they forced Danny to tell them the truth about himself by staging an intervention disguised as a birthday party. Only Danny *hadn't* told them. He took their ultimatum—tell us who or what you really are, or we're not friends—and made the wrong choice. They followed him home and it was the Greek Lockfriend, Hermia, who ended up telling them that Danny North was a Norse god, after a fashion. A gatemage, who could create passages through which people could pass instantaneously from one place to another.

Hermia also enlisted them as Danny's servants. She was very cold about it. They weren't Danny's equals, and so the only way to be his friends was to serve his purposes. They had all agreed, though they really had no idea what it meant at the time. At first it was really cool—the amulets he made for them, that brought them to this clearing in the woods; the occasional trips anywhere in the world. The time he enlisted Hal and Wheeler to help him dig out an ancient cave opening in Egypt. The time he had them memorize a proclamation, then gated them to each of the great Families to recite it to them. It felt so much bigger than anything they had ever imagined.

Laurette and Sin immediately got flirty with Danny in a way they had never been before, but it was Xena who quite openly started lobbying to have his baby. Danny rejected her advances, kindly but clearly refusing to father children on anybody. Xena hadn't let go of it—she imagined that because Danny wasn't actually cruel to her, he was secretly in love with her.

Pat saw all this with something halfway between amusement and disgust. The only girl who worried her was the Greek gatemage, Hermia. Because she was a mage like Danny, only weaker—she couldn't actually make gates, only find them and open and close them—he spent a lot of time with her. But Pat saw something about Hermia that Danny couldn't see—that she was using him, that she could not be trusted. Hermia didn't show any close bond to him. She wasn't *his*.

And when Pat went to his house late one night to warn him about Hermia, something happened. Pat ended up confessing to him something she hadn't realized until that moment: that she herself was in love with him—the only one of the girls who really *was*. And Danny responded by kissing her and telling her that he loved her in return. It was so overwhelming, emotionally, that if he had wanted to, she would have made love to him then and there.

But Danny refused. He wouldn't do it. He wasn't going to have sex with anybody until he actually made a lifelong commitment and married someone. Period. No exceptions, not even for true love.

After she left, Pat was stunned and humiliated by her own audacity in going to his little two-room house, alone, and practically throwing herself at him. She felt as stupid and obvious as Xena.

Except that Danny had *wanted* her. He *loved* her. So there was nothing to feel stupid about. That mantra kept her going.

Then Danny took them through a Great Gate to the world of Westil. He had been forced into making the Great Gate by Hermia's betrayal, and the purpose was to take the Mithermage Families through the Great Gate to Westil and then bring them all back to Earth, to Mittlegard. Passage through a Great Gate also brought mages to the peak of their powers. Danny had hoped that if any of his nonmagical drowther friends from Parry McCluer High had latent magical abilities, they would emerge after that passage.

None of the others reported having any changes in them. But that didn't prove anything, because a new power *had* emerged in Pat, and she hadn't told anybody. Though it was hard to imagine any of the others keeping something like that secret. Maybe Hal. But the others would blab or brag or be so scared they would have to talk to *somebody*.

Pat had no such need. She recognized what was going on the moment she felt the air of Westil moving against her skin. Then, moments later, when she returned to Earth, the same feeling was there. It wasn't *Westil's* air that mattered to her after passing through a Great Gate—it was air. Air in motion. Air with power.

She had always loved the wind, from breezes to gales. She was not surprised that this turned out to be her affinity, and she began to be able to spin little whirlwinds, to raise a breeze, even a wind. A few times, walking alone down a steep hill, she had created a wind that lifted her off her feet and carried her several yards in whatever direction she chose.

I can fly, she had thought. Yet she told no one, not even Danny.

She *meant* to, but it never came up. And she was afraid he'd see what she could do and say, Is that all?

No, Danny would never show disappointment. He'd be very encouraging. But she'd see in his eyes that he was *not* impressed.

So she held off, working on her windmagery privately so she'd have something worth showing when she finally told him.

But today something happened that made her own pathetic magery seem utterly unimportant. Because Pat had reason to believe that Danny was in grave danger.

No. Not *danger*. She had reason to believe that the worst thing had already happened to him.

"So what is this meeting about, Pat?" asked Hal.

He must have arrived while she was in her reverie.

"I don't think this meeting should take place here," said Pat.

Everyone seemed exasperated. "Then why did you bring us here?" demanded Wheeler.

"Because this is where the emergency escape gate is," said Pat. "What I tell you about, I want to say in front of Danny's friend in DC. Stone."

"Why?" asked Hal. "We don't even know him."

"But Danny does. And Stone knows about magery. He can tell us what to do, and what not to do."

"About *what*?" demanded Sin. "You're being so bossy and creepy."

"About Danny," said Pat.

She couldn't watch everyone at once, but it seemed to her that all the other girls flinched or stiffened or looked away when she spoke of doing something about Danny.

Pat rose to her feet and walked to the tree that held the small gate leading to DC. She touched the spot under the tree limb and just like that, with no physical sensation but the change of air, she was in a dark attic room.

By the light slanting through the shutters of the east-facing cupola window, she saw the low table with a stack of pennies on it. They were the arsenal Danny had created; each penny had gates on either side. If they arrived with an enemy in pursuit, they were to handle the pennies by the edge only, and throw them at the pursuer. The gate would hurtle their enemy to some far-off, awkward location, almost all of them with police or military close by.

But her pursuers this time were her friends, and she stepped away from the gate so they could come through without bumping her out of the way. Danny had told them about a time when he gated himself into a space occupied by Coach Lieder's hand, shattering the bones of his fingers into slivers inside little bags of flesh. Pat didn't want that to happen to her whole body.

She glanced over only long enough to see that it was Laurette who had come right after her. "Move out of the way of the gate," said Pat, "and keep the others up here. I'm going to find Stone."

"Can I turn on a light?" asked Laurette.

Pat was already out the door and heading down the stairs.

She found Stone in the kitchen, talking earnestly with two men in suits. For a moment Pat thought: We're betrayed, he's talking to the enemy. But then she realized that whatever enemy she was thinking of was not all that likely to be wearing suits, and there were a thousand perfectly honorable reasons Stone might be having such a conversation.

"Good to see you," said Stone cheerfully. He turned to the men. "I'm so sorry, but I do believe our time is up. I have to deal with some of my guests."

"What are you running here, a hotel?" asked one of the men, pretending it was a joke.

"A hospitable home," said Stone with a smile. "You'll see, someday."

"I hope not," said the other man. "He makes a terrible houseguest."

Stone took Pat firmly by the hand and led her out of the kitchen and up the stairs. He bounded upward with surprising speed and agility, for someone who looked to be middle-aged. But then, he had passed through a Great Gate too. He was in perfect health.

After the third-floor landing, he spoke to her softly. "What kind of mage are you?" he asked.

"Mage?" she replied.

"Whatever you've got," said Stone, "it's strong. Scary strong. I thought Danny's friends were all drowthers."

"That's why he passed us through the gate in Maine ahead of everyone else," said Pat. "Nobody knows about me."

"I'll keep your secret." Then he hesitated a moment. "Wind, I'm betting."

"You win," said Pat.

"How many of you are coming? Anyone in pursuit?"

"All of us," said Pat, "and no."

"Why are you here, then?" asked Stone. "If this is just a field trip to the nation's capital, I'm not in favor of it. There are buses and trains."

"There's something wrong with Danny, and I want you to hear about it along with the others."

Stone didn't ask any more questions. Most adults would have demanded that she tell more, right then. But he actually heard her request that he hear her story along with the others. He respected her decision and complied with her plan, undoubting. What other adult did *that*?

They were all sitting on the cot or the rickety old chairs, except Sin, who sat on the floor. "Hello, Mr. Stone," said Laurette.

"Not 'mister,'" said Stone. "Just 'Stone.'"

"My mother would kill me," said Laurette. "I was raised with manners."

"An admirable skill, manners," said Stone. He gently pushed Wheeler off the firmest chair and sat on it himself. So his respect for teenagers didn't extend to everybody. Maybe it only extended to fellow mages.

Wheeler didn't protest. He just sat on the floor and gathered his legs and arms into a position that Pat knew would leave him aching in only a few minutes.

But it was her meeting, and it was time to start. "Danny's changed," said Pat. "And it's enough of a change that I'm afraid he might already have been possessed by Set. By the Belgod."

Everyone became attentive.

"It's going to sound stupid and vain," said Pat, "but I think it's important."

"Instead of discussing the merits of 'it,'" said Stone, "please just tell us, straight out, what 'it' is."

Pat realized that Stone was right, she was talking around her observation because there was so much potential for embarrassment. But embarrassment didn't matter if Danny was in danger. "Every one of us girls made a play for Danny," she said, though she loathed comparing what *she* had done with the way the others had flirted and teased. "And he turned us all down."

"Hard to understand," said Stone. Pat wondered if any of the others knew he was being ironic.

"It's just a fact," said Pat. "He told us all he was interested, he liked girls, but he wasn't going to make any bastards or be the kind of god who went around having sex with . . . drowthers."

Stone nodded. "That was a wise policy, and I'm not surprised Danny had the strength to stick to it."

"Not surprised because you don't think we're all that attractive?" asked Xena, her ear always attuned to the possibility that she had been insulted.

"Stick to the point, Xena," said Pat.

"I don't know the point, you haven't told us," said Xena.

"The point is this. Nicki Lieder—the coach's daughter—she came to me this morning during lunch and told me, very quietly, that she was pregnant, and Danny was the only possible father."

"That little mouse?" said Laurette disdainfully.

"Mouse?" said Hal. "Have you *seen* her since she came back to school?"

"What does she have that we don't have?" said Xena.

Wheeler looked as if he wouldn't mind making a list for her, so Pat forestalled him. "That's my point," said Pat. "Why would he sleep with her, but not us?"

"She raped him," said Hal.

"Ha ha," said Sin.

"She told *me*," said Pat, "because he wasn't in school today and she needed to tell him about the pregnancy. She's going to tell her father this afternoon."

"Coach Lieder's going to kill Danny," said Hal.

"Not likely," said Stone.

"She wanted to give Danny a heads-up," said Pat. "Because she reported the encounter to the police the morning after it happened. She reported it as a rape."

"She accused Danny?" asked Xena.

"No," said Pat. "She didn't name names, she said she didn't see his face and couldn't even say what race he was, or how tall or anything. She said she didn't know her assailant."

"Oh, good," said Sin. "So I won't have to kill her."

"The point is that Danny's DNA is out there as a rapist," said

Pat. "I don't imagine Danny's DNA is in any database, but if he's arrested for something else . . ."

"Gross," said Laurette. "He left it in her."

"I thought when you reported rape, they, like, took care of it," said Xena. "The pregnancy."

"She didn't let them," said Pat. "She told them she had a religious objection to anything like abortion."

"She wanted his baby," said Xena.

"So did you," pointed out Wheeler.

"But I wouldn't have pretended he raped me," said Xena.

"No, you would have bragged it was him," said Hal. "She reported it as rape so that if she got pregnant, she could give the police report to her father and he wouldn't pester her to find out who the father is."

"Smart girl," said Stone. "She was protecting Danny."

"I haven't told you the important part yet," said Pat.

They fell silent again.

"Nicki said that it happened at Danny's house. She went there in the middle of the night. It was the same night after he made the gate in . . . that place. Remember how tired he was?"

"No," said Laurette, "which makes me think *you* were over there pestering him the same night."

"Well, you'd be correct," said Pat.

The other girls made a show of being shocked.

Pat looked Stone straight in the eyes. "Danny and I are in love," she told him. "I wanted to spend the night with him. To move in with him if I could. He said—and demonstrated—how willing he was. Eager. But he still wouldn't do it. For the same reason as always. He said he wasn't going to be a typical god."

"That's how he turned us all down," said Xena.

"But that same night, Nicki says she walked there at two a.m. and just opened his door and went in and there he was, mostly undressed, lying on top of his bed, and . . . she said he was ready for her. Sexually." Pat blushed, knowing why Danny was in that state, and then hated herself for blushing, and blushed all the more because of that. Thank heaven the attic was so dark.

"So she was, like, a succubus," said Wheeler.

"You don't get pregnant from that," said Xena.

"A succubus is a female demon that comes and has sex with you in the night," said Hal. "According to ancient lore. The male equivalent is 'incubus.'"

"Sounds like a medieval attempt to explain wet dreams," said Wheeler.

"And single girls' babies," said Hal.

"Well, she wasn't mythical," said Pat. "She undressed him the rest of the way and she was all over him before he even woke up."

"How much did she *tell* you?" asked Stone. "Was she trying to cause you pain?"

"No," said Pat. "She was apologizing. She was explaining. Because it wasn't really her."

They all looked at her blankly.

"OK, then why is *she* pregnant?" asked Laurette.

Stone knew. He was looking at the floor instead of at her.

"It wasn't her making the decisions," said Pat. "That's the whole reason we're having this meeting. Nicki has never heard Danny talk about the Belgod and how he possesses people, and how he can jump from one person to another and live forever and all that. But what she tells me, out of the blue, is that *she* was controlled, her *body* was controlled by something else. It would sometimes talk to her, using her own voice. And it would make her do things, strange things, stupid things. Then let her have control of her body for hours. Then make her do something bizarre again."

"Wheeler does that and *he* isn't possessed," said Xena.

Stone impatiently held up a hand to signal Xena to stop talking.

"Then right at the moment when Danny . . . got her pregnant . . ."

"Orgasmed. Ejaculated," said Laurette. "Come on, we all had sex education."

Pat shuddered, as she had when Nicki told her. "The thing left her body and went into his. Then it used *his* voice to talk to her. But no, I'm telling it out of order. Just before the . . . transfer . . . it used *her* mouth to say to *him*, 'You want me inside you.'"

"And he said yes," whispered Stone. His face looked like a portrait of despair.

"Yes," said Pat. "Only she told me it made no sense, because she wasn't inside *him*, it was the other way around. It only makes sense if you think of it as the Belgod asking Danny to let him in. To invite him."

"And he did," said Stone.

"So this is true?" asked Hal. "Because I was thinking it was all just a lie Nicki told to explain being pregnant."

"It might be exactly that," said Stone, "but then she certainly knows a lot of details that she shouldn't know."

"That's what I thought," said Pat. "That's why I thought this was important. Because ever since that night, Danny's been different. Not himself."

"In what way?" asked Stone. He was asking Pat, but looking at each of the other kids in turn, as if for confirmation.

"He came on to me," said Pat. "Which would have been fine, only he was weird about it. Came up behind me and cupped my butt with his hand. Right by my locker, with people around."

"Who cares?" said Xena. "I thought you two were in love."

"We are," said Pat. "*Were*, anyway. But he knows I don't like people to just . . . touch me. Out of the blue. He *knows* that. And the way he talked. He called me 'baby girl.' Guys who talk like that make me sick."

"Me too," said Wheeler.

Stone was nodding, though. "Not Danny's style."

"Danny knows better than to treat me like that, talk to me like that. He was crude. Like the only thing on his mind was sex. Like he thought he owned me. Like I see other guys act with girls, and they get all fluttery, but not me, and Danny knows that. Knew that."

"What did you do?" asked Stone.

"Pulled away from him," said Pat. "And told him it wasn't happening. He kept trying for a minute, and then he gives me a little shove and a tiny slap on the cheek and says, 'Your loss, baby girl,' and that was it. Walked away."

Laurette sighed. "You told him no? What else is he going to do?"

"Danny wouldn't have asked. Not that way. Not like he had the *right*. It wasn't Danny, and you all know it."

"What's your name?" Stone asked Pat. She told him.

"Pat," he said, "you did right. Not to tell him what you were thinking."

"I didn't know what the Belmage would do, if he was really in possession of Danny, and I told him I knew he was there."

"Good thinking," said Stone. "What about the rest of you? Anybody else notice a change?"

"Yes," said Hal. "He hardly talks to me and Wheeler anymore. Walks along the corridor at school smiling at people and saying hi to them."

"He's friendly," said Laurette.

"Especially girls," said Wheeler.

"I didn't notice that it was especially girls," said Hal.

"But it was."

"I'm not arguing," said Hal, "I'm just saying what *I* saw. It's like we could hang around if we wanted, but Danny didn't care, and maybe he was even a little annoyed to have us there."

"Maybe?" said Wheeler. "What about when he told us to get lost while he talked to Rosann?"

"Rosann?" asked Hal.

"You know, Rosann the queen of the universe—"

"I know who Rosann is," said Hal. "I just don't remember Danny talking to her and—"

"Oh, right," said Wheeler. "It was after lunch and you had already peeled off to go to—"

Stone interrupted them. "Has anybody seen Danny use a gate?"

"Like, constantly," said Xena.

"That's just not true," said Pat. "He hardly ever uses gates these days. He's trying *not* to clutter up the world with gates, remember?"

"I mean specifically *since* he took you through the Great Gate to Westil," said Stone. "It's been more than a month. In that time, has he ever?"

They were silent.

"This is kind of impossible," said Sin. "How can we remember what *didn't* happen since a certain day?"

"Since we went through a gate to another planet?" said Pat. "No, Stone, I haven't seen him use a gate since then. Not even to come up to our place."

"Place?" asked Stone.

"Where the emergency gate is," said Wheeler.

"Any of the rest of you seen him use a gate since then?" asked Stone.

Nobody could remember it if he did.

"The reason I'm asking is, a Gatefather like Danny knows when people pass through his gates. He can feel it. So when you all gathered at your *place* and then all came here, he would know that."

Pat understood. "Why isn't he here?"

"Exactly," said Stone. "All his friends are having a meeting, using his gates to get there. A meeting with me. Shouldn't he be curious? And if he's curious, why not come find out what's going on?"

"So you're saying the Belmage is keeping him from coming?" asked Xena.

"The Belmage would be even *more* curious why we're gathered here," said Stone. "Hard to think why he wouldn't come to see if we pose some kind of danger to him."

"So it's a good thing that Danny isn't here?"

"Maybe," said Stone. "I mean, he might also just be busy or he might respect your privacy. All kinds of reasons. But it might also mean that somehow Danny is keeping the Belmage from getting access to his gates."

"I thought when the Belmage gets you, you're, like, *gotten*," said Sin. "Possessed. Owned."

"Exactly," said Stone. "So if Danny found a way to keep the Belmage away from his gates—"

"Then he's beating the devil," said Wheeler. "Cool."

"Semi-cool," said Stone. "It's excellent because otherwise, the Belmage could just whip up a new Great Gate and go to Westil and that's it, he takes all his followers, the Sutahites, and Westil is lost. They won't even know what hit them."

"And we do?" said Laurette.

"The human race at least knows what possession *is*," said Stone. "Or movies like *The Exorcist* would never have been made."

"So does that work?" asked Wheeler. "Exorcism? Do we need to find a priest and—"

"No," said Stone.

"But how do you know that?" asked Wheeler. "Maybe *some* exorcists actually know what they're doing, like Buffy the Vampire Slayer, only with demons."

"Shut up, Wheeler," said Hal.

"If exorcism never works, then why are there exorcists?" asked Wheeler.

"Bleeding never worked and yet doctors carried leeches around for centuries," said Hal. "And Stone knows."

"Thank you," said Stone. "Exorcism might work or it might not, against the lesser Belmages, the Sutahites. But we're talking about *the* Belmage. Set himself. And there's only one way to get him out of a person if he doesn't want to go."

"So whatever it is, let's do it," said Wheeler.

"Let's not," said Pat.

"If Danny's being controlled by this Belmage guy, I'm pretty sure he wants him gone," said Wheeler.

"Wheeler," said Sin, "get a brain. The only way to get rid of this Set guy is to kill the host."

"Stone?" asked Wheeler.

"Not the host of this party—which doesn't even have refreshments," said Xena. "The host *body* where the Belmage is living."

"We're not killing Danny," said Laurette.

"Danny told us more than once," said Stone, "that if he was ever possessed, we should kill him without a qualm, if that's what it took to stop Set from using a Great Gate."

"Never," said Hal.

"So you'd leave him a slave forever?" asked Laurette.

"It's about saving the world," said Pat.

"I thought you said you loved him," said Xena.

"*If* it was necessary," said Stone, "then we couldn't do it anyway. Gatemages are hard to kill, and Gatefathers are the hardest. They don't stay put long enough to die."

"In his sleep?" asked Hal. "I mean, if Nicki could get his clothes off without—"

"Danny was undoubtedly under the influence of Sutahites,"

said Stone. "They can influence dreams. Make dreams that explain what's happening to your body. So *if* somebody slipped Danny a drug, maybe he could be killed in his sleep. But you're not thinking. We only *need* to kill Danny to save the world. The *worlds*. But if Danny is somehow keeping the Belmage from getting access to his gates, that means he'd be *easy* to kill, but we also don't need to, because the Belmage isn't dangerous."

"So let's stop talking about killing Danny, please," said Pat.

"No," said Stone. "Because if Danny's keeping Set away from the gates, then Set is seriously angry. He's not nice, you know. He didn't get a reputation as Satan or the devil or whatever because he was generous and merciful."

"You think he's going to punish Danny?" asked Pat.

"How?" asked Hal. "He's inside Danny's body, too. Whatever happens to Danny, happens to him."

"Until he leaves," said Stone.

"So he could, like, make Danny cut his own throat," said Wheeler, "and while he's bleeding to death, the Belmage leaves and goes into somebody else's body?"

"When Set leaves Danny," said Stone, "he's not going to be nice about it. He's going to cause Danny maximum pain, if he's angry at him. But you're right about Set feeling whatever Danny's body feels. So he's likely to do something much worse than just killing Danny."

"What's worse than that?" asked Wheeler.

Stone made a sweeping gesture, indicating all of Danny's friends.

"Oh, shit," said Hal.

"Exactly my point," said Stone.

"What?" said Xena. "What did you all get that I'm not getting?"

"Pretty much everything all the time," said Hal. "Let's say the Belmage wants to punish Danny. So he makes Danny murder one of us in a public place, lots of witnesses, and then jumps out of Danny's body into somebody else's and goes on his merry way."

"They couldn't *arrest* Danny," said Wheeler. "He could gate away."

"But the one of us that he killed would still be dead," said Hal.

"It would probably be Pat," said Stone. "And he'd probably make Danny do it with his bare hands. Danny would have an indelible memory of doing that murder. So yes, that's a possibility. But he could also cause Danny to cut off a hand. I'm not sure passing through a gate can heal damage like that. Or make Danny a mass murderer, like shooting up a kindergarten. Or all of the above. Don't underestimate the creativity and malice of pure evil."

"So we should stay away from Danny?" asked Xena.

"I don't know what you should do," said Stone.

"Then why are we here?" asked Laurette.

"I didn't invite you," said Stone, "you just came. But I'm glad you did. Because I can talk to some people who might know what to do about it."

"Danny would rather that we kill him," said Pat, "than let his body be used to hurt other people."

"Every time I hear people talk about what somebody else 'would want,'" said Hal, "it's always pretty much the opposite of what they'd *really* want."

"You're a perceptive young man," said Stone, "but in this case, Pat has a point. Danny North is a good man. Not perfect, because gatemages are all pranksters and brats, but he wouldn't want his body used to harm other people. So here's my hope: If he still has enough control to keep the Belmage from getting the use of his gates, then maybe he can stop him from doing other things, too."

Pat noticed that the other three girls all reacted to that idea. Laurette with a little nod, Sin by resting her head on her hands,

Xena by staring off into space as if remembering something. As if the idea of Danny stopping the Belmage from using his body to do harm meant something to each of them.

Don't read too much into body language, Pat told herself. You're a windmage, not a mind reader.

But maybe Stone noticed it, too. Maybe it really was something.

"I think Xena asked the right question," said Hal. "Should we avoid Danny? Or would that just tell the Belmage that we're on to him, and put Danny in worse danger?"

"You think this Set guy might possess one of *us*?" asked Sin.

"He'd prefer a mage," said Stone.

Pat appreciated the fact that he didn't look at her when he said it.

"But in a pinch, any body will do. And I mean it that way— not 'anybody' but 'any . . . body.' He could go into a dog or a horse or—"

"Pigs," said Sin. "The Gadarene swine."

"Anybody who comes near Danny is a potential target," said Stone.

"How near?" asked Wheeler. "Do you have to be touching him? I mean, Nicki was, like . . ."

"We know what Nicki was doing," said Stone, "and no, there doesn't have to be physical contact. Some people have more resistance than others, though. I think Danny is particularly strong, and that's why the Belmage set up a situation where he could trick Danny into inviting him in. That gives Set way more access than if he jumps in out of the blue. There are stories of how it can sometimes take a long time to worm in and take full control. Since this subject first came up, Veevee's been doing a lot of research and trying to work up a sort of biography of Set. Though it's hard to distinguish what's done by Set himself and what's really the work of the Sutahites."

"So it wouldn't really make any difference, whether we're close by or not," said Hal.

"If he wants one of you, he'll find a way to get close enough."

"So we should act like nothing's different?" asked Xena.

"For the time being," said Stone.

"Except Danny felt us all come here," said Xena, "so he'll *know* we did something without him and he'll ask us."

"Field trip to our nation's capital?" suggested Sin.

"Oh, right," said Wheeler.

"I was being ironic," said Sin.

"Just tell him you're planning a surprise Christmas present," said Stone. "But don't volunteer it. Make him pry it out of you."

"And if he really pushes, tell him we couldn't think of anything," said Pat.

"Yeah," said Xena. "What do you get for somebody who can shoplift anything he wants without ever getting caught?"

"Danny doesn't steal," said Pat.

"Unless he needs to," said Stone. "Don't impose your moral values on Danny. He's trying to overcome it, but he was raised in one of the Families, and to them, stealing from drowthers isn't really stealing. It's like snacking."

"Ah," said Xena. Snacking she understood.

"So Danny's living in hell right now," said Hal, "and we can't do anything at all to help him. We just have to pretend that everything's normal? Doesn't sound very loyal to me."

"Just until I can talk it over with the others," said Stone.

"What others?" demanded Pat.

"The others," said Stone. "Marion and Leslie. Veevee."

Pat waited.

"Oh, I see," said Stone. "No, not Hermia. That treacherous little . . . not her. And not Danny's family. The last thing we want anyone to know is that Danny's under somebody else's control.

Half the Families would try to kill him, and the other half would try to bargain with the Belgod to get some kind of advantage."

"Even Danny's own family?" asked Laurette mournfully.

"It's about power," said Stone. "Most people respond to power by trying to control it, to get the use of it. And if they can't own it, then they try to destroy it."

"The more you say about how bad the Families are," said Hal, "the more they sound like normal humans."

Stone chuckled at that, but didn't dispute the point. "I take it you can use your own amulets to get back home?"

"To our meeting place, anyway," said Hal.

"Then you should get back there before your families miss you. And just in case it occurs to one of you to try to save Danny by *inviting* the Belmage to jump into you, don't even try. Because he wouldn't come into you himself, he'd just have one of his followers take you over."

"But we could resist one of *those*," said Wheeler.

"Danny could," said Stone.

"And you think we're all weak?" asked Wheeler.

"Please don't take this as a challenge," said Stone. "Being possessed by the devil isn't a recreational drug. It's losing *everything*."

"It's like being murdered," said Hal, "only you have to stay and watch."

"Exactly," said Stone. "And yes, kid," he said to Wheeler. "I think you're weak. Because you *are* weak. Danny seems to be fighting this thing—and even *he* is barely holding on. There's not a chance in hell that any of you are even *close* to being as strong as Danny is. Get it?"

"Got it," said Wheeler.

"Go," said Stone.

"You're supposed to say 'Good,'" said Wheeler.

"This isn't *The Court Jester*," said Stone. "Go."

They all took out their amulets and gated away. Except Pat.

"Please tell me what you find out," she said to Stone. "Please don't cut us out of this just because we're drowthers."

"Give me your phone number," said Stone. "Danny can sense whenever you come here like this, but he can't tell if I text you or call."

She wrote it down.

"But you're the only one I'm telling," said Stone.

"You can trust Hal to keep his mouth shut," said Pat.

"Think a little harder," said Stone.

She did.

"Oh," she said. "I'm not a drowther."

"Goodbye, windmage," said Stone. "Thank you for telling me. I think you've done everything right."

"We don't even know what 'right' is," said Pat.

"But you didn't keep it to yourself in order to avoid being embarrassed if you were wrong," said Stone. "You didn't try to fix it or talk to Danny about it directly. A lot of really wrong things that you didn't do."

"Yeah, I guess it's comforting to know I could be even dumber."

Stone gave a short little bark of a laugh. "Nobody could ever call you dumb, kid. I saw you notice the other girls' reaction when I said Danny might have blocked the Belmage from doing other things, too."

"But I don't know what it means," said Pat.

"Maybe nothing," said Stone. "But you noticed. Now you'll hold that in the back of your mind, and maybe something will happen to explain it. Or maybe it won't, because maybe it was nothing."

Pat didn't think it was nothing, but he was right. Just wait and things will get clearer. Or they won't.

"Meanwhile, Pat, practice your magery," said Stone. "Get it under very good control. Weaponize it."

"Why?" said Pat. "I don't want to hurt anybody."

"When somebody's trying to destroy a person you love, even pacifists find themselves wishing they had a gun." Stone chuckled again. "Or a rocket launcher."

He seemed to be referring to something, but Pat didn't know what. She'd Google "rocket launcher" later. But it probably didn't matter—if it did, Stone would have explained it.

She touched her amulet and found herself back in the clearing. The others were already gone, though she could hear Wheeler and Hal talking loudly, well down the slope.

Pat sat down in her usual place. She hadn't really thought about having a "usual place" before, but yes, they all did. Like first grade, everybody in an assigned seat. Only it wasn't assigned.

How did I choose this place? It isn't particularly comfortable. But I wasn't the last to sit down, this isn't "last pick."

Danny sits there. So I wasn't trying to get as close to him as possible. But I'm also not directly across from him.

I sit where I can always see him, but he isn't looking right at me all the time. Off to the side. Just the tiniest bit outside the circle.

She heard footsteps.

She knew it was Danny before she looked. Because he knew they were here, and he'd have to know why. He or the Belmage. And waiting to get one of them alone made sense. Especially her. If the Belmage knew what she was to Danny.

If she was right and it *was* the Belmage. Maybe Danny just started acting like a jerk to make her fall out of love with him. Maybe he got Nicki pregnant because he liked her better.

He came up behind her and started playing with her hair. She couldn't help feeling a kind of thrill at his touch.

Then he knelt beside her and put one hand on her shoulder and slid the other hand down into her blouse.

She threw herself away from him, off to the side. "What are you doing!" she said.

"You liked it well enough the other night," said Danny.

"The other night, you didn't just grab me like you had a right," said Pat. "Or have you forgotten everything we talked about?"

"What I remember," said Danny, "was that we finally stopped talking." And he gave this little shit-eating grin that he only ever wore when he had just brought off a prank.

Only it wasn't Danny who was fooling somebody, it was the Belmage. He's feeling smug and clever, and so Danny's face shows it, but the Belmage doesn't even realize that it's a giveaway to somebody who really knows him, who has spent weeks and weeks studying everything he says and does.

The Belmage wasn't inside him that night, thought Pat. He doesn't know what we talked about. Is that because Danny didn't even remember it, the conversation was so unimportant? Or is it because the Belmage only has access to Danny's physical memories? He can remember Danny and Pat going at it, but not the conversation leading up to it.

"Danny," said Pat—knowing that she was talking to the Belmage, but hoping to get a message through to the real Danny, who was surely listening very closely. "I love you. That's not going to change. But like you said, we're not married, and so we're not going there. I didn't like it at the time, but I agree with you now. And you should remember what *I* said about personal space and being touched without me inviting it."

"Of course," he said. "I'm sorry."

But he didn't sound all that sorry. It was just words. The real Danny would really have been sorry. In fact, the real Danny would never have tried to cop a feel right out of the blue like that.

"Until we're in a position to make something real out of this," said Pat, "out of whatever it is we feel for each other, then physically we're just friends. That's what you wanted, right?"

"It's what I wanted *then*," said Danny's mouth.

"Oh, and just walking up behind me in the woods, suddenly you were overwhelmed with passion?" She laughed.

After a moment—too long a moment—he laughed, too.

The Belmage might have had a lot of practice, but he still wasn't good at this—pretending to be the original person so other people didn't notice the change.

"If you knew we were up here," said Pat, "why didn't you come along?"

"Because you didn't *stay* here," said Danny.

Pat wanted to laugh at how dumb the Belmage was. Danny North wouldn't need them to stay long enough for him to *walk* up the hill to join them. He would just gate to them—or gate to wherever they went from here.

"Well," she said, "it's a good thing you didn't, because that would have spoiled everything."

"Spoiled what?"

"It's hard thinking of a Christmas gift for somebody who can go anywhere and get anything he wants," said Pat. "And no, we're not planning some big stupid group gift, we just wanted to share ideas and make sure we didn't all get you the same thing."

"The same thing lots of times over can be very nice," said Danny. His face didn't really go well with the leer it was wearing as he said that.

"But not very individual," said Pat.

"So do it as a group," he said. "Or make me a video." There was that grin again.

"In your dreams," said Pat. She got up and started walking down the hill. Despite their effort to come and go without making a path that other people could follow, the ground sort of forced them into a couple of routes, and paths *were* forming. Some random hiker might find this place and already be here when one of them showed up by gate. But if they used the amulets all the time in order not to make a path, somebody was going to see one of them disappear.

He didn't call after her. He didn't follow her.

Danny would have. But the Belmage, caring nothing for the relationship, and apparently believing that "no" meant "no," didn't bother.

It was hard for Wad to find a time to visit Bexoi's inert body, for he did not want to let anyone else see him, and King Prayard made sure that she was almost never left unattended. Nor could he constantly watch through a viewport; he had other things to do. But now and then he thought of her, the Queen whose life he had saved, who had taken him as a lover, who had borne him a child, who then murdered that child and then burned to death his friend Anonoei.

Bexoi, the woman whom he hated above all other human beings, yet whose life he was going to protect until she bore King Prayard's baby.

One night he saw that both the doctor and the young servant girl who attended her had fallen asleep, and King Prayard was gone. So he made a gate and came in person to sit on the floor beside the bed where she lay in a coma, responding to no word, never opening her eyes, but able to drink and swallow some of whatever was poured into her mouth. Her dress was stained with old spills, damp with new ones. Behind the liberally applied perfume she smelled of various kinds of putrescence, and Wad passed a gate over her, in case she needed healing.

Did she feel it? Did she know that he was there? Was she afraid that he would kill her? No one in Iceway had more cause. But no, he had promised her that he would not harm the baby, and she knew that was a promise he would keep.

He put his hand in hers. It was warm. Her chest rose and fell slightly with each shallow breath. But as he held her hand, it gave no motion, responded to him not at all; nor did her face change in any way.

Wad had found her like this, though covered with burns. A firemage of Bexoi's power should never have been burned. The man named Keel had witnessed the event, and even though he was hanging upside down, in terror for his own life, his account was clear and did not change. When Anonoei stepped through the gate Wad had made for her, she found Bexoi waiting, and soon Bexoi set Anonoei on fire. But to Keel's surprise, Anonoei stepped to Bexoi and clung to her.

At first Bexoi did not burn, and she laughed at Anonoei. But then she did burn after all, even as Anonoei's body slumped into ashes on the floor. It was as if Anonoei were a firemage after all, as if she had stolen some of Bexoi's magery, that's what Keel said.

But Wad knew that such a thing was not possible. Anonoei was a manmage. She had no way of acquiring someone else's skill.

She might, however, have taken over Bexoi's body in that last moment of her life. And in a brief struggle, she might have kept Bexoi from protecting her own flesh from the fire. Then Anonoei died and Bexoi was so badly injured that she fell into a coma.

But Wad had healed her the moment he saw her, for the baby's sake. He and Keel had made sure that she was found, floating in the waters of the port; she had been kept warm and comfortable, and if anything went wrong with her body, Wad healed it again and again. Why was she still unconscious?

Or was this an elaborate prank? A diversion? Wad knew well that Bexoi had the power to create a clant of herself that could talk and bleed and show all other signs of life. Was this only her clant? Keel swore that it could not be—he had been conscious the entire time, and he swore that the woman in the coma *was* Bexoi. There could have been no substitution.

Besides, no clant could survive passage through a gate. It would crumble into its constituent parts.

What are you hiding from, Bexoi? Why can't you allow yourself to return to the world? King Prayard weeps and prays for you. The kingdom awaits your baby. All your plans are coming to fruition. How can it benefit you to pretend to be asleep like this?

Or is this real? And if it is, what could possibly ail you that passage through my gates did not heal?

The servant girl stirred, and with her small noise, the doctor awoke. Wad knew that he would go to the corner and urinate, then return to Bexoi's bed and check her pulse to make sure she had not inconvenienced and endangered him by dying on his watch.

With the trickle of urine into a jar to cover any noise he made, Wad leaned close to Bexoi's ear and whispered, "When the baby is born, I will kill you. You cannot hide from me."

He gated away from Bexoi's bedchamber before the doctor turned around.

Wad found himself in a certain clearing in the woods at the southern end of the Mitherkame, where a nameless treemage was teaching the Earthborn windmage Ced how to control himself. It seemed to Wad that the lessons were going all too well.

Whenever he came to visit, Ced was in some kind of meditative trance and the treemage would tell him almost nothing about Ced's progress.

This time was no different. Ced was sitting in absolute stillness, and there was not a breath of wind in the clearing, though breezes blew through the trees only a dozen yards away. The treemage stood with his back against an old beech, only his eyes moving to follow Wad's movement through the grass.

"He does well," said the treemage.

"I didn't ask," said Wad.

"You asked before, and now I have an answer," said the treemage.

"I find that I've sworn to kill an evil mage, but because she's lying in a coma I don't know if I can do it."

"Do men refuse to cut down a tree because it doesn't speak or walk?"

"Cut down a tree and you can build something. A house or furniture or a fire. Cut down a sleeping mage, and all you have is a mass of flesh and bone and bodily fluids, rotting as quickly as it can."

"And then it becomes part of the soil, or part of the bodies of crows and maggots," said the treemage. "What form does her evil take, when she's awake?"

"She deceives everyone, kills whomever she wants, and seeks to rule two kingdoms. To start with; I think her ambition will never end."

"If she can't wake up, then her ambition will only be fulfilled in dreams, where it harms no one," said the treemage.

"But I don't *know* that she can't wake up," said Wad. "I only know that she seems to be asleep, and has not seemed to wake up yet."

"So if you knew that she *could* not wake, you'd leave her alive," said the treemage, "because being alive would be useless to her. But if she *might* wake up, and thus make use of her life, you need to kill her."

"She murdered my son," said Wad. "And Anonoei, the woman who used to come here with me."

"The manmage."

Wad had not realized that the treemage knew what she was. "A good woman," said Wad.

"A mother, as I recall," said the treemage. "I believe you left her sons on Mittlegard."

"I did," said Wad. "Because we thought they were in danger."

"They are, I'm sure," said the treemage. "What did they say about their mother's death?"

"I haven't told them," said Wad.

"What makes you think that they don't know?" asked the treemage.

"Because they're on one world, and their mother died on another."

"These are not ordinary boys," said the treemage.

That was true enough.

"You imprisoned them with their mother for more than a year," said the treemage. "Then separated them so she could help you seek vengeance on Queen Bexoi. You owe them a conversation. You owe them the truth, that they are orphans no matter which world they're on."

It was true that Wad owed a debt to them—their imprisonment had been terrifying and wrong, and it was all Wad's doing. Now their mother was dead because he hadn't realized that she was calling to him until it was too late.

And now that he thought of her, it was as if he could hear her voice in his mind. Why haven't you told my boys yet how I died?

"I can't tell them how she died," said Wad. "It's too terrible."

"Not telling them is terrible," said the treemage. "Children heal better than adults. Tell them now, while they're still children."

"They're on Mittlegard," said Wad.

"Then you're the only person on Westil who can get to them," said the treemage.

"I'm not going to make a Great Gate, and I'm not going to use any of Danny North's Great Gates either, because then the Belmage will know that I'm on Mittlegard."

"Then make a Great Gate after all. Use it and eat it so it's gone."

Hearing it spoken aloud made it seem so obvious. He didn't dare to make a permanent Great Gate, and the two that Danny made posed a serious danger to both worlds. But to make a temporary gate and then close it permanently—the Belmage couldn't use *that* to get to Westil.

Unless he struck while Wad was still on Mittlegard. Danny North would sense Wad's arrival—indeed, he would know that a Great Gate had been made. But would that knowledge be available to the Belmage? Would he understand it if he felt it himself? Danny was still able to make gates, using the captive outselves of long-dead gatemages; if the Belmage understood what was happening, he could force Danny to bring him directly to the Great Gate; Wad would have no choice then but to eat the gate before the Belmage could use it to go to Westil.

It would require alertness. But since Wad held all of Danny's gates inside him, Wad would be aware of whatever Danny did. There would be warning.

But it was still a risk; why chance it just to tell two boys that their mother was dead? Surely that was information that could wait a week or two more.

No. Wad had harmed the boys enough. He owed them honorable treatment now. To leave them in ignorance of such a terrible transformation of their lives was wrong. It had to be done.

Wad made the Great Gate in the clearing where Ced was studying with the treemage. "If anyone but me comes through this Great Gate," said Wad, "kill him immediately. Or her. Whoever it is."

"Even if they come with you?" asked the treemage.

"Especially if they come with me," said Wad.

"And what if the Belmage has entered *you*?" asked Ced.

"Then it's all over, because you won't be able to kill me," said Wad.

"We could try," said the treemage.

"You would fail," said Wad. "And you wouldn't know the Belmage had me, anyway. Not quickly enough. So I need you to watch for anyone *else*. It means they snuck through when I wasn't looking."

"And the penalty for that is death?" asked Ced.

"The fate of this world is at risk here," said Wad. "If someone comes through it means I failed and something's seriously wrong. It probably means I'm dead. Whoever comes through will be powerful and dangerous, and if you don't kill them at once, they'll probably kill *you*."

"Remember, only *you* can prevent forest fires," said Ced.

"I have no idea what you mean by that," said Wad.

"I'm saying that we'll do what it takes," Ced answered.

"Ced and I will talk about this when you're gone and reach our own decision," said the treemage.

"I'm making such a huge mistake," said Wad.

"Probably," said the treemage. "But we treemages know that doing *anything* is usually a mistake. And so is doing nothing. Almost everything is a mistake. Have a nice visit to Mittlegard."

Wad turned slowly a couple of times, and cast a Great Gate with both ends sealed against anybody but himself. But since there were Lock- and Keyfriends on Mittlegard, it would not guarantee anything.

He found the two boys, Eluik and Enopp, racing each other through a pasture behind the home of Marion and Leslie Silverman. They were running toward the Great Gate, so they saw Wad arrive and changed direction, both at once.

For a moment Wad thought the older boy, Eluik, might have brought his ka out of his brother's body, but no. His eyes were still dead and empty. Yet he had been running, as surefooted as his brother. He must have been using his own eyes to see—the pasture was too clumpy and uneven for him to have been relying on Enopp's eyes to see for them both.

But either way, Wad knew that both boys would hear and understand whatever he said, even if Enopp was the one who would speak for them.

"That's a Great Gate you came through, isn't it," said Enopp.

"You're speaking the local language very well," said Wad, "but you should speak to me in Icewegian."

"You understood me," said Enopp. "Because we gatemages are very good with languages."

"I only have a few minutes here," said Wad. "And if Danny North shows up, I'll leave immediately, because the Belmage has possession of him."

"Is Danny the enemy now?" asked Enopp.

"The being who's controlling him is the enemy. If Danny somehow gets free of him, he'll be a good friend to you again. But for now, he can't be trusted."

"Bummer," said Enopp.

"I came to tell you that something very bad has happened on Westil. Your mother was surprised by Queen Bexoi."

Enopp immediately grew very serious. "Why didn't you gate her away?"

"She knew I was busy. I warned her that I couldn't watch over her, but she insisted on going anyway. She was sure she'd be safe. By the time I knew she was in trouble, it was too late."

"What does 'too late' mean?" asked Enopp.

"Queen Bexoi is a firemage," said Wad. "Your mother was consumed by fire."

Enopp regarded him steadily. "You're telling me the truth," he said.

"Yes," said Wad. "I would never tell you something like that if it wasn't true."

"You think that Mother is dead," said Enopp.

"I know she is," said Wad. "Her friend Keel saw her die. There's no mistake."

"Eluik says that she's alive," said Enopp.

"Eluik isn't part of this conversation unless he talks to me himself," said Wad.

"That's a poor excuse for not listening to someone who knows things that you don't know."

"I have no evidence that Eluik knows anything. How can she be alive? Keel saw her body consumed in a flash of fire. I saw the ashes. Boys, your mother is truly dead. I'm deeply sorry and I would have prevented it if I could. But that's the truth."

"No, it isn't," said Enopp. "Mother is alive."

"There's no way you or Eluik could know one way or the other," said Wad.

"Just because you don't know of such a way doesn't mean it doesn't exist," said Enopp. "When we were in the cave, Eluik came to me. Came into me. He helped me calm down and not scream or cry. He also helped Mother."

"So even though the three of you were in separate caves, Eluik made contact with you and Anonoei?"

"He had to stay with me all the time at first, and then he just got used to it. But he could *feel* Mother the whole time. He made it so I could feel her, too, and she could feel us."

"She never told me that."

"So what?" asked Enopp. "Why should she tell you anything? You were the one who imprisoned us."

"You're saying that Eluik can feel her *now*?" asked Wad.

"Yes," said Enopp. "If she were dead, he'd know it because he wouldn't be able to find her."

"He can't even find his own body," said Wad. "I'm not going to believe anything he says unless he says it with his own mouth."

"Why do you get to make the rules?" asked Enopp.

"Because I'm the most powerful mage in either world," said Wad.

"I thought you were down to your last few gates because Danny North is stronger," said Enopp.

"The Belmage got him but Danny gave all my gates back to me and gave me all of his, too."

"He really trusts you," said Enopp.

"Yes, I guess he does," said Wad.

"Why can't you trust me and Eluik?" asked Enopp.

"Because I'm not as trusting as Danny North," said Wad. "He's a kid, and I'm more than a thousand years old."

"A thousand years inside a tree," said Enopp. "That made you so much wiser, I guess."

Wad couldn't believe this conversation. He had expected to comfort two grief-stricken boys. He had thought maybe his news would bring Eluik out of his trance, put his ka back in his own body. Instead, they were pretending it wasn't true and Wad didn't think there was any urgency about forcing them to believe. "Believe what you want," said Wad. "I have to get back."

"What are you going to do?" asked Enopp.

"I'm going to leave you here for the time being. You're still King

Prayard's illegitimate sons. You look like him. So there are still people who'll want to use you and people who'll want to kill you."

"Not about us," said Enopp. "Eluik wants to know what you're going to do about Queen Bexoi."

"I'm going to kill her," said Wad. "As soon as she has her baby. Your brother. Once he's born, you're not as useful and not as dangerous. Maybe you can go home."

"Don't kill her," said Enopp.

"You don't get a vote on that question," said Wad. "Even if I don't kill her for killing your mother, I'll kill her for murdering my son."

"Don't kill her," said Enopp. "Eluik says you can't."

"Eluik said nothing," said Wad. "I watched his lips."

"Eluik says that's where Mother is."

Wad thought about this for a moment. "Inside Bexoi?"

"The way that Eluik is inside me," said Enopp. "That's what he says. Only farther in. Completely in. It's the *only* place she is."

Wad wondered if it might be true. "You mean she has Bexoi the way the Belmage has Danny North?"

"No," said Enopp. "She isn't in control. They're still fighting each other."

"Are you and Eluik fighting each other?" asked Wad.

"Why should we?" asked Enopp. "He still has his own body. Mother doesn't. She's got nowhere else to go. Bexoi can't throw her out and Mother's afraid to let Bexoi leave the body for fear it'll die. So they can't either one of them do anything with their body."

"How can Eluik know any of this? They're on separate worlds."

"Why can't you believe children know what they're talking about?" asked Enopp. "Why are you so stupid?"

"Because this isn't something that manmages can do," said Wad.

"Just because you never heard of a manmage doing it doesn't

mean it can't be done," said Enopp. "That's not Eluik talking, that's me."

"Anonoei's inside Queen Bexoi's body?"

"That's what Eluik says, and he wouldn't lie about something like that. If Mother weren't there, he'd tell you to go ahead and kill that murdering bitch."

"If Eluik's so smart, why doesn't he go back into his own body?" asked Wad.

Enopp didn't answer.

And Wad finally got it. "You won't let him go," he said.

"He can go whenever he wants."

"You don't want him to leave you," said Wad. "You're afraid to let him be a separate boy again."

"I'm not making him do anything," said Enopp, "and he isn't making *me* do anything, either."

"When he thinks about going, you become afraid and so he feels like he can't leave you."

"I'm not afraid," said Enopp.

"You're still terrified that if he leaves you, you'll feel the way you did back in the cave, when you were first a prisoner there."

Enopp said nothing.

"I'll tell you what," said Wad. "I'll think about what you *say* that Eluik says about your mother. And you think about what I'm saying about you and Eluik. Maybe I'll believe you, maybe I won't. Maybe I'll keep Bexoi alive, maybe not. Maybe I'll think of a way to help your mother get complete control of that body and get Bexoi out of there. But when I come back, let's see if you figured out a way to let Eluik go back to living his own life instead of being trapped helping you live yours."

Enopp said nothing.

"I'm going now," said Wad. "Think about it."

"Don't kill Bexoi until Eluik says you can."

"When Eluik talks to me with his own mouth," said Wad, "then I'll take the two of you seriously. Do you understand me?"

"You'll kill Mother if Eluik can't get back to his own body?" asked Enopp.

"I don't know," said Wad. "First I've got to figure out a way to prove whether she's in there or not."

"Eluik says she's there, that's your proof."

Wad only smiled. "Eluik says nothing, so there's no proof. I've been here too long. I'm going now."

"If Danny never gets free of the Belmage, who's going to teach me to be a gatemage?" asked Enopp.

"Nobody," said Wad, "as long as you've got your brother trapped inside you."

Wad stepped back into the Great Gate and arrived in the glade with Ced and the treemage. He immediately ate the gates that comprised the Great Gate, then saw that the two men were watching him intently.

"Just me," said Wad. "I know Danny sensed it when the Great Gate was made, but he didn't make a gate or try to find me any other way. As far as I can tell, he hid it from the Belmage."

"Is that even possible?" asked the treemage.

"No," said Wad. "But then, Danny's the most powerful gatemage in all of human history. Just because other mages couldn't resist the Belmage doesn't mean that Danny can't."

And then Wad thought: What kind of mage has Eluik become, after the things he did in the caves to comfort his brother and, apparently, Anonoei? How can I be sure he doesn't know what he's talking about? And how do I know that in the moment of her death, Anonoei couldn't possibly have leapt, inself *and* outself, from her dying body into the living flesh of Bexoi? How do I know what's possible anymore?

"What are you thinking about?" asked the treemage.

"How ignorant I am," said Wad. "And how many new things there are in the world."

"Your face looked like hope," said Ced.

"Yes," said Wad. "That would be right."

"What are you hoping for?" asked Ced.

"That maybe one of the people that I've loved might not be dead."

"That would be cool," said Ced.

"Why does he always talk in temperatures?" asked the treemage. "It makes no sense."

"He's from Mittlegard," said Wad. "And so am I. It makes us strange."

"Did you get rid of that Great Gate?" asked the treemage.

"I did," said Wad.

"The Belmage wouldn't have done that," said the treemage. "So I guess that I won't kill you this time."

"Thanks," said Wad. "I'm going to rest now until Bexoi is alone again."

"Going to kill her now?" asked Ced.

"Maybe I won't kill her after all," said Wad.

"That's good," said the treemage. "People are so shallow rooted. It's a shame to cut them down. They don't grow back."

3

Pat knew it was safer to stay away from Danny. Mostly because it wasn't really Danny. Danny's face, but not the same smile, not really—now he was too knowing, condescending like one of the jock athletes. It only made her angry and afraid and sick at heart and *lonely* to see him walking through the halls at school or sitting there in class, looking bored or annoyed or amused. None of it was Danny and she missed him.

Missed him and wanted to do something to help him, but there was nothing she could do.

At least he no longer came and sat at the same lunch table as Pat and her friends. Hal and Wheeler still came, but that was all right, even though before Danny they would never have dared—Laurette would have withered them with a look. Now, though, everybody seemed so miserable that who would *want* to sit with them? Just pack the food into their faces, that's all they did.

Then it was Friday and Hal and Wheeler either cut school or had some errand or assignment during lunch because they weren't there, it was just Laurette and Sin and Xena sitting with Pat at one end of their table. Nobody else could hear them—nobody would try to listen anyway—and it soon became clear to Pat that the other three were working up the courage to say something.

"Just say it," said Pat.

"Say what?" said Xena and Sin at the same time.

"Whatever it is none of you has the guts to say," said Pat. "The longer you take, the worse I expect it to be."

"Well it's bad," said Laurette, "and you're going to hate us."

And then Pat guessed what it was. "Danny," she said. "You made a play for him and you don't have the guts to tell me."

"But we *didn't*," said Xena miserably.

"We would never," said Sin.

"Yes, but not the way you think," said Laurette. "We were all flirty with him. Offering things we didn't mean to do—"

Xena rolled her eyes.

"OK, so *Xena* meant to," said Laurette. "But after you took us to DC and told us that stuff with Stone—"

"I thought we didn't talk about things like that here at school," said Pat.

"Do we have to go to the place even to *breathe*?" asked Xena.

"We didn't want to make a big deal out of this," said Sin.

"It's a big deal," said Laurette. "But we didn't understand it till that conversation. We knew something was weird but—"

"And we didn't know about each other until after," said Xena.

"We each thought we were the only one," said Sin.

Pat knew they'd never get it out unless she helped. "You said it wasn't the way I think," said Pat. "So whatever you think I think, what is it really?"

"He came on to us," said Laurette.

"Not *us* like a *group*," said Xena.

"That would be perverted," said Sin.

"Why don't you each tell me what happened one at a time?" said Pat.

They all looked miserable and nodded and then just sat there, saying nothing.

" 'One at a time,' " said Pat. "Not 'nobody at once.' "

"I can't," said Xena.

"I can," said Laurette. "He showed up at my door. I was upstairs studying—yes, I do that sometimes, I like getting good grades—and the doorbell rings and then my mom calls from downstairs, 'Laurette, honey, Pat's boyfriend is here to study with you,' which was bizarre because *a*, Danny doesn't study, and *b*, the only way my mom would know he was your boyfriend is if that's how he introduced himself and I thought you two were being all stealthy about it."

"I didn't know that's what we were," said Pat. "But how nice. Go on."

"So he comes upstairs and closes my bedroom door behind him and I say, 'Why did you come to the front door?' and he just reaches down and pulls me up from my chair and *kisses* me."

Pat kept her face from showing anything. She knew it wasn't Danny, and she wasn't surprised that the Belmage would try something like that. But she also knew that Laurette would not have put up much of a fight.

"So when he came up for air I said, 'I'm not sure that's something Pat's boyfriend ought to be doing.' "

"How loyal of you," said Pat.

"I *was* loyal. Trying to be. But he says, 'It's not like that, and if she doesn't know, do *you* care?' or something like that, and then—I swear this is true—it was almost like magic, he gets his hands at my waist and in like two moves he has me"—and now she whispered—"naked."

"Two moves," said Pat.

"He's *strong*," said Laurette. "And he didn't tear anything or pop any buttons and I couldn't believe it. And I was cold. For about a second. Because then he's got me on the bed and he's all over me and—"

"Are you going to say you were raped?" asked Pat. She almost added, Like Nicki Lieder, but decided not to say her name out loud. Nicki had been possessed by the Belmage and then she was protecting herself from her father's wrath and she didn't accuse Danny so Pat couldn't blame her for anything. Laurette, on the other hand . . .

"No," said Laurette.

"That's just it," said Xena.

"Oh, were you there?" Pat asked her.

"Same thing with all of us," said Sin. "Same move, same everything—"

"Except I was home alone and he did it right there at the front door," said Xena. "Didn't even *close* the door before he had me starkers."

"Disrobed," said Sin.

"I'm really trying to figure out why you think I want to hear about his advanced skills," said Pat.

"Because it matters," said Laurette, "so if these two will let me tell it, since they *didn't* want to say anything *till* I started telling—"

"Go," said Sin. "It's all yours."

"He couldn't do it," said Laurette. "He wasn't, like, ready."

The other two nodded.

"He was impotent," said Pat, not believing it.

"Yes," said Laurette. "It was all his idea, and it's not like we were fighting him off or anything—you're right, we're terrible people and disloyal friends and you should hate us forever or I hope for maybe just a year or a week or maybe not at all because it took us completely by surprise and then *nothing* happened."

"You're naked on the bed with the man I'm in love with," said Pat.

"Living room carpet," corrected Xena.

"Not exactly nothing," said Pat.

"Nothing," said Laurette. "And believe me, *he* was more surprised than we were. It's like he couldn't believe it."

"He must have come to me last," said Sin, "because he *did* look like he expected it and he was totally pissed off."

"At *me*, I thought," said Xena, "and I said, 'You think I'm fat and ugly,' and he says, 'How are you doing this?' and I realize he isn't talking to me. He's talking to himself."

"Only now we realize that he was talking to Danny," said Laurette. "Do you see why this matters? Danny didn't like what he was doing—because he really *is* in love with you."

"Or he thinks I'm ugly," said Xena.

"So Danny found a way to make it so his body couldn't do the job," said Sin. "He's still in there, and he's got a little bit of control."

Pat couldn't help it. Her eyes filled with tears and she covered her face with her hands.

"What are you doing?" asked Xena.

"Pat doesn't cry," said Sin.

"Shut up," said Pat. "Just for a minute here, eat your stupid carrot cake."

"I hate the carrot cake," said Xena. "And I like *all* cake, so you *know* it's bad."

"She wants us to give her a second," said Laurette.

"A minute, actually," said Sin.

Pat took her hands away from her eyes. Emotions under control. "You're right," she said. "That's good news. Danny's still in there and he's doing something that victims of the Belmage aren't supposed to be able to do."

"What?" asked Xena.

"Resisting him," said Laurette. "Don't you even understand why we're telling her?"

"I just thought we were confessing," said Xena.

"Resisting," said Pat. "The Belmage isn't completely controlling things."

Xena looked like it was finally dawning on her. "So it was the Belmage who was trying to . . . whatever . . . to me! Not Danny at all."

"Quiet," said Laurette fiercely. "This is supposed to be a private conversation, for pete's sake."

"Nobody understands what we're talking about," said Xena.

"They know who Danny is and that we're friends with him," whispered Laurette.

"But they don't know what 'whatever' is," said Xena.

"Anybody who hasn't had a frontal lobotomy knows exactly what 'whatever' is," said Sin.

"Except I don't know what a full frontal bottomy is," said Xena, "only it sounds really dirty. And kind of hard to do."

"Was there anything else?" asked Pat. "When he made his play and failed?"

"No, he just got mad and left," said Laurette.

"Chewing himself out," said Sin.

"Chewing *Danny* out," said Xena, full of newfound understanding.

"If that's all, then I think we're done here," said Pat. She got up from the table, shouldered her purse, and picked up her tray.

The others started to get up.

"No," said Pat. "You stay here till I'm gone."

"What, are you playing spy or something?" asked Laurette.

"I'm not playing," said Pat. "I sat down here to have lunch with my friends. Only now I know I don't have friends. So I'm leaving, and you're staying."

"Come on," said Sin. "Nothing happened."

"Not by *your* choice," said Pat.

"True," said Laurette softly. "But Pat—"

"Stay away from me," said Pat. Then she dumped the garbage and returned the tray and left the cafeteria, trying not to show any emotion to anybody because it was none of their business.

She didn't go on to her next class. Instead she walked out of school and kept on walking, not to the place up in the woods and not home, either, but down the road and on and on, mile after mile. Not her most comfortable shoes today, but she didn't actually mind a little pinching or the blisters that were almost certainly forming. It would be good to feel some pain, now that Danny had lost the power to pass them through gates and heal them.

Though of course she could always pass through the gate on the amulet in her pocket. It was thoughtful of Danny to provide for emergencies. Except for his own emergency. With that, he was completely on his own.

Her thoughts raced everywhere but kept coming back to that. Danny is completely alone. The only time he comes to his friends is when the Belmage is trying to force him to have sex with them, and *then* all Danny can do is protect them—always protecting other people—but he can't do anything to save himself.

And what do I do? Supposedly his girlfriend who supposedly loves him? I get jealous of my stupid friends for acting exactly the way I would have predicted they'd act, and as for Danny, I completely stay away from him.

That's what Stone told me to do. That's what makes *sense*.

Right, it makes sense to leave the man I love completely alone while he's going through the worst thing in his life.

But if I try to talk to him or go to him, then he'll just be worried about me and have to try to protect me, and what if he *can't* stop the Belmage from using me?

Well, so what if he does? Just because it's the Belmage doing it doesn't mean I can't still be making love with Danny. And with me, Danny won't have to do whatever he did to make his body useless to the Belmage. He can go ahead because whether the Belmage is there or not, it's what Danny and I both want to do so guess what, Belmage—we win!

Stupid, she told herself. Stupid. Danny doesn't want it that way, with an onlooker, with somebody else *riding* him like a pony. With a *monster* watching. And neither do I, because it won't really be Danny. No way does Danny have some kind of magical trick to undress women in a couple of moves, if that's what really happened. Danny's not experienced, he's not smooth, he's just a kid, and *that's* who I want to make love with, not a thousand-year-old incubus who uses up women like kleenex.

But if I just talk to him. Just tell him that I know, that I—

That's the opposite of what Stone said to do.

When did Stone become my boss?

He became my boss when I went to him and asked him for advice and he gave it to me and I realized he was *right*. What good will it do if I let the Belgod know that we've figured him out, that we know Danny's a captive? That would make me even stupider and more selfish and more disloyal than Xena and Sin and

Laurette. As long as I stay away from him, Danny won't have to worry about me.

That's the circle she kept running through, around and around in her mind, and underneath it all this nagging thought: Why did the Belmage go to all three of them and try to get Danny to have sex with them but he didn't bring Danny to *me*? Can he read Danny's mind and figure out that Danny doesn't actually want me that way? Or was that gross encounter up on the hill the only try he's going to make? *That* sure wasn't smooth or experienced, *that* was just crude.

She wasn't sure where she was. She had been so lost in thought that she was probably lucky not to have wandered into traffic. Now she only knew she was on some rural road south of Buena Vista.

Not that it mattered. She could get back to the school grounds whenever she wanted.

She fingered her amulet, and then realized that using it would not only get her back to their little clearing in the woods overlooking the high school, it would also be noticed. By Danny, perhaps—though maybe he could hide his perceptions of his gates from the being who possessed him. But also by Danny's friend Veevee. The one who pretended to be his aunt. Danny had said that she could sense whenever someone used his gates. Maybe she would come to see what Pat was doing. Maybe not. But if she came, Pat could talk things through with her. Stone said that Veevee had done a lot of research into the Belmage. Maybe she would know things that could help Pat make a rational decision.

So Pat pushed her finger into the amulet.

She was relieved that none of the others were in the clearing. The last thing she wanted was their company.

She walked to the downhill side of the clearing and looked out over the school. Pat had been walking all afternoon—but not really, because school was still in session and the buses hadn't even assembled. Some poor unfortunate PE class was running the hill with Coach Lieder watching them. Soon to be a grandpa, Coach Lieder. To the child of a Gatefather who was seduced by a succubus. Your daughter.

Don't dwell on that.

"If you want to be alone I'll go away again."

Pat turned around and gave Veevee a half-smile. "I was actually calling you. Or at least I kind of hoped you'd notice me and look into why someone was using Danny's gates."

Veevee frowned. "They aren't Danny's gates."

Pat had no idea what this meant. "They go where Danny made them go."

"All very complicated," said Veevee. "I don't think I could have made sense of any of it before I went through the Great Gate. But here's what happened. Loki—Wad—the Gate Thief—he gave his gates to Danny."

"But Danny already took them."

"But now they weren't stolen, they weren't imprisoned. They belonged to Danny. But you knew that. The thing is, that's how Danny learned that gates *could* be given. So when the Belmage took over Danny's body and started trying to get him to make a Great Gate, Danny *gave* all of Loki's gates back to him. And then— and this was such an act of genius—he gave all his *own* gates to Loki as well."

"Including my private gate?"

"Everything. Stripped himself bare."

"And he could do that? The Belmage didn't stop him?"

Veevee shrugged. "He *didn't* stop him. But maybe he didn't know what was happening until the gates were gone."

"So the gate I went through is Loki's gate now."

"Oh, it's more complicated than that," said Veevee. "Because Loki took up all the gates."

"Ate them?"

"No, no, they're his now, so he just took them up. Like gathering up your knitting and putting it in a bag. So that he was sure none of them were left for the Belmage to use, probably. He doesn't explain himself to me. All the gates I've been using disappeared, which terrified me—how long would it take me to get to Danny without gates to bring me here? I had already bought a plane ticket to get me to Roanoke when all of a sudden all my gates were back. Every one of them. Exactly where Danny had made them."

"That was . . . tidy of the Gate Thief."

"It was incredibly generous. Not at all typical of the behavior of gatemages *or* Family members. And you know whose gates he put back first? Yours. And then Danny's other high school friends'. And he only put back the ones I use last of all. Maybe because I'm a gatemage of sorts. Or maybe because he wanted to make sure he wasn't inadvertently putting back a gate Hermia might use."

"So the Gate Thief isn't our enemy anymore."

"He was never *your* enemy, darling," said Veevee. "But now, I don't know. Because I think I'm seeing a lot of brightness in your outself. What are you?"

Pat was a little confused by the question.

"You went through the Great Gate like the rest of us," said Veevee. "And now you've learned how to do some magery. What do you do?"

"Wind," said Pat.

"Are you any good at it?"

Pat shrugged. "That's not why I called you."

"No, you called because you're in love with Danny and you have some fantastical idea of helping him and you want to know what you might do that would be of any use."

Pat sank to the ground. "And because you didn't come straight to that point, I'm betting that you're going to say that I can't do anything."

"Only because it's true. Believe me, dear, if I thought anything you might do would help Danny, I'd send you off to do it even if it killed you."

"That's rather heartless of you," said Pat, "but—"

"It's not because I love Danny and don't give a rat's petoot about you," said Veevee, "because Danny cares for you very much, and that means that the one thing I can do to help him is try to keep you safe. For him. In case he ever gets out of this."

"Which you don't think he can do."

"Well, not without dying," said Veevee. "Or having the Belmage find somebody else who is more useful to him. But compared to the greatest gatemage who ever lived, who would *that* be?"

"Loki?" asked Pat.

"Loki is no fool," said Veevee. "All this stuff he did with gates— he did it *from Westil*. That's quite incredible—to manipulate gates, make and unmake them, on another world—what a mage he is. But no, he'll never get anywhere near Danny while the Belmage has him."

"So the Belmage, Set, he wouldn't want a windmage?"

"Oh, how noble of you," said Veevee. "I'm not mocking you, it really is noble. But you're an untrained novice at this, and there are some highly trained windmages who went through the Great Gate. There are about five hundred people on Mittlegard who are likelier targets for the Belmage than you. But it doesn't matter. Even if the Belmage decides to abandon Danny, he's a spiteful bastard, and he'll probably kill Danny as he leaves."

"What's the point?" asked Pat in despair.

"To punish him for getting rid of his gates. To the Belmage, that must seem like the ultimate perfidy. 'I took over a gatemage, and now he has no gates? Somebody's got to pay!'"

"Danny can't go through this alone!"

"He got into it alone, didn't he?" asked Veevee. "He didn't phone you up and ask if it was a good idea for him to do the bouncing bedcovers with the coach's daughter, did he?"

Pat shook her head. "But he *did* keep the Belmage from using his body to . . . sleep with my friends."

Veevee made her explain it all. Pat hated going over it again, but she made herself remember what the other girls had said.

"Oh, this is splendid," said Veevee. "This is unprecedented. In all the cases of possession by the Belmage himself—at least the ones we're pretty sure were him—nobody was ever able to resist him to the slightest degree."

"So Danny's doing well," said Pat.

"And no doubt pissing off the Belmage even more."

"Well, that goes without saying," said Pat. "Are you saying that Danny's as good as dead?"

"I don't know," said Veevee. "He's already done things that nobody has ever done to resist the Belmage. I'm very proud of my clever clever nephew."

"He's not really your nephew, is he?"

"The school records say so," said Veevee, "and they're *very* official."

Pat sat in silence.

"Do you mind putting down that wind?" asked Veevee. "You're scaring me."

Pat had no idea what she was talking about. Then she looked around and realized that there was a gale blowing in a circle all the way around the clearing. A wind so strong that it was bending the nearly leafless trees. It was making a kind of suction in the middle that had already raised her a few inches from the ground. Veevee was clinging to a branch.

Pat reached out and stilled the wind. "Sorry," she said. "I didn't know I was doing that."

"Undisciplined," said Veevee. "Not your fault, but you really do have to keep the wind from picking up on your moods and acting them out."

"I didn't know I was . . ."

Veevee was looking at her with amusement. And, it seemed, pity.

"Yes," said Pat. "I did know. But I didn't notice. It just felt . . ."

"Natural," said Veevee. "Listen, Pat. I love that boy almost as much as you do."

"But in a different way," said Pat.

"Don't kid yourself," said Veevee. "All the ways of loving people overlap more than we're comfortable with admitting. Possessing, controlling, exploiting—we do those things and call them love just as we act kindly and unselfishly. And call it love."

"But *real* love—"

"Do you really love Danny North? You've known him for only a few months. I've known him for a few years. But the people who loved him most and first—his parents—they were ready to kill him if they had to, for the good of the whole Family."

"But it wasn't a good family, so the good of the Family wasn't *good*."

"And which family do you have in mind, when you speak of good families?"

"Most families are mostly good," said Pat.

"How much do you love Danny North?" Veevee asked again. "Do you love him enough to kill him?"

Pat turned away, her face flushing, because she knew exactly what Veevee meant. What if Danny's only escape from the Belmage was death? Did she love him enough to set him free from that bondage?

"I'm not saying that's what you should do," said Veevee. "He's showing so much more freedom and control than any other possessed person I've read about. But he's still not *free*."

"That's like asking if you should let someone in a coma starve to death," said Pat. "If you don't know that they're never going to wake up, what right do you have to—"

"I'm not talking about killing him to set him free," said Veevee. "Dead isn't free. Dead is dead."

"Then why would I kill him?"

"If it looked like Set was going to be able to use Danny to make a Great Gate, and Danny couldn't stop him, then what would Danny want you do to?"

"He'd want me to do whatever was necessary to take that power away from the Belmage," said Pat.

"Which means killing Danny, not to set him free, but to accomplish the purpose for which he went to war."

"So you're saying that Danny was on a suicide mission," said Pat.

"Danny was like any other soldier," said Veevee. "He knowingly put his life on the line. More than that—he knew he was the person in the most danger in this war, because he had the power the enemy most wanted. He told me and Hermia explicitly: 'If the Belmage ever has me, kill me before I can make a Great Gate for him.'"

Pat nodded. Danny had said pretty much the same thing to her. Not for *her* to kill him, but for *someone* to do it.

"But it's pretty hard to kill a Gatefather," said Veevee. "He gets away too fast. So when Danny gave away all his gates, he wasn't just keeping Set from making a Great Gate. He was keeping himself from being able to get away from any attempt to kill him."

Pat was crying and didn't particularly care if she ever stopped. "He *healed* that little . . ."

"She couldn't help it. Danny *could* have helped it, but his body's drive toward reproduction trumped his brain. Everybody who dies has a whole bunch of if-onlys. If only he had left one minute earlier, he wouldn't have stepped in front of that bus. If only a kid's parents had married somebody else, their genes wouldn't have combined to give him cystic fibrosis or sickle cell or whatever. But here's the truth, Pat: Everybody dies. Some die younger than others. Soldiers at least die in the service of something larger than themselves . . . but they're still dead. If I had to arrange for Danny to get blown up or poisoned or something, it would tear me up forever. But I would do it, knowing that Danny isn't just this boy that I love so much, he's also the most terrible weapon in the world."

"But disarmed now," said Pat.

"Yes," said Veevee. "But now he is possessed and controlled by the most evil creature in the world, and Danny has really pissed him off. Who knows how Set will punish him? So you wanted me to tell you what I know. Here's what I know: That boy loves you. Maybe he's been able to conceal that from Set, or maybe not. But if you come anywhere near him, and Set realizes what you are to Danny, then how can he hurt Danny the most?"

"By hurting me."

"Yet I must be honest. Because what would give Danny the most joy? Seeing you again. And what would scare Danny most? Seeing you in the power of Set—because whatever Set might do to you, he would do using Danny's body, so to Danny it would feel as if *he* were doing it."

"I get it, yes," said Pat. "The worst, most terrible thing I can do is come anywhere near Danny North."

"And also the best and kindest thing. He misses us all, but if he doesn't miss you most of all, then I don't know my Danny."

"How do you even know that? Danny and I only just realized it the day before the Belmage took him."

"Danny and you might not have known it," said Veevee. "But all the rest of us knew it. We also know that it's young love and unlikely to last forever or even till next year. But that doesn't mean it isn't real. No love is stronger than adolescent love—it's overwhelming, all-consuming. It's what inspires the most passionate, godawful poetry in the world. It's what makes people get moony over the stupidest love songs and the worst movies. It's *real*. He would die for you."

"I would die for him, too."

"I believe you would," said Veevee. "But if you die, it won't be *for* him. It'll be used against him. It'll make his imprisonment even more hellish."

"So what am I supposed to do?" asked Pat, trying to keep her voice from rising into a whine.

"Go to high school, if you can bear it, what with Danny North's body running around like a fellow student. Or go on a long vacation. I'm not suggesting you run away from home—why torment your family?—but tell them you're going, and I bet Stone will take you in. Or maybe Leslie and Marion. Or, now that you're a real mage, maybe Danny's real family would take you in. As his betrothed."

"I don't want to be in their power," said Pat.

"Smart girl. I'm just saying you have options."

"But Danny doesn't," said Pat.

"No, he doesn't," said Veevee. "We can pity him for that. But we can't change it. I don't see how he can get out of this without dying."

"Death is so final," said Pat.

"Mostly," said Veevee.

"What do you mean? Are there exceptions? Are you suddenly Christian? Do you think Lazarus came back from the dead?"

"Oh, *that* is likely enough. All those miracles Jesus performed—they mostly seem within easy reach of a Gatefather. And if Lazarus was only in some kind of low-metabolism coma when they buried him, a Gatefather could easily bring him back. But not *from the dead.*"

"Because gatemages can't raise the dead."

"If you're really dead, then they're just dragging a corpse through a gate. It does nothing."

"So what did you mean about death being *mostly* final?"

"Well, remember who we are. We Westilians. You've been hearing about us your whole life. There are stories. Katabasis."

Pat had heard the word in English class. "The descent into the underworld. Orpheus and Eurydice. Odysseus. Gilgamesh searching for Utnapishtim to find out how to bring Enkidu back from the dead."

"Oh, you really are an educated girl. How could that happen in a podunk town like this?"

"There are books. There are good teachers."

"Osiris also dies and comes back."

"Yes, well, he was cut into pieces, so that doesn't seem likely," said Pat.

"Adonis dies and Aphrodite brings him back," said Veevee. "That might be another gatemage thing. But then there's Hermes, who rescues Persephone from Hades."

"But Hermes is a gatemage," said Pat. "Isn't that right? Loki among the Norse, Hermes among the Greeks, Mercury with the Romans, Thoth with the Egyptians . . ."

"Yes, he's a gatemage," said Veevee, "but he doesn't take a *dead*-seeming Persephone and bring her corpse back to life. She is taken into the underworld, and Hermes goes there, finds her, and brings her back. So even though he's a gatemage, it isn't gatemagery, it's katabasis."

"But how does anybody go into the underworld to bring somebody back?" said Pat. "I don't know if I even believe in some underground place beyond the River Styx or Lethe or whatever."

"Oh, I don't, either. Remember that 'Mount Olympus' was really a whole planet called Westil. So it's probably not underground. But it's *somewhere*. The souls of the dead go somewhere, if those stories have any truth in them."

"Well, *do* they?"

"The Families believe them," said Veevee. "And so *something* happened, even if nobody knows exactly what. Here's where I feel a tiny shred of hope: All my study of the Belmage gave me a strong impression that Set comes from the same place where human souls come from when we're born and go back to when we die. Another world, I think. Danny thought so, too. We called it the world of the Belmages. But it's not really—it's more like heaven, which Lucifer was cast out of and sent to Earth."

"So I should take that literally?" asked Pat.

"Danny and I did," said Veevee. "Oh, not word-for-word. But Set is Lucifer. He dwelt somewhere in the sky before there was war in heaven and the great dragon was cast down to Earth. He came from a *place*, another planet, and Danny and I thought maybe it was the same place where souls go when we die."

"Souls," said Pat.

"Oh, you're such a skeptic. Don't you get it? We mages—we *know* that people have souls. We call them inself and outself, and since Danny's little Egyptian expedition we started calling them ka and ba. But we *know* we have souls. And we know that Set is nothing *but* a spirit, a ghost, a soul without a body. So we can't afford the pleasant ignorance of unbelievers."

"Are you suggesting that if Danny dies, I might be able to go and fetch him back?"

"I have no idea," said Veevee, "but I wouldn't count on it."

"Then what's your point?"

"I don't know if I even have a point. You said that death is so final, and I merely pointed out that every now and then there's been a special case where somebody goes to the land of the dead and brings somebody back."

"Only Persephone had to keep going back," said Pat.

"Oh, now that part of the story is just silly," said Veevee. "That's a just-so story. 'When Persephone returns to the world it's spring, and then when she goes back to the underworld, it's winter.' That was added on to the story later, along with the absurd claim that Persephone's mother was Demeter, the goddess of harvest and such."

"She wasn't?"

"Oh, human storytellers have had their way with these stories for ages. Hermia told me that the Greeks—pardon me, the Pelasgians or Illyrians or whatever—they believed in Persephone, rescued by the Hermes of that time, but she had nothing to do with any of the Demeters, who all come from a completely different tradition anyway. The earth-goddess tradition has nothing to do with the Indo-Europeans and therefore has nothing to do with the Westilian Families."

"How do you sort it out?"

"Remember that *Bulfinch's Mythology* is just a feeble attempt to rationalize all the god stories as if each name went with only one person. And Ovid's *Metamorphoses* were just as feeble at the same task. The Families started a lot of the stupidest stories themselves, the way that people lie to children for their own amusement. 'Santa Claus won't bring you presents if you're bad. You'll get a lump of coal.' What does punishment of naughty children have to do with St. Nicholas? And how is it a punishment to get something that can keep you warm in winter?"

"So with one breath you tell me to believe in the old myths, and in the next breath I'm supposed to think of them like Santa Claus putting coal in stockings."

"Exactly," said Veevee.

"You look so triumphant that I think *you* think you actually explained something."

"Oh, my poor darling, of course I haven't *explained* anything. I've read all the same stuff that Carl Jung and Joseph Campbell and a whole bunch of other philologists and psychologists read, and like them I've tried to fit it all together. The difference is that *I* don't think I succeeded, and so I didn't write a book."

"But what am I supposed to *do*?" said Pat helplessly.

"The very best you can," said Veevee.

"But if I go off to do my best, what's to prevent me from doing the very *worst* thing?"

"If my reading has taught me anything," said Veevee, "all the best stories arise from unintended consequences. You *think* you're doing one thing, but you don't have enough information, so you end up doing something entirely different. But then in the happy-ending stories, everything works out anyway."

"And in the tragedies . . ."

"Well, there's that," said Veevee. "Sometimes you're rescuing Andromeda from the monster Cetus, and sometimes you're bringing home Medea, who will murder your bride and her own children to punish you."

"And how do you *know*?"

"You don't. You can't know. Nobody ever knows *all* the consequences of the things they do. Which is why I told you that you're supposed to do the very best you *can*."

"But I can't know it's the best if—"

"You don't know it's the best! There's no 'knowing.' There's only *doing*. The best you *can*."

"I'm trying to think how your coming here has helped me at all," said Pat.

"Well, before I came, you were hopelessly confused and had no idea what you should do, but you knew you couldn't be happy unless you did something."

"Which is exactly where I am now," said Pat.

"Oh, no, not at all, darling," said Veevee. "Now you know that the wisest person you know—me—doesn't know anything more than you, except that almost anything you try to do has the potential to be a disaster. Including doing nothing! So as the person who quite possibly loves Danny most, and as the person whom he most certainly loves most, you're in the best position to think of what is the best thing to try."

"But it will all turn disastrous!"

"Since every path is disastrous, I don't know how anything you can do will make it worse."

"I'll find a way."

"Quite possibly, but it will make a good story," said Veevee.

"Yes, I'll go down in history as an idiot, like Psyche with her stupid lamp."

"Don't forget Pandora and her little casket of all the ills of the world," said Veevee helpfully.

"I always thought *that* was a metaphor."

"Oh, it most definitely is. And not a *nice* one, either. Look, my dearest ignorant lovely sensitive well-meaning child, what you have to decide is which action has the best chance of success."

"I can't know that either," said Pat.

"No, I said it wrong," said Veevee. "You decide which action has a chance for the best success."

Pat covered her face. "I'm tired. What in the world is the difference?"

"If you think of an action whose best outcome is that Danny's still a slave to Set, but he got you pregnant or something, what have you actually accomplished, except horribly complicating your own life and giving Danny no real happiness because it will feel to him like a failure. You see? Even if you succeed exactly, the outcome won't have changed anything that matters to Danny—only to you."

"Since I wasn't thinking of going to him to get pregnant, that really doesn't—"

Veevee laughed. "You liar. As soon as you found out that the coach's daughter was carrying Danny's baby, you've been insanely jealous."

Pat couldn't argue with that.

"I'm telling you that you could probably succeed in that. Unless Set decided *not* to impregnate you, but instead makes Danny torture you to death."

Pat shuddered. "But anything I do might end that way."

"I know," said Veevee. "And Set may make Danny search for you until he finds you, so that even if you do *nothing* that could still happen. As I said, all the awful outcomes are on the table. So you have to do something that at least offers a possibility of a really *good* outcome."

"The only good outcome is Danny alive and Set out of his body and gone from the world."

"It's not a good outcome if he's gone to Westil and comes back with an army of a hundred thousand mages under his control, my dear," said Veevee.

"Danny alive and free, and Set *not* in a position to harm anybody ever again."

"Now you really are too ambitious, my pet," said Veevee.

"Best outcome," said Pat. "You can't deny that that's the best outcome."

"Yes, it's victory in the whole war against the Belmages."

"*And* Danny alive and free."

"I wasn't forgetting that. But darling, you're a novice windmage—though pretty skilled, judging from the highly localized cyclone you whipped up when I first got here. I don't think there's any plan you can come up with where *your* actions can lead to the defeat of Set. Still, it's lovely to dream."

"I don't have any plan at all," said Pat. "But you're right. Because you came to me here and we had this conversation, I'm now looking for a different *kind* of action. Not the action of Juliet, stabbing herself to death because she thinks Romeo is dead. That's just melodrama and self-indulgence. Just *emotion*. I'll find something rational, or I won't do anything at all."

"Rational?" asked Veevee. "Who does anything *rational*?"

"Me," said Pat. "If I can think of something."

"Well, if you refrain from action until you have a *rational* plan, then both you and Danny will be safe from any screw-ups you might otherwise perpetrate."

"At least I'll be thinking instead of just walking around crying and wanting to scream," said Pat. "So . . . thank you for coming to me."

"And thank *you* for talking to *me*. Aren't we a pair of shopkeepers? Thank you. No, thank *you*."

Pat laughed.

Veevee came to her, raised her up from the ground, and gave her a hug. "You're a dear," said Veevee. "Danny could have chosen *so* much worse."

"Oh, I know," said Pat. "But I do aspire to be something better than not-the-worst."

"You're doing very well so far," said Veevee. "And if you do take a trip to the underworld, do come back and tell me about it."

"You'll get a full account. Though I might have to tell it to you through a weejee board."

"Never," said Veevee. "I hate those things. I think it's Set's buddies who run those things, and not the dead people that you *think* you're talking to."

"I think it's just some jerk in the group, deliberately guiding the pointer to some outrageous message."

"Well, you know *your* friends, and I know mine," said Veevee. "Good luck, dear girl. I'd say God bless you, only then I'd have to specify *which* god, and I'm just not in the mood for metaphysics."

Veevee walked to the tree that held their emergency escape gate.

"That leads to Stone's house," Pat warned her.

"I know where all gates start and where they end," said Veevee. "But Stone is my husband, and there's a gate from his house leading to my place in Naples. Loki put them all back, right where Danny had them. So this is my fastest route home. Goodbye, Pat."

So at the last she rated a name rather than "darling" or "dear girl."

Pat sat there until the end of school, when it was likely that the others would use their amulets to gather there in the woods on the hill. Pat didn't use the escape gate, because she didn't want to go to DC. She just walked away along a secondary path, heading down to the parking lot in time to catch her school bus, since she was *not* riding with Laurette or Sin or any of them. Not today. Because she couldn't help Danny if she was in jail for assault and battery. Or attempted murder.

N o matter how Wad explained it to him, Ced seemed puzzled. "Isn't Bexoi the great Firemaster you wanted me to
help you fight?"

"Yes," said Wad.

"And she's in a coma."

"So it seems," said Wad.

"Seems or is?" asked Ced. "Is she faking?"

"I think it's real. She can raise an incredibly believable clant,
but no, I think this is her, that she's unconscious. Unresponsive."

"But not dead."

"Definitely not."

"Pregnant."

"That's why I haven't killed her yet."

"You're all heart," answered Ced.

"She killed my baby," said Wad.

"I remember that."

"I'm not killing hers. I'm a very nice man. Not a forgiving man, but nice."

"That's exactly how I see you." Ced smiled. "And while we're at it, she also killed Anonoei. I liked Anonoei."

"Me too," said Wad.

"What I don't understand is why we're still preparing for war."

"Bexoi may turn out not to be a threat," said Wad. "But I told you all along that we had to prepare for an onslaught of powerful mages from Mittlegard."

"Even though you now have control over all the gates in both worlds."

"That was true for fifteen hundred years. And then the universe popped a little surprise on us. Or, I should say, the world of Duat, which sent the soul of Danny North into a gatemage's body."

"He's a very nice boy," Ced reminded Wad. "Even when he was burgling houses, he saved people's lives."

"He's a nice boy who built a Great Gate and put both worlds in enormous danger."

"Now he's paying for that," Ced pointed out. "Lost all his gates, and he's possessed by this Belmage, probably for the rest of his life."

"Only because Set will probably kill him when he gets tired of living inside a gateless Gatefather."

"I'm not blaming you, Wad, but all your enemies seem to be . . . more or less neutralized at the moment. Danny North has no freedom and no gates. Set caught himself a gatemage but now he's got no power to pass between worlds. Bexoi killed everybody until she got herself into a coma. It seems to me the universe is on your side, man."

"Yes, that's how it seems," said Wad. "But my guess is that

nothing is as it seems. Or if it is, it won't stay that way. Because mine is not the only will that's working in these worlds. Danny North is already proving himself to be resourceful and oddly undefeated. What if Bexoi comes out of her coma? Set has infinite patience, when it suits his purpose, and no scruples at all. And who knows what the world of Duat will send us next? We still need to get Westil into shape to cope with that influx of mages. And why are you even resisting this? For the next few weeks, or days, or hours, you're the most powerful mage on Westil."

"Or years. It's also not true, because you're here."

"Yes," said Wad. "Ced, I can't do anything. Not compared to you."

"Because I'm such a likable fellow."

"So you *were* listening. You're the windmage who devastated fifty leagues of the Hetterwold and made them love you for it."

"It wasn't a trick. I was really sorry, and I worked hard to try to help them rebuild. They treated me better than I deserved."

"I'm a good liar, Ced, but I don't know how to make myself seem as sincerely miserable and repentant as you."

"Because I'm not lying."

"I know! That's why I can't do what you can do. If you make yourself master of Westil, they'll love you for it."

"So what does that mean?" asked Ced. "That only fifty assassins will be trying to kill me, instead of the usual two hundred?"

"Oh, it'll still be all two hundred," said Wad. "But you have me watching out for you."

Ced only shook his head.

"Anonoei went on that little jaunt of hers against my advice, and while she was in the greatest danger, Danny North held my attention by using my gates to explore *my* memories."

"And nothing will *ever* come together just wrong so that you can't protect me either."

"Ced, there are no guarantees in this world. Anonoei didn't think anybody could kill her, because she could make people want *not* to have her dead. Except she came up against Bexoi, who had no human feelings, and so she had nothing to manipulate."

"Your hypothesis."

"No, it's a fact that she has no human feelings," said Wad. "The only part I'm guessing about is that that's why Anonoei had no defense against her."

Ced shook his head and laughed. "Wad, you seem to filter out of your memory anything that doesn't fit your preconceived notions! Anonoei apparently *did* have a defense, because Bexoi, the firemage, got *burnt*. It nearly killed her and she only survived because you passed her through a gate."

"I have no idea why that happened," said Wad.

"But it still happened, whether you have any idea of why or not," replied Ced. "And even after you healed her, whatever Anonoei did to Bexoi, she hasn't come out of it yet. Am I right?"

"Yes."

"Take everything into account, Wad. I keep dreaming of Anonoei."

"Most men who met her have those dreams," said Wad. "It's part of her power."

"Not *those* dreams. I was once married to a *succubus*, please remember. I liked Anonoei but I didn't faunch after her like most men apparently do. The dreams I have are truly weird. Anonoei is inside a coffin, knocking and knocking to get out. But when we open the lid of her coffin, all that's inside is a moth. Or a dead . . . thing."

"A dead baby," said Wad.

"You've had the dream too?" asked Ced.

"People don't have each other's dreams, Ced. I saw the way you glanced at me and then said 'thing' instead of what you were *going* to say. What dead thing would you *not* be able to say to me? Dead baby."

"Well, yes. A mummified baby. And sometimes the whole coffin is full of spiders as big as my hand. It's not a pleasant dream. But I always know that it's Anonoei inside the coffin, knocking to get out."

"That's a strange dream indeed," said Wad. "I'm trying to think why that has anything to do with whether we go help the Doge of Drabway."

"Because you don't want to help him," Ced explained. "You want to use his fear in order to get control of him."

"He's a very lazy old man who doesn't do any of his own work anyway," said Wad. "He's already a puppet controlled by his Wazir, and *he's* a puppet controlled by Drabway's oligarchs and enemies in approximately equal proportions. Somebody's going to kill the Wazir and probably the Doge as well. So we'll be saving his life. And the Wazir's life, even if from now on he'll take his orders from us while we protect him from the people who will be discommoded by our takeover. They both get to keep their jobs, on a somewhat reduced income, and all their prestige and perquisites."

Ced shook his head. "You don't really think they'll regard this as a favor, do you?"

"No, they'll hate us. Or rather, they'll hate *me*. But you're so likable—"

"That's where we cross over into Bullshit Land. It's one thing to apologize abjectly to peasants who are used to bowing to powerful mages. But these clowns *are* mages, right?"

"Not in your league," said Wad.

"They're used to ruling, not being ruled."

"They take orders from other people all the time."

"Wad, I won't be good at this. And if I *am* good at it, then I'll hate myself for it."

"Neither one," said Wad. "You'll rule so benignly, so generously, that you'll even like *yourself*, I promise."

"I only ever tried to rule one person. Not even *rule* her, just *contain* her so she didn't destroy herself and hurt a lot of other people in the process. I couldn't do it. And also, likable as I am, she hated me for it."

"These aren't women," said Wad.

Ced shook his head. "Wad. You keep explaining this as if I didn't *understand*. I understand completely, I just don't *agree*."

"I know," said Wad. "But I don't know what else to do."

"Find a new plan," offered Ced.

"You're all I've got, now that Anonoei is gone."

"You've got her boys. Didn't you say they're already some freaky kind of conjoined-twin mage?"

"Ced, when I say you're all I've got, I mean it. If I had anybody else, would I still be here after you've told me no so often?"

"You still have *you*," answered Ced. "Do it yourself, and call on me if you need a big wind. Or a little tiny one with a lot of tightly-focused force."

"What did you want power *for*?" asked Wad, genuinely curious.

"I didn't want power over *people*, Wad. I wanted *wind*. I've had more than I want of people."

"But the world consists of people," said Wad. "We're humans, we have responsibility to the society we—"

"You sound like a politician."

"I was talking like a philosopher."

"A really boring one. Don't you get it? I'm a windmage. To me the world consists of a million different airs wandering over the surface, and people are just occasional obstructions that are fun to swirl around and take the hats off of, but I can always sweep them away and it's hard work to remember that it's not nice to do that. *Not* killing people randomly—that's the level of morality that I'm still working on. I'm not ready to take on whole kingdoms."

"It's only a small duchy."

"An incredibly wealthy trading city," corrected Ced. "I hated governing one crazy woman."

"But I don't care what you *hate* doing," said Wad. "I'm Loki. I'd rather be pulling practical jokes instead of doing whatever this is. Adult stuff. Business. Politics. I hate doing this even more than you imagine that you would hate it. It's completely contrary to my nature. I'm the brat in the back of the schoolroom, not the teacher. But when the survival of the world is at stake, then you do whatever you *can*, not whatever you *like*."

"And now we've come full circle, because I can't do this. I keep telling you, and you keep answering me, but your answers don't change anything. I still can't do it."

"Won't."

"Won't try because I know I can't succeed. Give it up, Wad. I won't interfere with you. I'll even help with whatever wind can do. Except assassination. But you want to capsize some of Drabway's ships? I can do that. Bring some sand into the city from the desert? My gig, exactly. But nothing that might kill anybody."

"Capsizing ships might kill people," said Wad. "And people die in sandstorms all the time."

"OK then," said Ced. "I won't do those things either. You keep lightening my load. You're all heart."

"Aren't you even curious?" asked Wad.

"Yes! I'm amazingly curious! But I'm not curious about the things you care about, Wad. I'm not from here. I'm not from the *time* you're from. You were inside that tree for fifteen hundred years, and you've been back to Mittlegard at least once. But you've never even asked me about cars, airplanes, the trips to the moon, nuclear energy, how stars form and collapse and explode—it's incredible to me how much you *aren't* interested in."

"I can't do anything about those things," said Wad. "And if you give it a moment's thought, you'll see that a gatemage has no reason to be curious about transportation."

Ced laughed. "I suppose not. You claim to care about the drowthers, but did you ever think of setting up a public gate just to get people from downtown to the suburbs? Like a magic railroad, a subway that doesn't need any tunnels. You just go through the turnstile and you're in the parking lot forty miles or a thousand miles away, where you left your car."

Wad could only shake his head. "There are billions of people. How many gates do you think I could make?"

"How many freeways and subways and airports have we built? There are fewer than two thousand commercial airports on Earth. You had way more gates than that. You could have established a handful of hubs, and people could just jostle their way through to their destinations. You don't have to load them into planes. No air traffic control. Clean. No fuel costs. No crashes. A farmer with a cart could get his produce to a market a thousand miles away without a middleman. And everybody who travels that way arrives completely healed! You could have been such a blessing to the world, and I bet it never crossed your mind."

"Airplanes are good enough," said Wad. "And I have other things on my mind."

"Well, I grew up in the drowther world. More specifically, I grew up on Mittlegard, where they have amazing technologies that would really help people here. So many things haven't been invented, because all the power in the world was in the hands of *mages*, so nobody cared about the needs of the people. The things you haven't invented here. Paper! Without paper there's no point in inventing a printing press because with parchment, a whole sheep has to die for every sheet."

"Paper? Papyrus?"

"Are you even literate?" asked Ced.

"Writing is language. I can write in any system I've read."

"Mittlegard made *all* its scientific progress because writing allowed scientists to share what they'd learned. And when books could be printed cheaply on paper, using movable type, the sharing and therefore the progress exploded."

"So you, a windmage, care about paper?"

"I can't do anything about paper. I don't know enough. But my mother made soap. Handmade artisanal soaps. A lot of the chemicals she used, I don't know how to get. But I read about soapmaking, I watched her, she talked about how it was done anciently, and I can make better soap than the vile stuff that they use here to strip the skin off children. No wonder nobody wants to bathe!"

"Personal hygiene, then? That's the magery you want to work with?"

"If midwives could approach every mother with *clean hands*, do you know how many lives that would save?"

"Then we'd soon have the same population problems as Mittlegard."

"Earth doesn't have a population problem," sighed Ced. "It has a distribution problem. And ultimately that's a political problem."

"So I'm offering you a chance to work with politics," said Wad.

"So that you can wage a war that you don't even know will happen!"

"Only the aggressor knows that a war will happen. But if his targets don't prepare in *case* there's a war, then the aggressor wins every time."

"How do I know *you're* not the aggressor, Wad? I don't think you are, don't bother defending yourself. All I know is that soap is a war on bacteria and other filth, and it makes the world a better place."

"So you've been up here working with a great treemage and what you come back with is soap?"

"I had to spend a lot of time making my windwork so habitual that it's like walking, or driving a car—I just do it, not thinking about it. But I couldn't think of *nothing.* So I thought about my childhood, and that brought me to the birds that fluttered around my mother, and it made me think of her at her cauldron—that's what she called it, 'I'm a witch and this is my cauldron full of brew'—and the smells of her soaps, and then the cakes aging, sometimes in the sun, sometimes in shadow. I thought about my own life."

Wad stopped himself from another retort. They had been through their arguments so often—but this was something new. Soap. Paper. Gates as a means of transportation. That's what Danny North had done, when he gave portable emergency gates to his friends. He created a hub for them, and amulets that would take them there, and allow them to transfer on to another point.

And those gates on tiny coins, that could be flung at an enemy to send him far away—that was brilliant. And it wasn't for Danny North or any of the Mithermages. It was for his drowther friends.

Instead of arguing with Ced, I should have been listening to him. He will never care about what I care about, unless I also care about what *he* thinks is important.

"So why aren't you making soap?" asked Wad.

"Here? Who would it be for? Treemages like to be covered with dirt. It makes them feel like they're rooting."

Wad laughed. "Maybe," he said. Then he remembered being inside the tree, feeling the life of the thing, how it clung to the soil, reaching ever deeper, gripping more tightly, drinking the elixirs of the groundwater, the fresh draught of new rain, while the branches and leaves fell ever downward toward the sunlight. For that was how trees experienced the world, upside down, their heads in the soil, reaching upward into the earth, while the visible part of the tree dangled, wading in sunlight during the day, but hardening and drying out for nighttime, for winter. Yes, trees loved the feel and taste of soil. So of course a great treemage would feel the same way.

"What if I help you with the soap?" asked Wad. "Help you get ingredients. Take you to where you can make the soap."

"I don't want to be a soapmaker, Wad. I want to *teach* soap-makers."

"Can't teach them without making it yourself, Ced. Let me help you. But let's do it in Drabway. They're a trading city. If your soap catches on with them, merchants can take it far and wide."

"I don't want to get *rich* from soap, I want to teach—"

"Teach soapmaking. But nobody will want to learn your methods unless they first learn to want your *soap*."

"Lawsy me," Ced intoned, clearly imitating a woman's voice. "You a capitalist, Wad."

"What dialect is that?"

"The old black woman who took me in when my mother died," Ced answered. "And that wasn't her real dialect. She was born and raised in Seattle, for pete's sake. That was the voice she put on when she was being sarcastically black."

"Dialects interest me more than soap," said Wad. "But that's natural for a gatemage. I'm just trying to think what soap has to do with wind."

"Nothing at all. I'm human before I'm a mage, Wad. Unlike you and your kind, my life isn't about power."

"Tell that to the—"

"This training you sent me to, it worked, Wad. I'm not the self-indulgent stormbeast I became when I first passed through a Great Gate. I'm myself again. But who will *you* be, when you get over being a gatemage? I think that's all you are. I think that without gates, there'd be nothing left."

Ced's words stung, because they were so obviously true. But Wad couldn't blame himself for it—there were only a few times when windmagery was useful or even possible. Whereas gates were a part of every moment of Wad's life. Ced could do tricks with wind. Wad's magery was as much a part of his life as walking. As breathing.

But if he couldn't. If Danny North had completely stripped him instead of leaving him his last eight gates . . . what then? Who would he be?

The kitchen monkey in Prayard's house? He *had* learned how to make a dough that passed Hull's inspection. Would I bake bread for a living? Or learn how to make noodles or fine pastry or . . .

"Got you thinking, didn't I?" asked Ced.

"Yes," said Wad. "I'm also a little hungry."

"Suppose I go with you to Drabway, and I'm making soap, and you come to me and ask me for something. What would it be?"

"A little demonstration. Power of a kind they haven't seen in fifteen centuries."

"You don't want me to kill somebody, I hope. Because I'm not really interested in doing that."

"I've seen you drive a twig through a sheet of metal. If they see something like that, and then imagine what the same twig might do driven through a shirt or a shield, they might become more interested in preparing to unify against the threat from Mittlegard."

"Why do you assume it's going to be a threat?" asked Ced.

"Because look what you did when you first came through the Great Gate."

"So you're not expecting an invasion. More like a plague of locusts."

"You're a decent guy, Ced. You didn't *want* to be some force of destruction. But you know that the Families are full of mages who are *dying* to be like that. The more drowthers weeping, the more powerful they'll feel."

"I only knew my mother, Stone, and Danny North. None of them were like that."

"But Stone must have told you about the Families," said Wad.

"Not much. But *you* told me about Bexoi. And I saw you and Anonoei. You were both drunk on your own power—and you're the good guys. I know the danger. I'll help you. As long as you arrange it so they don't know I'm the windmage."

"Seriously?"

"I can't gate away from assassins, Wad. My best armor is to be a soapmaker and nothing else, as far as anybody knows."

"Then how can I arrange the demonstrations I need?"

"Bring them near where I'm making soap. I don't actually have to be watching when I whip up a tight little tornado. The kind that can drive a dart a thousand times faster and harder than an arrow. The wind shows me where it is, where everything is. I can feel it. Trust me, Wad. You can make gates when you're a thousand miles away, right?"

"More like a few billion miles," said Wad. "I remade all of Danny North's gates after he gave them to me."

"On Earth? From here?"

"I'm really good at what I do," said Wad. "But so are you. So yes, I'll bring them into the city. Or maybe we go out in the woods at a time when I've arranged for you to be having a picnic or something. As long as you act as scared as everyone else—you don't even have to be good at acting. These aren't geniuses we'll be working with."

"I know you're trying to do good things, Wad. I know you're trying to save the world. I don't know if it's true but I believe that you believe it. So yes, I'll help. After what happened to Anonoei, I know that mages can be evil. And if I had seen that bitch queen set Anonoei on fire, I'd have driven a splinter through her brain in a hot second."

"I'm glad to know that you're not a complete pacifist," said Wad.

"I'm not a pacifist at all. I'm just not an assassin. And besides, you know that Anonoei couldn't help but make me fall a little bit in love with her and feel real loyalty toward her. My teacher made fun of her as a habitual rapist of the souls of men. Even as I felt it, he made sure I realized it was just her magery. But that didn't make the feelings go away."

"It never does," said Wad.

"Which is the reason why I think my dreams matter. Did she leave something behind in me? Is that why I'm still thinking about her?"

"Could be," said Wad. "She told me she left a little bit of her inside of everybody she needed to . . . influence."

"Including you?" asked Ced.

"I assume so."

"So are you still feeling drawn to her? Dreaming about her?"

"No," said Wad.

"Too bad," Ced replied. "I was kind of hoping that it meant she was still alive somehow. Trying to talk to me. But why would she talk to me? I was never anything to her."

"She was a memorable woman," said Wad.

"When are we going to Drabway?" asked Ced.

"As soon as I can make arrangements for a proper shop for you. In the right part of town."

"Good. Because I've got unfinished business here."

"What kind of business? Your teacher says you've learned all he can teach."

"But I haven't learned all that I can learn. Besides, even though I'm no kind of treemage, I've come to know this wood . . . intimately."

"You want time to say goodbye to the trees," said Wad.

"More or less. To tickle their branches. To touch the buds and leaves of spring. Nice thing about being a windmage—I can touch a million things at once."

So Wad gated to Drabway and within a couple of days he had rented a shop that once belonged to a baker who ran afoul of one of the rich families of the city. He only had to promise that no-body would make bread there. Otherwise the price was right and the place was alongside a wide and busy street, so it would serve Wad's purposes just fine. Ced's, too.

But as he performed these errands in Drabway, his mind kept returning to Ced's dreams. Because Wad had lied—he had thoughts of Anonoei all the time, waking and sleeping. His dreams were more like memories—Anonoei enticing him, or cuddling with him, or taunting him, or . . . but no, they weren't really memories. They were *like* things that had really happened. But always she said the same thing. "I'm here for you. Will you be here for me?"

He couldn't recall her ever saying that exact statement, though it was the implicit bargain between them. Why did it keep coming back to him, waking and sleeping?

It was like the way Anonoei called to him when she was facing Bexoi, before she fell silent. Not an actual call, but a feeling, an insinuation into his thoughts.

I'm here for you. Will you be here for me?

Was she alive? Was her ka calling to him from Duat? What could she possibly need from him, now that she was dead?

Maybe what he was feeling was those little bits of her that she left behind. Her outself, her ba, fragmented like a gatemage's gates. Danny North had been able to talk to Wad's own gates, to access his memories through them. Were Anonoei's bits of outself still talking to each other, still reaching out to talk to the people she had known and cared about?

Or was it the absurd idea that Anonoei's sons had told him— that Anonoei was still inside Bexoi's body? But that's not how manmagery works, the whole ka moving into the one possessed. That was Set's move. And while it might be hard to know which of Anonoei's sons was the more insane, it was reasonably certain that they were neck and neck, and way over the finish line.

They believe she's still alive because they want it to be so. And so do I.

I didn't love her enough to still be obsessing about her on my own. I didn't realize it, I thought I simply missed her a little, but Ced is dreaming too, and he didn't know her all that well and could hardly miss her. But dreams of her being trapped inside a box, beating on it to get out, but when he opened it, there was only a dead thing or a monster or something. What were the last scraps of Anonoei trying to say? What did they need, that would be within Wad's power to give?

5

Buck Harward's career had gone just fine up till now. He made a good impression on people at the Point, and while he wasn't sure which of the two generals he had served as aide was now looking out for him, it was obvious to Buck and everyone else that somebody was bringing him along. He made lieutenant colonel ahead of anyone else in his class, though not so early as to set a record. The real proof of someone's patronage was the kind of assignment he kept getting: at age thirty-five, he had already served three tours in combat zones, two stints in the Pentagon, and one with NATO.

Now he headed a Combined Arms Battalion, consisting mostly of recent trainees who had never seen combat. Because they were training in mountainous terrain in West Virginia, he assumed that they were preparing for possible future operations in Taiwan. He found this encouraging—*this* administration, at least, was not going to let China get away with gobbling up its neighbors. And Buck Harward would be in the thick of it with men he had trained himself. If he screwed up there would be no one to blame but himself—but he was fine with bearing responsibility. Because if he succeeded—brilliantly, he hoped—then the credit would all be his. That would help a soldier who hoped to end his career as Army Chief of Staff—or higher.

But one of the problems with commanding a training battalion within a hundred miles of the Beltway and five miles from Interstate 81 was drop-ins—VIPs who wanted to get a sense of what the Army was doing or vent their opinions or have a photo op with guys in tanks. And Buck Harward knew better than to complain about this—not to his superiors and not even to his underlings. Politics was an essential part of soldiering, today and in every other era. If Hannibal had understood that better, he might not have had to end his days in exile from Carthage.

Buck was teased sometimes because he spent so much time reading about the great strategists of history—not just Hannibal, but Alexander, Pyrrhus, Scipio, and Caesar. Learning from their successes and their failures, Buck struggled to find the balance between caution and boldness, but had recently come to realize that there was no perfect balance. Victory went to bold, cautious generals—if they were also lucky, or faced incompetent enemies. And the longer their careers, the more their enemies learned to use their own strategies and tactics against them.

Alexander had the right idea—conquer and move on, and when your men will no longer follow you on wars of conquest, die young and live forever in legend. If Alexander had died as a fat old man, he would certainly not have such a glorious reputation. Likewise, if Hannibal had been good at politics and stayed in Carthage, Scipio probably would have beaten him and had no choice but to bring him back to Rome to be strangled after Scipio's triumph. Even setbacks could be viewed as lucky, depending on what you hoped for.

I hope for everything, Buck admitted to himself in moments of candor. I want the name of Buck Harward to stand among names like Omar Bradley, George Marshall, Dwight Eisenhower, Ulysses S Grant. Or, if he was lucky enough, George Patton, Stonewall Jackson, George Washington, or Robert E. Lee.

Or Hannibal. Hannibal would be nice. And if he could perform brilliantly in Taiwan, against the high-tech hordes of China . . .

Meanwhile, there were more VIPs today. They had not been scheduled. They just showed up—but they were accompanied by the Army Chief, which meant that they were not just some senator's family.

But what a bunch of hicks. They looked presentable enough—their clothes fit and looked businesslike—but the moment they opened their mouths, Buck thought he might have stumbled into an old episode of *Andy Griffith* or *Beverly Hillbillies*. There were three of them, a married couple in their early forties, Alf and Gerd North—really, *Gerd?*—and a thirty-something nephew named, of all things, Thor.

Buck heard one of his staff try to joke with Thor about his name—could he see his hammer?—and Alf North cut off the conversation with, "Thor doesn't work with carpentry." Which suggested that these people never saw movies or read comic books.

"What can I do for you?" Buck asked the four-star when he ushered the hillbillies into his office.

"I want you to understand that the North family is very important to us and they are to have full access to everything."

Buck waited a moment, but since the four-star didn't clarify, he had to ask. "What level of security clearance are we talking about here, sir?"

"Full access to everything," said the four-star.

The Norths were looking out the window, as if this conversation was boring them.

"Yes, sir," said Buck. "But there's a lot of everything. What is it that you want to see, Mister and Missus North?"

"We need to look at a tank," said Alf. The way he said it, "tank" seemed to have three syllables.

So Buck started to delegate one of his men to set up a training tank. The four-star interrupted. "Not a trainer. Top of the line. They've studied the engineering specs for the M1A3, and that's what we need to show them. In operation, fully fueled and with ammunition."

"Yes, sir," said Buck. "Live fire demonstration?"

"Whatever the Norths want to see."

Buck looked at the Norths. Mrs. North was looking at him skeptically. Alf lazily turned toward him; Thor kept looking out the window. "We won't know what we need to see," said Alf, "until we're in the presence of a working tank."

"It might be safer at first *not* to have live ammunition," said Mrs. North. Gerd.

"I was hoping to see them blow things up," murmured Thor.

"Plenty of chance for that later," said Alf. "Try not to act like a twelve-year-old."

The rebuke sounded stern, but Thor turned to his uncle and grinned mischievously. "I'm up to twelve?"

"Barely," said Gerd. Then, to the four-star: "Can we please get on with this? All this empty talking wears Alf out."

Since most VIPs were all about empty talk, this surprised Buck. What in the world would these hillbillies do that *wasn't* just talk?

The four-star insisted on coming along. At first Buck wondered if this meant that he didn't trust Buck; then he came to understand that the four-star was more than a little worried about what the

Norths thought of him. Who *were* these people? Buck had never seen them as talking heads on the news—he would have remembered their hick accents—and if they were associated with some university or think tank, the four-star would have said so.

As they walked out to where a fully-fueled M1A3 was rumbling onto the asphalt, Buck tried to find out more about what the Norths' connection with the military might be, but the four-star shut him down at once. "No questions, Harward," he snapped. Then, more gently, he said, "Soon enough you'll understand."

As the tank came closer and grew louder, Alf North suddenly seemed to be filled with energy. He walked briskly toward the tank, getting directly in its path and striding toward it as if he meant to jump on. It was not a safe thing to do. The driver should have seen him coming and stopped the tank—crushing civilians was not generally regarded as a legitimate training exercise— but the tank didn't even slow down.

And then, when it was only a foot and a half from Alf North, it lurched to a stop. Alf seemed not to be aware of what a close call he had had. He reached out a hand and rested it on the metal of the front of the tank.

Meanwhile, the driver bounded out of the vehicle and rushed over to Buck. "Sir," he said, "I tried to stop it twenty yards back, as soon as he came out toward us, but the damn thing wouldn't stop. I thought he was roadkill for sure. And then it just stopped by itself. I have no idea what caused—"

But then the driver seemed to be aware of the fact that Thor was chuckling. "Sorry," Thor apologized. "But when Odin wants a machine to run, it runs, and when he wants it to stop, it stops."

"Odin?" asked Buck.

"Family nickname," said Gerd North. "Which we never use in front of outsiders."

Thor looked abashed. "Sorry," he said.

There was nothing going on here that needed Buck's eyes—he listened to them talk but watched as Alf—or Odin—walked around the tank, his hand never losing contact with metal, though he did move it up and down, touching everything as he passed. At one point, it seemed to Buck that the man's hand pressed into the metal of the turret, but within a moment the illusion had passed.

Then the tank started to move forward again.

"Hey!" shouted the driver. But Gerd's hand flashed out and touched his elbow and the driver staggered. "Ow!" he cried. "What did you—"

One of the crew stuck his head out of a hatch and shouted, "What the hell!"

"It's all right," said Thor.

And the four-star immediately shouted, "It's all right, soldier. Stay at your post."

The tank rumbled on, going through some maneuvers, with Alf walking directly behind it, his hand on the back almost as if he was pushing a six-year-old who had just got the training wheels taken off his bike.

"This is so . . ." But the driver saw the hard look in the four-star's eyes, and fell silent.

The tank stopped. The engine stopped.

Then it started again.

Then stopped again.

Buck had never heard the engine of the M1A3 stop and start so cleanly. In fact, as he listened he thought the engine sounded cleaner and smoother. Less rumble and roar, more hum. More like music.

Alf stepped back away from the tank. It started to rotate swiftly on its axis, a maneuver that was hard to learn, since it required perfect balance between the left and right tracks. And the turret rotated the opposite direction so perfectly that to the observers it seemed not to be moving at all, as the tank moved under it.

Then the direction of movement changed abruptly. Alf stood with his hands in his pockets, watching. And then not watching, as the tank sped up and began to make a wide circle across the pavement. Faster. Faster. The M1A3 was not supposed to go at full gallop like this during training—it caused too much damage to the equipment. It was something you did only in combat, knowing that the mechanics would work it over before you had to take it into combat again.

The circle grew tighter, spiraling inward, as the tank began to move faster than Buck had ever seen any tank move. The tracks' tolerances had long since been passed. But nothing seemed to be going wrong.

Once again, the tank headed directly toward Alf, this time at a breakneck speed. Once again, it came to an abrupt stop right in front of him.

The whole crew poured out of the tank, some of them rubbing their heads or limping a little. They were expostulating in highly colorful language.

"Attention!" Buck called.

They looked at him, recovered their composure, stood at attention.

"I see some of you rubbing your heads," said Buck. "Were you wearing your helmets?"

"No, sir," two of them answered at once.

"And here I thought you were a well-disciplined crew," said Buck mildly.

"We didn't know she was going to *move*, sir!" said the tank commander.

"How *did* she move?" murmured the driver.

"I think she moved very well indeed," said the four-star, in a tone that suggested it was the final comment in this conversation.

"Get back in your castle, boys," said Buck. "Nobody gave you permission to come out."

"No," said Alf casually. "We won't need them inside for a while." He strode to his wife. "Well, Gerd, did you get what you needed?"

"Those speeds took a lot of heat. A lot of *explosions* going on in that engine." She directed this at Thor.

"If I can't see it, it doesn't count," said Alf.

"I think I can draw enough ambient heat. Without the load of fuel, it'll be much more maneuverable."

Buck heard it, but was she insane? Without fuel, an airplane could take off more easily, too—except for that little thing about not being able to work up enough speed.

"About how much gasoline is left?" asked Gerd.

"Oh, at the speed we were going, we used up half a tank."

"Well, use up the rest," said Gerd. "I don't want to run the risk of the gas tank exploding when I get to work."

Buck took in a breath, about to challenge this insanity, but the four-star clicked his tongue. "Let's just watch and see," he said to Buck.

Alf did not go back to the tank; neither did anyone else. But it started moving again, as fast as before, and in a wide circle. Alf didn't even look at it. Instead, he came up to the four-star. "All of the design flaws I pointed out to you will need to be corrected."

The four-star raised an eyebrow. "Looks and sounds like she's running beautifully."

"I made some alterations of my own," said Alf. "It's better if it comes off the assembly line with a good design instead of having to jerry-rig it afterward."

Jerry-rig? By caressing the armor plating? But the four-star seemed to think this was all rational, and Buck held his tongue. Besides, it was obvious that *something* had controlled the tank, and it wasn't the crew. It made no sense, but Alf was in command of the tank as surely as if it was Bucephalus and he was Alexander.

It wasn't long before the tank's engine fell silent and it coasted to a very quick stop. "Empty enough for you?" asked Alf.

"You tell *me*," said Gerd. "I don't work with internal combustion."

"Till now," said Thor.

She didn't even look at him. Instead she closed her eyes for a long moment.

Then the engine came back to life.

"Oh, no, dearie," said Alf. "It can't run on hydrogen."

"And yet it is."

"Well, yes, but it's not the fuel it was designed for."

"Water vapor is everywhere," said Gerd. "I just separate it electrically and we have all the hydrogen we need. Then it burns and comes out as steam. I think it's elegant."

"There's a lot less water vapor in the desert," said Thor helpfully.

This time Gerd glared at him. "Those desert savages won't *matter* if tanks no longer run on petroleum."

"Hydrogen will require a complete redesign of the engine, dear," said Alf, "and we need quick results."

"But direct heat is so *inelegant*. And it becomes less efficient in winter or at high altitudes or extreme latitudes, where there's less ambient heat."

"We don't care about elegance," said Alf. "We just need it to never run out of fuel."

Buck couldn't believe what he was hearing. These people thought they could separate water vapor into hydrogen and oxygen on the fly. They thought they could extract ambient heat and put it in the engine.

And they could.

The tank went in circles again, faster than ever—and without a lick of fuel in it. It stopped only when the four-star asked if the crew could get back on in order to monitor the instruments.

"Just don't try to change anything," said Alf.

"Not that they *can*," said Gerd.

"But they could break bones trying," said Alf.

The tank went around and around. Alf and Gerd led Buck and Thor and the four-star back to Buck's office. Naturally, the four-star took the chair behind the desk, while Buck stood at attention to one side and behind him.

"I don't know what you did," said the four-star, "but I'm satisfied. Can you give us a redesign to allow all our future M1A3s to run like this? And what will it cost us? Because you can ask for the moon and I'm betting you'll get it."

What a clever negotiator the four-star *wasn't*, thought Buck.

"Oh, dear," said Gerd.

"You can't *build* it to do what we got it to do," said Alf. "Besides, you want your tank crews to be able to control their own tanks."

"Well, yes. But the fuel thing—do you have to be present for that to work?"

Alf nodded.

"No, dear," said Gerd. "He means the whole time, and the answer to that is no. We have to start it up, but once Alf and I have spent a few minutes with each tank, they'll all run like this . . . well, forever."

"We need to be able to shut them off," said Buck. "Do you need to be there each time the engine restarts?"

"Oh, that would be so *tedious*," said Gerd.

"No, it's a one-time treatment," said Alf.

"No cost," said Thor. "We don't need *money*, anyway."

"I think we do," said Gerd softly.

"What we need is a certain percentage of the tanks," said Thor. Silence.

Finally, the four-star showed he had a little spine: "I'm sorry, but it's illegal for private citizens to own tanks."

"We don't really want tanks per se," said Thor. "We want the tanks, their crews, all the supporting crew and spare parts and all that."

"It's *really* illegal for anyone to use the U.S. Army as mercenaries."

"Oh, we won't pay them," said Gerd. "Or rather, we'll pay for it all by the cost of the fuel you *won't* be buying. And by the lack of repair needed by the tanks that Alf has seen to. He's really very talented."

"I can see that," said the four-star. "But . . ."

"We won't use the tanks you give us anywhere on planet Earth," said Thor.

That information hung in the air for a moment.

"Think of it as foreign aid," said Thor.

"You aren't foreign," said the four-star.

Gerd rattled off something in a language that Buck didn't think he'd ever heard before.

"We're as foreign as we need to be, she said," Thor translated. "If we don't get the tanks, we can offer our services to someone else who'll think a ten percent tariff is a bargain."

Buck thought of calling for some Marines to come and blow these hicks to kingdom come. But he didn't think the Marines would get anywhere near the Norths.

"I will recommend to the President and the Joint Chiefs that they honor your request," said the four-star.

"We like the President," said Thor. "Auntie Gerd thinks he's weak, but it's a good sign that he wants our services. We're used to thinking of ourselves as Americans."

"Sort of," murmured Alf.

"We wouldn't want that to change," said Gerd. "But I can assure you that we have desperate need of these weapons on this world, too. But in respect to our agreement, we will explain the missions we need accomplished and the U.S. military can take care of the problem. *Our* tanks we'll only use off-world."

It made Buck's skin crawl, to see the four-star agree to everything. To treating the Army like these hillbillies' private security force.

But he said nothing.

"How many of these tanks do you already have built?" asked Alf.

"Besides the prototypes, only two dozen."

"Then you need to stop the assembly line and implement the simple design changes I outlined for you yesterday. Meanwhile, Gerd and I will retrofit the existing M1A3s. Fair?"

"Deal," said the four-star. "As long as you understand that only the President's word is binding."

"We're way past the Constitution and separation of powers and all that, don't you think?" asked Gerd.

"I do not," said Buck.

"You're a brave boy," she said. "But you must not bluster unless you can back it up. Which, at the moment, you cannot."

"You can't just come in and take over," said Buck.

"And yet we did. Last week. But we want it kept quiet. People should think the government is proceeding as normally. You wouldn't want to contradict that, would you?" She directed the question at Buck.

"I don't think it's polite to contradict a lady," said Buck.

But something must have surfaced in his voice, something that revealed his true feelings—utter loathing, and fear of what these ignorant peasants would do with so much power. Thor must have detected something in his manner. Because he got up and put an arm over Buck's shoulder so he could whisper in his ear. "In case you're thinking of pulling out a gun and hurting somebody, please remember that Uncle Alf could whip the gun out of your hand or make it jam. Auntie Gerd could stop your heart with a bolt of lightning. And I could pound you to a pulp with my hammer."

So he *did* have a hammer!

Thor burst out laughing. "Lighten up, my man, don't be so grim. We're going to help you be victorious in all your confrontations. We'll save hundreds of thousands of lives. Not all at once, but in the long run."

"I'm sure you will," said Buck.

The four-star took them out of Buck's office, and Buck slumped down on the couch. "Those are seriously dangerous people," he murmured to the junior officer who had happened to be in the outer office waiting for him when the Norths arrived. "I can't tell anybody what I saw because they'll assume I'm out of my mind."

"But you're going to do as they said, isn't that right, sir?"

" 'One nation under God,' " said Buck. "But now I think that might need changing. To the plural."

6

Danny North had never thought of his life as particularly boring until now, when he was a mere spectator, forced to endure the company of people he did not like, while finding the words coming from his own mouth to be stupid and unfeeling.

Whether Set was deliberately making Danny sound mean, vain, and unwitty in order to punish him, or because Set was incapable of better, was a matter of no importance. Danny only thought about it because there was so little else to think of. What good is it to wonder about this or that, when he had no means of finding out the answer. As for changing what Set used his mouth to say and his body to do, Danny was nearly powerless. Only when Set had determined to sleep with every girl who seemed interested, was Danny able to interfere with him, and then only in the crudest way, by thinking of the aunts and the cousins back on the North

Family compound, which made his body incapable of any kind of romantic involvement.

This had been an important discovery, that Danny's body still remained at least a little bit under his control or, at least, responsive to his feelings and thoughts. Since then, he had tried to think of other indirect ways that he could frustrate the Belgod and perhaps encourage him to lose interest in continuing to dwell inside him and overmaster him. But no ideas occurred to him, or if they did, a quick trial showed that Set was able to overwhelm his resistance.

My control remains in the most basic, least volitional parts of the brain, Danny told himself, and then tried to remember what it was that the limbic system controlled. It involved the formation of memory, but Danny hardly wanted to shut that down, since if he ever won back his freedom, he would have to deal with the consequences of whatever Set had made his body do; therefore it was essential that he know exactly where he would have to make amends.

It was, if Danny remembered right, the nucleus accumbens that controlled pleasure and sexual arousal in the brain. Was it possible that this was the *only* part of his own brain that responded to Danny's will in any way?

He hadn't actually controlled it, anyway; he had tricked his own pleasure center into thinking that its sexual arousal was being directed toward the females against whom every instinctive taboo protected him from mating with.

If Danny tried to *do* anything, Set seemed to notice the attempt at once, and blocked him; if they were alone, he'd make Danny's lips say, "Tut tut tut, naughty North boy," or "When will you learn, you poor ignorant gateslave?" or "None of your tricks, Loki."

But Set seemed incapable of interfering with Danny's private thoughts or plans, or even sensing them until Danny tried to put any of them into motion. And because Danny still had access to memory formation, especially kinetic memory, he was able to get his way now and then—through indirection and trickery, but it worked.

For instance, if he had tried to go to his cell phone and check his email and text messages, Set would have blocked him—and would have started making guesses and assumptions about Danny's motives.

But if Danny lightly stirred up memories of emails—especially the seemingly endless solicitations from porn sites—Set often responded. *Usually* responded.

It meant that Set would spend way too much time searching through anatomically complete but soulless pictures of women behaving in ways that Danny had never found particularly alluring; but it also meant that Danny could at least notice the subject lines of emails as Set used his eyes to glance through them.

That was how Danny came to realize that someone who knew his situation was trying to pass messages to him. After a couple of days, he realized that the pertinent emails all seemed to come from three senders, none of whom he recognized: Persephone@Hades.org, Eurydice@Dis.org, and Isis@Duat.org.

All three of these referenced classical women who went to the land of the dead and returned. Well, Isis didn't go to the land of the dead—rather she gathered up the fragments of Osiris's murdered body—murdered by Set—and put them all together. Lacking only one piece, his penis, she made one out of gold, attached it to his corpse, and then brought Osiris back to life by the use of a spell she had learned from their father, the earth god Geb. He lived only long enough to impregnate her with Horus, though he continued to be worshipped as the god of the dead, among many other things.

The other two women, though, were definitely taken down to

the land of the dead. Eurydice stepped on a snake and died from its bite, and her husband, Orpheus, went to Hades to retrieve her. He sang so sweetly that Hades' heart was softened and he allowed Orpheus to take her home. Some versions of the story included a don't-look-back warning, which mythic people always ignored, and so Eurydice was snatched back to Hades until Orpheus himself died.

Persephone, though, was particularly interesting because *she* was rescued from Hades by Hermes—the traditional name for gatemages in the Greek Family. Of course, Persephone wasn't really one of the original Westilian names, because her cult was practiced around the Aegean long before any of the Indo-European tribes arrived. Hades' kidnapping of her was sometimes viewed as a symbol of the conquest of the female-deity-worshipping Aegean by the male-deity-worshipping Pelasgians or Phrygians or Danae or Hellenes or whatever name the first Indo-European invaders used.

But because the Earth wept and suffered with Persephone in the underworld, Zeus decreed that she must come back to the surface. Hades, having tricked her into eating six pomegranate seeds, was able to make her come back to the land of the dead for six months of the year. All very just-so, but it mattered that Hermes was the messenger that Zeus sent to Hades to bring her back to the surface.

Though the three addresses were different, the emails all repeated the same kind of subject line. First it was, "Take me home and find out what I know." Then, "You can be a god if you follow me into the shadows." And finally, "I'm old enough to decide. Don't make me go home alone."

All three subject lines sounded like sexual come-ons designed to evade spam filters. And when Set clicked on two of the mes-

sages, probably searching for porn, the URLs in the emails did lead
to sites specializing in underage-looking women posing explicitly.
But Danny knew that the contents of the emails didn't matter,
because whoever sent them knew that Danny couldn't choose to
open any email message. All that mattered was the sender's email
address and the subject line.

All three dealt with people who were brought back from death.
All three subject lines could be taken as advice or requests to
Danny. I'm going to die, they seemed to say. It's your job to follow
me to the land of the dead—Hades, Dis, or Duat—and "find out"
whatever it was that Duat had to teach him. And one of them
asserted that she was "old enough to decide," which meant he
shouldn't feel bad about her dying, but should instead use the
opportunity to learn whatever he could.

Danny didn't allow himself even to attempt to take action, but
his anxiety grew with every letter. Since all the addresses were
female, he assumed that they came from a woman—from the
same woman. "I'm old enough" implied that it wasn't Veevee or
Leslie. It was either one of his high school friends from Parry
McCluer High, or it was Hermia from the Greek Family.

Hermia seemed unlikely, if only because she was the one
who betrayed him by moving the Wild Gate and letting all the
Greeks go through, turning loose the power of augmented
mages—gods—in Mittlegard again.

And of the girls at Parry McCluer, the only ones educated
enough to think of the names of these three mythical women were
Pat and Laurette.

Danny might be wrong, he knew, but he believed Laurette was
way too selfish to put her own life at risk, even in a noble cause.
So the letters came from Pat. Pat was planning some insane move
to try to break him free from the power of Set. Clearly her plan

involved going to the land of the dead—which meant, from what Danny had been able to learn, Duat, the third planet, the one from which all the kas and bas of humankind derived.

Don't do it, Pat, he thought. And then stopped himself from thinking it, because whatever he thought *too* clearly, Set could understand, at least partly, and he didn't want to alert his enemy to how important Pat was to him.

Still, he had to admit it was clever of her to figure out a way to deliver a message to him. This way, if he should run across her dead or dying body, he would know that her plan was for him to somehow follow her into death. And then, with luck, bring her back with him.

The problem with this clever plan was that he had no idea how to do it. He hadn't seen that much death in his life. At least not deaths of humans. So he had no idea of whether he could even *find* Pat's dying ka and somehow attach to it in order to hitch a ride into hell. Or heaven. Whatever.

And Persephone only made it back for half-years. Eurydice was cheated at the last moment because Orpheus looked back. Osiris's resurrection was only temporary. The track record for returning from death was pretty poor even in the stories.

Yet the emails hinted at ideas that fit within conversations that Pat and Danny had before Set took him over. He himself must have given her this really, really bad idea.

So if she died and he couldn't find her departing inself, let alone follow her, he'd bear the added guilt of knowing that she had died trying to save him, and that words of his had, unintentionally, led her to her death.

We all die in the end, he thought. All we can influence is the timetable. Not the outcome. Even if everything works according to the plan Pat seems to be proposing, and I bring her back, she'll still die eventually. Or we'll both stay dead. Which might not be all that bad, compared to living until Set gets tired of me. Everybody dies.

"Well, isn't that the truth," said Set aloud, using Danny's mouth.

Danny pretended not to know what Set was talking about—he tried to shrug. Set blocked him, but then did an elaborate super shrug. "Oh, I didn't mean anything," said Set in a whiny caricature of Danny's voice. "But I heard you, North boy. 'We all die in the end.'"

Again Danny shrugged; again Set overdid the gesture.

"But you're wrong, Danny North, philosopher. *I* won't die. Bummer, huh? *You* can die. You *will* die. But your final comfort as you lie there dying can be this: The Mighty One who taught me how to live will continue to live on after me, in another body, and another after that, forever and ever. Your greatest happiness will come from knowing that you were once my sock puppet. Do you like that one? Sock puppet! Except that I didn't come in through your butthole."

Crude as always. Set was as disgusting as a seventh-grader. Danny was surprised he didn't spend all day drinking soda pop in order to produce ever longer, louder flatulence.

The message emails stopped coming, but Danny didn't stop looking. He'd bring up the memory of checking emails, then Set would check the next batch of emails and Danny would scan them quickly to see if any of them looked like a message. None of them did. Then one night, when it was almost dark, someone knocked on the door.

Set used Danny's body to spring up and open the door.

It was Pat. She looked him steadily in the eye. "Danny," she said. "I can't just leave you alone in there."

"He's not alone," said Danny's voice.

Pat's eyes turned cold. "I'm not talking to you."

"Good thing," said Set. "Because I'm not talking to *you*, either."

Danny's right hand flashed out and gripped Pat's shoulder. She winced and cringed at the pain and pressure. Then Danny's left hand leapt forward and slashed across her throat. Only then did Danny realize that he—that Set—was holding his knife. Blood geysered from Pat's throat and splashed into Danny's eyes.

For a moment, startled at being blinded, Set's attention was distracted. Danny could have made one of the captive gates right then and passed it over her. He could have healed her and then given the gate back to itself.

But that wasn't what Pat had come for. The plan she proposed was for Danny to follow her to Duat. Or Hades. Or Hell. And for that to work, he had to let her die, even though healing her was within his power.

Instead, Danny watched for her ka and then he realized—I don't have to find her ka, I need to find her outself, her ba, because I *know* what those feel like. They feel like gates. Pat is a windmage now, not a gatemage—but she has a ba and as she is dying, it's going to flow back to her and I can see it, I can find it, there it is. Her ba, returning, guiding me to the ka.

It was like when Danny swallowed the Gate Thief's gates, only instead of breaking the connection between Pat's ba and ka, he left the connection open, and when the ba found the ka and reunited with it, Danny held them both within his grasp. Whatever it was in him that did the grasping.

He waited for Set to recognize what he was doing and stop him, but either Set didn't sense it or Set couldn't stop it. Or perhaps Set wanted it to happen.

Danny hadn't *taken* Pat's ba and ka, but he had a grip on it, he knew where it was. He felt it withdrawing from her body, like a million-armed squid pulling its arms out of sucking mud.

And the moment that the last link between Pat's ka and her

body was severed, Danny passed one of the captive gates over her body. Almost every cell in her body was still alive, even if the ka was missing. Her body healed.

Danny gave the gate back to itself and it disappeared.

"What are you doing?" demanded Set, using Danny's lips. "You're too late, you know that doesn't work."

For a moment Danny thought her ka would leap back into her body, and perhaps it might have, except that he could feel her resist the impulse and let go. In that moment she chose to go ahead and die, even though he had given her the choice.

Her ka hovered nearby. Am I holding you back? thought Danny. Is my light grip on you enough to keep you here instead of letting you return to Duat?

Yet if I let you go, how can I follow you?

No, my grip on her won't hold her back—it's my grip on my own body that keeps me here. It's not enough for me to have a grasp on her. I have to let myself float free.

As soon as his attention turned inward, he realized that the strongest anchor holding him to his body was not his own ka—it was the captive gates he still held within his hoard.

So he made all those gates and gave each one back to itself, all of them in a few moments, all gone. Set screamed in rage until it hurt Danny's throat and left him nearly voiceless.

But Danny hardly felt it, for he was unburdened now. He had not understood what a heavy weight those prisoners had been to him.

He could feel Pat tugging on him. She was trying to move away, trying to go to wherever dead souls go. To the planet Duat. But Danny's grip still held her back.

Yet now her pull on him began to draw him away from his own body. He could feel his own ka trying to suck its tendrils out of his flesh.

"No!" Set shouted hoarsely.

But he had no power to stop Danny from doing what he was doing now. It was Danny's body that Set had overpowered, not Danny's ka, and he could not stop Danny from discarding the skin and bones.

If I die completely, thought Danny, can Set continue to use my body? He can't make gates because all the gates are gone. Will he leave? Whose body would he take? What poor bastard will be his next victim?

Plenty of time to answer that when Danny returned. If he returned.

Besides, whoever Set possessed next would not be a gatemage. So if Danny's death turned out to be permanent, the worlds were in far less danger than when Set owned a gatemage's body.

As more and more connections with his body pulled free, Danny could feel that the remaining ones became more attenuated. Thinner. Stretchier. Pat's tugging drew him farther away, and faster, and faster, so that when he had only three connections left, his grasp on her stopped being any kind of barrier and he was with her, traveling on.

He tried to talk to her but he had no mouth, no more power to make speech than when he was in a body controlled by Set. Instead of feeling liberated at losing most of the connection with his body, he felt imprisoned; it was the body that had given him so much strength and power. It was the body that ran, that ate, that ached, that slept, that healed. The body, with all its demands, had given him tremendous powers and now he didn't know how to function without them. When possessed by Set, at least he had still *felt* things.

Only when his grasp on Pat tightened and her movement slowed did he receive a communication from her. Not words—there were no words between two kas, just as Danny had not been able to use actual language to communicate with Loki's gates when Danny held them. But he understood the sense of what she was trying to communicate: It worked. It's working. Let's keep going.

Danny did not know what their movement consisted of, or how it was done, or how he even knew it was happening. He had no eyes to see. But he knew that they had left the world of six billion human kas and were in the vast space between worlds, between stars.

And then they weren't. Far faster than they could possibly have covered the actual distance, they were now approaching another world with trillions, quintillions of kas. More than the total number of people who had ever lived on Mittlegard and Westil combined. More than the total number of animals and plants. Enough to populate the worlds through all their history ten times over.

He had no idea how he knew this. He could not identify or label or count any other ka besides his own and Pat's. And yet he knew how many they were, a number for which he truly had no name. A number that could represent all the particles of any kind or size in the universe, and still have more left over. Yet because kas, like geometric points, had no dimension, there was room enough for them all on this world. On Duat.

He could not see the world. He could not tell where life left off and rock began. Could it be a gas giant? Could Duat be the surface of a star? Unable to see, to sense heat or cold, to feel pain or even the hardness of a rock, Danny could sense only the life around him.

He made sure his grasp on Pat remained firm, because he feared that if he ever lost his hold on her he would lose her in the chaos of this place.

Not chaos. There was no chaos here. There was perfect order. A place for every ka, and every ka in its place.

How did he know that?

Without words, a powerful ka unfolded to him the answer: You knew because I gave you the knowledge. I put the wisdom into you, and now you have it as if you thought of it yourself.

Though he understood this, he did not "hear" it. There was nothing sequential about it, nothing like the orderly flow of language, one word after another. Instead, the knowledge wasn't there, and then it was.

Who are you? Or at least it was Danny's intention to ask that question.

I am I.

Or maybe it was, I'm myself. Or "me." Or "this one." There were no words, but Danny caught the idea of the deep self-understanding of the being who was talking to him. Danny had no such understanding of himself. By comparison to the depth of his guide's self-knowledge, Danny was trivial, a bit of dust on a breeze, a grain of sand being churned in the belly of a wave.

Except that because he was talking to This One, Danny was *not* wave-churned or windblown. He was very still. And tucked beside him, inside him, was Pat. He was also aware of her.

Who is that? asked This One.

Pat, Danny answered. Only there was no *word* Pat. Instead, his answer was to convey at once all that he knew of Pat, all he remembered, all they had meant to each other, the plan that Pat had come up with and acted on, the murder in the doorway of his house, done by Danny's own hand but not by his will.

You did not want her dead? asked This One.

I want to be alive with her, answered Danny, and there flowed from him all that he hoped for out of life, the companionship of marriage and family, children to raise, friends and work and learning and making, all the things that have value in a mortal human life.

Yes, said This One. That's why we sent you there.

I did not want Pat to die, Danny tried to explain. And yet she chose to come where death was waiting, and when Set killed her I stood by and let her die even though I could have healed her, so I consented to her death so she could bring me here. And she consented to her death because when I healed her body she could have leapt back into it and she didn't. She is here by her own choice.

And yet you hold her prisoner, answered This One.

I enclose her because otherwise I would not know where she was.

You would know, said This One.

In that moment Danny knew that whatever This One told him, it had to be true; that in the telling of it This One *made* it true.

So Danny let Pat go.

The moment he did, Pat seemed to grow, to explode until her presence with him was almost overwhelming. It was not that she was greater or larger or brighter or louder—words that meant nothing here—but that she was vastly present to him. When he had held on to her, her ka seemed elusive and faint; now, set free of him, she was so powerfully focused on him that she seemed to fill half the space around him. By the intensity of her devotion to him, she made him greater than he had been.

And this was not just some illusion. The other nearby kas sensed it too, and turned to him. Not a physical turning, but a focusing of their attention, and he grew and glowed brighter and became warmer and saw farther and understood more because of the brightness of their attention. But brightest of all, Pat.

Something like amusement from This One.

No. Pat was not the brightest of them all. She was only the brightest of those close by who were not This One. This One's attention to him was like the ocean compared with the single raindrop of Pat's attention. And the perception of all the others was like flecks of mist compared to her.

That is love, said This One.

Pat loves me, I knew that, but why do *you* love me? And these others, whom I do not know, how can they love me?

Because they saw you let go of Pat and set her free. They saw that you did it because you trusted my promise that you would know her even if you no longer held her. For those two things they love you, and because of their love you are larger than you were. And Pat is larger because she willingly died for you. For that love they are in awe of her.

We don't want to be dead, said Danny, and he understood that Pat was explaining the same thing in her own way at the same time.

There are many here who did not wish to be dead. But here they are, content for the time being, content to be with me.

Are you God? asked Danny.

A being who makes others obey him against their will? Never. A creator out of nothingness? It cannot be. The absolute ruler of heaven and earth? No such, or if there is, I do not know it.

Then who are you?

Is that what you came here for? To know me?

I don't know. I came here to find out what I need to know in order to keep Set from overmastering two worlds and ruling with cruelty for ten thousand, a hundred thousand years. Forever.

In this place you will never learn how to force another to bend to your will against his own inclination. Have you learned nothing of power?

Danny thought of all the teaching of the Mithermages: To gain power from trees, you must love the trees: Pay them attention, serve their needs, protect them from their enemies. As you show your love for them, they give you whatever power they can share with you, because they trust you to act in their interest. Then the eagle lets you ride inside him, and follows your wishes as if they were commands, because his life means more obeying you than it ever did in his solitary freedom. But if you betray that trust, then you are worse off than those who have no influence with plants or eagles, rock or rain.

All this memory flowed into Danny's mind, and This One assented to the memory. This One seemed to say, I'm glad they have kept that much understanding: that power comes from willing obedience, and willing obedience flows from trust and love.

But they love only the thing they serve as mages, Danny answered. They love nothing else, and harm many against their will.

All of them? asked This One.

And Danny suddenly understood that by his testimony he was causing This One to judge all the Mithermages. And so he immediately remembered those he knew who never used their power to harm others. Marion and Leslie. Veevee. Stone. And for all Danny knew, countless others among the Families and the Orphans. Even inside the North Family, there were Uncle Mook and Aunt Lummy.

And Thor and Mother and Father meant well—Danny could see that now, and understood that when his parents came to see him that day at Parry McCluer, they weren't seeking some advantage as he had feared, but rather they truly loved him, attended to him, wanted to serve his happiness, wanted his love and trust in return.

This One answered him: I see that many do harm, and mean to. And many do harm without meaning to. And many do good without meaning to. And many do good by deliberate action, and at great cost to themselves, and act with courage and strength to serve the happiness of others. Yet you do not love them.

I fear them, replied Danny honestly.

That is wise yet childish of you, answered This One. You fear that you cannot trust their love, so you do not trust their love, and thus you can never know if you can trust their love. Your fear protects you from harm, yet it exposes you to the pain and terror of loneliness, so it harms you through another door. Why do you think that you, of all the ones who come home to Duat, should return to Mittlegard?

Not me, not for my own sake. Not Pat either, not for her own sake and not for mine. I'm here to learn how to free myself from Set or to overpower him so he cannot harm another or acquire the power to rule the worlds.

He cannot rule here, because no one rules here.

Not you? asked Danny.

Those who do as I ask of them, do it because they see my purpose and they want my plans to come to fruition. That's why they joined me in assembling the worlds you live on, and growing the lives of both worlds, and sending so many of my friends to dwell there and learn to live in the body, with all its walls and powers.

You compel nobody, Danny echoed.

Nobody ever compels anybody, said This One. It cannot be done. You can hurt them in the body or damage them in the soul, but only they can choose what to do about it. But look now, Danny North. I already knew you and understood your worth, because when I sent you to be born on Mittlegard, a billion others chose to follow you into your body and become a part of your very self, and give you the power that is in them. They are what you call your gates. Because you gave your own following to the one called Wad, he now has great power; but the moment you call them back to you, all that you ever had will be yours, because they want to do your will.

My gates are really not a part of me?

They are part of you. The part of you that is able to travel through enormous distances in moments. Every ka and every ba possesses simple power to move from here to there, and there to here. That power of movement is harnessed and put to work to make things like gravity and engines, light and wind. But left to themselves, how can they discover where "here" is? Someone needs to establish the baseline, so that all the particles can organize themselves and form worlds and atmospheres, landforms and climate zones, fish and animals and birds. All of these are made from molecules, which are made from atoms, which are made from particles ever smaller, and smaller yet. But ultimately the building block of everything is the thing you call *ka*, but which in other places and times has been spoken of as *pret*. Prets are the ones who wait, doing their duty to *me* all the while. Always ready to obey as soon as they know what law applies to them.

They are drawn to love and power. They were drawn to you. The millions of gates in your hoard are those who loved, admired, and followed you, to be a part of you, perfectly obedient even when you imagine you can give them away. They went with you the way the Sutahites went with Set.

I don't want to be like Set, answered Danny.

Then don't be, said This One.

Tell me what to do, and I will go back and do it.

You know what to do.

Danny North hated enigmatic answers. They smacked of trickery to him, and he didn't want to try to outthink someone who was obviously much wiser and better informed than he.

Without answering, his thoughts became his answer.

I am not tricking you, said This One. I simply cannot choose for you. Nor can I tell you how to do what has never been done.

You can't tell me . . . because you don't know?

There is a law that keeps you here, once you come. If I make an exception to that law, it will not be to serve myself or to indulge some mortal's whims. All the laws exist to protect and promote the happiness of all. If I give you a plan and send you back, then you will be acting as my tool in Mittlegard, and your acts will be my acts. I will not do that, because the good order of Duat and of all the worlds depends on my never doing that. You and all the others must be free to choose. I offer. I teach. But I do not manipulate. I do not force. I do not rule.

I think the world would be a better place if you did.

The worlds of men and women are free to obey me whenever they choose. Meanwhile, they're also free to obey and disobey each other.

I am not free to disobey Set.

Then how are you here? He did not want you to come.

He ruled my body. It obeyed him, not me.

Your body never obeyed anyone but you.

Danny hated this thought the moment he grasped it; but he also knew that if This One said it, it had be true, even if only in a way that Danny did not understand.

In all the weeks that Set had ruled over his body, controlling his speech, his actions, was Danny North somehow doing what Set commanded?

Why didn't my body do my will? Set blocked me every time.

Set blocked *you*. Not your body.

Danny tried to remember what it felt like, to attempt something and be blocked by Set. He would will his body to do something, like move an arm or say a word, and then he was blocked. Wasn't that Set controlling his body?

No.

So it was Set between his will and his body. It was Set blocking his desires.

Still wrong, but less wrong.

It was Set telling him that he did not want what he had thought he wanted. It was Set contradicting him, and then Danny himself backed down.

Why did I do that? demanded Danny.

Why did you do that? answered This One.

I was afraid.

What were you afraid of?

Danny tried to remember. Tried to analyze it.

Then Pat spoke—or rather, had an idea and pushed it into the dialectic: You were afraid your body would not obey and so you countermanded your own command.

Yes, This One affirmed.

Would my body have obeyed me?

No answer.

Because I *did* keep pushing, I *struggled*, and I couldn't get past Set's contradiction.

Couldn't?

Pushing is not how you get your body to obey, Pat suggested. Pushing is compulsion. There is no compulsion between the body and its owner, its ka and ba.

I felt Set as if he were blocking me, so I pushed. But pushing accomplished nothing because my body doesn't respond to pushing, and neither does Set.

Understanding flooded through Danny. When I make a gate, I don't *push* the gate, I *invite* it. My own body is controlled the way a mage gets his heartbound to obey: by invitation, by trust, by willing obedience.

Danny, Pat murmured. I think we barely know our own bodies. I think we ride them like leaves on the wind, blown about by the body's desire, and only rarely persuading the body to follow a higher plan. You knew how to block your body's fulfilment of desire— that's how you resisted the girls who wanted you. How you resisted me. But resisting your body is not the same as knowing it.

Right, replied This One.

I can't expel Set, thought Danny. So I can't stop him from interposing himself between my body and my will.

But that idea was immediately set aside by This One. Or rather, Danny immediately felt sluggish-minded and stupid, which is how he experienced This One's "no."

I *can* stop him from getting between me and my body. By making sure they are not two separate things. By truly becoming one with my body. So there's no interval into which Set can push through and block me.

But if I do that, Set will give up and leave, and then we won't know where he is.

Tomorrow's battle, Pat answered. Your freedom, your control of your body: today's battle.

This One said nothing.

I think I can't learn how to do this here, away from my body, thought Danny North.

That is right.

Please make an exception to the rule and let Pat and me go back to our bodies. We will learn how to know our bodies better, so no one else can come between us, so that our bodies will respond perfectly to our will.

And how will I explain this to all the wights who have asked for exactly that, and been denied?

Explain that I will try to make the worlds safe from Set.

You are already one of the great ones here, Danny, replied Pat. I saw it the moment we returned. They knew you, they remembered you. They rejoiced to see you but they were also puzzled, because you haven't yet done the work appointed for you.

How was I ever supposed to do that work if no one ever told me what it was?

We choose our own works, said This One.

Am I choosing well? asked Danny.

You are choosing, and noticing your choice, and taking responsibility for it.

But is it the right way?

Why do you think there is only one right way to do your chosen work?

Because there are so many wrong ways!

You want me to always tell you what's the right way so you never get it wrong. But if you come to count on me, then once again, am I not the one doing it, and not you?

Yes, you'd be doing it, and I'm content with that! Let me help *you*. Please don't make me guess.

It doesn't work that way.

Change the rules until it does!

The rules are not of my making. They're in the nature of things. Power comes only by persuasion, by love and service. It comes from trying and learning.

A quote from *The Empire Strikes Back* that Hal and Wheeler always used came to mind. "Do. Or do not. There is no try."

This One responded with sadness and scorn. The opposite is true, This One seemed to say. There is only try, and try again, until you can persuade the world to work according to your new plan for it. There is no "do" because everything has a mind of its own, and follows the laws it already understands.

So you can't change the laws, Danny replied to This One. Not because you are blocked from changing them, but because without the laws there *is* no doing, no making, no knowing. The laws *are* the universe, and we kas and bas, we inselves and outselves, we prets—we can only find a place within those laws, and by obeying them gain a measure of power.

Closer. Closer. Close enough for now.

May we go back? asked Danny North. May we be alive again

on Mittlegard, in our same bodies, using what we've learned here to *try* to make the world safe from that old liar Set?

There was no answer; there was no *time* for an answer. Because Danny immediately felt the overwhelming rush of sensation. He was in his body again.

He could hear: the noises of the street outside, the highway two blocks over. He could feel: the vibrations in the floor. He could smell: the iron stink of spilled, congealing blood. Pat's blood.

Danny opened his mouth to speak.

His mouth spoke.

"Welcome back, Danny North," his mouth said. "Brought your girlfriend, too, I see. Let's kill her again and see how many times we can do this."

Danny paid no attention to the message from Set. Instead, he now could sense how his ka connected with every cell of his body. Only that wasn't enough. He tried, for a moment, to push the tendrils of himself deeper. Only there were no tendrils and there was no pushing. Instead, he asked his body to receive him more deeply, and now he was aware of the minute workings of the cells, the business of life at the most basic level.

And still he knew that it would not be enough.

Let me be a part of you. Let me know you well enough to serve you.

The cells of his body became large to him, because his awareness reached so deeply inside them, all at once. He felt the weight of large molecules drifting through the liquids in the cells. He sensed the businesses and processes, the atoms jostling, shifting from one molecule to another. How can I know this? Because this is the body that was given to me. The body that gives itself to me.

This deep knowledge of his own flesh and bones filled him with light and fire. There was a larger world inside himself than outside, or so it seemed.

He opened up his mouth to speak. "Pat, are you all right? Are you back?"

And then that welcome voice, that crazy voice that had volunteered to die. "Of course," she said. "And it's scarcely been three minutes since I came to your door."

Danny's mind reeled. The death of Pat, the journey to another world, the long, elaborate, wordless conversation with This One on Duat, and it all took place in such a brief period of time that their bodies had not begun to decay.

By reflex, without thinking, Danny tried to pass a gate over Pat to make sure that she was well.

Only he had no gates.

Yet still, something passed over her, something of Danny's making, and she was well.

"I have no gates," said Danny. "How did I pass you through a gate that I don't have?"

"I don't know, but I was in pain and felt logy, and now it doesn't hurt at all, and I'm sharp and clear again."

"But I didn't make a gate."

"Maybe you don't need gates to do it anymore," said Pat. "Maybe it's enough for you to ask every part of my body to be healed at once."

Danny wanted to think about this, but he was interrupted by a feeling that it took a moment to identify.

Set was trying to leave him.

"Please don't go," said Danny. "I don't think you're ready to wander off without me yet."

And just like that, Set stayed.

7

Hermia recognized the girl the moment she appeared. It was Danny's drowther girlfriend, Pat. Only she was no drowther anymore.

"What ill wind blows you here?" Hermia asked.

"Danny and I were curious about how you're doing these days," said Pat.

Hermia laughed a little. "How do you like my cell?"

Pat looked around expressionlessly. "You gave your Family a Great Gate. Do you expect me to believe that exile on the island of Arkoi was your reward?"

"They exiled me to Patmos, where my Family owns a little bit of . . . well, everything. But the place was crawling with Christians who thought that because God gave John such a wild dream on

Patmos, he'll keep pumping out deep revelation to seminarians and pious tourists."

"No gratitude from your Family, then?"

"They were grateful—till the Great Gate disappeared. Good old Gate Thief, still in business after all." Hermia knew that this visit wasn't prompted by curiosity and certainly not by friendliness. She was going to have to face Danny's judgment sooner or later. So if Pat wouldn't bring up the subject, Hermia would. "You know that I didn't choose to betray Danny."

A hint of a smile? The girl's face was so hard to read. "The devil made you do it," she said.

Such hypocrisy. "That's the excuse Danny's using these days, isn't it?" Hermia saw the moment she said it that this was a mistake. Pat was loyal. It was her main virtue. Only a fool would speak ill of Danny, even as a joke.

But Hermia was a gatemage—a gateless one, so all she had left was her perverse sense of humor. It was too much to expect Pat to understand this.

Hermia felt a sudden wind roil her hair, and then a gust threw her off balance and she fell, chair and all, onto the tile floor.

"Oh, very good," said Hermia. "Clever windmage, to knock down a powerless prisoner."

"You're not *my* prisoner," said Pat.

"I am now," said Hermia, "since I can't get away, and you're the one in the room with all the power."

"You chose to betray Danny," said Pat. "There's always a choice."

"You're right," said Hermia. "But oddly enough, I think I made the choice Danny North would have made. If you can stop blowing things over long enough to listen, I think you'll agree with me."

The air was suddenly still. "It was wrong of me to use the wind that way," said Pat. "I'm sorry."

"I'm not much for forgiveness, but—"

"I wasn't apologizing to *you*," said Pat, her voice thick with scorn. "Tell me your story. Not so I can judge you, but so that Danny can hear. For some reason, he thinks he owes you a hearing."

"How is he listening?" asked Hermia. "There's no gate in this room and there never was. How did you get here?"

Pat paused a moment, perhaps to make a point of the fact that she wasn't going to answer Hermia's questions. "I think you were going to explain why you moved the Wild Gate and wrecked Danny's plan," said Pat.

"I didn't believe in Danny's 'plan' because it was never going to work."

"Not with *you* subverting it," said Pat.

"But I wasn't going to subvert it," said Hermia. "I was going to let it fail under the pressure of all its inherent errors."

"I'm not here so you can critique Danny's plan. It failed because of what *you* chose to do."

"And here's why. My clever Family put together a list of Danny's friends. You, the three stupid girls, and Hal and Wheeler."

"The other girls aren't stupid."

"Compared to you they are," said Hermia. "Compared to me, of course, you're all stupid except maybe Hal. But the point is that Danny cared about all of you. And the Family was perfectly willing to spend you, all at once or one at a time, in order to get Danny to give them exclusive use of a Great Gate."

"So we were hostages even though your Family didn't have any of us in custody."

"Silly child," said Hermia. "Families don't have to have you in *custody*. They only have to know where you are and how to get to you. Which of you would have been able to stand against a single dogsbody, let alone a mage with real power."

"Nobody had *real* power till the Great Gate."

"Compared to you and your friends, they *all* had power."

"But we could get away."

"Not quickly enough," said Hermia. "They knew about your amulets."

"Because you told them."

"Because you all fingered them while delivering your messages. And I had one, too, remember. Do you think the Families can't figure out *obvious* things? They may have had old-fashioned, out-of-date powers, but their brains are the latest model *Homo sapiens*, and when it comes to the use of coercive power against drowthers, you have no idea how skilled they are. The Iliad didn't begin to plumb the depths of what they could and would do."

"So you moved the Wild Gate in order to save me and my friends." Pat sounded skeptical.

"I don't give a rat's ass about you or your friends. But *Danny's* friends, now—I knew they were his hobby and you were the momentary love of his life."

"Momentary. Cute."

"Oh, grow up, Patty. Everybody in the Families is notoriously fickle, but gatemages most of all. Most of the really good Eros stories are the escapades of Gatefathers. And even though Jupiter gets the credit for Leda and Ganymede and all the other kidnapped lovers, it was always a gatelord who did the carrying off. Danny may not know it yet, but he'll lose interest. Maybe not as quickly as most of them, but 'faithful gatemage' is an oxymoron."

"So I'm Danny's *momentary* conquest. You've hurt my feelings. Boo hoo. That's your whole story?"

"I knew that they probably couldn't kill all of you, but they could hurt most of you, scare you all, and maybe kill a couple. Even if I warned Danny, it wouldn't matter. He couldn't be everywhere at once, but the Family could. And of course, anything *we* knew, other Families could figure out, what with all the spying we all do all the time. Ratmages have their role to play; there are mice in the walls and floors. As an example of ruthlessness, the Hittites found Danny and me and blasted him with a shotgun without asking questions. He lived, of course, because he could gate himself away before he died. But if it had been me they blasted, I couldn't have used my amulet quickly enough. Ditto with you and your chums. So yes, I took the threat seriously. I knew Danny would rather revise his hopeless plan than lose any of you. So I moved the Wild Gate. But I pretended it was harder than it actually was, so Danny would have plenty of time to realize it was gone from the Silvermans' barn so he could set up an alternative. Maine, wasn't it? But I didn't tell anyone where his Great Gate was. I was playing as nicely as I could, giving him every chance to keep the Families in balance."

"*Brava*," said Pat. "You're such a *princess*."

"My Family realized that I wasn't really playing for their team. And once they discovered that my amulet wasn't working anymore, then the same people who once plugged a bunch of tracking devices into my body decided that keeping me on a heavily guarded island was almost as good an idea as killing me."

"Yes, I imagine that Danny will believe all of this and agree that you made the right choice," said Pat.

"But you don't think I did right, keeping you alive?"

"I'm not the judge," said Pat. "I'm just a novice Orphan windmage of as-yet-unmeasured powers."

"Oh, that indoor wind thing was pretty impressive," said Hermia. "You'll hold up pretty well in the coming war."

"I'm not in that war."

"Oh, don't kid yourself, kid," said Hermia. "The Orphans will be brushed aside before the *real* mage-to-mage fighting begins."

"Fine," said Pat. "Then I'll be dead."

"Dead is pretty final," said Hermia.

"No doubt," said Pat. "Except for one tiny thing." And right in front of Hermia's eyes, Pat shifted about a meter to the left. Without changing her posture or moving her hand or anything.

What was the girl trying to show her? "You have an amulet to move you a meter? Do you get to choose the direction of this incredibly useful move?"

Pat shifted rapidly from point to point around the room. Then disappeared completely, and returned about ten seconds later.

"How many gates were created?" asked Pat.

"None," said Hermia. "None at all."

"Not surprising, since I'm not a gatemage."

"So Danny's doing it."

"Danny is with Veevee, teaching her how to do what I just did. In fact, while I was out of the room I checked in and told Danny you were about ready."

"Ready for what?"

"For him to decide whether you can be trusted with any of the things we've recently learned. Or whether he should just get you out of here. Me, I'm for leaving you right where you are, but he thinks he owes you something for past help. Danny's even more loyal than I am. Though perhaps that will turn out to be momentary, too."

"For an American high-school girl, you certainly have mastered snottiness."

"For American teenage girls, snottiness is an Olympic event, and we're all training to qualify for the national team. Starting in middle school."

Hermia laughed. "I can see why Danny likes you," said Hermia. "*I* like you, even though all I really care about right now is how Danny was able to give gatemaking abilities to a windmage, when he could never give them to me."

Pat cocked her head a little. Thinking? Listening? "He didn't give them to me," said Pat. Apparently she had reached her decision, and she was going to tell Hermia something about what was going on with these gateless gates.

"Oh, please," said Hermia. Because challenging Pat with scorn seemed to work better than simple inquiry.

"Everybody has the ability to move like that," said Pat. "It's not even a secret, if you just think about it. We all get from Duat to our newborn baby bodies, without any detectable gate, and when we die, back we go. Gateless again."

Hermia realized Pat was right—it was obvious enough. "But those aren't gates."

"They're not only gates, they're Great Gates, since they go from one planet to another. And we all know the way. We just don't leave a trace of our path behind us."

"Somebody from Duat manages all that," said Hermia.

Again, the cocked head. The decision. "No," said Pat. "Not the way you think. The ability to move *from* anywhere *to* anywhere is inherent in all of us. What's tricky is bringing along our baggage." And she indicated her own body.

"Danny told you to tell me this?" asked Hermia.

"He left it up to me. Because simply telling you doesn't help you at all," said Pat. "You can only learn it by doing."

Hermia tried to make sense of this. "So *you* learned it, and you didn't learn it from Danny. What did you do, die?"

"Yes," said Pat.

Hermia had meant the question as a joke. But Pat's response was honest enough. So Hermia thought through what that implied. "He followed you to the afterlife and brought you back?"

"That's the simplest version."

"You were actually completely dead," said Hermia.

"If you're not dead, you can't get to Duat. Except that Danny held on to me, mostly detached from his body, and let me pull him there."

"So you've been dead, and you came back."

"Which is how I know what it feels like to move—without leaving a gate behind me that somebody else might follow."

Hermia began to realize the implications of this. Danny had given away all his gates, and a few days ago he got rid of the last of the captive gates, too. But now he could go anywhere without needing to have any gates at all. His outself was in Loki's tender keeping, and yet Danny's movements were not restricted. "So that makes you a windmage *and* a gatemage," said Hermia.

"I can only move myself," said Pat. "But in the long run, that's all anyone can do. Danny and Veevee have talked about it, about how gates usually work, and I suspect they want you to hear their ideas and see if you can come up with alternatives."

"Did they lock you out of the room, or do you know what they think?"

"If explaining it could give you the ability to do it, Veevee would already have learned it."

So you think that if Veevee can't learn it, neither can I? But Hermia did not say that. Instead, she said, "If I can't learn it by hearing about it, you might as well tell me."

Pat gave one little derisive laugh—but then went ahead and told. Maybe not everything, but something. "The movement I can do now is the only kind of movement there is—a ka relocating itself in relation to other kas. Only in Duat they seem to think 'ka' should refer only to the human inself. The generic term for every entity capable of such movement is 'pret.' All of us are prets. And the ba—the outself, right? It acts like a part of us, but it isn't. It consists of the handful or dozen or thousand or billion prets that chose to follow us into this life, into our bodies."

"So Danny's not really a man with a billion gates, he's just the chairman of the board?"

"The prets that make up the ba seem to be as obedient to our will as our bodies are. That's why you can make a gate and then die, and yet the gate stays there, guiding people back and forth between locations."

Hermia saw that Danny and Pat may well have had a glimpse behind the curtain, and it excited her. Even as a prisoner, trusted by nobody, she still loved to learn how things worked. To make sense of the world. "So you're saying that every gate is somebody else's ka, but it's your slave, bound to obey you?"

"Not a slave, not *property*. It follows you because it chooses to, because it's bound to you by some kind of unbreakable oath. Or at least *it* can't break the oath."

"What was the word?" asked Hermia. "Pret?"

"Gatemages don't forget words," said Pat, "so you know it is."

Hermia summarized what she thought the girl had told her. "You and I and every other human *is* a pret that has an entourage. A body, maybe a ba, maybe a thousand gates. But all those parts in the entourage, they're really independent beings that could have been people in their own right."

"I don't think they could be people," said Pat, "or they would be. In Duat it all seems to be about some kind of ranking. If you're at a certain level, you can be born as a human, and take along whatever other prets choose to bind themselves to you."

"A patronage system. Our outselves are merely clients, along for the ride."

"Hardly," said Pat. "They're the source of our power. When I guide the wind, I do it by using the prets of my outself. Nothing like so many as you have, and not persistent enough to become gates. But they love to guide the air into becoming wind. That's how I see it."

"This is all very interesting, but what is it you actually *do* now that you know about these 'prets.' "

"I can sense where things are," said Pat, "and I can go there. My body comes with me when I do. No gate, I just go, and the others follow without my having to tell them to. But if you're like Veevee, you can sense other mages' gates, but you have only the vaguest idea of the outselves of other kinds of mages, and you can't sense anybody's ka or any of the nonmagical prets."

"Correct so far," said Hermia, "though you can be sure I'll try to find out whether this is true or you're just playing with me."

Pat said nothing.

"You can't tell me it surprises you that I'm not taking you at your word."

"I expect nothing from you," said Pat, "so you can't very well surprise me."

"When did you do all this dying and journeying to Duat?" asked Hermia.

"A few days ago. Danny got rid of the captive gates the moment after he healed my body. I had just died. That's when he followed my instinctive journey to Duat."

"No coin for the ferryman at the river Styx?" asked Hermia.

"There's no river and we all know the way."

"And our outselves are prets that voluntarily bound themselves to us, when we were born," said Hermia.

"We don't know how they sort themselves out," said Pat, "but yes, that's pretty much what we were told."

"So how could the Gate Thief take them away from other gatemages? How could Danny strip my outself away from me? Did they suddenly decide they liked him better?"

"No, they're still yours," said Pat. "Only captive. You can't use them, but the Gate Thief can't use them either, or not safely, anyway. Which is how that Wild Gate was created in the first place. The prets *wanted* to be part of a Great Gate, and once they weren't locked inside Danny's hoard, they weren't bound to obey him."

"But how could they be stolen?" asked Hermia.

"I'm not a gatemage," said Pat. "But from what Danny and Veevee were saying, I think their current guess is that your gates, your outself, your . . . entourage? . . . was invited to leave you for a time, and they accepted."

"Just like that?"

"They were asked by somebody far more powerful than you. Far more attractive to a pret. But they still belong to you because that oath seems to be unbreakable."

"You sound so sure," said Hermia.

"I'm sure that that's what Danny and Veevee said. I'm sure that they're completely unsure about whether they're right. I'm sure that I can't do any of those things because even though I can move wherever I want, I'm not a gatemage, so I will never experience any of what *you* experience."

"And apparently I will never experience it again," said Hermia. "Because even if Danny were inclined to return my gates to me, they're now in the possession of the Gate Thief, and he doesn't give anything back."

"Whatever," said Pat. "Danny's heard all he needs to. So I have only one question now."

"What's that?"

"Do you want to get out of this place?"

"I'm like the Wild Gate," said Hermia. "If Danny sets me free, what makes him think he can control me?"

"He doesn't," said Pat. "Because he doesn't think he can control anybody."

"He controls *you*," said Hermia, knowing that it wasn't true, knowing that these words were designed to cause pain to someone who had done her no harm. But it was in her nature to say it. It was her *pleasure* to say it.

In that moment, without any awareness of a gate, Hermia found herself sitting in a chair on the balcony of Veevee's condo in Naples, Florida. Veevee was lying on a chaise, taking the sun. Danny was sitting on the floor in a corner, looking for all the world like a frightened child.

"So I'm worthy to enter the august presence," said Hermia.

"Don't be a bitch, dear," said Veevee. "You know that by all the rules of the Westilian Families, you should be getting thrown from this balcony—perhaps after having most of your skin removed."

"I know that," said Hermia. "But I also know that Danny isn't like that, and neither are you. And neither is *my* Family, for that matter, because here I am, alive and as spunky as ever."

Pat appeared in a chair beside Veevee. "I think she believed everything I explained, and she thinks she can try to learn it by watching what we do."

"Maybe she can," said Veevee. "Can't stop her from trying."

"I don't think any of this can be learned just by clicking your heels and saying, 'No place like home,'" said Danny quietly.

"He's saying that because this old dog couldn't learn any of the tricks," Veevee explained to Hermia.

"Maybe it just takes time," said Hermia. "It took time for you and Danny to figure out anything, before you had me to show you what I could do."

"But Danny has shown me his new powers. It blows me away, Hermia, darling, but I have no idea what he's actually doing."

"Pat knows how to do it because she was with me in Duat," said Danny. "I didn't have to teach her anything except how to move. She already *saw* what she needed to see."

"Prets?" asked Hermia. "Pret—is it really the French word? As in *prêt-à-porter*?"

"I don't know," said Danny. "The word was put in my mind. Our minds. By somebody who doesn't actually use language to communicate. So who knows the origin of the word?"

"You're such gatemages," said Pat. "Worrying about etymology when you're talking about the fundamental power of the universe."

"I know I can't teach you, Hermia, because I can't teach Veevee," said Danny. "And I actually trust *her*."

"I assume you listened to what I told Pat?" asked Hermia. "I was not betraying you."

"Oh, I assumed all along that they did something to manipulate you," said Danny. "But I think that just gave you the window-dressing to do what you really wanted—to have control of a Great Gate and pass your Family through."

"Probably true," said Hermia. "In fact, I'll say you nailed it. I wanted them to make me do it. But it doesn't change the fact that they really would have messed up your friends."

"I'm not your judge," said Danny. "I'm not anybody's judge."

"You're everybody's judge," said Hermia. "People with power are always judges, deciding whom to treat well and whom to ignore. And this power—gating without gates . . ."

"Moving myself and others without using my outself," said Danny. "I don't know if I was meant to end up with this power, or if it's just something that comes with katabasis."

"She really died?" asked Hermia.

Danny held up his hand and looked at it somberly. "Out, damned spot," he said softly.

"Set used your own hand to kill her?"

"It's the only hand he had the use of," said Danny. "So, yes."

"You remember killing her."

Danny nodded. "And I remember my own choice to let her finish dying and stay dead."

"So you could follow her to Duat," said Hermia.

"It was *my* plan," said Pat.

"What made you think it would even work?" Hermia asked her.

"Persephone," said Pat. "Isis. Eurydice."

Hermia could hardly believe that was all Pat had to go on. "Ancient lies, long since augmented and altered and . . ."

"She took an extravagant chance," said Veevee, "and laid her own life on the line. What did *you* do?"

"I caved in at the first opportunity," said Hermia. "So toss me off the balcony into the Gulf."

"The Gulf isn't directly below the balcony, and you don't deserve a soft landing," said Veevee.

"Nobody's dropping anybody off of anything," said Danny. "All I have right now is that Pat can move herself around at will, and I can move myself and others, all without taking any of my gates back from Loki. I can't teach this to anybody who hasn't died and come back. I have no idea how to turn this into anything."

"Maybe you can't," said Hermia. "And in the meantime, where's Set?"

Danny patted his chest.

"You mean he's still *in* you?" asked Hermia.

"Where else?" asked Pat. "Where would Set go if Danny let him loose?"

"You mean you're holding him prisoner?" asked Hermia.

"I don't think so," said Danny. "I asked him not to leave me, and he stayed."

"So he could jump from you into any of us," said Hermia.

"Why would he?" asked Veevee. "Danny has powers that no one has ever had. Set probably thinks he can take back control whenever he wants."

"Maybe he does," said Danny, "but I don't think he's that stupid."

"I think he really can't go anywhere," said Pat. "You should have heard Danny when he 'asked' Set not to go. Danny has authority now. No, he has Authority. Capital A. Or maybe it's AUTHORITY—all caps."

"Like drunk people texting?" asked Hermia.

"The shift button doesn't activate because your blood alcohol level reaches a certain threshold," said Veevee.

"Set is listening to everything? *Watching* everything?" asked Hermia. "Aren't you afraid he's learning it all? If he ever figures out how to gate between worlds without actually using any gates, then all these elaborate precautions you and the Gate Thief took are pretty worthless, aren't they?"

"He can't do any of it," said Danny. "Because he's incapable of rooting into a living body."

"You're sure?" asked Hermia.

Pat murmured, "Idiot."

"I wouldn't have done the things I've been doing if I weren't sure," said Danny.

"What *happened* on Duat?" said Hermia.

"We were dead, and now we're not," said Pat.

"None of it happened in language," said Danny. "Or with the normal human senses. It all keeps fading in and out, like a half-remembered dream. But parts of it are clear. And then other parts are clear. But I can't put it all together into a coherent report. 'How I Spent My Vacation in Hades.'"

"'Captain Stormcloud's Trip to Heaven,'" offered Veevee. "Mark Twain."

"If you've got Set as a captive inside you," said Hermia, "then you've already won the big war. What's left for you to do?"

"I won't live forever," said Danny.

"Get Loki to teach you how to live for a thousand years inside a tree," said Veevee.

"You think I haven't thought of that?" asked Danny. "But as Loki proved, even a thousand years isn't all that long. And during that time, Set got smarter and more powerful."

"Oh, don't flatter him," said Veevee. "You know that when you talk that way, he just *preens*."

"I have no idea what he thinks or feels. If anything," said Danny. "Even when he was controlling my body, he didn't actually *feel* what I felt."

"So what's *in* it for him?" asked Pat. "Why does he do it?"

"He's in it for the power," said Danny. "The control. The puppeteer doesn't feel what the puppets feel. Nor does he care. He just likes to make them dance."

"So if he ever gets loose again . . ." said Pat.

"I don't know how he could do anything worse than the kinds of things he already did." Danny shuddered. "And while he's here, the Sutahites are still out there, doing whatever they do."

"I keep telling Danny that there's no reason to rush out and do anything," said Veevee. "Just let things play out and see what happens. Maybe it will become obvious when Danny needs to intervene."

"Sitting on this balcony is already a decision to do exactly that," said Hermia.

"We brought *you* here," said Pat. "So we aren't just sitting around."

"No, you merely added another sitter," said Hermia. "And I was already doing that on Arkoi."

"Danny can send you back," offered Pat.

"You said you cared about the drowthers," said Hermia to Danny. "But you're not doing anything to stop the carnage."

"What carnage?" asked Veevee.

"The war among the Families is about to erupt, and it's going to be fought by drowthers, using drowther weapons. It's going to make the Trojan War look like an amusement park ride."

Danny shook his head.

"That's the problem," said Pat. "We were given some . . . I don't know, *rules*. Danny isn't supposed to take away other people's power of choice. Including the Families."

"No, I can . . . I can do things. Save people. Some people. Heal people. But I can't *stop* them from waging their war, or at least I think that's how it's supposed to work. If I can *persuade* them not to . . ."

"They've all been to Westil now," said Hermia. "You don't have any leverage."

"Persuasion isn't leverage," said Pat. "Leverage is coercion. Persuasion is to help them see things differently and change their minds, on their own. Not because they're afraid of Danny, or because they want something he can offer."

"That's the only kind of persuasion that works in the real world," said Hermia. "People don't actually change their minds, they just claim they did when they realize that they'll get more advantage out of behaving differently."

"I wish you were just being cynical," said Veevee, "but sadly enough, I think you're right."

Danny sighed. "You think I don't know that? But rules are rules."

"What an ungatemagely thing to say," said Veevee.

"Ungatemagely," repeated Hermia. "Oh, that *is* a word that needed to be said, at least once, in the history of the language."

"The person I need to have here for this discussion is Loki," said Danny.

"Text him and see if he comes," said Hermia.

"There aren't many cell towers on Westil," said Danny.

"And Danny can't go there himself," said Veevee. "Because he'd carry Set with him. And what if he got out after all?"

"So you sit here on the balcony taking in the sunlight," said Hermia.

"What were you doing in the Aegean?" asked Pat.

"I was a prisoner there."

"And we're prisoners of our ignorance," said Danny. "But I appreciate the conversation, because now I think I understand where I'm *not* going to get any answers."

"From us?" asked Veevee.

"From the data available to me so far," said Danny. "If we had enough information, you might very well be able to come up with good ideas. So if you don't mind waiting here for a while . . ."

"I mind," said Hermia.

"I'll escort you back to Arkoi," said Pat. "I think I've learned enough of what Danny does to take a willing passenger."

"Are you two a thing now?" asked Hermia.

Pat stared back at her blankly.

"She's asking if you're sleeping together, dear," said Veevee.

"I know what she's asking," said Pat. "And I was giving her the answer she deserved."

"I was just wondering if Danny was going to be worried about the pregnant girl carrying his baby," said Hermia.

"That's not me," said Pat.

"I don't want to go back to Arkoi," said Hermia. "I'm not sure I want to stay here among people who have every reason to hate me and no reason ever to trust me . . . but since that also describes my family, especially after my astonishing escape . . ."

"Stay here," said Veevee. "I do indeed hate you, but Danny's free of Set's control and he and Pat are back from the dead, so I honestly think it's not as awful as it was just a few days ago, and I might as well have you where I can watch you."

"And what if I decide to walk away from here?" asked Hermia.

"Do what you want," said Danny. "But if you leave, then you aren't part of anything we do from then on."

"Ever?" asked Hermia.

"You've already betrayed us once," said Danny. "Fool me twice, shame on me."

"Fair enough," said Hermia.

"And the food here is pretty good," said Veevee. "You aren't a prisoner. You can go grocery shopping or whatever. Just so you come back at night. And we know where you are and whom you're seeing."

"We don't have to know that," said Danny. "She's not a prisoner. I've had enough of keeping prisoners."

"Except the one," said Pat.

"Well, yes," said Danny. "The Father of Lies and all that. I can't very well encourage *him* to do whatever he wants. But I'm not sure he's actually a prisoner, either."

"And *I'm* not a prisoner," said Hermia, "but if I go too far off the reservation . . ."

"You're on parole," said Pat.

Hermia considered that for a moment. "Is that how it stands, Danny?"

"Close enough," Danny answered. "Do you promise to be a good girl and check in with Mom?"

"Oh, please, I'm nobody's 'mom,' " said Veevee.

"He meant me," said Pat.

"I meant Veevee," said Danny. "Because I hope *you'll* stay with *me*."

Veevee hooted. "Oh, the two of you, really. Danny, don't you know why chaperones were invented in the first place? I think you two should get married so it's all legal and you can make the beast with two backs without breaking any rules."

"We're too young," said Danny. "And I don't think it's legit for a third party to propose marriage to the two of us on each other's behalf."

"Just suggesting," said Veevee.

"Always looking out for others," said Hermia. "You're such a saint, Veevee."

"Sainte Voyeuse, patroness of oglers, panderers, and dirty thoughts," said Veevee.

"I don't think the Catholic Church will ever accept *that* particular saint," said Pat.

"Everybody has a patron saint," said Veevee. "You gotta have somebody to pray to."

To Hermia this was completely incomprehensible. Didn't they understand that gods were just members of the Families, and prayers were just . . . sucking up?

Then she looked over at the corner and Danny was gone.

And that was that. He was off doing something, somewhere.

"I'm surprised he didn't even say goodbye to *you*," Hermia said to Pat.

Pat just looked at her with something like pity. "I know where he is."

"Where, then?"

"If he wanted to tell you, he would have," said Pat.

Hermia rolled her eyes.

"Oh, she knows where he is," said Veevee. "It's the most romantic thing, apparently, being dead together. She never loses track of him, and if he needs her, she can be there in an instant."

"That sounds like hell to me," said Hermia. "Never being able to get away from each other."

"You notice I'm not with him right now," said Pat. "I don't *cling.*"

"I just realized," said Hermia. "Every power that somebody has takes away something from somebody else. Danny can never have any secrets now as long as he lives."

"And vice versa," said Veevee.

Hermia laughed. "Oh, really. Pat can have all the secrets she wants, because it doesn't matter what she's doing."

"She's the one who insisted on taking you out of captivity," said Veevee.

"My point exactly," said Hermia. "What happens to me isn't even interesting, in a world that has Danny North in it."

"But for a couple of minutes a few days ago," said Veevee, "it didn't have Danny North in it. He was with her, in the land of the dead. So Hermia, you can try to hurt Pat or offend her or impress on her how unimportant she is, and it's not going to matter, because she's already done more with her life than you and I will ever do."

True enough. But when Hermia looked at Pat again, she could see that the girl had tears in her eyes.

"I'm sorry," said Hermia. "I can't help being catty."

"Meaning you're proud of it and don't want to quit being bitchy," said Veevee.

"Sorry," said Pat, brushing a sleeve across her eyes. "I wasn't listening. Were you talking about me?"

"If I didn't hurt your feelings," said Hermia, "what were the tears about?"

"The children. The boys. Danny's with the boys. It just makes me sad."

"Hal and Wheeler?" asked Veevee.

Pat shook her head.

"Oh, you mean the boys from Westil," said Veevee.

"Sorry," said Pat. "I think he needs me."

"Meaning you need him," said Hermia.

"Meaning that he just said that he needs me," said Pat. And she was gone.

Hermia sat on the balcony, watching Veevee bake in the sun. "Florida does have its advantages in the winter," Hermia said.

"Oh, sweetie, you don't have to stay out here and talk with me," said Veevee. "I think you're a despicable traitor and I don't enjoy your company right now. So why don't you go make yourself a sandwich or watch something on YouTube? Indoors, with the air-conditioning. Or go shopping."

Hermia was beginning to think she wasn't wanted. She went down the elevator to the beach and walked for a couple of miles. She knew perfectly well where the gates were, but she couldn't really celebrate her new freedom by using gates that were under the control of the Gate Thief. It was walking aimlessly that made her feel free. Something that any drowther could do.

Danny was right. Everything that matters, drowthers can do, and probably better than any Westilian. But the games of power, those belong to us, and when we play, everybody loses.

8

Pat did not know where she was going. She simply went where Danny was. Ever since her passage to Duat and back, enfolded—or so it seemed to her—in Danny's inself, she knew at every moment where he was, and could join herself to him, taking her body with her.

She found herself in a living room—no, a parlor—with Danny, two boys, and two adults.

"Thank you for coming," said Danny.

"When did you invite her?" asked the woman.

"And why?" asked the man.

"I thought about her, and the fact that I needed her, and she came," said Danny.

"What kind of magery is *that*?" asked the woman.

Instead of answering, Danny made the introductions. But now

Pat remembered them from the Great Gate in Maine, when she made her momentary visit to Westil and awoke her latent wind-magery. Marion and Leslie Silverman, Danny's foster parents. And they seemed to know exactly who she was, which was encouraging—it meant that Danny had talked about her. And had said good things, because they were warm in their welcome to her, though Pat also suspected there was a tinge of pity in the way Mrs. Silverman spoke to her.

"We're glad to have you here," said Mr. Silverman, "and especially so if Danny needs you."

"Though I hope you don't sit around doing nothing, waiting for his call," said Mrs. Silverman. "Devotion is fine, but he'll lose interest in you if you don't have a life of your own."

"That's not an issue," said Danny. "It's impossible for us not to be aware of each other at all times, and she carries on her life just fine."

That was not actually true, but Pat knew that Danny had little knowledge of what her life had been before she died and he brought her back, so how could he compare?

"She's not agreeing with you on that," said Mrs. Silverman.

Pat was startled. Nobody could read her face; what had she given away? "Mrs. Silverman," Pat said.

"Leslie," said Mrs. Silverman.

"Miz Leslie," said Pat. "Nobody's life is 'just fine' right now."

"A southern girl," said Leslie. " 'Miz' Leslie. I like that."

Mr. Silverman cleared his throat. "Are we all friends now? Can we move on?"

"Grump," said Leslie.

"Why do you need her here, Danny?" he asked again.

"Because I can't fix what's wrong with these boys, and there's a good chance that she can."

Pat's immediate thought was, And there's an overwhelming

chance that I can't. But she said nothing, because she had no idea what kind of fixing they needed, or why a windmage would be involved in it.

"There's nothing wrong with us," said the younger boy. Pat thought back to what Danny had called him in previous conversations. Enopp. The silent older one was Eluik.

Danny had told her that Enopp thought he was a gatemage, while it seemed Eluik had some of the powers of a manmage, like his mother, because during the boys' terrifying confinement in separate caves in Iceway, on Westil, Eluik had somehow sent his ba into his brother, to comfort him. Now he was stuck there, because, in his inexperience, he did not know how to return; or, fearful now himself, he was afraid to let go of his brother. Danny had speculated that, no matter how it began, it wasn't the older brother comforting the younger anymore. It was Eluik now who was afraid to let go, and instead he communicated with Enopp and Enopp spoke for him to the others.

Only now Pat could sense things that were beyond the reach of other mages. She and Danny were the only living souls who had been to Duat and then returned. In the process, not only had they become capable of detecting each other's inself and outself, but now they understood that the inself, the ka, was the original self, while the outself, the ba, the wanderer, the doodlebug, was really someone else, an independent entity or entities that their guide in Duat had taught them to call "pret."

The pret or prets that made up a mage's outself had entered into this close bond voluntarily, but now it could not be broken. That's why, as soon as Danny gave them back to themselves, the wild captive left-behind gates immediately returned to Duat, to rebind themselves with the masterful pret to whom they had bound themselves before he or she was born. They could be kidnapped, as the Gate Thief had done, or lent out, as Danny had done when he "gave" his gates to Loki; but they could never belong to anyone but the ka to whom they had bound themselves as ba.

So what Pat *should* have seen, expected to see as she looked at the two boys from Westil, was that Eluik's ba was inside Enopp's body, riding him like a heartbeast.

But this was not the situation at all. Eluik was not a manmage, half dwelling inside his younger brother. Instead, it was Enopp whose ka, whose very self, had left his own body and now dwelt inside his older brother. Until now, Danny had completely misunderstood who was riding whom. Eluik was silent because he had as little access to his own body as Danny had had when Set was controlling him. And Enopp knew what his brother wanted to say because he was inside him, intercepting all his attempts to speak with his own voice.

Meanwhile, Enopp was able to use his own body freely, because even though only his ba—the thousands of prets that proved him to be, in all likelihood, a potential gatemage—was inside his body, there was no rival trying to control it. It was his own body that he rode like a heartbeast, using his outself to control it.

Danny looked at Pat searchingly. "Do you see?"

"The opposite of what you thought," said Pat.

"Say no more than that," said Danny. "Nothing more can be said aloud."

For a moment, Pat wondered why Danny didn't trust the Silvermans. Or did he think that naming the situation for what it was might damage the boys further?

Then she realized that there was a seventh person present—Set himself, dwelling silently inside Danny North. At the moment, Danny seemed to have him under control, but there was no assurance of that continuing. It was quite possible that Set would realize that Enopp's body *had* no ka dwelling in it, and he would take it. Or perhaps the very process of helping Enopp bring his ka back into his own body would teach Set how to take full possession of a body—and he might use that understanding to take control of Danny again, only this time deeply and irrevocably.

Whatever could be done to restore Eluik and Enopp had to be done without Danny, and therefore Set, present.

"I have no idea if I can do it," said Pat.

"We only learned how to do the things we can do now by experiencing it," said Danny. "Maybe Enopp and Eluik can learn the same way."

And there was the warning, almost explicitly stated: They could not afford to let Set see, or he, too, would learn.

"Leave, then," said Pat. "And I'll do my best."

"That'll be good enough," said Danny.

"You don't know that," said Pat, mildly amused.

"If it's all we can do, it's good enough," said Danny. "We can't do more than is within our power." He went to Leslie Silverman and kissed her cheek. "I'm sorry for all the trouble I caused you."

"If Pat can do the job," said Mr. Silverman, "then we'll still need to find another hiding place for the boys."

"And for yourselves," said Danny.

"In time of war," said Leslie, "sometimes you have to become a refugee in order to survive. We've made arrangements for a friend to tend the cows. They'll miss me, but they'll be well cared for."

"It's a good mage who leaves her heartbound for the sake of strangers," said Danny.

"Don't be absurd," said Leslie. "These boys are *not* strangers."

"We like them much better than you," said Marion. "They're way less trouble."

"Only because on average they talk half as much as I did," said Danny.

"That's probably it," said Marion.

"Plus, they stay where we can keep an eye on them," said Leslie.

"I was a brat, wasn't I. You poor, patient oldsters."

Marion winced at "oldsters." "What a horrible word," he said.

"A brat, yes? We agree on that?" Danny grinned, and then he was gone.

Pat stood looking at the boys, who were seated beside each other, Eluik in a wooden side chair, Enopp on the floor beside him.

"Eluik won't sit in soft chairs," said Leslie. "And Enopp won't stray far from him."

No wonder, thought Pat. Enopp wants to keep his own body close by, since he uses it for all his talking.

Did Enopp understand that he had captured his brother's body? Almost certainly not.

"Maybe this will go better," said Pat to the boys, "if you close your eyes."

"I don't like surprises," said Enopp. "And Eluik only closes his eyes when he feels like it."

"I'm afraid I won't be able to do this clearly enough for you to understand what I'm doing," said Pat. "And since it can't be seen by physical eyes, I thought you'd want to be undistracted by visual stimuli."

Enopp shrugged and closed his eyes. Eluik's remained open, but since he didn't seem to be focusing on anything in the room, that would probably be all right. It's not as if Pat had any idea what would or would not work, or what might interfere with a good outcome.

Instead of saying anything to them, Pat sent her ba—a group of her prets, she now understood—inside Eluik. There she probed until she found Enopp's ka, his inmost self, with the roots he had sunk into his brother's body. Not as deeply as the roots of Eluik's ka, of course, since the body belonged to him, but Enopp was definitely more closely entwined with Eluik than Set had been with Danny North.

It occurred to Pat that maybe Eluik had spent years in deep frustration, as Enopp controlled and silenced him, while speaking for him. Yet it might be that Eluik really did want to comfort and protect his little brother, and if he had to sacrifice his own ability to speak in order to do it, maybe he didn't resent it.

Would he resent being liberated?

Was he being liberated? Ultimately, it would be up to Enopp. Would he understand what Pat was showing him?

Still she did not speak with her mouth, but rather communicated as This One had communicated with Danny and her, showing the boys her understanding of what she was discovering inside Eluik's body. This is you, Enopp. You are in him; he is not in you. You can give him back to himself, by pulling away here. And here. And here.

Then Pat sent part of her ba into Enopp's own body, showing the empty place—if it could be called a "place"—where Enopp's ka should be, and how inadequately his thousands of gates substituted for Enopp's missing inself.

Time seemed to have no meaning when communicating ka to ka like this; Pat was very thorough in her demonstration, and she could sense that Enopp understood well enough to pull parts of himself, tendrils of his control, out of Eluik's body. But as for moving his entire ka back where it belonged?

It was time for Pat to give him a choice, which meant also giving him time to choose. She pulled her ba back into herself, and then murmured, "It's time to let Eluik have his body back, Enopp. He has served you so kindly, and you have also been his friend. You didn't know what it was costing him, or even where you were. But now you know. Will you give him his freedom back? Will you take up your own bones and live?" She kept up this low incantation, always asking, never demanding, but still urging him to decide.

"Shhhh," whispered Enopp. But whether that was a command for her to be silent or simply an escape of air, Pat could not tell.

"Eluik," murmured Pat, "it's all right now for you to tell him what you want. To let your brother resume his place. His body isn't a lonely cave, it's his inheritance, his kingdom to rule alone. As yours was also meant for you alone. Stand beside each other now as brothers, not inside each other with all this confusion, with one of you helpless and the other lost."

She realized that now she *was* urging an outcome; but why not? Neither of them could have any kind of life until this conjoinment at a metaphysical level was replaced by the proper distribution of souls in bodies: one for one.

And then, having said all she could think of several times over, Pat wearied of her own words, and fell silent.

The boys sat unmoving, expressionless, Enopp with his eyes closed, Eluik with his eyes open but focused on nothing.

Pat turned to Marion and Leslie Silverman, intending to shrug, to communicate her helplessness, her growing certainty that this had been beyond her ability after all, that if Danny could not do it, then it could not be done.

But their faces stopped her from shrugging, for Leslie was openly weeping, tears flowing down her cheeks as she looked unwaveringly at the boys. And Marion, though tearless, was no less focused on the boys. How much had they seen and understood?

A sound from the boys turned Pat back to them, and to her surprise, Eluik was looking at her, his eyes focused. His face still expressed nothing, but Pat could see that his lips were moving slightly, and a few sounds emerged, like a phone coming in and out of a good reception area.

At the deepest level, she could sense Enopp's action as he with-drew his ka almost completely from Eluik's body. Pat could only imagine what it felt like to Eluik, to have his body back, to have it now respond to his will, for the first time in years.

But to Pat's consternation, then worry, then fear, Enopp's ka, coming free of Eluik's body, was not returning to his own body. Instead, Eluik seemed to be gathering his ba out of his own body and drawing it back to himself. And Pat realized: He is starting to die. He is preparing to make his way back to Duat.

"No," she said aloud. "That is wrong," she said. "Enopp, I forbid you to die. This body has been waiting for you all this time. Don't abandon it now." And to reinforce her words, she sent her ba into Enopp's body. She could feel that the body was preparing to die, as its controlling mind and will withdrew from it. Back and forth she sent her ba, from Enopp's ka-and-ba to the body he was leaving derelict.

It couldn't be that Enopp did not sense what she was doing—if he had understood her before, he could surely under-stand her now. No, he was doing this because he didn't *want* the body. No, not that. As her ba drew near to his ka-and-ba, surrounding it, she could sense his answer to her words. It was overwhelming surprise and shame at what he had done to his brother.

You didn't know, Pat told him silently. There is no blame, no shame; no harm was intended, and so no guilt ensues. It's not time for you to return to Duat now. Take up your body and live the life you were sent to live. You still have much to do, and it can only be done with a body, with the power of the gatemage you were born to be.

Enopp seemed to ignore her—he made no move to reinhabit his body—and yet he also did not rise up to make the quick voy-age across the lightyears to Duat. Is it because he wants to stay alive, but doesn't think that he deserves to have a body after depriving Eluik for so long? Or am I holding him here by surrounding him with my outself?

I have no more right to hold his ka than he had to inhabit his brother.

Pat pulled her ba back inside herself.

And then felt Enopp's ka-and-ba start to rise. His last connections with Eluik's body began to attenuate and break. He had chosen. He was going to die.

At that moment, Eluik threw himself clumsily from his chair to land on top of Enopp, where he sat on the floor. It knocked Enopp over. Eluik lay on top of him, embraced him awkwardly, and he began shouting something. Weeping and shouting.

Pat was not a gatemage. She had no gift for languages, and did not understand the language of his cries.

But she did understand—for who could fail to understand?—what Eluik's ka was communicating to Enopp's ka. So much force. It felt like shouting. This One had not used even a fraction of this power when communicating with Pat and Danny on Duat. And the message was simple and pure: Stay with me. Live.

Enopp's ka stopped its upward movement.

Eluik began clumsily punching and slapping Enopp's arms and chest, as if to wake up his senses, or even to provoke him into striking back.

Pat felt it, empathically, as Enopp's ka returned to his body and thrust its tendrils, or rather its influence, into every place in his body where those connections needed to be complete.

And as he did, he let go of his last few connections with Eluik's body. In a moment, Enopp's ka-and-ba existed only inside his own body, and almost at once his connection was deep and complete. More complete than most people's self-connection.

Now he was connected to himself as Pat and Danny had learned to connect with their own bodies.

Eluik, too, had learned how it was done, and his ka reached deep inside himself. Like Danny, his domain could not be usurped again.

The hitting and punching stopped. Eluik rolled off his brother and they both lay on the floor against the wall, their bodies touching at many points, but their inself and outself completely distinct for the first time in years.

"Good choice, Enopp," said Pat. "Eluik, you were the reason he stayed. You saved your brother again."

A single great sob convulsed Eluik's body. And then he lay there, weeping desperately, like a heartbroken toddler.

Enopp half-rolled so he could reach his hand to touch his brother's face. "I'm sorry," he said in English. "I didn't know."

Eluik answered him in another language, but this time Leslie saw that Pat didn't understand, and murmured a translation. "He's saying that it's all right, he didn't mind. Neither of them had to be lonely in the caves, and that was good."

Not for the first time, Pat thought, Loki has much to answer for. Imprisoning these boys, almost forcing them into the tortuous intertwining they had lived with all this time.

Then she remembered: Loki had been commanded by his queen, by his lover, to kill them. And yet he decided he owed more to his conscience than to Queen Bexoi. He kept them alive. And now here they were, tormented and suffering . . . but alive. Still able to choose, to act, to live their lives. All the entanglement was now untangled. They were themselves again.

Danny had trusted her to do this, and even though she hadn't known what she was doing, she muddled through, and what she couldn't control, the boys had settled for themselves, between themselves.

"I'm just wondering," said Leslie, "when people are going to start thinking about lunch. Now that we've all decided to stay alive."

Enopp rose easily to his feet, but Eluik was out of practice controlling his body. Marion had to lift him up, and then Eluik leaned on his little brother and on Marion to make his way to the kitchen table, where Leslie had stacked plates and was now setting out slabs of homemade bread and various sliced meats and cheeses, vegetables and spreads.

Once the boys were seated at the table, and Eluik had proven that he could put together a sandwich and bring it to his mouth, Marion came to Pat in the kitchen doorway. "Well done," he said softly. "You did things I didn't imagine were possible. I saw things—well, *understood* things in a way I never did before. You were brave and patient and wise. Danny's a lucky boy. I hope he's smart enough to know what you are."

"If he isn't," said Leslie, "I'll tell him in a way he can't mistake."

Pat smiled in relief, feeling tears coming to her eyes. She didn't like to cry in front of other people, but she also didn't want to leave.

"Oh, don't worry about a few tears," said Leslie. "Sit down and let them salt your sandwich."

So Pat sat at the table with the boys as they ate their first meal together as independent souls, each bound to his own body, each free to make his own choices and act on them.

What they just won, with such effort, is possessed easily by almost every human being on Earth and Westil, thought Pat. The difference is that, having been without that independence for so long, they know what they have.

I hope they never forget. I hope *I* never forget. How precious it is to be alive, to have a body of my own, to be free to act on this physical world in whatever way I choose.

"What I want to know," said Enopp, "is whether you can sing."

Eluik answered in the other language, and both boys laughed until they cried.

Marion interpreted this time. "What he said was, 'I never could before.' And apparently that's hysterically funny."

Pat couldn't help grinning—a huge grin, stretching her cheeks because she rarely called on them to show so much happiness.

"And I see that you agree," said Marion.

"Let the girl eat," said Leslie. "She's had a busy day."

9

King Prayard no longer showed any surprise when Wad appeared in Bexoi's heavily guarded chamber. Whether he guessed at Wad's connection to the Queen—as her lover or as her enemy—was not a particularly interesting question to Wad. The baby in her womb right now was Prayard's. So whether Prayard resented past betrayals was not a matter of concern to Wad. He had no grounds for feeling betrayed *now*.

Of course, Wad also knew that people judged whether something was right or wrong by their own standards, and those standards were rarely rational. Wad's own standards were as mad as could be. Yet they felt viscerally right and true to him, so that if he did not live by them he felt a deep unease until he made things right. That was why he couldn't simply kill Bexoi and have done with her—because if killing *his* baby had been wrong, then killing her baby must be just as wrong. Because the crime in killing his boy Trick had not been the offense to and betrayal of Wad, it was in depriving that wonderful, clever, beautiful boy of his life. So taking vengeance on Bexoi by killing a child that was just as innocent would not be vengeance at all, but a new crime, a new injustice. Wad knew this was the law he had to live by, but he did not know why he felt this way, or where his moral code came from. He only knew that he could not bear the idea of doing something as vile as the crime Bexoi had committed.

Yet Prayard might have a completely different moral code, one in which cuckolding a man was not such a bad thing, but cuckolding a king was treason. Or in which a wife's womb, once it had borne bastard fruit, could never bear a truly legitimate heir. Prayard himself probably did not know how he would feel about Bexoi's adultery, particularly since it happened at a time when Prayard himself was not acting in such a way as to conceive a child. Not that such a distinction would necessarily matter to Prayard.

There were times when Wad was curious about how Prayard would decide to act if he knew the whole truth about the past. He toyed with the idea of telling him. And then he had to recognize that one not-unlikely response Prayard might have would be to kill Bexoi forthwith. And since by that act, Wad would be indirectly causing the death of the baby, he could not take the chance. Could *never* take the chance. This baby would be Prayard's true child. Prayard should not be given any reason to doubt it. So Wad kept his peace.

Yet he also made it a point to come to Bexoi's sleeping body only when Prayard himself was there. If he came to her when Prayard was away, the King might suspect that Wad was hiding something from him. That would provoke suspicion and Wad did not want to provoke suspicion.

"There's been no change in her," said Prayard softly.

"Except the baby is growing," said Wad.

"Nearly to term now," said Prayard. "And how can a baby be delivered when the mother is asleep?"

"Maybe the coming of the baby will waken her," said Wad, though he did not believe it.

"And maybe not," said Prayard. "Maybe the baby will be ready for birth, but her body won't know it, won't work to squeeze it out. Maybe it will stay within her, growing and growing, until it bursts her belly and she dies, and the baby dies."

"I won't let that happen," said Wad.

"And how will you stop it? Is midwifery among your talents?"

"You can have a surgeon cut the baby out."

"I know of that procedure," said Prayard. "The mother always dies, and the baby often dies, or it was already dead."

"If I'm here," said Wad, "then the Queen will *not* die, and the baby will *not* die, and I can promise you that as of this moment, the baby is healthy and alive. Why do you think I come so often? It's to make sure that this remains true up to the moment when the baby is born—or is taken."

"Do you really think I'll let anyone cut into my lady's belly? Do you think I'll allow a knife anywhere near her?"

"Yes, I do," said Wad. "If your choice is between the knife and her certain death, you'll choose the knife, with me watching to keep her safe."

"You can heal her from the knife, but not from this . . . this *sleep* that is on her."

"She is not asleep," said Wad. "I believe she hears all, knows what is happening, listens to this conversation. She's helpless to respond, because her body is not under her control."

"So is she under the control of a manmage?" asked Prayard.

"Don't imagine manmages to be all that powerful," said Wad. "This is a weak age of the world, with no Great Gates to enhance the power of mages. No manmage could steal this woman's body from her."

But Anonoei *had* been through a Great Gate. And Enopp and Eluik had some weird power over each other that had left Eluik as silent as Bexoi, though not quite so inert. Wad had no idea if what he was saying to Prayard was the truth. He almost hoped that it was not, because that might mean that Anonoei was somehow still alive, trapped—at least her ba—inside Bexoi. So when it came time to kill Bexoi—after the baby was safely born—then killing her might also liberate the remnant of Anonoei, setting her ba free to return to Duat, the way Danny North had set the captive gates free by giving them to themselves.

As if he had been called by Wad's thought of him, Danny North suddenly stood behind King Prayard, his hands in his pockets, slouching like a boy who isn't sure whether he's going to be in trouble or not.

How could Danny North be here on Westil? If he had made another Great Gate, Wad would know it, not just because he could sense any gate that was made on either world, but also because all of Danny's gates were under Wad's control, and could not be used without Wad's knowledge.

Only Wad now realized that Danny had appeared here without the use of any gate at all, or at least none that Wad could see. And Wad could see *all* gates. How had Danny come?

Prayard must have noticed Wad's surprise, because he turned to look where Wad was looking.

Danny North wasn't there.

But he wasn't dodging Prayard's notice. Danny North was now kneeling at the head of Bexoi's bed, and he reached out a hand and touched her forehead.

"Who are you?" asked Prayard quietly. "You came as this one comes. Are you a gatemage?"

"He is," said Wad. "But he has no business here."

"Then send him away," said Prayard.

Wad tried. He made a gate and passed it over Danny North—but Danny did not move. It was unthinkable—nobody could resist the power of a gate. And yet that's what he had done.

"I just tried to do that," said Wad, "and it didn't work."

"You can't gate me away," said Danny. "And you don't want to, either. Because I'm here to bring this woman out of her coma."

"That's not within your power," said Wad.

"You don't know my power," said Danny. "I say that I can bring her back. But I think you don't want me to."

Wad had no answer for that, because if he told the truth to Danny, Prayard would hear.

So they looked at each other in silence.

"I understand," said Prayard. "You have secrets of gatemagery to discuss, but can't speak freely in front of me."

"It would be helpful if you weren't here," Danny said.

"He's the King," said Wad, "and this is his wife."

"If he loves her," said Danny, "then he'll do whatever it takes to bring her back. Even if it means trusting me, a stranger, enough to leave this place while I do what I have learned how to do."

"Is that Other still inside you?" asked Wad.

Danny North knelt there silently, looking at Prayard.

"I'll go," said Prayard.

"There's no need for you to leave," said Wad, "because whatever this foolish *boy* thinks he's going to do, I forbid it."

"You can't stop me," said Danny, "and King Prayard doesn't want me to be stopped."

Prayard rose up from the stool on which he had been keeping vigil. "As long as Wad is here to keep you from harming her, I'll trust you."

"This boy isn't even from our world," said Wad. "You can't trust him."

"I know he isn't from Westil," said Prayard. "Look at him, listen to his accent. He's obviously from Mittlegard. Yet he came here in spite of the Gate Thief. And you didn't have the power to send him away. So of all the mages in this room, I think that he's the most powerful."

"I am," said Danny North, "but I won't harm anyone."

"You'll harm everyone," said Wad.

"No," said Danny. "I know what's keeping her silent and still, and I know how to remedy that, and you don't know, and you don't want to know."

"I don't want to know," said Prayard, though he obviously knew Danny's words had been aimed at Wad. "But I want my wife back."

"And the baby safely born," said Danny.

"When the time comes," said Prayard.

"The time is now," said Danny. "And Wad knows it."

Prayard looked at Wad. Apparently Wad's ability to look innocent had left him, because Prayard immediately said, "When were you going to tell me, Wad?"

"It *could* be now, or it could be in a week, or two weeks," said Wad. "I'm waiting to see if she goes into labor on her own."

"He knows that the time is now, and that Bexoi must be awakened before the birth, and he hasn't got the power to waken her, and I do."

"So you say," said Wad.

"I came here, didn't I?" said Danny North. "And you couldn't detect my coming, or send me away, or even understand how I came. I *will* do this, Loki. If you try to stop me, then I'll take away from you the power to interfere."

"Come with me, Wad," said Prayard. "This is a mighty mage, young though he seems to be. Old men like us need to recognize when someone else has the mastery of us."

"King Prayard speaks wisely," said Danny, "and he's leaving. Now, Loki—will you go or will you stay?"

"I'll stay."

"I'll go," said Prayard. And he did. Because he wore slippers to keep the cold of the stone from his feet, there was a hushing sound as his steps took him from the room. Then the door swung shut and Wad was alone with Danny.

"The last thing that Westil needs," said Wad very softly, "is this bitch awake again, to do more killing."

"I agree," said Danny. "But that's only half the story. You want the firemage to stay powerless. But what about the manmage?"

Wad felt a flood of relief. "So she died with her ba inside the Queen," he said.

"No," said Danny. "She is inside this body, ka and ba, and she and the Queen struggle equally for control."

"Manmages can't send their ka," said Wad.

"Except for the ones who can," said Danny. "Anonoei's boys, Eluik and Enopp? I've seen what's really happening there—it's Enopp who is inside Eluik; that's why Eluik is silent. Enopp's ka is inside him, and all that remains in Enopp's own body is his outself, as if his own body were his heartbeast."

"Not possible," said Wad.

"I agree. And yet my friend Pat has just drawn Enopp out of his brother, and now she and Eluik are trying to keep Enopp from dying."

"And by 'dying' you mean—"

"I mean going back to Duat," said Danny North.

"And is that what you plan to do here?" asked Wad.

"This case isn't simple, because where Enopp and Eluik love each other, these two are at war. A constant bitter stalemate which neither of them can win."

"Two kas in the same body," said Wad.

"Of course the manmage has no right to be there. The body belongs to Bexoi, and Anonoei is a thief."

"If that's what you think—"

"That's what *is*," said Danny, "and you know it. But you also know that Bexoi murdered Anonoei. She burned up her body and Anonoei made this jump in that last moment of her death agony. So now there's a serious question here. What does justice demand? That Anonoei get out of a body that she has no right to be in? Or that Bexoi make restitution to Anonoei for the body she burned up, by leaving *this* body so Anonoei can go on living? There's something proportional in that, don't you think? Even though the law would normally demand that we go the other way."

"How do you know any of this? You can't *know* it."

"I not only know it," said Danny, "but the whole time my lips have been talking to you, my own ka has been showing things to them. Hearing what they have to say for themselves."

"I only care about one thing at this moment," said Wad. "Is the dragon still inside you?"

"If he were, could I be here?" asked Danny.

"That's an evasion, not an answer," said Wad.

"Set has no more power over me," said Danny North. "But yes, he's still inside my body."

"And you brought him here?" asked Wad, his fear and fury rising.

"I did not," said Danny North.

"Which is it? He's inside you or not? Which?"

"He's inside me, but he isn't here," said Danny North. "Instead of getting angry, why not listen to what I'm saying and try to understand it?"

"He's inside you, but you didn't bring him here. That's a contradiction."

"And yet it isn't a contradiction, because you're making one false assumption."

"And what is that?" said Wad.

"You're assuming that I'm here," said Danny North.

"I can see you," said Wad.

"You once saw Bexoi die a bloody death on her bed, even as she stood beside you watching herself die," said Danny North.

"It was her clant," said Wad. "A brilliant clant, so real that it even bled. But you can't be a clant, because gatemages don't make clants."

"Until now," said Danny North.

"You really did die," said Wad. "You died and went to Duat, and then came back, and now the things you're doing . . ."

"I learned some things on Duat," said Danny, "and other things I've figured out since then. I make gates now without my ba. Or, to speak truthfully, I transport myself and other things and people without making gates at all. I simply go."

Wad had no choice but to believe him, because he got here somehow, and yet he did not make a gate.

"Every living person has that power, because when we die, our ka goes back to Duat, without a guide, without a ferryboat, without a spaceship, without a gate, we simply go. The power is in all of us. So my friend Pat no longer needs me or my amulet. She simply goes."

"You were able to teach her? A windmage?"

"I taught her nothing," said Danny North. "She died and went to Duat, and she saw all that I saw, and learned all that I learned."

"So which will it be, Danny North? Will you waken the Queen, and drive out what's left of poor Anonoei to return to Duat?"

"I can't really do that," said Danny.

"Meaning that you really can't, or that you choose not to because it would be wrong?"

"Both," said Danny. "When Bexoi killed Anonoei, she forfeited her right to have a body of her own."

"So you'll drive out Bexoi and leave her body for Anonoei?"

"I can't do things that aren't within my power," said Danny.

"And here I thought you could do *anything*. Mage of mages."

"I don't have power to do things that can't be done," said Danny. "I can't send Bexoi back to Duat—she has to want to go there, and given the kind of life she's led, I don't know how happy a reunion that will be for her."

"I don't care whether she's happy there," said Wad.

"But *she* cares," said Danny North, "and if she doesn't want to go, I can't make her."

"Then what *can* you do?"

"I can show Anonoei how to sink deeply and completely into the body. But that will only work if the body itself recognizes her as its rightful owner."

"How can it?" asked Wad. "It's Bexoi's body."

"It began as Bexoi's body, and grew up as Bexoi's body, but now its hands are covered with the blood of babies. The body doesn't like to be dishonored like that. It may be done with her."

"So if her own body rejects her . . ."

"It won't happen that way," said Danny North. "Her body won't expel her. Instead it'll accept someone else as its rightful owner. And I think that will happen only if the powers that be on Duat tell her body to do that."

"So you might end up expelling Anonoei after all. Killing her."

"It's up to the body to decide."

"The body's just a—a puppet made of meat. It can't *decide*."

"So I thought, too, until I went to Duat, leaving my body behind. Set had it all to himself, but he couldn't even begin to get control of it. It waited for me. It continued to be mine. But Bexoi's body deserves better than a mistress who used that body to commit terrible murders. Don't you think?"

"This is starting to sound like theology," said Wad. "Justice and mercy. An eye for an eye. Not Christianity, with all its talk of forgiveness, but the older law, tit for tat, eye for eye, where the law always rules and can't be tricked."

"Why should I care what it sounds like? If it's true, then it would be surprising if the idea didn't crop up everywhere, in one form or another."

He had a point, but Wad knew that there were rules, and somehow Danny North wasn't following them. "How can you be a clant, when I have all your gates and you have none?"

"I've never made a clant, so I don't know if that's what I did. I asked a lot of particles to form themselves into a second body for me. And they did, so here I am."

"Then you passed this clant through a Great Gate?"

"There is no Great Gate," said Danny North, "and I didn't pass the clant from Mittlegard to here, I *made* it here. I made it right here in this room. I made it out of the air in the room, plus the light and heat of the fire, plus my inner knowledge of how my body works, of what it truly is. And the prets in this place saw what I needed to make, and they helped me make it."

"So you formed a clant, clothes and all, right here? Just now?"

"You can marvel at my newfound talents later," said Danny North. "This baby's due, and we need to resolve who's going to have the use of the mother's body before it's born."

10

Anonoei listened to everything that was said, not because she really understood what Danny North was going on about, but because she had nothing else to do. Bexoi was asleep, or in some other kind of trance, and so her thoughts, when they rose to the level of consciousness, were *something* to pay attention to. Anonoei was desperately lonely. She could hear what Bexoi's body heard, see what she saw; but her eyes were generally closed, and since Bexoi wasn't *doing* anything, it was like being a passenger alone on a boat that was trapped in the winter ice.

So Wad's conversation with Prayard had passed the time, at least, and then when Danny North appeared, things got interesting. Anonoei heard things which, if she had a body to allow her to *feel* anything, would have made her hopeful. But there were no emotions without the body. She could understand things, but dispassionately. Oh, *this* might be possible. Oh, *that* might not.

Do I even care whether I live or die? Am I really alive here in Bexoi's body? Did the vital part of me perish in the flames of my original corpse, and now I'm just a shadow, less real than the clant of a gatemage?

It was hard to hold on to Bexoi. Anonoei had to keep such a careful balance. Since she had thrown herself out of her own dying flesh and plunged into her enemy's body, Anonoei had known that she could not stay here without Bexoi herself. For the body was Bexoi's and if her inself broke free and returned to Duat, the corpse would be left behind to rot, no longer a single continuous organ, but just a heap of tissues, food for the scavengers that always waited, a heartbeat away, for the first sign of death.

I am one of them, a scavenger, a fungus growing inside Bexoi, unable to sustain a life of my own, feeding instead on hers.

And Anonoei couldn't even be sure how much of this situation Bexoi understood. Maybe, having come so near to death, Bexoi really did believe herself to be dead, or something like it. Maybe she couldn't fully reattach to her body. What was holding her back? The baby, perhaps?

But it was just as possible and, knowing Bexoi, far more likely, that the Queen knew exactly what was happening, and kept herself hovering on the edge of consciousness, waiting for Anonoei to grow weary of the continuous tug of war.

If Anonoei pressed too hard, Bexoi would leave the body and it would die. But if Anonoei relaxed her grip, Bexoi would take back full control and Anonoei would be left with nothing, no part of this life. Then Bexoi's attempt to murder her would at last be complete.

And maybe that would be best. Maybe it was not heroic but pitiable that Anonoei was so desperate to keep some part of her alive. If this miserable existence as a shadow lurking inside the body of the Queen counted as life.

Anonoei was powerless to make Bexoi's eyes open and look at Wad or at Danny. Oh, she could do it—but that was just the kind of thing that made Bexoi's inself detach itself in some unfathomable way. Anonoei could sense it happening, but she had no idea what sense was sensing it. Not some message from Bexoi's body, she had long since realized. Anonoei could sense Bexoi's inself letting go of her own body at some level where only the inself and outself existed. At the same time, Anonoei knew somehow that wherever Bexoi was going, there would be no coming back. Anonoei would be left alone in a body that was not hers, that she couldn't control. She could stop Bexoi from doing anything, saying anything. But she couldn't do anything herself, not without taking so much control that Bexoi would leave.

The message was clear: I may not be able to get rid of you, but I won't be your puppet. If I can't rule here, no one will.

Which was, Anonoei understood, the fundamental principle that guided Bexoi's life. She was going to rule everything within her reach. Anyone who blocked her from ruling had to be destroyed. Anyone who could help her rule had to be exploited. No partial success was enough to settle for, and if thwarted, she would refuse to stay in the game.

So now, Danny North, with all your wisdom, will *you* see what's going on?

"Yes," said Danny.

But no, no, he did *not* say it, and Anonoei did not *hear* it, not through Bexoi's ears. Nor was it even a word. Anonoei had framed a question in her mind—if it *was* her own mind—and Danny had answered without language, in a place so deeply inside Anonoei that no part of it touched Bexoi.

"That's the problem," said Danny. "You have to reach deeper.

This body might accept you, if it knows that you will never use it to kill innocents, as Bexoi did. Or it might not. But it can't accept you if you don't reach deep and offer yourself as an alternative to Bexoi."

Again, it was not a matter of words. In fact, the idea that Anonoei understood as "reach deep" was a concept that she could not have understood if Danny had not pushed something into Bexoi's body. His outself? His own inself? Danny North was a gatemage, not a manmage. He shouldn't be here, shouldn't be able to do . . . anything.

Yet his urgency could not be evaded. Behold this, he was pressing her. Pay attention to what I do.

But how could she pay attention? She had no bodily senses to pay attention *with*.

Gently he drew her. Come look at this. Come see. Come feel this.

If she were a poetic person, she thought, she might be able to find words for what Danny North was doing. It was as if his inself took my inself by the hand—no, by the very heart; no, he took the entire inself, enveloped it, guided it.

Yet at no point was Anonoei being compelled. Enticed, perhaps. Come, try this. Feel this. Watch this.

She began to understand what was happening when Danny North insinuated himself into Bexoi's body. Not the whole of him, the way Anonoei was entirely present inside the confines of Bexoi's body of flesh and bone. Something like a dagger, though, would lick out, darting like a snake's tongue, and penetrate Bexoi's body, probing into places that Anonoei had not understood before. When Bexoi had tried to die, she drew herself out of these places.

This is how you own a body.

Not quite, said Danny North in his silent, wordless way. You can't take it. But you can ask it to give itself to you.

That was never true, Anonoei knew it. In all her years as a manmage, she had always *taken* what she could, or at least what she needed. She hadn't *asked*.

Yet now she could sense how Danny insinuated himself into Bexoi's body, even though it was a woman's body and Danny was no manmage. He didn't take control of anything. He offered himself to the bits out of which the body was made, like a man reaching over a cliff to offer a hand to someone who was clinging to a single vine. Take this! he was saying. Take *hold* of this and don't let go. But at no point was Danny forcing the body to fragment itself, to choose between following Bexoi or himself. It was only an offer: See what's possible. See if this would please you better. See what I am.

And to Anonoei's surprise, she could feel the body responding. At a level deeper and more primitive than mere physical sensation, she could sense how the body was becoming more and more responsive to Danny.

But Danny doesn't need this body. I need it. It's all I've got, and I don't have it.

That is right, said Danny, without sound, without words. You haven't "got" anything at all. The best you can hope for is that this bone house will invite you to be mistress here. But this is how you offer yourself.

It wants *you*, thought Anonoei. Look how each part you touch leaps out to meet you. Like a magnet drawing iron filings to itself.

You do it, said Danny. The body wants to be part of something better than Bexoi. It's weary of leading a monster's life.

But how could he know that? And why was he so sure that Anonoei herself was not just as monstrous?

That very doubt is proof that you are not like Bexoi. The very idea that something you want might not be *right* says that you

believe yourself to be part of a larger world. That you're account-
able. That something matters more than you do.

My children, thought Anonoei.

But no, that was not enough. Her sons were part of her. Their
survival was *her* survival.

What is it that tells me there are some things that I mustn't do?
Can't do? Don't *want* to do.

What if I'm as bad as Bexoi? What if this body would be trading one evil for another? A strong mistress for a weak one who
was no better?

Even as she doubted herself, she reached out into the body as
Danny had done. Into the deep places, the tiny places, the unfathomable depths of the body, where the tiny selves clung to her like
dust.

They don't find me despicable.

Her surprise, her gratitude seemed to draw more of them.

But not the brightest of them.

Let them see the woman who lets nothing stop her, said Danny.

That would be Bexoi.

The woman who endured imprisonment. Loss of her sons. And
yet kept her sanity.

If I did.

Don't you understand that it's not your fear but your boldness
that makes you fit to rule? Offer who you *are*, not what you are
ashamed to be.

How can I lie to them? They aren't deceived.

Exactly, said Danny. So let them see it all.

See? There was no seeing, there was no telling.

Even though she did not understand, there was some part of
her that knew what to do. She thought of all the things she had
done with her manmagery. The way she played on what other

people wanted, persuaded them that *she* was the object of their deepest desires.

I won't lie to you, she said silently. No promises except this: I don't kill babies. I don't kill at all, if I can help it. This is a world full of life and I want to stay in it. I want to see my sons grow up.

This baby growing in Queen Bexoi's body—I will raise him up to be the best man he can find inside himself. I won't punish him for being his mother's child. He will never know that I am *not* Bexoi. He is made from this body, and from this body he will have a mother's love. As best I can. That's a promise I can make, if you let me be mistress here. I could never kill a child of my own body; I couldn't harm a child born to my enemy. If you let me dwell here, truly rule here, then this baby will be both. Child of my enemy; child of my own body.

And the true child of a man I love.

Was that even true? Did she still love Prayard?

Without a body to feel emotion, she didn't know.

But love was *not* an emotion. She and Wad had discussed this more than once. Love was a *decision*. Your happiness before my own. But not *instead* of my own. Alongside me.

What I offer Prayard, I offer you. I will be part of your pleasure and your pain. I will decide where to guide you, but you will always be able to urge me and draw me toward your desires as well. You did not want to kill the baby that you made, did you? I will never grieve you like that.

The body gathered to her. There was no physical movement; the limbs did not move, the eyes did not twitch. But she felt herself reaching deeply into it. Knowing it far more deeply than its muscles or bones, nerves or veins.

More deeply than Bexoi knew it.

And in that very moment, Bexoi must have realized what was

happening, or at least that *something* was happening. That she was losing her power here.

She could feel Bexoi try to make a sound, a scream, a shout. The meaning was also clear: No! But Bexoi's possession of her own body was so shallow, so tenuous that it was already weak compared to the control that belonged to Anonoei.

In her panic, Bexoi tried to force her body to obey her. But of course that did not work. It *could* not work. The body had once been hers, but now it belonged, mostly, to someone else. To Anonoei.

Not completely, no. Because Danny had been there before her. Danny had shown himself to the bits that made up this body, and they had recognized his power, his enormous, dazzling strength. And also, perhaps, his goodness. Certainly his goodness, or at least his desire to be good to other people. To be good to whatever body belonged to him.

Then he retreated, and all that was left to entice this body was Anonoei. Compared to Bexoi, that might well be enough—no, it *was* enough.

But if Danny asked, if Danny *offered*, then it would all be his.

Yet he would not ask. He would not offer. He had come here only to show her what she needed to do. How it could be done.

All these years, ever since she first recognized her manmagery, she had imagined that she was tricking them, seducing them, and then, when she needed to, forcing them. But no, it was never that. They all gave themselves to her. Not as completely as this body was giving itself to her. But to some degree, they had been won over, they *wished* for what she offered. The weakest of them had accepted her complete domination. But the strongest of them also became her willing allies. Her followers.

As Bexoi's body now was.

I am you now, she said to this body, all the parts of it, the whole of it. Let's be alive together, she said, and the body came to her and clung to her and now she willed the legs to bend.

They were stiff from lack of movement, and could not easily respond.

In that instant, Danny North sensed what was happening and she felt a wave of healing, of strengthening, pass through her. Had he taken her through a gate? No, this was something else. This was him giving the body permission to heal itself. And now her legs moved easily. She swung them off the bed, leaned up on an elbow.

"Who is she?" asked Wad.

"You mean, which of your lovers?" asked Danny softly. "Which do you want her to be?"

"I can see what body it is," said Wad tersely. "Is it the mother or the monster?"

"She is the woman the body wanted to be," said Danny. "But the monster isn't gone yet."

"Make her go," whispered Wad.

Danny only gave a low chuckle. "You saw how I did this," he said. "How Anonoei did it. You know that neither of us can *make* Bexoi do anything."

"Then we'll never be rid of her," said Wad bitterly.

"Perhaps not," said Danny. "But it's not about us or what we want."

Is it about me? thought Anonoei.

And from Bexoi came a wave of rejection and hatred.

Anonoei felt it as emotion because now she was directly connected to the body as if it were her own.

No, she was connected to it because it was her own. It belonged to her now.

She could feel the urgency of Bexoi's demand: Where can I go? I don't want to die.

Anonoei had no answer. Nobody wanted to die, and Anonoei couldn't think of a good reason why Bexoi should be willing to die when her body remained alive, in someone else's possession.

"It doesn't want you now," said Danny, and Anonoei realized that now he was using his voice. "It's been offered a better life. A better self. What can you offer?"

Again Bexoi reached for the body's voice, but she was not connected to it anymore. Yet Anonoei knew, without words, what she was trying to convey: It's mine.

"It's yours because you were such a powerful pret, back on Duat," said Danny. "Such brilliance and strength. Of course it wanted to follow you. But look what you did with it. You might have felt no shame, but the beautiful beast you dwelt in was ashamed of how you made it live, what you made it do. Back then it had no choice. Now it has one. It's hard to imagine a living soul that it would not rather be."

Bexoi raged—or would have raged, if the body had obeyed her. What do you know about me? I don't know you, you're nothing to me, a boy, a stranger!

But Danny responded with perfect calm. "Bexoi," he said, and the very act of naming her pulled her even farther out of the body which she was still desperately trying to control. "You know me. At this moment, you know me better than you have ever known anybody. I'm hiding nothing. You know me, Loki knows me, Anonoei can see me plainly. And you know that I have done nothing to you. Everything that grieves you, you did to yourself. You took life away from others without a moment's regret. Did you think that meant that *you* would not also someday die?"

Anonoei felt Bexoi's fury turn to a mix of fire and fear. She was trying to burn up Danny North, and she was terrified because her body gave her no such power now. It would not harm Danny North.

And then Anonoei realized why. All the power to burn things was part of the body still, but Bexoi could not consume young Danny with that fire, because Anonoei did not wish to harm him, and it was Anonoei's will that the fire responded to now.

Danny's words had finally reached Bexoi's deep understanding, and her inself echoed the wordless understanding beneath his spoken words. Everybody dies, and Bexoi realized for the first time that there would be no exemption for her.

"This is that day," said Danny—gently. Even kindly. "No one has harmed you. No one else is causing your death. You gave up any claim on life when you killed your little boy. You handed your life to Anonoei when you burned her own body out from under her. You know that I have done nothing but teach Anonoei how to love your body better and more deeply than you ever did. And in return it serves her, as faithfully as it served you, and more joyfully. Now go home to Duat, Bexoi. There is One there who remembers what you meant to be, when you left there and came to Westil. He knows your whole story, while you know only a part of it. Go home and find out who you were, and who you are, and who you might yet become."

Only then did Anonoei recognize another presence in that place. Not really in the *room* they occupied, not here in the palace of Prayard. But wherever he was, he had decided to let them sense his . . . attention. The watchful concern of Duat.

Danny seemed unsurprised. Anonoei could feel his relief. Whoever this was, whatever powers the stranger had, Danny welcomed him, because to him this one was no stranger at all.

Anonoei felt something like a shudder, not in the body, but in Bexoi's inself; Bexoi was not prepared to endure the visitor's attention. Yet it could not be escaped, so she shrank. Whatever part of Bexoi it had been that tried to reach into the body and control it now withered, and any part of the body that still clung to Bexoi's inself was now stripped away. She was only herself now, the ancient part of herself that had once been given such power. Nothing but her naked self, small and terrified. Pain and loss. Alone.

Are we all this small in death? Anonoei didn't mean to ask the question; she barely knew she had thought of it.

But the answer came immediately and clearly, not from Danny but from the one who had come for Bexoi:

You will be as small or as great as you made yourself.

Then the stranger was gone, and Bexoi with him.

Anonoei was in sole possession of the body. It was now *her* uterus that held the baby. *Her* hands now clutched herself with a fervent mix of gratitude and unworthiness. Why am I being given such a chance to live?

"You'll have to speak aloud now," said Danny. "I could only communicate with you that directly because you weren't fully in the body. Now I sense that you're asking something, but I don't understand it."

That disappointed Anonoei more deeply than she could have expected. It had only been a few minutes that she had felt such a deep connection and communion with Danny North—but she missed it already.

"I miss it too," said Danny. "With you. With Pat—the woman I love."

"I know who she is to you," whispered Anonoei.

"I miss it with This One."

It took Anonoei scarcely a heartbeat to understand whom he meant.

" 'This One'?" It was how she had thought of him, too.

"It's what he called himself when we first met. I have no other name for him. But 'This One' is name enough for him, when dealing with us. Maybe we're not capable of understanding his real name."

"Does he come to everyone who dies?" asked Wad.

"I don't know the rules of Duat," said Danny. "But when I die, I'd be so . . . grateful. Honored. If he came for me."

"I was grateful that he didn't notice me," murmured Wad.

"He noticed you," said Anonoei. "He noticed everything."

"I know," said Wad. "But he didn't make me answer him. I'm not ready to answer him."

"Yes, you are," said Danny. "Answering him is easy, because he already knows."

After months of darkness, Anonoei realized that she did not have to remain blind. The eyes were hers now, and she opened them for the first time in months. She had felt so many other sensations in these minutes since the body became truly her own, but now at last she was ready to join the world again, ready for sight.

Wad was closer to her than she had thought. And he was kneeling beside the bed. Seeing that she could see him now, he reached out a hand to touch her cheek. She welcomed the touch, though it made her tremble, having been so long without sensations of such intensity and power.

"I know what happened here," said Wad. "I don't know *how*, but I understood it as it happened. And yet when I look at you, it's still the face of Bexoi."

"But not the heart," said Anonoei.

"Well," said Danny, "organically speaking, it is."

"Not the mind. Not the *will*," said Anonoei.

Wad pulled her closer to him as he half-rose from the floor. He kissed her lightly and then sat beside her on the bed. "Yes," he said. "I loved this face once, and these hands. And then, another time, later, I loved this heart and mind, though they wore a different face."

"You never gave up on me," said Anonoei.

"No lies," said Wad. "I didn't understand at all what was

going on here. I kept such close vigil because I was afraid that Bexoi would suddenly wake up and begin killing all the wrong people. I didn't even believe your son when he told me that you weren't dead."

"I mean," said Anonoei, "that you were willing to believe that I was here after all."

Wad shook his head. "Danny *showed* me where you were. I saw what he was doing, and I saw you learn from him. I never really understood till now how we connected with our bodies."

"You still don't," said Danny.

"But I'm closer," said Wad. "I saw Anonoei take true possession, because the body gave itself to her."

"This is the last time," said Anonoei. "The last time you can say who I am and call me by my own name."

"I know," said Wad.

"From now on, I have to answer to *her* name." Then she realized something else. "I'll have all her enemies."

"Not all," said Wad. "You will have, as your friend, her worst enemy." And he bowed his head with false modesty.

Anonoei wanted to kiss him, as a lover this time. But then she realized: "I have to be faithful to Prayard."

"And it's about time *I* was his faithful friend and subject, too," said Wad. "I won't offer, and you won't ask. Friends now, and nothing more than that."

"And nothing less." Anonoei kissed him again—not long, but not too briefly, either. "After your long vigil, Wad, will you be kind enough to go invite my husband to come and welcome me to the land of the living?"

Wad looked at Danny, and Anonoei could see that Wad was asking permission, or so it seemed.

"We'll talk about it after you've brought Prayard here," said Danny.

"I can't explain *you* to him," said Wad.

"Gatemages don't have to explain anything," said Danny with mild amusement. "But I'll wait somewhere else. What about returning to Ced? I want to talk with him, too."

"You know where he is?" asked Wad. And then: "Of course you do. The gate marks him."

"Don't worry. Set is *not* here. You know that now."

"When This One came," said Wad. "I could see everybody's ka as bright as fire. Set wasn't here. And neither was Danny North, though when This One arrived, I knew exactly where you were, and how many billion leagues away."

"This temporary body of mine is a good one, a good gift that gave itself to me. I'll be able to hold on to it until we talk again."

"The important thing is that Set is gone," said Wad.

"Set isn't gone," answered Danny. "He's still inside my body back on Mittlegard, and I don't know whether he's capable of taking control again. I know that if he sees a chance, he'll try. So I'm not coming to Westil, not in person."

Wad nodded. "I think I need to go and get the king. His wife misses him." He smiled at Anonoei, and to her relief, the smile was kind and gentle—though not without irony and just a touch of bitterness. That was the best part—that he seemed to harbor some regret that she would never again belong to him.

"If I didn't have so many reasons for hating Bexoi," said Anonoei, "I would be jealous of her now because she carries her babies so high and lightly. I know the baby's due in a very short time, and yet I barely feel pregnant, compared to what it was like with both of the boys."

"That's a comparison you should avoid making," said Wad. "Because Bexoi only had one other son, and you never saw him."

"And you did," said Anonoei. "I'm so sorry that what *you* lost can't be restored to you."

"I'm content," said Wad. "The monster is gone." Then he looked at Danny. "Or, well, one monster."

Danny laughed. "Go and tell the king."

Wad left at once. By gate, not by walking.

Anonoei laughed. "I think you're the only person that Wad could possibly obey."

Danny looked flustered. "I didn't command him."

"You didn't even say please," said Anonoei.

"But I wasn't—I didn't—"

"No, you didn't," said Anonoei. "But if you did command him, do you have any doubt whether he'd obey?"

Danny shook his head. But then the sound of shouting came, and someone running down a stone-floored corridor. When Anonoei looked up to suggest that Danny really ought to go, he was already gone.

11

Pat knew she should dislike Hermia so intensely that she would hate every moment she spent in her company. And for a while, stuck in Veevee's condo with Hermia, Pat tried to resist any kind of conversation. Terse replies, a clear sense that whenever Hermia spoke to her it was an inconvenience, a burden.

But that wasn't how Pat was raised. It bothered her to treat anyone with open rudeness. Pat knew how to be self-protectively quiet, but she also knew that she must answer politely when spoken to. The first rule of good manners was to make the other person comfortable.

I don't want Hermia to be comfortable.

You're not her jailor. You're not one of the Furies. Punishing her isn't your job.

And, when Pat was honest with herself, she had to admit that

Hermia was not only personally charming, she had also experienced many things that Pat envied. World travel—even before gatemagery had reared its head. All the perks of being from a wealthy family. Superbly educated—far beyond anything available to Pat in Buena Vista, Virginia. And more than that—Hermia had seen Danny's wide-open gates and followed him, then practically *forced* him to learn how to close his gates. She took bold action at the first opportunity, and then tried to help him.

Compare that to how Danny and Pat first met—at a high school lunch table, hiding her bad acne under long straight hair, and Danny's first action was to heal her by passing her through a gate. And what was her response? Not helpful.

Here was the huge question that nagged at Pat all the time. Danny knew Hermia. Danny had learned from Hermia. So why was Danny in love with Pat, when Hermia was right there? Hermia was everything Pat had always wanted to be—pretty, outgoing, clever, funny, smart. What did Pat have that Hermia lacked?

It couldn't just be that Hermia was years older than Danny. Nor that she was from a rival family. Neither fact had kept them from being friends. Danny was a normal heterosexual boy, he couldn't possibly have missed Hermia's prettiness. It was quite possible he was oblivious to the way Hermia made herself look available to him—the occasional touches, the looks, the covert eye rolls. As if she and Danny were the only two who got the joke, whatever it was. She was always including Danny in her conversation—even on the balcony, when she had already betrayed him, she was flirting—no, not flirting, but—yes, she was *including* him, making it clear that in some way she belonged to him. He couldn't possibly be unaffected by that, even if he wasn't consciously aware—Danny's ability to remain oblivious was quite remarkable. Yet because Hermia was far better at it than Xena or Laurette or Sin, Danny never had to speak up to shut it down. Therefore he might be perfectly aware but simply chose not to respond.

Why didn't Danny North fall in love with Yllka Argyros— called Hermia because she was a gatemage?

And was Hermia really in love with Danny, or was she just playing with him? Or was it something even more nefarious— was she *playing* him, running some sort of Greek-god con?

I'm jealous of her, even though Danny has never given me the slightest sign that he's interested in anybody but me. I'm jealous because I know that she is the kind of woman who *deserves* a man like Danny, and I'm not.

Crazy thoughts, Pat knew. Yet they kept coming back.

Danny doesn't have a crush on Hermia. *I'm* the one who can't stop thinking about her. Wishing I could be like her. Knowing that I never can. Not believing that anyone could prefer me to her.

"I'm no threat to you," said Hermia.

Pat was so startled that the book she was reading flipped out of her hands. "I didn't think you were," said Pat, retrieving the book.

"You keep studying me," said Hermia. "I know what you're thinking."

"Do you?" asked Pat.

"You're thinking, Danny North is going to fall in love with this amazing Greek bitch goddess, only you have nothing to worry about, it'll never happen."

Pat would have denied it, but since this was exactly what she had been thinking, she didn't bother. "If he hasn't fallen for you already, I expect he isn't going to."

"Oh, he will, someday. When all this nonsense is over and he's able to concentrate on something other than saving the world and keeping control of that devil he's got trapped inside him. But don't worry. I'll wait to let anything happen until you're already out of the picture."

Pat shook her head and returned to her book.

"You don't fool me," said Hermia. "You aren't actually reading, you're just trying to keep from making some acid retort to my teasing you about how faithless the gods are. *You're* the one who's right, I admit it. Danny North isn't your typical strutting god-boy. If there's anybody in any of the Families who might actually make a decent, reliable husband, who might actually be there to help raise his kids, I think you've found him."

Pat felt tears begin to well, or at least that thick feeling around the eyes that told her it was about to happen, so she turned away from the feeling. "Hermia, I'm really not trying to answer you tit-for-tat, but . . . it seems to me that the real reason you keep taunting me about how Danny and I are doomed not to last is because you really are hoping that he'll turn to you someday."

"Well, of course I am," said Hermia. "He's the best—and believe me, I've seen *all* the godlings, so I know. Of course, when my Family brought me along to look at the Norths, Danny didn't exactly stand out. I didn't know he was the maker of all those gates until long after. The day he made that abortive attempt at a Great Gate and sent all those schoolboys flying into the air over the high school. But since then, I've had a chance to compare him to all the others and I'd be a fool not to want him."

"I'm sure you make all your romantic decisions based on such stringent analytical processes."

Hermia laughed. " 'Romantic,' " she repeated. "Oh my, you *are* such a drowther."

Maybe this was why Danny didn't like Hermia so much. "The thing that we poor ignorant drowthers call 'romance' is the fundamental human longing to be part of a pair bond. You gods may pretend not to have that desire, but you have it. Don't most of you marry and remain faithful?"

Hermia was about to answer scornfully, but then she turned thoughtful. "Well, you have a point. And you're right, we have all the fundamental human drives and desires. So all right, Pat, I'll call it 'romance,' too. In fact, let me go way out on a limb and admit that I 'love' Danny North."

This was not something Pat wanted to hear. "You say 'love' as if you were putting air quotes around the word."

Hermia took just a moment to respond, and so Pat demonstrated air quotes, drawing the first two fingers of both hands downward to make quotation marks in the air. "Love," she said, giving it the air-quote intonation. "I admit that I 'love' Danny North."

Hermia giggled like a girl. "Oh, yes, I really *did* that. As if I have to deny the admission even as I make it. No, Pat, I'm not lying in bed pining over the boy, but yes, I care about him and the worst thing in my life right now is that I've given him every reason to hate me forever and I don't know what I can do about it."

"Don't look to me for advice," said Pat. "I think he doesn't hate you enough."

"Well, he *is* Danny North. He doesn't hate *any* of his enemies enough."

"Are you one of his enemies?" asked Pat.

"*He* thinks so, and with good reason," said Hermia. "And he's not surrounded by people urging him to forgive me. Why couldn't he have fallen in with a Christian crowd in high school?"

"We're Christian," said Pat. "More or less."

"Point proven," said Hermia. "But yes, I still put 'love' in air quotes because I don't know if what I'm feeling toward him really is love or even all that romantic. Fascination bordering on obsession—but that's easily explained by his power. He *cannot* be ignored. He's the ultimate mage, the Gatefather beyond all Gate-fathers, and now what you and he can do, gateless gating, how can I possibly *love* him when I have no choice but to *worship* him?"

Pat thought about that without answering. Worship. Is that what I feel about him? That's Xena and Sin, even Laurette, but not me. I don't worship anybody. I've never been able to even be a fan—no actor, no singer, no athlete, *nobody* that I admired enough to shiver and be all excited to see him in person. I know other people feel that, but . . .

"I don't see you as a quivering worshiper of Danny North," said Pat finally. "You've always treated him as an equal."

"Oh, I've treated him as being somewhat beneath me. I'm not talking about how I act. I'm talking about what I feel. We're having a discussion about 'feelings.'" Hermia made the air quotes again.

"How very high-school of us," said Pat.

"When you think about this discussion later, you'll conclude that I was just playing you to try to get you to bond with me so I can be excused from this house arrest you and Danny have me under."

"Never crossed my mind," said Pat. "Until now."

"It would have," said Hermia. "Because you're smart, and it's true. Until you like me, you won't trust me. I want very much for you to trust me."

"I've been pissed off all afternoon because I already like you and I find that shameful and annoying."

"Teach me how to do the gateless gate thing that you and Danny do."

And there it was. Cut to the chase. Here's what she really wants—not Danny, not me, not trust, not friendship. Power.

And yet the power came to me because I was stupid and got

myself killed, and for some reason This One decided to let me come back to my dead body and revivify. Why should I guard it?

Because Hermia has already proven her willingness to use whatever power she has to hurt Danny.

"I don't think I *can* teach you," said Pat. "If Danny couldn't teach Veevee . . ."

"Veevee is *not* a quick learner," said Hermia. "She's not dumb—gatemages are never *dumb*—but she's so full of her own thoughts and her own ego that she really can't observe anything. I know that about her because she and I worked together trying to learn how to move gates and other useful skills back when Danny had gates and we were still on the same team. You notice that *I* learned how, and she didn't."

"Yes," said Pat.

"I'm just as full of my own thoughts and my own ego," said Hermia. "But I know that about myself, and I can switch it off long enough to really concentrate on things outside myself. I've spent this afternoon concentrating on *you*."

Pat found this flattering, which annoyed her. She hated being so manipulable. "I haven't done anything," said Pat.

"Oh, you've sat there not-reading that book whenever you wanted to not-talk with me. When you and Danny brought me here, I should have been baffled because there was no gate. But I already knew that you hadn't made any gates in all your moving around back on the island. So when Danny took me—I know it was Danny and not you, because you followed an instant later—I didn't look for a gate. I'm not a cat, constantly trying to catch the laser pointer. I didn't look for anything outside myself at all. The things you had told me—you led me to look inside myself. To see if I could sense, could *grasp*, whatever it was that Danny grabbed hold of in order to drag me here to Florida."

Pat had to admit that this sounded far more sensible than anything else Hermia might have done.

"And I think I did sense it. Not the way you sense something outside yourself, like a smell or a sound. And not even the way you see yourself in a dream, in the third person, as if you were hovering just over your own shoulder, watching what you do. No, what I sensed was the part of me that Danny tugged on. Only it wasn't a tug. It was more like an invitation that was so powerful that I fell into it. Like gravity. I fell here. That's what it felt like."

And now that Hermia had put it into those words, Pat realized that it was true, or at least truish. She thought of the headlong rush to Duat and yes, it was like falling. As inevitable as gravity. And so was coming back to her body.

"So I thought, 'That's who "I" am,' and yes, I'm putting air quotes around 'I' because it's *not* the thing I've thought of as myself for my whole life. It's not this face or these hands or this body that eats and pees and walks and reads, it's not my eyes or any of my senses. But when Danny tugged on it and I fell here, it was *me* doing the falling, and all those other things came along with. So it's me. It's who I am. But there isn't much of it, is there? If I were really stripped down to that tuggable thing that fell, it wouldn't really be *me*, would it. Just a fragment."

"The fragment that makes all the decisions," said Pat.

"Ah. Yes. That's what it comes down to, doesn't it. Whatever part of us *decides*, that's our true self."

"Ka," said Pat.

"Inself. Or . . . pret," said Hermia. "Names for the part of myself that's always listening to my thoughts, always observing me. The judge who evaluates everything I do. But whenever I've ever been aware of that watcher, that judge, it flies away, recedes out of reach. Until now. Now I know where it is. I can tug on it too. Because Danny showed me how to find it."

Because of what Hermia said, Pat felt her own inself in a curious new way. In Duat, that's all she had been, just that ka, naked and almost but not quite alone. Because Danny was there. She was always aware of him, and therefore always aware of where *she* was in relation to him.

But now she was also aware of Hermia. Not of the woman, but the ka within her. The way she had been able to sense the ka and ba of Enopp and Eluik. Those, Danny had shown to her. And now Hermia was showing herself to Pat.

Showing it for a purpose. Showing it so that Pat would tug on it.

Only Pat didn't know how. She had never done it.

Except that even as she thought this, she made the contact—just as she had contacted Enopp and Eluik, as she had communed with This One. Only she didn't want that kind of intimate wordless communication with Hermia. Hermia was too strong and dangerous, she could not be trusted. And so Pat recoiled from her, and instead of that recoil taking a physical form, Pat moved her ka across the room and she was standing by the window facing into the room. . . .

And Hermia was not sitting where she had been sitting. She was standing only a few feet away from Pat. Smiling.

"I see," said Hermia.

"I didn't mean to do that," said Pat.

"I don't care," said Hermia. "You were running away from me, I get that. But you were in contact with me. I felt that. Not a tug, just a touch. But when you moved, I kept the same position. See? I'm exactly as far from you as I was before. You're standing, so I'm standing, but the *distance* is the same."

"How very Mr. Science of you," said Pat.

"I mean I *know* the distance. Not the *name* of the distance, but its exact length, and I was able to hold on to that. Is that how it is with you and Danny? You know where he is, and you can always jump to him."

Pat nodded.

"So right now I'm anchored to you the way you're anchored to him," said Hermia.

"I don't know," said Pat. "He had to send me to you, because the only thing I know how to do is move a few feet, to a place I can see—or to go to Danny."

Hermia closed her eyes. A long time. And then she was back near the door.

"Very good," said Pat, feeling pleased at Hermia's achievement and frightened by it. What would Danny say?

"But that's inside the room," said Hermia. "And I don't know where Danny is, so I really *don't* love him as much as you."

"That's not about love," said Pat. "That's about going to Duat together. That's about dying and having him surround me. I lost my body, but I still had Danny North."

"Ah," said Hermia. "So the connection I feel to you isn't at all the same. But look, I can choose what position to be in, relative to you. . . ."

Hermia appeared in rapid succession in places all around the room.

And then she was entirely gone.

No. She was out on the balcony, and now she walked back inside the condo. "Veevee would know how to do this, too," said Hermia, "if she could just pay attention."

"But it's still quite limited," said Pat.

"Oh, I know. But don't you see how useful this is? Each time I move, I'm healed. Just like passing through a gate. I think what happens is that all the prets that make up my body—am I getting that right?—they jump right along with me and reassemble. Only they reassemble according to the right plan, and not whatever accidental injuries or weaknesses I might have developed along the way. Do you think I'm right?"

Pat didn't have to answer. Hermia just went right on.

"So now I'm not helpless. If I had come home to that shotgun blast that Danny took, I could gate away instantly, by reflex. Even if I stayed in the same hotel room, I'd be completely healed. They shoot me again, I just move again. Unkillable. Uncatchable."

Pat couldn't help but laugh. "I think at some point they'd run crying out of the room."

"Men who depend on guns don't know what to do with people who aren't afraid of them," said Hermia. "People who won't die when they're shot."

"So this is useful," said Pat.

"The real question is, if I can anchor on you, a person who barely knows me and definitely doesn't like me, can I perhaps find another ka? Someone I know well? Let me ask you—you know where Danny is right now, yes? Is it far?"

Pat almost answered: He's in two places. His body is in his little rented house in Buena Vista, with Set locked away inside him, but he's also operating a clant on Westil. A perfect copy of his body, so that in a way, Danny is completely on Westil, only without Set inside. Except that the body on Westil is just an illusion, it isn't a part of him, it isn't bonded to him like his real body in Buena Vista here on Earth.

But Pat didn't think it was wise to let Hermia know that Danny could be in two places at once. She had already taught her too much.

"I wonder if I have a sense of my mother," said Hermia. "She's a ruthless, frightening, selfish, despicable human being, but she *is* my mommy."

Pat realized that in all these days since she had died and learned how to sense other people's ka and ba, it hadn't even occurred to her to look for her mother or father. What kind of unnatural child am I, not to have a sense of them?

A woman leaves her father and mother to cleave unto her husband, or some such wording. That's why she never thought to look for them. She was "cleaving unto" Danny North.

"No sense of where she is, though," said Hermia. "And I'm really content with that. I like being away from her. And Daddy. But surely there's someone else. Veevee?"

Just raising the question made Pat think of Veevee and, to her surprise, she knew exactly where Veevee was. In a car, driving along Tamiami Trail, having just left Trader Joe's. Why do I know that? Have I been unconsciously tracking her?

"Please," said Hermia.

"She might wreck the car if we—"

But the words "car if we" came out of her mouth inside Veevee's car. Hermia and Pat were sitting in the back seat, side by side.

"You little brats, you're practicing without me," said Veevee.

"What else do you expect?" said Hermia.

"From you, nothing better," said Veevee. "But Pat isn't a brat, she isn't a *gatemage.*"

"She is now," said Hermia. "Maybe the brattiness follows."

"I didn't realize I was tracking you," said Pat. "Or that I knew how to find you so quickly."

"And now Hermia knows," said Veevee.

"Not really," said Hermia. "Pat knew where you were, and I just came along for the ride."

"Did you?" asked Pat. "Because I never decided to make the jump."

"You must have, or we wouldn't be here."

"It is *so* hard to concentrate on driving," said Veevee.

"And yet you're doing it," said Hermia.

"My body is driving by reflex," said Veevee. "I'm more distracted than if I were texting right now."

"Still in the lane," said Hermia.

Pat let them bandy words. She was trying to find the ka of someone important to her. But she had experienced Veevee's ka when Danny was moving her around, trying to teach her. Had Pat ever really sensed anybody else except those Westilian boys?

But maybe it wasn't just a matter of finding people. Maybe . . .

And there she was, in the clearing in the woods above Parry McCluer High School. Just like that. It was a place she knew well. A place she had gated to before.

There was somebody there. It was during high-school hours, but there were a girl and a boy, vigorously snogging.

Xena. Yes, of course Xena. And . . . oh, not possible. Wheeler.

Before she could make a sound, Pat was gone again. To another place she knew very, very well. The bathroom mirror where she had spent so many hours of her life washing her acne-plagued face with benzoyl peroxide soaps. A place she knew better than any other.

I don't have to go where Danny is. I can go to places that I know well. And when I was there in the gathering place in the woods, I didn't recognize Xena and Wheeler by *face*, I knew them by their kas. I *knew* them. I could find them again no matter where they were.

But at this moment, she didn't *want* to find them because she knew where they were and what they were doing and she couldn't imagine that she would be a welcome visitor.

There were two people looking into the bathroom mirror. Hermia was beside her. "You came here?"

"Second choice," said Pat. "I went to the clearing in the woods first."

"I thought you made two jumps," said Hermia. "But I'm not good at this yet."

"Places I've been to a lot," said Pat. "Places that were emotionally important to me. Easy to find them. To just *go*."

"Are you really so vain that your bathroom mirror is—"

"I had terrible acne till Danny healed me," said Pat. "I wasn't being vain when I stared into this monster movie screen."

"You poor dear. And also, lucky you." Hermia squinted.

Even squinting, she was pretty. Pat really should hate this woman.

"So what *place* has ever been so important to me?" asked Hermia.

And then she was gone.

It was Pat's turn to follow her. She knew the place at once— behind the gym down at the high school. "Where you first met Danny, knowing he was a gatemage," said Pat.

"Knowing he had started to make a Great Gate," said Hermia. "I don't know how I understood that, because it's not as if I had ever seen one. But it was all entwined. Lots of gates together. So . . . I knew. And there he was."

A moment's pause, and she was gone again.

Again, Pat followed.

A large building made of stone. Almost monumental. "Library of Congress," said Hermia. "See? There's the Capitol dome. We're behind the Library of Congress right here, but this is the spot where I sat while I was showing Danny how to close his gates. And it was here that he . . . made a gate into me. Oh, it was such a powerful feeling, such a . . . but you know that. It has to be like what you experienced when . . . only I wasn't dead, so, not the same after all."

Danny had never talked about any kind of powerful experience with Hermia at this point in their story. She didn't like that it bothered her. Maybe it was more powerful for Hermia than it was for Danny.

"Shall we go back to Veevee's condo?" asked Hermia. "Do you know the place well enough to get there?"

"Do you?" asked Pat.

"Well, it was never very important to me until today. My liberation from jail and all that. And the place where I learned how to . . ."

Pat didn't hear because she had jumped to Veevee's apartment.

"Gate from one place to another without making gates," said Hermia.

"Did you follow me?" asked Pat. "Or jump here on your own?"

"I don't know," said Hermia. "I just came here. I think. But now I think we need to separate."

Pat knew immediately that this was the dividing line. Hermia had learned all she needed to from Pat—or all she thought there was to learn. One of those. But she was done with Pat now, and wanted to go do things that she didn't want Pat to see.

"You're really not a nice person," said Pat to Hermia. Not angrily or bitterly. It was simply the truth.

"I *am* a nice person," said Hermia. "I could have just gone."

"No, you couldn't," said Pat. "Because I might have followed you, and you don't want me to. So you had to tell me *not* to follow you, and you knew that I'd comply, because I, in fact, *am* a nice person."

Hermia smiled at her. "Very accurately expressed. For a wind-mage, you have a way with words."

"Don't go to Danny," said Pat.

"Why not?" asked Hermia. "I assume he's at home, so even if I can't find his ka, I can find his *house*. That place is *very* import-ant to me."

"Please don't go to Danny," said Pat.

"I don't pose any threat to you, and you know it."

Pat closed her eyes. "He's doing something very difficult and dangerous, and you already know too much. If you go there, and Set sees what you know how to do . . ."

Hermia gave a low chuckle of understanding. "You're afraid that if Set saw that I could make gates, or whatever we do now, he might jump to me."

"And whatever Danny's doing, your arrival won't help him," said Pat.

"Well, I've already interfered with his plans too often as it is," said Hermia. "I won't bother Danny until I really need to. And Pat. You treated me better than I deserved."

"Yes," said Pat. "But with any luck, we all get treated better than we deserve, from time to time."

"You deserve Danny," said Hermia, "and Danny deserves you. And that may be the most completely true and *nice* thing that I've ever said to anybody in my life." Hermia leaned close and kissed Pat on the cheek. "Work on your windmagery, darling—it's nice that you can make quick getaways, but you need to make sure you have a powerful offensive weapon, too, when the war starts in earnest."

And then she was gone.

Pat just stood there in Veevee's apartment, trying to think of some reason why it wasn't completely disastrous for Hermia to have gained this ability.

Then Pat walked out onto the balcony and worked on whipping up a powerful twister with edges so clearly defined that nobody on the beach felt even the slightest uptick in the wind. The twister whirled at monstrous speed fifty feet up, and reached high into the atmosphere. Pat then brought the top of it down so that the twister was no thicker than a frisbee, though it was half a mile wide, a disk of intensely destructive wind.

It was so exhilarating.

She slowed it. She sped it up. She narrowed it, then widened it. She took care to keep it out of the flight path of any airplanes, though she couldn't resist capturing a couple of hopeless kites and whipping them away at such speeds that they were instantly torn to shreds. The wind was so hungry to feel that power and kites were cheap and easy to replace. The young men who were flying them would have a story to tell. "The kite just . . . disappeared. A jerk on the line and then it was dead, and there was *nothing* left, like some invisible bird came and ate it whole."

Everybody wins. And I have an offensive weapon already. If I ever need it. Oh, please, let it be that I never, never need to use this against a person.

Veevee came out onto the balcony after a while. "Playing with your windmagery?"

"Better than teaching a traitor how to move around the world on seven-league boots."

Veevee made a show of pouting. "*Her* you can teach?"

"Now that I've seen *how* she learned, maybe I can teach you," said Pat. "If you really want to know."

"Of course I—"

"Hermia thought that you weren't willing to concentrate on the things that are actually pertinent."

"The word 'bitch' was invented just so she could grow into it," said Veevee.

"You gatemages know all the secret facts about words, not me," said Pat. "I'm going to take you through what Hermia and I did. Step by step. If you're willing to let me lead you that way."

"Whatever it takes, kid," said Veevee. "If *she* can learn it, I'm damn well going to learn it too."

It took until well after dark, but by then they were in Stone's house in Washington, DC, and it was Veevee who had led them there.

"It's not the regular way," said Veevee to Stone. "I still can't do that, but Peter Von Roth, I can *move* like a gatemage through the world."

Peter seemed so genuinely proud of her—and so moved that Veevee had actually come to him to brag about it—that Pat gated herself back to the clearing in the woods so they could be alone.

It was dark. The snogging party was long since over. Just the night noises of the woods, and some distant traffic noises. And yes, wait, yes, there was a noise of distant cheering. There must be some kind of athletic event down at the school. Or a party. Something. Happy sounds.

It made Pat glad—glad that other people were happy, and glad that she was by herself, not trapped inside a happy throng.

Only she wasn't by herself. Because after only a few moments, Danny was beside her.

"I didn't come while you were teaching Veevee," said Danny. "You were succeeding where I failed—I wasn't going to interfere with *that*."

"I'm glad you came to me here," said Pat. And then she burst out laughing.

"What?" asked Danny.

Pat told him about Xena and Wheeler.

"Inconceivable," said Danny.

"You keep using that word," said Pat. "I do not think it means what you think it means."

He seemed not to get the *Princess Bride* reference, and instead of explaining it, she kissed him. Now that this was established as a snogging site, it seemed appropriate, and he went along with it willingly enough.

12

Eluik sat by the window on the flight from Dayton to Lexington. He hadn't asked for the seat, but Enopp told him, "You should be able to look out the window." Eluik wondered if Enopp was afraid of what he'd feel, looking down from such a height, but no. Enopp thought of it as the best place, and he was giving it to his brother, and Eluik accepted the gift as it was intended.

The distance was slight—it wouldn't have taken two hours to cover it by car. There had been so much ritual associated with getting through airport security and getting on the plane that as they walked through the terminal Eluik wondered aloud if it might not be faster for Marion or Leslie to drive them.

"It would be faster," Enopp said quietly, "for us to simply *go*."

Eluik saw Leslie, who was walking ahead of them, hesitate a bit. But then she must have realized that nobody who overheard them would have the faintest idea of what they were talking about, so she kept moving and didn't stop to hush them.

"Do you know where it is?" asked Eluik.

"No," said Enopp. "But Pat or Danny could have taken us. Or shown us where. I know you learned as well as I did how to move from place to place."

"I don't have your reckless confidence."

"I'm not reckless," said Enopp. "I'm very careful *not* to try to do more than I know how to do."

"You just think you know how to do far more than *I* think I know how to do."

"Gating, or just going, whatever we call it," said Enopp, "is quicker. But I think Marion and Leslie wanted us to experience flying in an airplane. Most people in America have flown, so why shouldn't we? When we get back home, there won't be any airplanes."

Then they were at the gate, and Leslie gave the paperwork to the gate agent, and then she returned to Eluik and Enopp. "I know you're going to enjoy this," said Leslie.

"Which means you're afraid we won't," said Enopp, "and so you want us to know we're *supposed* to enjoy it."

"I'm not going to miss your snottiness one bit," said Leslie.

"Which means you know you *are* going to miss it," said Enopp.

Leslie turned to Eluik. "Am I really such a liar?" she asked him.

"You're just speaking the way adults always speak to children," said Eluik. "Only a child as snotty as Enopp would be rude enough to point it out."

"I hate being a typical adult," said Leslie, "but I'll only brood about it constantly while you're gone. Anyway, it's time for you to be handed off to the attendant who's taking you on." Leslie glanced out the window. "It's really not much of a plane. But then, it's not much of a flight, either."

"This is just a regional jet," said Enopp, "and it won't ever reach a high cruising altitude, so we'll get a much better view of the ground."

"You say that as if it's a good thing," said Leslie. "I always like to fly above the clouds so I can't *see* the ground. Everything looks so pillowy and soft."

In other words, Eluik realized, Leslie was afraid of flying. Maybe he should be, too. Except how *could* he be afraid, since he and Enopp both had the power to simply *go* to the ground, if something went wrong with the plane.

We could probably take the other passengers with us. Or a couple at a time, and then go back for the others. Long before the plane crashed.

Leslie had been right. It *was* disturbing to have a clear view of the ground, especially when the plane juddered and jinked in the turbulence. He and Enopp had both looked up everything they could about flying, so they knew the turbulence shouldn't bother them. But when the plane shifted like that it was disturbing not to be able to see anything holding them up.

But Eluik had kept looking out the window anyway, to get used to it. It wasn't the same thing as being trapped in the cave, when it was so hard not to slide down to the cave mouth and start to fall. *That* had been terrifying. But he had gotten used to trusting that the gate at the cave mouth would always catch him and bring him back up. And he was getting used to this, too. And getting over the feeling that he was as much a prisoner inside this airplane as he had been in the cave, because that feeling was completely irrational. *Now* he had the power to leave this plane whenever he wanted. So he didn't want to. Mostly.

"You'll get a crick in your neck from keeping your head twisted toward the window the whole way," said a woman's voice. In a strange version of the language of Iceway.

Eluik was startled, but didn't show it. Slowly he turned his head and then his body until he could see the woman who was sitting in Enopp's seat. Enopp had gone to the toilet. This woman had not been in the waiting area and she had not boarded the airplane, because Eluik had made a point of memorizing everybody on the plane.

"When Enopp comes back, he's going to want his seat," said Eluik.

"Since we both know that you and your brother could simply gate yourselves to wherever you're going . . ."

"You must be Hermia," said Eluik.

She smiled. "You were warned to watch out for me?"

Eluik almost laughed at her vanity. "Because you speak a version of the Icewegian language, so you're a gatemage, and that's a very short list."

"You should really learn English," she said.

"Enopp will be back soon," said Eluik, "and the airplane's full, so if you have something to discuss . . ."

"It's really quite simple. This airplane is headed for Blue Grass Airport in Lexington, and I can't think why you might be going there."

"That's where the airplane lands," said Eluik. "So it seemed prudent to choose the same destination."

"Something or someone near Lexington."

"If Danny wanted you to know . . ."

"Are you his dog now? On his leash?" asked Hermia. "I know he's keeping you safe. I know that the Silvermans' farm isn't all that safe now."

"Because of the games you played with the Wild Gate," said Eluik.

"All my fault, I'm so wicked," said Hermia. "And you lived in a cave for a year or so, weren't you the silly one."

"Not my choice," said Eluik, "and so you're claiming that your moving the Wild Gate wasn't your fault. But I'm a child and had no choice, and you're . . . older and definitely had choices."

"Just tell me where you're going," said Hermia, "so I know whether you pose a threat to me or my Family. It will save me hours of spying, and if I believe what you tell me, it might make it possible for me to keep my Family from interfering."

"Just don't tell them where we are," said Eluik. "But wait—I'm sure you'd *have* to tell them."

"Or they'd kill my pet kitten," said Hermia. "As you said, Enopp will be back soon."

Eluik thought it through. Hermia's actions were the reason that all the Families became aware of Silvermans' farm. Maybe they knew about Eluik and Enopp and maybe they didn't. But if word was out, and somebody made it to Mittlegard from Westil, then they might be in danger. How would it help to tell Hermia?

Then again, if she couldn't be kept from gating into a moving airplane, she probably couldn't be kept from spying on them wherever they were.

"There's a farm near Danville, Kentucky," said Eluik.

"Whose farm?"

"A retired Air Force officer. *Not* a mage of any kind, but he and Marion are friends."

"So they don't think you need any more protection or training," said Hermia.

"Protection?" asked Eluik. "We can do what you do. We don't need protection. We just need beds and a roof and some food and water."

"So here's the million-dollar question. Are you hiding from your enemies on Westil, or is somebody in Mittlegard looking for you?"

"None of the Families know we exist, unless you told them," said Eluik.

"I didn't," said Hermia, "because you two were seriously troubled. All better now, I see."

"So now you'll tell?"

"If I told, word would spread, and *some* Family would get the crazy idea of kidnapping you and forcing one of you to gate them around or they'll kill the other."

"Wouldn't work," said Eluik. "We can both do it, so which of us would be the hostage?"

"This Air Force officer—"

"Retired."

"Can he pilot a jet?"

"That was never his job. He was in theory and doctrine and history and intelligence."

"Just wondering."

"Because you need a pilot," said Eluik.

"Because I wonder if Danny thinks he needs a pilot."

"He needs somebody willing to take us into his home in a remote place and help us stay alive a while longer. But the longer we talk, the more I'm thinking maybe we should go back to Westil so we don't have you on our back."

"I can go to Westil, too," said Hermia. "No escaping me. But I don't wish you any harm, and I'll keep your location secret."

"Then you didn't need to ask me anything," said Eluik. He turned back to the window.

"Maybe I just wanted to see if you were really talking now," said Hermia.

"Or maybe you just wanted to test your Icewegian accent. You gatemages and your vanity about languages."

The plane bounced a little, and the pilot started talking about being on the initial approach to Blue Grass Airport near Lexington, Kentucky.

"Enopp's coming back," said Hermia. "Thanks for the chat. Happy landing."

Then she was gone. In a few seconds, Enopp plunked down on the seat and refastened his seat belt.

"That wasn't Pat," said Enopp.

"Hermia," said Eluik. "Wanting to know where we were going."

"Did you tell her to go . . . well, I never realized, we don't have a Westilian equivalent of what I wanted to say in English."

"I told her that we were going to stay with somebody who isn't a mage."

Enopp nodded. "True enough."

Eluik looked out the window again. "The ground's a lot closer."

"That's an essential part of landing," said Enopp.

The pilot warned them not to use laptops from now on.

"Do you think we'll ever go back to Westil?" asked Enopp.

"To Westil?" asked Eluik. "Probably. To Iceway? Probably not."

"Because our father doesn't need us now. Because Bexoi gave him a son."

Eluik shook his head. "Because *Mother* gave him a son."

"Bexoi's son."

"Bexoi's *body's* son," said Eluik. "And it's Mother's body now."

"Our half-brother," said Enopp.

"I think he should spend a couple of years in a cave, don't you?" said Eluik.

"Nobody should spend a *minute* in a cave that keeps rolling you out into empty space," said Enopp. "That baby did nothing to us."

"Wisely said," Eluik answered. "The important question is: Do we go right back and tell Silvermans that Hermia found us on the way?"

"What's the point?" said Enopp. "She can follow us anywhere. If she wants to tell people where we are, she can."

"So if we can't do anything about it," said Eluik, "it doesn't matter what we do."

"We keep working on learning how to be mages," said Enopp. "And I'm not sure how we can, because now I'm in the habit of going places *this* way instead of using my gates. And we still have no idea what *your* magery is."

"If I'm not drekka," said Eluik.

"Drekka or drowther, you can *go* wherever you want and heal yourself in the process. So we'll figure out more and more about this new kind of magery, and meanwhile we'll also try to work on our own *natural* mageries. If any."

"Eloquently said," Eluik replied. "That's why I never minded having you speak for me. You always said things better than I could have myself."

"I'm sorry I didn't understand that I was the one keeping you silent."

"That was the hundredth apology," said Eluik.

"Oh, is that my limit?"

"All apologies after the hundredth have to come in the form of money."

"I don't have any money."

"Then that was your limit."

Eluik went back to looking out the window, and when the plane gently touched the runway and then slowed down with great suddenness, Eluik marveled as so often before: These machines the drowthers make here in Mittlegard—why didn't anybody in Westil learn how to make airplanes?

Different worlds, different ways.

Colonel Diamond was waiting at the gate for them. He had already shown them his identification, apparently, because he thanked the flight attendant and introduced himself to Eluik and Enopp and that was it, they were racing to keep up with him as he strode through the terminal toward the exit.

Hermia was standing at the curb when they came outside, as if she were waiting for a ride. Eluik pretended not to know her, and she pretended not to know him. He just hoped she didn't think it would be funny to pop into the back seat of Colonel Diamond's car on the way to his farm. He didn't know how much Diamond already knew about Mithermages. Eluik certainly didn't want to have to explain people popping into existence and then disappearing again.

"Can't wait for you to get out to Persimmon Knob," said Diamond.

Eluik gave Enopp a little half-smile. If he really couldn't wait, they could go there instantly. But of course that was just an expression. An idiom. Eluik didn't have to be a gatemage to understand *that*.

The scenery was trees and hills and blacktop, just like in Ohio. And nothing like Iceway. Eluik looked out the window the whole way. He decided that he didn't miss the bare-stone craggy cliffs and tors of Iceway. This softer landscape of deep deciduous forest alternating with meadows, pastures, and cultivated fields gave him a greater sense of peace.

Does this mean that I'm a treemage? That I have some affinity with vegetation, so that in a stony, icy place I feel tense and bereft? Or is it simply an echo of the simple reality that in Iceway, I was always in danger and suffered terrible things, while here in Mittlegard, in America, in Ohio and now Kentucky, I really am more safe?

Though with that weird Greek woman able to pop in and spy on me whenever she wants—or kill me, if that idea appealed to her—maybe I'm not all that safe after all.

"What kind of mage are you?" Enopp asked Colonel Diamond.

Diamond hesitated. Perhaps it took a moment for him even to make sense of the question. Drowthers in Mittlegard weren't used to the idea of mages, or so the Silvermans had warned them.

"I don't think I'm a mage at all," said Diamond. "Not even interested in being one, to tell the truth. I think what people like you can do is cool, in a potentially destructive kind of way. I've been hearing that some of the Great Families have been getting involved with our military and some of my friends are scared. But I guess we'll all just have to get used to a world with these strange abilities in it. Doesn't mean I want to have any myself, though."

Eluik thought that Diamond's answer showed that he had clearly given the matter some thought. And when he said that he didn't want any powers himself, Eluik figured that meant that he really wished he had them, but knew it was never going to happen, and therefore kept himself happy by pretending not to care.

"Maybe if you went through a Great Gate," said Enopp, "you'd find out that you had powers you never thought you had. Like what happened to Danny's girlfriend, Pat."

"Maybe," said Diamond, not revealing any particular interest.

"There aren't any Great Gates in the world right now," said Eluik to Enopp.

"I know," said Enopp. "But there *could* be."

"You planning to make one?" asked Eluik. "Because the Gate Thief is still very much alive, and lots more powerful than you are."

"I know he's alive, but he's also Mother's friend, and I don't think he'd do that to me."

"He did it to Danny."

"Before he even knew who Danny was," said Enopp.

"It doesn't matter to *me*," said Diamond. "I didn't think you'd believe me when I said I didn't want any magery, but I really don't.

Besides, what if I turned out to have some really dangerous power. Or an annoying one. Who wants the ability to summon mosquitoes? Or make somebody's hair fall out?"

Enopp laughed. "There's no magery for that."

"That you've heard of," said Diamond. "I'm probably the first."

"If you're not interested in magery," said Eluik, "I wonder why you're taking us in?"

"Stone told me he had a couple of kids from another country who had already suffered a lot and still needed to be kept out of sight. We don't have a lot of security at the farm, but we have plenty of obscurity, and Stone was pretty sure that would be enough."

"One of the Great Families already has a spy watching to see where we go," said Eluik. "And don't bother with evasive maneuvers. She doesn't use cars."

Diamond chuckled. "Stone said that Hermia would probably find you no matter what we did. His wife apparently has a low opinion of her. But they both agreed that she probably wouldn't cause you any harm."

"Probably not," said Eluik.

"How do you know Stone?" asked Enopp. "We don't know him all that well, we mostly just know the Silvermans. And Danny."

"I've never met any of them," said Diamond. "Unless you count the phone calls setting up your flight. I know Stone because I met him when I was stationed at the Pentagon. One of the times I was stationed there."

"So you were an important guy in the Air Force?" asked Enopp.

"I was a colonel when I retired," said Diamond. " 'Important' starts with a general's stars."

"You were important," said Eluik. "Stone said that you know everybody."

"I know everybody that I know," said Diamond. "Still a few

billion short of 'everybody.' I collect friends, and help them share information and ideas with each other. A few generals in that group, a couple of civilian leaders, some scientists. And now a couple of mages. Pretty eclectic group."

"So you'll be sharing information about us?" asked Eluik.

"Not about you in particular. But mages in general? 'Westilians' or whatever you call yourselves? That's a pretty hot topic. What to make of these planes and tanks that run without friction and gather their own fuel from the air. How to maintain security when every hawk or eagle or crow might be a spy. Whether there's any chance of drowthers like us remaining in control of our own government and military. Little things like that."

"So you'll study us," said Eluik.

"I may ask you questions, if it seems pertinent, but no, I'm not studying you. I'm sheltering you. You can ask me questions, too. I don't want to make you my subjects of study, I hope to make you my friends."

"Because it would be useful to have friends among the mages," said Eluik.

Diamond laughed. "I guess you'll just have to get to know me and reach your own conclusion about my motives. But yes, it's useful to have friends. It also makes me happy. And I'm happier when I have friends drawn from many different groups and classes and nations and ethnic groups. You're definitely not from any ethnic group I already knew. And *nobody* could look at you and decide what race you are."

"Human race," said Enopp. "Pretty much."

"Close, anyway," said Eluik.

Diamond chuckled. "Oh, you're fully human, all right."

"And you have as much of the blood of the Mithermages as anyone else on Mittlegard," said Eluik. "So don't rule out the possibility that you have an affinity for some branch of magery."

"My first rule of intellectual inquiry: Don't rule anything out till you have no choice."

"Good rule," said Enopp. "But in this case, the only way to rule it out is to go through a Great Gate and see what happens."

"Shouldn't my affinity, if I have one, show itself before I actually go through the gate?" asked Diamond.

"If you had been trained from childhood, then probably, unless you're a gatemage," said Eluik. "That doesn't show up."

"Stone told me that gatemages were always killed," said Diamond. "If everybody needs gates, that seems counterproductive."

"It wasn't always that way. Gatemages are rare, but their gates can last for centuries," said Enopp. "So every Family on Westil and here on Mittlegard had access to lots of gates, whether they had a gatemage or not. But then Loki stole all the gates. Suddenly nobody had gates. So whoever got a gatemage first would have a huge advantage."

"Still doesn't explain why any Family would kill their own gatemage."

"The only Family that everybody monitored was the Norths," said Eluik, "because Loki was theirs. The others probably all cheated when they thought they could get away with it. But any gatemages who tried a Great Gate ran into the Gate Thief and lost all their gates, and that was the end."

"Till Danny North," said Diamond.

"He got away from his Family in time—with some help, I understand," said Enopp.

"And he was stronger than the Gate Thief," said Eluik. "He stole the Gate Thief's gates."

"You sound happy about that," said Diamond.

"The Gate Thief was the one who kept us imprisoned," said Enopp. "He's sorry now. And he's also the one who saved our lives when the Queen tried to have us killed."

"Sort of like Stalin," said Diamond. "Started out as a very bad enemy, until an even worse enemy attacked him, and then he was our ally."

"I don't know about that," said Enopp dismissively. "What's the point of our learning Mittlegard history? We're not going to stay here forever."

"When will it be safe for you to go back?" asked Diamond.

"I don't know," said Enopp. "But Mother is free now, and so it's only a matter of time."

Eluik shook his head. "She may never be able to bring us back," he said. "She's in the other body. She has to pretend to be her."

"She's still our mother," said Enopp.

"In our enemy's body," said Eluik.

"Your mother has changed bodies?" asked Diamond.

Eluik realized at once that he had said too much. Why? He and Enopp were very good at keeping secrets. Their lives had always depended on it.

There was something about Diamond that made Eluik let down his guard. To trust him.

And then it became clear. "I know what your affinity is," said Eluik.

"Really? What?"

"You're a manmage, if you're any kind of mage at all. And I think you are. A strong one."

"Now you're just trying to flatter me," said Diamond.

"Enopp and I never tell secrets," said Eluik. "We're *never* lulled into talking freely. Until now, with you."

"Well, I'm glad you trusted me. Your secret is safe. I'll never tell."

"Our secret is only safe if nobody else knows it," said Eluik, "and we never tell. Only we told you."

"And that makes me a manmage? Isn't that the other kind of mage that the Families all killed?"

"And they weren't joking about it, either," said Enopp. "The manmages of Dapnu Dap ruled all of Westil for a while. They were impossible to fight."

"But you fought them and won," said Diamond.

"Not *us*," said Eluik. "It was five thousand years ago. And we only defeated them because some of the most powerful manmages changed sides and worked with us. Afterwards, when all the other manmages were dead, the ones who helped us killed themselves. The law was: No manmage could ever be allowed to live."

"So calling me a manmage wasn't nice," said Diamond.

"Mother is a manmage," said Enopp. "We think killing manmages is a bad idea. Because some manmages are good."

"What Stone told me," said Diamond, "is that manmages ride other people the way a . . . blood brother? No, Clawbrother, the way they ride inside animals."

"Or a Bloodfather," said Enopp. "And yes, the most powerful ones can. But Mother never did that."

"Yes, she did," said Eluik. "But you have to remember how riding a heartbeast works. A Clawbrother can't get inside a hawk or a bear and make it act like something other than a hawk or a bear. The creature is still itself. The Clawbrother can guide it, but it can't change its nature."

"So people are still themselves," said Diamond, "even if a manmage is riding them?"

"Yes," said Enopp.

"No," said Eluik. "It depends on what you mean by being yourself."

"As if you know," said Enopp.

"Mother told me years ago, when she first told me what she

was," said Eluik. "You only become a manmage the way you become any other kind of mage. By truly loving and serving your affinity. Sandmages serve the dry sand, Tempesters feed the storm, Trunkfathers love trees."

"So manmages love people," said Diamond.

"Like you," said Eluik. "You collect people. A huge network of intellectuals and decision-makers all around the world. You don't rule them, you don't try to organize them, you just know when one of them needs to meet with one of the others to exchange ideas. Did I remember that right? Did the Silvermans get it straight?"

"I never thought of it that way, but yes, I'm pretty good at networking."

Eluik laughed. "That's a nice way of putting it. So you love those people, right? You care about them. You try to get them what they need."

"When they have to solve a problem, I rarely know the answer, but I usually know someone who *might* know what to do."

"Manmage," said Eluik.

"Why didn't we see that right away?" asked Enopp.

"Why didn't *Stone* see it? Or Leslie, or Marion?" asked Eluik.

"Because it's not magery," said Diamond. "It's just . . . being a good friend."

"The way a Rootherd is a friend to corn, or a Stonefather to a mountain," said Eluik. "Mother said that she sees what a person really loves and cares about, and then she can talk to them and help them realize how the thing she wants them to do is exactly what they already wanted to do."

"Ah," said Diamond. "But I don't do that. My friends decide for themselves what they want."

"You haven't been through a Great Gate," said Eluik. "And do they really? Don't you sometimes persuade them to accept ideas that they didn't like at first?"

"Everybody does that," said Diamond.

"But manmages always succeed," said Eluik.

Diamond laughed sharply. "If I let you keep talking to me, you'll persuade me that I know how to ride a hawk and fly."

"Not a Bloodfather, not a Clawfriend, not even a Furboy," said Eluik. "Manmagery isn't like beastmagery. You can't use words with a hawk or a lion or a horse. The beast has to trust you and let you in, because of how you treat them, how you feel about them."

"Well, as you said, there aren't any Great Gates anymore, so we'll never know about me," said Diamond.

"I'm a gatemage," said Enopp.

"You might *become* a gatemage," said Eluik. "You might even become a Gatefather like Wad or Danny. But it won't matter because if you try to make a Great Gate, the Gate Thief will stop you."

"He doesn't do that anymore," said Enopp.

"What makes you think that?" asked Eluik. "He didn't block Danny because Danny was stronger. But he ate the Wild Gate that Hermia had moved, didn't he? He has all of Danny's gates and he didn't give them back."

Enopp fell into a thoughtful silence.

"I'm probably wrong," said Eluik to Diamond. "You're probably not any kind of mage at all. You're just a really nice man who makes friends easily and holds on to all of them."

"That's what I think I am," said Diamond. "Or what I try to be, anyway. My kids will tell you I'm not *always* a really nice man."

"Your kids don't always do what you want?" asked Enopp.

"Are you kidding?" asked Diamond. "I tell them what's the right thing to do, but they're free to choose, and . . . then they do whatever they damn well please."

"So . . . not a very good manmage," said Enopp.

"No, an excellent manmage," said Eluik. "Like Mother. She didn't control us. She left us free."

"Because she loved us more than anybody," said Enopp.

"Hardest thing I've ever done," said Diamond. "Letting my kids do some of the insane things they chose to do."

"Doesn't mean you're not a manmage," said Eluik. "Just means you're not the kind of manmage that needs killing."

There were fields on the left side of the car when they turned off to the right, plunging into trees and winding up a narrow lane through deep woods. "Almost home," said Diamond.

"I can see why somebody might think you're a treemage," said Enopp. "This is serious forest."

"I love trees," said Diamond. "I know most of the grand old trees on my property by name."

"Name?" said Enopp. "Trees don't have names."

"He just means the name of the *kind* of tree," said Eluik.

"No," said Diamond. "I mean: Annie's Sycamore. Elm by the Brook. The Reading Oak. Things that we've done with or on or under or near the tree. They all have a story and that becomes the tree's name. We love these trees."

"Treemagery is a lot safer," said Enopp. "Nobody kills a treemage."

"That settles it, then," said Diamond.

The car crested a rise and emerged at the top of a hill. The ground was meadow for a ways around the house on all sides, but as soon as the ground started downward again, the trees came back. In every direction, they could see miles and miles of tree-covered hills, but hardly any houses at all.

"It almost looks Westilian," said Enopp. "Like there aren't any paved roads or big houses except this one."

"That's why I love this place," said Diamond. "Surrounded by life—beasts as well as trees—but the trees are the mothers and fathers of all. They shelter everybody, provide for everybody. Look down there, in that glen. Those are trees that have never been clear cut. There are some thousand-year trees there."

"For *this* world, that's really old," said Enopp.

"The Indians used to walk among those trees. And really ancient creatures walked among the ancestors of those trees. This place was never a killing ground for trees. That means something to me."

"You were in the Air Force," said Eluik. "The Air Force drops bombs and blows things up."

"Sometimes it's a job that has to be done," said Diamond. "But that doesn't mean that a soldier doesn't dream of finding a place that's full of peace."

Eluik thought about that. Full of peace. Kind of a backward way of looking at it. Eluik would have thought that peace was the absence of war. But maybe war is the absence of peace. Maybe when you leave a place alone, for all the creatures to live their lives, the place fills up with peace, and the peace spills over. Like a lake with a stream running out of it, so that people downstream can drink up all the peace they want, and be filled with it.

"You know, Westil might be full of magic," said Eluik. "More than Mittlegard. But what neither world has very much of is this."

"Trees?" asked Diamond.

"Plenty of trees in Westil," said Enopp.

"Peace," said Eluik. "No peace in either world. Except maybe in little islands like this."

"Then it's a good thing we've come here, isn't it," said Diamond. "Now come on inside, I know Annie will have all kinds of food for you. Regular food. Plain food. Bread and meat and cheese and fruits and vegetables. Nothing fancy but everything is good for you."

"In Westil," said Enopp, "that's all anybody knows how to make."

"Then you'll feel right at home," said Diamond. "Come on inside."

Eluik and Enopp got their bags—the ones that Diamond didn't grab first—and followed him up the porch stairs into the house.

Eluik took one glance back at the trees beyond the car and he thought maybe he caught a glimpse of somebody. No, not "somebody." Hermia. Probably not his imagination. Probably she knew exactly where they were. Can't be helped. But if anybody can damage the peace of this place, it'll be her.

Living with the Silvermans had prepared Eluik and Enopp for the American way of life. None of the customs of Iceway applied, and while there were differences between the Diamond kitchen and Leslie's cooking back in Ohio, the ways of procuring the food—buying packages in stores, keeping everything in refrigerators and freezers, baking and frying and grilling and nuking things according to an arcane set of principles that Eluik couldn't begin to guess at—were very similar. The colonel joked about cooking up the native fauna—about raccoon and squirrel stews, and how oily and nasty possum meat tasted ("but it would keep you alive in a pinch")—but nothing like that was served.

Eluik and Enopp had grown up on wild game, when there was meat at all, and Eluik missed it, though Enopp professed that when it came to eating, he never wanted to leave Mittlegard, or America, or even stray more than a hundred miles from the Ohio River. But that was a matter not at all under their control.

Mother would call for them sometime. Probably not soon, because as Danny North explained, Anonoei had spent years setting up the destruction of Queen Bexoi, and now that she had to live inside Bexoi's body and pretend to *be* her, she had to find a way to undo all her plotting—preferably without betraying people who had, after all, trusted her when she had her own body. It was a very tricky thing to do. Of course it would take time. Of course.

Enopp seemed not to mind, but to Eluik, Mittlegard was not home. Maybe it had to do with his having been older, having a clearer memory of life in Kamesham and inside the palace of Nassassa before they were abducted and thrown into prison. To Enopp, Mittlegard was simply the world he knew; to Eluik, it was an alien place where he didn't really belong.

And maybe it was also because Enopp was already coming into his magery. Danny and Pat and Veevee and even Hermia spoke as if it were merely possible that Enopp would grow up to be a gatemage. But Eluik could see clearly that while Enopp was not a Gatefather at the level of Danny North or Wad, he still had a very large number of prets that would serve as gates inside him.

So to Enopp, who could go anywhere and leave a gate behind, what did it matter where he lived? He would have gates enough inside him to make a Great Gate all by himself. So the differences between worlds were less important.

Eluik knew that even without gates, he could travel from place to place, leaving no trace of his passage. He had learned that from Pat as she helped him and Enopp separate. He had seen and understood the prets, had seen how dazzling and powerful Enopp was, how many prets had chosen to follow him.

But what am I? Eluik could not help but wonder. His own pret had no dazzle or spark, and if he had a troop of followers he could not detect them. My younger brother is the great mage. What am I? Here on Mittlegard, he was likely to be, not drekka, but a drowther, and while the drowthers were mostly oblivious to magery, Eluik would know the vast gulf between those with and without power.

In Iceway, he would be just as lacking in magery, perhaps— but he was the firstborn son of King Prayard, though born to a mistress rather than a wife. There were people eager to exploit him; others who would like to have him dead. But he mattered.

So maybe it's pure vanity that makes me see Mittlegard as an alien place, where I do not have and will never have a home.

Enopp needed company, needed people to talk to, and the Diamond home was always full—not only of the Diamond family, but also of the many visitors that the Colonel was always inviting, or who came by uninvited. With Enopp happily occupied listening in on all the conversations of adults or playing videogames with the Diamond boys, who were older but seemed to enjoy teaching him, Eluik had plenty of time to himself.

That's how he wanted it. When the conversation was in full swing, Eluik would say enough to make it clear he was there, and then drift out of the room and . . . jump.

If he had been a gatemage, then another gatemage might have been able to track him. But because he simply *went*, his pret going without any kind of gate at all, no one could have tracked him in any way.

Eluik liked Diamond's farmstead, especially the wilder country, the deep woods, the glens, the hilltops. On summer evenings, when there was plenty of light, he would simply go. Even when he jumped to places that he could not see, he never appeared partly or fully inside a tree or a rock. Perhaps the other prets that were already there protected him against such a destructive collision. Eluik was content to know that it worked.

Sometimes he also jumped back to Ohio. Never into the Silvermans' house—he did not want to let them know he was there, and he certainly didn't want to spy on their private conversations. He would simply go to some corner of their property, or some nearby place in Yellow Springs, and sit and think for a while.

Not many of his thoughts were happy, and some were angry and some were sad. He hated that he would never see his mother's face again, that she would wear Bexoi's simpering face and he would have to find some way to believe it was really

Mother. He hated Wad and yet knew he had no choice but to trust him, and he seemed really to care about Mother and, for that matter, about Eluik and Enopp. Veevee was too overpowering; Hermia always had her own agenda. Danny and Pat were the ones he liked best. So he would think about them and work up whatever emotions attached to them. And then he would think of something or someone else.

What he thought about most was going back to Westil. Enopp talked about someday making a Great Gate and Eluik always warned him that the Gate Thief would eat it, but what Eluik *really* thought was: Who needs a Great Gate? That's only for when you want other people to be able to make the passage.

Why shouldn't I just . . . go? I know Iceway better than I know America; if I can jump to Ohio or other parts of Kentucky, why can't I jump to Iceway?

Two things stopped him. First, he didn't know how Great Gates worked, so how could he be sure he wouldn't need one? What if his jump took him only partway, and he ended up in the vacuum of deep space?

Second, he wasn't sure he could come back, once he returned home to Westil. Because it *was* home, and this place wasn't, it might be possible that he could bridge the gap between worlds, but only one time, and only one-way.

So he didn't try that jump. He just kept imagining making it—thinking of where his arrival point might be. The palace? The prison? The poor little farm up in the mountains? On board a ship? The house where Mother took care of them when Enopp was a newborn?

Could any of the gatemages find me? Could Wad? Could Danny?

Eluik hoped not. There had to be some way to get himself out of playing a bit part in other people's dramas.

13

Gerd North was not happy. "I don't like Taiwan," she told Alf. "We won't be here much longer," he replied.

"I miss our quiet life on the farm."

"We didn't *have* a quiet life on the farm. We were always traveling here or there, doing diplomacy with the other Families, working on honing and expanding our mageries, harmonizing them. And I think that right here, in this war of survival for Taiwan, we're proving that we've achieved more than any other mages in history."

Gerd heard him, but the words felt empty. "Alf, I know you're right, but I can't bring myself to care whether one group of Chinese people is ruled by another group."

"The Americans care, the world cares, so it's a good demonstration."

"Of what? For what?"

"That whatever nation has our protection is going to prevail in battle. It's what we've always done."

"And in the end, what difference does it make? More dead drowthers on one side than on the other. Rich and powerful drowthers strutting around as kings or emperors, making little token donations to priests who pretend to care about pleasing us. Alf, didn't the centuries without gates teach us *anything*?"

"Taught us we don't like being without Great Gates," said Alf. "Which, to all intents and purposes, we still are."

"Danny took us through his gate."

"Last. Came to us *last*. There's no loyalty in the boy."

"He's loyal to those who are loyal to him. When did he see any spark of loyalty from the Family, when he was growing up? And when he made his first Great Gate, who showed up to try to kill him?"

"Defend him, fine," said Alf. "I even agree with you. But he has to get over it."

"Whether he does or not," said Gerd, "here we are on this mountainous island with barbarous food and unintelligible language, constantly fiddling with airplanes and weapons and tanks and even rifles and machine guns, and somebody said something about battery packs for night vision and communications, and it's very boring work. I mean listen to what I just said: *work!* I might as well be the employee of some corporation."

"Magery is work. Only drowthers think it isn't."

Gerd knew he was right. She hated hearing the hint of a whine in her own voice. But she was *not happy.* "Is this all we were hoping for? When we kept Danny alive? That our powers would be magnified so we could make drowther weapons work better so they could kill each other more efficiently? Didn't we used to dream of going home to Westil?"

Alf came out of the bathroom, his mouth still full of toothpaste and the toothbrush in his hand. "When did we *ever* talk about going home to Westil?"

"Constantly!" said Gerd.

"We talked about going *to Westil*, because that would mean our powers would be fantastically increased, we would be gods again! But going 'home' to Westil? None of us has lived there for fifteen hundred years. I don't even know if our version of Westilian language is even spoken there."

"But we'd have enhanced powers there, too," said Gerd. "And they don't have all these terrible weapons. Or at least I hope they don't."

"Maybe they have worse ones," said Alf.

"If I can't just live peacefully in Virginia, Alf, then why not go to Westil and see what our ancient homeland is like? Why is it wrong for me to feel nostalgia for a land I've only glimpsed for a second or two? Americans all feel nostalgia for whatever homeland their ancestors came from, whether they've lived there or not."

"Sounds to me like you already want to retire."

"Maybe I just need to get a good night's sleep."

"If the mainland Chinese will cooperate by not sending bombers or commandos or—"

"If we're such hot stuff, Alf, why do the mainlanders still *have* any bombers or helicopters?"

"Because they make them faster than we can blow them out of the sky."

"When do the Taiwanese with all these enhanced weapons we've given them take over and do all the fighting for themselves?"

"They're doing all they can. Pilots can only fly so many hours. Planes run out of ammunition. We're dealing with finite numbers here."

"So we have to keep waking up in the night to take their planes and choppers out of the sky."

"In a word, yes," said Alf. "Because when the world sees what we are doing for Taiwan, they take us seriously."

"They take America seriously."

"Oh, come on, Gerd. America *is* us, now. Last week, all it took was the President announcing that America was sending sixteen enhanced jets and fifty enhanced tanks to Israel, and the Islamic armies pulled back from the borders and the jets stopped intruding in Israeli air space."

Gerd thought about that for a moment. "So maybe with all the killing here, we're saving lives there."

"Yes! That's the point! A powerful demonstration, and then our enemies back down."

"America's enemies."

"When we take a nation under our protection, then their enemies are our enemies. That's what it means to be gods."

"The Iliad doesn't read that way."

"The story of The Iliad was put together by clowns who didn't know what they were talking about."

"The old stories make it all seem so personal. What happens when a great mage from another house takes us on? What good will our jets do against a Watersire who can make America suffer from a drought? Or a Rootherd who can make plants die of some uncontrollable blight—but only within America's borders?"

"Enough bombs and they'll decide to stop."

"Oh, Alf, come on. We know enough history—enough *recent* history—that we can be sure there aren't enough bombs to do that. If America is starving, America will submit. And besides, how would we even know *which* of the other Families was doing it?"

"You have a point. Taiwan and Israel only face enemies who have no mages protecting them."

"But our enemies can all see the limitations of our power because we're showing everybody all that we can do," said Gerd. "And they'll gang up against us because the other Families have hated us for centuries. Us against everybody. I want to go home to Westil!"

Alf stood there in silence for a moment, and then put the toothbrush back in his mouth and brushed as he returned to the bathroom.

Where he was standing, a young woman suddenly materialized. Gerd recognized her immediately.

"You," said Gerd. "That Greek girl."

"Hermia by title," said the girl. "Yllka was my birth name."

"It seems the Great Gate has made a real gatemage out of you after all."

"No," said Hermia. "And Danny took all my gates anyway, so it wouldn't matter."

"Yet here you are."

Alf was now standing behind Hermia, fury in his eyes and stance.

"There's nothing you can do, Odin," said Hermia, giving him his title. "Danny and his girlfriend taught me a different way of moving without gates at all. I can be gone—and healed from any damage you do—almost before you do whatever you're thinking. Gone and with no trace of where I went."

"Aren't you the powerful one," said Alf.

"You know that I'm not," said Hermia. "Everything depends on gatemages, everybody's power, healing in battle. But that's all we are—transportation and medical. Everybody else has more real power."

"How modest of you," said Gerd. "Though of course you can 'transport' your enemies to the bottom of the ocean or deep into space or the heart of the sun or miles up in the sky. So I can't really think of you as just 'transportation and medical.'"

"All right," said Hermia. "I'm very powerful. So powerful that I could listen to your whole conversation tonight without your knowing I was here. My purpose was only to gather information, but something occurred to me and I realized that you're missing an opportunity by not doing *exactly* what Gerd is yearning for."

"None of your business," said Alf.

"Even if we can't stop you from listening," said Gerd, "we don't have to empower you by listening to *you*."

"'Empower,'" Hermia repeated. "You are *so* American."

"In gods we trust," said Alf. "What do you want, Yllka?"

"I had a thought, that's all. And since you're the only people in either world who can do anything about it, I might as well say it to you and see if it leads anywhere."

"Then say it," said Alf.

"These planes and tanks you've enhanced—never run out of fuel, parts never wear out cause there's no friction, make their own electricity, practically fly themselves, weapons that don't miss—"

"We know what we did," said Alf.

"You made them more powerful and useful, but you're still just working with stuff drowthers made."

"We're working with the world around us, the way mages always have," said Gerd testily. She didn't like the implication that they somehow depended on drowthers. Though she knew that it was true.

"Oh, I know. But still, your planes may win more fights than theirs do—but they've got pretty good planes. They have to refuel more, they miss more, but they don't *always* miss, so the two of you have to fight them directly. Go outside in the middle of the night and take them out of the sky with lightning, or by making their parts crumble so they stop working."

"We know what we do, girl," said Alf.

"Alf, she's setting up to suggest that we take some of those planes and tanks to Westil," said Gerd. "Where the other side won't have tanks and planes at all. Ours don't need to be refueled, and if we could get them there at all, we could get more missiles and bullets and artillery shells. Only we wouldn't have to use up many, because once they saw what the cannons and missiles on a jet could do, who would fight us?"

"What 'other side'?" asked Alf.

"Whichever side is against the side we choose," said Gerd. "We don't care which side here, either. But once we pick, then our side has to win."

"So we invade Westil, is what you're saying," said Alf. "Live here for fifteen centuries, wishing we could go home—but we go home with heavy armaments and blow stuff up."

"Sounds like the essence of magery," said Hermia. "Why fight where the other side has a fighting chance?"

Alf chuckled. "Well, ain't that something."

"We'd have to bring pilots with us," said Gerd. "They wouldn't be all that happy to leave Mittlegard."

"Doesn't have to be for very long," said Hermia. "Take the ones that want to go, use them to train locals on Westil, and then let the ones from Mittlegard go home. With lots of pay, of course."

"The North family isn't rich like you Greeks," said Gerd.

"The North family has complete access to the treasury and the credit of the United States of America and every bank within its borders," said Hermia.

"Oh, that," said Gerd. She felt foolish that she hadn't remembered. They weren't an obscure family on a compound in Virginia anymore.

"What's in this for you?" asked Alf.

"Well, that's just it. You know Danny would never make a Great Gate for you to take armaments to Westil. Or Pat. Certainly not the Gate Thief. So if you're going to get there, it has to be with my help."

"What's your price?" asked Alf.

"Not money," said Hermia. "And besides, I'm not *sure* I can do it."

Gerd didn't have to turn and look to know that Alf was rolling his eyes.

Hermia held up a hand. "I *think* I can, but I had no reason to try. It would just irritate Danny and Loki, for no good purpose. I have no business on Westil right now, except *your* business. I had some thoughts of going there and offering to take local mages to Mittlegard and back, spice things up a little there, but the problem is that with this new way of going from place to place, I'm not sure if it will have the enhancing effect of a Great Gate."

Alf raised a skeptical hand. "Well, now, if—"

"Think," said Hermia. "You've already made the Great Gate passage, so you don't need any enhancing effect. All you need is to get from one place to another. What I don't know is, does the enhancement come from just traveling between Mittlegard and Westil? Or does it come from passing through an area of dozens of gates aligned to carry people between the worlds? No way to know until we try."

"The way you travel now," said Gerd. "Without making a gate. Does it still heal the traveler?"

"Yes, absolutely," said Hermia. "So it gives me hope that the Great Gate enhancement will work, too. I just don't know yet."

"If there's no actual gate," said Alf, "how do you find it again?"

"I don't," said Hermia. "I won't *send* things through a gate, I'll *take* things with me when I go."

Alf laughed. "So you'll be hand-carrying jet planes and attack helicopters and tanks."

"Maybe it won't work," said Hermia. "I don't know. What do you lose by letting me try?"

"One big problem," said Gerd.

"Only one?" asked Alf.

Gerd raised a finger. "Runways."

"Oh now," said Alf. "That *is* important. Airplanes need a long straight smooth wide road for takeoffs and landings. How much paved road do you think they have in all of Westil?"

"Cobbled? Many miles," said Hermia. "Straight? None. Smooth? None. So maybe no planes after all."

"Good," said Alf. "Because it's a lot easier to learn how to drive and aim and fire a tank than a jet. And if you screw up, you don't fall thirty thousand feet."

"You're thinking of training locals, then," said Gerd.

"As soon as we can."

"So you're thinking of doing this," said Gerd, feeling herself slump inside.

"Hermia has a point."

"Hermia also has a record of betrayal," said Gerd.

Hermia only looked at her. Calmly.

"She isn't arguing," said Gerd.

"How can I?" she said. "It's true. Danny gave me orders and refused to listen to my arguments. He assumed that because I stopped arguing, I would do what he said. But he was wrong. His plan was stupid and doomed to fail. Two mages per Family? While the Orphans would all get to go? My way, we aren't actually at war with each other yet. His way, and the war would have been immediate. So I moved the only Great Gate I had access to and sent my family through. I made it all take time, so Danny had plenty of chance to respond and do the only thing he could do—take all the other Families through his own new gate. Don't you think that was a better plan?"

"It was," said Alf. "But you betrayed Danny."

"I disagreed with Danny and failed to obey him," said Hermia. "Please tell me, in all your lore of gatemages, whether you ever heard of an obedient one."

Alf chuckled.

Gerd did not. "We will be totally dependent on her," she said. "She can take us anywhere and leave us stranded."

"I could do that right now," said Hermia, "and you couldn't stop me."

Gerd wondered if a jolt of static electricity could stop Hermia's heart before she could jump and heal herself. No, she would need to make that jolt strike Hermia's brain, short-circuiting everything, including whatever part of her brain triggered jumps.

"Before you try to kill me," said Hermia, "you should be aware that this kind of jump has nothing to do with any part of my physical body. You could fry my brain and I could still do it, and heal myself in the process."

Gerd smiled. "It's nice to know that we think alike."

"I'm not like Danny," said Hermia. "I grew up as a valued member of a Family, and so I learned to think like one. Your isolation of Danny allowed him to become soft."

"Compassionate," said Gerd.

"He's a dear," said Hermia. "He loves the drowthers and thinks their lives and their happiness are as important as ours. On even-numbered days I see his point. On the other days, though, I recognize that power only exists if you use it to increase your power. Every time you fail to act to protect your interests, you embolden your enemies to defy you more and more openly, until finally you have no influence at all, except whatever raw power you have. Danny doesn't understand this. He has—or had—so much raw power that he didn't understand that *real* power comes from getting other people to obey you before you have to compel them. But here you are in Taiwan, showing me that *you* understand that."

"We do," said Alf. "So here's my question. Mittlegard is a known quantity. There are vast and terrible weapons here, but Gerd and I are uniquely qualified to use or neutralize them. We can and will dominate this world."

"And every Family knows that you two are the ones that they must kill," said Hermia.

"If you meant to do that," said Gerd, "we'd be dead."

"But we know nothing about Westil," said Alf. "They've had fifteen centuries since our last map, our last history. We don't know what kingdoms are where, which are on the make and which are declining."

"And we don't know what condition their magery is in," said Gerd.

"They haven't had Great Gates at all," said Hermia, "and you have. Loki is the only one who can make Great Gates now, and he won't do it. So *if* I can take you to Westil, and regardless of whether my version of travel will enhance your powers, you'll still be the most powerful mages in Westil."

"Except for Loki," said Alf.

"And anyone else he or Danny brought from here to there," said Gerd. She thought she saw a hesitation, a momentary deadness in Hermia's eyes as she concealed something that she knew. There *was* someone from Mittlegard that Danny had taken to Westil. And maybe vice versa, for all they knew. That was a mystery that deserved a little prying into.

"Why should we go from the known to the unknown?" asked Alf.

"Besides," said Gerd, "Odin and I have shaped and honed our magery to be able to control and enhance the technological arti-facts of Mittlegard. There won't be any electronics or heavy machinery on Westil, will there?"

"I don't know," said Hermia, "but I doubt it."

"I can't do anything with wooden machinery," said Alf. "Like the kind in water and windmills."

"Anything that lasts will be metal," said Hermia.

"Showing that you know nothing about the tolerances of cast iron compared with wood," said Alf.

"So don't go," said Hermia. "I'll go back and see if my Family wants to see if I can transport a fleet of ships to the oceans of Westil."

"One good windmage or seamage would put them on the bottom of that ocean," said Gerd.

"But we have mages to prevent them, and *ours* have been through a Great Gate. We'll do well enough."

"So why did you come to us first?" asked Alf.

"Because my Family thinks they own me, the way you stupidly thought you owned Danny. They held me prisoner on a miserable little Aegean island."

"How do you hold a gatemage prisoner?" asked Alf.

"I was between gates," said Hermia. "Danny had taken all of mine to punish me, and I hadn't yet learned how to jump without gates."

"It seems to me that every power you have is owed to Danny," said Alf.

"And I'm grateful to him. I taught *him* a lot as well. I think we're even," said Hermia.

"I have an idea," said Gerd. "Take one of us to Westil right now and let's see if we even have anything to talk about."

"One of us?" asked Alf.

"If her plan is only to get us out of Mittlegard, then she can't do it to both of us at once," said Gerd. "You'll be here to destroy her Family and continue to keep these weapons working until you bring Mittlegard into obedience and the other Families into submission."

"She would just come back and kill me. Or take me wherever she wanted. Gatemages of any kind are uncontrollable," said Alf.

"Except by other gatemages," said Gerd.

"Good call," said Hermia. "If I betrayed you by stranding his mother on Westil, Danny *would* take steps."

"He could kill you whenever he wants, I think," said Gerd.

"Well, I'm hard to kill, even for him," said Hermia. "But he isn't the killing kind. No, he would simply bring you back to Mittlegard and stop me from doing anything to either of you. So there it is—you have a guarantee that this particular trickster god won't bother trying to trick you."

Gerd held out her hand. "Take me," she said.

Hermia took her hand, then looked at Alf. "You can bear to be separated from the woman you love?"

"It won't be for long," said Alf.

"I think you both need to see Westil long enough to judge for yourselves what you might accomplish there," said Hermia.

"You've never been married," said Gerd.

"We've worked in close partnership for decades," said Alf. "Gerd will see anything that I would see. She will know anything that I would know. And I know she's safe with you, or my vengeance will be terrible."

"Danny's vengeance," said Hermia.

"You won't care about the difference," said Alf.

AND THERE SHE was on Westil. In a circle of standing stones, just like before. Her hand was still in Hermia's hand—at least the girl hadn't abandoned her to make her own way.

"Where are we?" asked Gerd.

Hermia looked around. "I find it interesting that the passage between worlds still has some element of randomness. I thought I was taking you back to the gatecatcher that we used before. But here we are in mountains overlooking a sandy desert. The obvious guess is Dapnu Dap, but I have no way of knowing if *this* desert is part of something that vast."

"So the passage between worlds is random," said Gerd. "Now we're in a particular place, and you should be able to go to any other known place."

"In Mittlegard, yes," said Hermia, "because I know most of the places we might want to go. It's not as if I ever set up housekeeping here."

"Then take me back to Alf."

"We have things to learn," said Hermia. "Let's go spying."

"Shouldn't we change clothing first?" asked Gerd. "I'm betting these outfits will stand out."

"The shoes are certainly impractical," said Hermia. "You really walked around Taiwan in *those*?"

"I walked around my *house*," said Gerd. "And with you holding on to me, I don't expect I will actually have to do much outdoor walking here, either."

"Danny has a point about the arrogance of the Families," said Hermia.

"Beginning with you, my dear," said Gerd. "Let's find a place where we can go shopping."

"None of them take American Express."

"But all of them accept the five-finger discount," said Gerd. "As long as we can make a clean getaway. What do you think of our chances?"

"I wonder how bad our accents are," said Hermia.

"You gatemages have such a way with languages that I'm betting yours will be superbly local within moments," said Gerd. "And I'm content to let you do all the talking."

By nightfall, they had the costumes of ladies of high station in the riverport city of Ny, the capital of Nefyryd, and knew a surprisingly large amount of interesting but probably useless information about the cotton and weaving trades, and the shipping and overland routes that brought wealth into Nefyryd from all the other kingdoms.

Alone in a very rich house that Hermia had learned was standing empty, the two of them began to figure out their next move.

"We can assume," said Hermia, "that the rumors of a great Tempester in Hetterwee are true, and that Danny has somehow managed to curtail the depredations of the Orphan Cedric who didn't come back from the first Great Gate he made."

"It still doesn't tell us where Danny is," said Gerd. "I'm surprised he hasn't come to us already."

"We didn't make a gate," said Hermia. "Not the kind that he and Loki would instantly recognize. The kind of jump we did, maybe Danny can detect it or maybe he can't. Loki almost certainly can't. And if Danny can, maybe he's just waiting to see what we do."

"Or maybe he's busy," said Gerd.

"More to the point," said Hermia, "how do you assess your potential power here on Westil?"

"The machinery is trifling," said Gerd. "Not even a good clock. And no indication that there's any higher technology elsewhere, because they have enough wealth here to import anything of real value or interest from anywhere else in the world."

"Comfortable climate," said Hermia. "We're almost in the tropics here, if that term applies, but it's not as suffocatingly hot as, say, Manaus, or even Havana."

"I have no interest in this city in particular," said Gerd.

"Ny rules over one of the largest nations of Westil, and one of the richest," said Hermia.

"A one-crop economy," said Gerd.

"Not very observant of you," said Hermia. "Like America, they also export food. Especially to the northern islands. They are self-sufficient in most metals, because the northern marches of Nefyryd reach well into the foothills of the High Mountains—"

"Mitherkame," said Gerd.

"The locals avoid that word," said Hermia. "Too sacred."

"It always has been," said Gerd. "That's why we refer to this world as Westil instead of Mitherhame, let alone Mitherkame. But I see no reason not to name things by their right name, when it's just the two of us talking."

"Do you think some tanks and attack helicopters here could make an impression?" asked Hermia.

"Of course," said Gerd. "But Cortés and Pizarro didn't win with those primitive muskets and cannon they brought with them. The Inca and Aztec soldiers could have overwhelmed them in moments. They learned enough about the local culture to overcome them with mind games."

"They also made allies," said Hermia. "Or at least Cortés did."

"So yes," said Gerd, "there are possibilities here. And . . . even though I'm no Meadowfriend, it seemed as if every grain of pollen in the air was welcoming me. As if this was the atmosphere I was meant to breathe. It's quite an overpowering sensation."

"It is, isn't it?" said Hermia, breathing deep. "So we should probably return to Odin and reassure him that I haven't buried you deep in the ice somewhere in Antarctica."

"And yet I still feel . . ."

"You sound as if you want to do something very wicked," said Hermia. "I didn't know anyone but gatemages ever felt that way."

"We've been deliberately invisible the whole time we've been here," said Gerd. "And that was a good plan. Only . . . shouldn't we let them know that a Lightrider has been here? I can't turn off their computers or cellphones with an electromagnetic pulse. But a dazzling display of lightning in a clear sky?"

"Impressive, of course," said Hermia. "But will that be enough? If the idea is to come here and make an alliance with Nefyryd, shouldn't you give your display some kind of purpose? A point?"

"I don't want to show myself in the open yet," said Gerd.

"Oh, I agree. Let's leave it anonymous. But show, by what the lightning *does*, that you're on their side. A god has come—to protect them."

"Who were their trading rivals? File Apwor, Barliham, Ru, Nix—"

"Nix is in the far north," said Hermia. "And I think Loki's work is all in the far north. From things Danny has said."

"So the lightning singles out the ships of Nix?"

"I don't think you should *destroy* any of them. I wouldn't want us to start a naval war."

"No, but . . . show their vulnerability," said Gerd. "I'm thinking—vast lightnings in the sky, but only a bit of dancing light on every ship carrying the banner of Nix."

"Maybe just . . . *little* fires at the tops of the masts?" asked

Hermia. "Nobody dies, no ship sinks, but they have to scramble to put out the fires, and maybe refit a little before they sail away?"

"If only the ships of Nix are affected," said Gerd, "are we saying that we're the friends of Ny or the enemies of Nix?"

"I don't think it matters yet," said Hermia. "It's just enough to start rumors flying. The way the Tempester of Hetterwee has the whole world talking. They're speculating that a Great Gate has opened again, somewhere. Let's give them a little more to chew on."

From the terrace of the house they had a fine view of all the ships docked at the wharves or anchored in the river. And once Gerd had a fairly steady stream of lightning dashing back and forth across the sky, it was easy to see which banners flew from the various ships. They marked five Nixy ships and Gerd drew down wisps of lightning to illuminate them, and then intensified them all at once, at the tops of the masts, so they burst into flame.

The banners immediately flared, and there was an immediate hurly and bustle on the docks. Two of the ships were at a berth, and men from shore could rush on board to put out the flames. Two others were anchored near to shore, so that boats could reach them quickly and join the men aboard who were already fighting the flames.

In every case, they immediately unstepped the highest portion of each burning mast, cutting the sheets and lines so that they could be pitched overboard. There was no machinery to bring water to the tops of the masts. Something for Alf to invent for them, perhaps, thought Gerd. A system of pumps. A fireboat that could stand off from a burning ship and put out the fires.

"Uh-oh," said Hermia. "That one's getting out of hand."

The ship that was anchored farthest out in the river was now burning right down to the deck. Nobody seemed to be fighting the fire on board, and if one of the boats from shore was headed out there, they weren't going to reach it in time.

"They should have left some of their crew on board," said Hermia. "Instead of letting them all go drinking and whoring in town."

"They might *be* on board," said Gerd. "Asleep below deck. Where they couldn't hear any of the shouting from closer in to shore."

"Probably all so drunk they couldn't be wakened by anything. Or the thunder would already have woken them," said Hermia. "You put on quite a noisy show."

"You have to go waken them so they can get off the boat," said Gerd.

"There's nobody on board," said Hermia.

"You don't know that," said Gerd. "If this is to look like a great mage announcing herself, there shouldn't be any deaths."

"I get it," said Hermia. "You expect me to go out there, into a burning ship, and wake them up?"

"Gate them to land, if that's what it takes," said Gerd.

"I can only do it one at a time. What if there are too many of them?"

"You said a moment ago that there's nobody. Go now, before the ship is gone and it's too late."

"So I have to clean up after your clumsiness," said Hermia.

Before Gerd could shout at her to *move*, Hermia grinned. "I bow to your vast wisdom, O ancient lady." And she was gone.

A few minutes later, Hermia was back on the terrace. "Only one man, and yes, drunk as a skunk. He was actually on the verge of death from smoke inhalation, but I got him out into the water, and of course the movement immediately healed him."

"Did it teach him how to swim?" asked Gerd.

"Don't sailors all know how to swim?"

"A Greek should know the answer to that," said Gerd.

"Well, *now* it's required of every sailor on every ship in our fleet," said Hermia, "but in ancient times . . . and yes, you're right, he's already completely underwater."

Hermia disappeared, and this time when she returned she was soaking wet. "I wasn't really in the mood for a dip tonight," she said, shaking herself a little. "But I got him right over to a boat that's headed for his ship, and they're pulling him in. Of course he got undrowned in the process. It's nice that some aspects of this take no effort."

That farthest ship was burning to the waterline.

And the two boats that had been pulling toward it suddenly reversed direction and raced over the river, heading back toward shore.

"Well, well," said Gerd. "I think we will have accomplished more than we hoped for."

"What do you mean?" said Hermia. "Obviously they saw that it was hopeless and they're heading back."

"At that speed?" asked Gerd. "No, I think somebody has invented gunpowder or some other explosive, and that ship is full of it."

As if in answer to her statement, the burning ship was replaced by a fireball and then the boom of an explosion, so forceful that the terrace trembled and Gerd could hear glassware and ceramics in the house breaking.

"It must be explosives used in mining, that's all," said Hermia.

"Mining is done with the help of Cobblefriends and Rockbrothers," said Gerd. "This is Westil, where magery isn't a secret and technology isn't a solution."

"Good point," said Hermia.

"Nix was bringing explosives here for some other reason. I think it will be nice for us to allow the Nixies to explain why they anchored that ship so far out in the water, with only one watchman aboard. What *were* they going to do with it? Why did they bring it right upriver to Ny itself?"

"You have a gatemage's heart," said Hermia.

"In a box on my closet shelf," said Gerd. "Now take me home to my husband. I think he may conclude that we need to find out if Nix has reached a technological level that Alf and I can work with."

14

I wish you wouldn't," said Wad, but Anonoei knew that he couldn't stop her. And, because he couldn't, he wouldn't even try.

"You're free to come along and watch," said Anonoei.

"You think I oppose this because I'm afraid for you," said Wad, "but I'm not. I know you can escape instantly. I still don't understand what you do, or how Danny North managed to teach it to you. But you're safer alone than you are with me."

"Why do you oppose it, then? The last thing we need now is for Frostinch to invade Iceway, and I intend to prevent it."

"I know you've been practicing with Bexoi's powers, since you have them along with your own."

"I'd be a fool not to," said Anonoei.

"I don't want Frostinch's life to end in flames," said Wad.

"There's no reason why it should," said Anonoei.

"He's a selfish little cretin and he poisoned his own father, but only because you persuaded him to."

"I take responsibility for that," said Anonoei.

"No, you don't, and you never will, because if you did, people might realize that Bexoi's lovely body no longer contains Bexoi's ugly little pret."

"Inside my own mind, I take responsibility for it."

"And feel not even a spark of guilt."

"Frostinch's father was the Jarl of Gray, who forced King Prayard's father to accept humiliating terms and compelled Prayard himself to take Bexoi as his wife. I can't mourn too much for his unfortunate demise."

"And when you're there in the presence of Frostinch, his murderer and successor, it will occur to you that Frostinch frightened is not half so useful as Frostinch dead."

"Now it won't occur to me there," said Anonoei, "because you said it to me here."

"There are larger issues in the world than whether Iceway or Gray is the dominant power in the North."

"Larger to you," said Anonoei. "Wad, don't you see? Danny's the one in control of things now."

"Danny has no gates," said Wad.

"Danny doesn't need them," said Anonoei. "And if he *did* have gates, then Set would have been able to use them."

"Danny thinks he has Set under control, and so he's going to try to do stupid things."

"Danny told you that he knows that whatever control he has over Set can't be relied on, and he will never bring him here."

"Until he changes his mind," said Wad.

"So only you are wise," said Anonoei.

"Only I am a thousand years old," said Wad. "I've learned to be relentless, and Danny North hasn't."

"You're telling me to abandon the liberation of my own people, who are currently under the control of a conquering enemy, in order to help you prepare for a struggle that's *over*, except in your nightmares."

"Exactly," said Wad. "Because my nightmare is infinitely worse than the petty humiliations that Gray exacts from Iceway."

"Let's not quarrel," said Anonoei. "I promise not to kill Frostinch."

"You shouldn't put King Prayard's baby in danger."

"There's no danger."

"What you really mean," said Wad, "is that it's not your baby. But it's the child of that body you're wearing, and that's the only body you can ever use to have a child, so you might as well consider it to be yours."

"I have two sons of my own, *real* sons, back in Mittlegard," said Anonoei. "When I bring them home—"

"King Prayard will have them killed, because they're bastards born to a mistress and now they pose a threat to his legitimate heir. What story will you tell him, *Bexoi*, to explain that you're secretly his mistress after all? How will you convince him that you're not insane?"

"Wad, I came to you as a courtesy, because I thought you were my friend. I see that you want to control me—"

"I'm trying to *persuade* you," said Wad.

"You want me to do your will," said Anonoei.

"I want you to help me save Westil."

"I have Bexoi's powers," said Anonoei, "plus my own, all enhanced by passage through a Great Gate. When I've resolved things in the North, I'll help you wherever you need me."

"I know you mean what you're saying . . ."

"Wad, you know that if I wanted to use my powers to persuade *you* . . ."

"I know you've told me that you never have."

"And I spoke the truth. If it *weren't* true, do you think I'd waste time arguing with you now?"

"I think you know that I'm right, and so you don't want to meddle with my superior wisdom." He said it with a slight smile, meaning her to take it as irony, as wit.

But Anonoei decided to distract him with something true. "Wad, I know that there's more danger to Westil than whatever Danny North poses. That selfish, irresponsible Greek girl brought someone else from Mittlegard several days ago. A week, now, come to think."

"There was no Great Gate, and she can't make gates anyway. . . ."

"How long did you think it would take trusting, sweet-tempered Danny North to teach her to do what he taught *me* to do?"

"This power of movement can carry you between worlds?"

"Without the creation of any kind of gate."

"And you can sense it?"

"Just as you can sense gates," said Anonoei. "I can also sense every person who dies, from the moment their pret moves away from Mitherhame to return to Duat. It's distracting but not unpleasant. Like a kind of music in the background of my life. A lot of people die, every hour of the day and night."

"Where is the Greek girl?"

"She took the woman back to Mittlegard," said Anonoei. "They were only here for a day. In Ny, though I can't think why."

"Did you go there? Watch them? Listen?"

"I can't peep through tiny gates the way you can, Wad. Either

I'm there or I'm not. And I'm pregnant. I have no idea what powers the mage she brought with her might have. So I'm not going
to put the baby at risk."

"If you had told *me* she was here, *I* could have listened and
watched to see what this was all about."

"So go now," said Anonoei, "and ask people if anything strange
happened a week ago."

"I needed to know what they were *planning*."

"Then go to Mittlegard and interview her yourself. I couldn't
tell you she was here, because I didn't know where you were. This
is the first time you've come to me since it happened, and so you
can see that I told you at the first opportunity."

"You know where I am all the time," said Wad.

"I suppose I do," said Anonoei. "But I can't very well show up,
a pregnant queen, when you might be involved in some delicate
conversation."

"While you wear that face," said Wad, "it's better if you don't
make foolish excuses or gloat about having deceived me."

"I'm not doing either," said Anonoei. "I'm not trying to control *you*, I'm trying to give you your freedom as you used to give
me mine."

"Nobody can control you, so you have your freedom," said
Wad.

"I do," said Anonoei. And with that she moved herself instantly
to a corridor in Frostinch's palace.

The truth was that she *didn't* know exactly where Wad was, the
way he could instantly track every gate and leap right to it. She
had a bit of herself in Wad, just as she did in Frostinch and every
one of the others she influenced—her heartbound, if truth be
known. But unless she actually chose to take control of him, she
couldn't locate him precisely in space.

Nor did her new pret-sense help much. She could tell whether

a pret was in one world or the other, so she had known immediately when Hermia brought that North matron to Westil. But it
had taken her several hours of moving from one place to another
until she finally found them on the streets of Ny, stealing from
shopkeepers in order to dress themselves as fine women. She had
thought of talking with them, but decided it was better if they
thought that nobody knew they were there. She also thought of
telling Wad, but she was tired. Being pregnant took the strength
out of her when she stood and walked and simply stayed awake
too long. She had devoted hours to finding them, and because
of that she could tell Wad to look in Ny to find out what, if anything, they were planning. More than that was beyond her
power.

I have so much power, and yet so many things remain beyond
me. The power of the gods is much overrated. We are still so limited in what we can do. Except Danny North. *He* seemed to be able
to do whatever he thought of.

Someone was coming along the corridor toward her. This
was not a good moment to be discovered. So she moved down
the corridor—jump, jump, jump—making not a sound, staying out of sight. Until she found an open door and stepped
inside.

The people who passed the room she was in were talking, but
about nothing important. They said nothing to tell her where
Frostinch might be.

Well, she knew how to find his bedchamber and, for that matter, his toilet. If she could not stealthily locate him, she could wait
for him to come to her.

Or burn the castle down.

No, no. That isn't my purpose here.

Besides, stone does not burn.

But the ceilings are of wood, and all the hangings and the carpets are of cloth.

And perhaps when a Lightrider of Bexoi's power ignites a fire, stone may heat and crack and crumble. A castle might come down, if the fire is hot enough.

She could imagine Wad saying, "What a subtle way to announce your power. So many dead, who did nothing but serve their jarl."

She could imagine Danny looking at her coldly and then going away. Despite the fact that she had known Wad so long and loved him so much, it was Danny's disapproval that made her tremble.

Why? What would Danny do to her? There was nothing he *could* do, especially if he continued to refuse to come to Westil because of the creature he carried inside him.

Yet even as she told herself that Danny was powerless, she found herself obeying an order he was not even here to give. There would be no flames in Graywald tonight. No common folk would die. It was Bexoi who killed to get her way—who killed even when she did not need to. Anonoei had come here to prevent a war that she had once set in motion in order to defeat Bexoi. Now she *was* Bexoi and needed to stop her own plots. She was a manmage, enhanced by a Great Gate, and now with the added power of moving as swiftly and invisibly as a gatemage herself. Manmage, firemage, gatemage, all in one, all in *me*; surely I can win Frostinch's obedience without killing anyone.

He came to his bedchamber alone—of course, for Frostinch's lack of interest in women was a prime target for speculation within the jarldom of Gray. He did not see Bexoi until the door was closed and half his clothing was off.

"Are you an assassin?" he asked, looking at her in the shadows where she stood. He looked more closely. "Pregnant. An odd choice for such a mission."

"I'm not here to kill you," said Anonoei. As she spoke, she kindled the part of her outself that she had left within him, making him feel relief, the beginnings of trust. He could believe this woman, he could feel that.

"Then you won't mind if I go to my privy," he said. "I had to flee the dining room to vacate my bowel without offending the company."

"Don't fall in," she said merrily. "Our conversation will profit us both."

This close to him, she could sense all that he was feeling, everything that he desired. It was true that his bowels were causing him considerable distress. It was also true that he did not feel safe going into his privy. She well remembered how she had first accosted him there.

Why did I come myself? she wondered. Bexoi had the power to raise a clant so real that it could bleed. I haven't even tried. To send a clant on this mission . . .

But then she would not have been so close, so easily able to understand him, to influence him. So she waited patiently, wondering if it would weaken her influence over him if she sat on his bed. It was so *wearing* to stand, and her back hurt.

She stood. She bore the pain. She listened to Frostinch's noisy evacuation and was glad she wasn't sharing the room with him.

Then she saw that Wad was standing beside her. "I thought you'd want to know," he whispered, "that Hermia and Danny's mother showed off a bit in Ny. They're trying to provoke a maritime war between Nix and Ny."

"Birds of a feather, fight together?" asked Anonoei.

"Are you referring to Nix and Ny, or to Hermia and Gerd?" asked Wad.

"Is that Danny's mother's name? How unfortunate."

"How are things going here?"

"I waited for him to come to his bedchamber, so we could have a private interview. But now I can sense that he is fully . . . relieved."

"Allow me to witness your conversation," suggested Wad.

"You don't trust me," said Anonoei.

"This is Bexoi's body, and she was a creature of astonishing rage and cruelty," said Wad. "Are you sure you have these passions under control?"

"I'm a manmage, you miserable witling kitchen boy. Go away, please."

"I can't watch the master of manipulation at work?"

"Go."

"Afraid I'll recognize the techniques you use on me?"

"Nothing that works on Frostinch would work with you. He's coming, so go."

The privy door opened; Anonoei didn't have to look to see that he was gone. Whatever else Wad might be—and he did have the trickster streak—he would not deliberately subvert what she was trying to do here.

"So who are you?" asked Frostinch. "Since your intentions are so benign."

"Don't you remember me, my darling boy?" said Anonoei.

Frostinch took a candle from a sconce on the wall. "Cheeks fatter, but that's the pregnancy. I do believe you're my Aunt Bexoi, Queen of Iceway. Astonishing that you could have come here without any ceremony. Or invitation."

"So much diplomacy and back-and-forth, if I were to come with fanfare," said Anonoei. "We have so much that we can work out between us."

"I believe," said Frostinch stiffly, "that any problems are between Prayard and me."

"History is the huge chain we drag behind us. A thousand years ago, Iceway conquers Gray, seizes half our coastline, moves their ancient capital of Kamesham to an inlet of the sea in what was once our land, and then becomes a mightier seafaring nation than Gray ever was."

"Don't forget that they forced the King of Gray to accept his reduction to the rank of jarl."

"A title that your ancestors have changed into a synonym for king."

"Not all of history works against us."

"Ancient hatreds. So your father fed on that ancient hatred and defeated Iceway in turn. Not so decisively that those ancient wrongs could be reduced—especially since the people of what used to be *our* lands are now so committed to being Icewegian."

"I was once told," said Frostinch, "that you were plotting to kill Prayard as soon as your son is born, rule in his name, and conquer Gray again."

"Do you believe everything you're told?"

"I was told that you're a great firemage."

"So many rumors about a poor Feathergirl."

"Why are you here?"

"I'm your father's sister," said Anonoei. "I grew up in Gray. I don't want a single man of Gray to die, nor a Grayish wife to become a widow. And now I'm queen of Iceway, too—and I want no dying in that land, either."

"So you're here to make peace. Why should I believe you?"

Because I'm filling you with trust and contentment.

Except for the tiny problem that she could only work with desires that were already present. And in all of Frostinch's soul, she could find no yearning for peace. What an odd thing.

"I know that you care nothing for peace," said Anonoei.

"Peace is just another word for 'biding my time,'" said Frostinch. "But give me an inducement, and I'll bide my time."

"Let me help you with the definition of 'biding your time,'" said Anonoei. "I'd like it to mean, 'as long as you live.'"

"Why not? As long as I live, peace. There. Agreed."

Anonoei shook her head. "After all your labors in that little room, *still* you're full of shit."

Frostinch shrugged. "I'm eager to please you, because I assume you have a gatemage helping you. How else could you have gotten into this castle undetected?"

Anonoei moved directly behind him before she spoke. "Why do you think I need some mage's help?"

He was halfway turned around when she moved to the side that he had been facing.

"The woman who came to you before, I know every word she spoke to you. She was a manmage, you know. She took away your own volition. I know you would never have murdered my brother otherwise."

He stumbled as he tried to turn back around to face her. "I don't know what you're—"

"She came to you in your privy. She convinced you that I was a monster. But she finally overreached herself. I caught her once without her gatemage friend and I'm afraid my temper got the better of me. She tried to control me the way she controlled you, but I'm made of stronger stuff. While she turned out to be . . . flammable."

Anonoei, having learned to control Bexoi's magery quite precisely, began to heat Frostinch's body. Just a little fever. He began to sweat.

"Feeling warm?" she asked. "Is it uncomfortable? Are you coming down with something?"

She allowed him to cool off, drawing the heat away quickly. He shivered.

"And now . . . is that the ague? Why are you shaking? Not fear of your own aunt, is it?"

It was easy to make all the candles in the sconces flare up brightly, and then go out. She felt his fear, and knew just how to push him, and in what direction.

She could hear him moving in the dark. Heard a draw of metal.

She made the candles light again just as he plunged a dagger into her pregnant belly. Into the baby.

She jumped at once, and both her body and the baby's were healed completely, in the instant. "Frostinch," she said. "Did you think it would be that easy?"

He held the dagger in front of himself, pointing at her. "You aren't even bleeding. I know that it went in."

"Went in what?" she asked.

"There, where the cloth is torn. Into your belly."

"Frostinch, let me explain this to you. The manmage who came to you before could not control me. You can't kill me. Any ship you send against Iceway will burn to the waterline. Send an army overland, and every icy peak will release its snow at once. Those who don't die in the avalanches will die in the floods. You're really quite helpless here."

She filled him with fear and despair.

"Unnecessary for us to fight each other. I want you to keep your jarldom—after all, you traded your father for it, you should get *something* out of the bargain."

"How can I believe you speak for King Prayard? You're only a woman, he's the king."

"*Now* you're thinking like the clever boy you used to be. If I'm going to save your life and your jarldom, we need to convince my husband that you can be trusted."

"I *can* be trusted," said Frostinch. And at this moment, terrified at the power she had over his body, he meant it.

"I don't think that your holding a dagger toward me, claiming that you stabbed me in my womb, will help Prayard to trust you more."

Frostinch tossed the dagger onto the bed.

"So here you are," said Anonoei. "Wearing only a tunic, completely weaponless. That's a start. But of course, here in Graywald, my husband can't see how harmless you are. I think we must go to Kamesham."

"No," said Frostinch. "My life wouldn't be worth a rusty nail there."

"You have a point," said Anonoei. "But by a happy coincidence, I do believe that my waters are about to break. In fact, I think my baby is going to start coming right now."

Anonoei sat on the bed, lay back, and then raised her knees up high and began to groan. "Oh, nephew Frostinch, I think you need to be found helping me give birth."

"I don't know how to—"

"Just stand there at the foot of the bed, between my legs, exactly, that's very good. Now grip my legs just below the knee, both of them. Just like that. And when King Prayard finds you, let *me* do the talking."

"But you can't—"

"Hold my legs, my darling nephew, and stop blathering."

He obeyed, and in that moment she jumped to her own bed. To her relief, Frostinch came with her. She didn't know if it was because he was gripping her legs, or because she tried to include him in the penumbra of her own pret and all its servants. Perhaps it required both touch and intention.

Two of her women were in her room when she appeared on the bed. She immediately moaned as if she were in labor. She remembered it well, and pushed.

The women shrieked. "Who is that!" cried one. "Is the baby coming?" asked the other.

"Bring the midwife!" cried Anonoei. "And the king!"

Both women rushed from the room.

"Are you really giving birth?" asked Frostinch softly.

"Of course I am," said Anonoei. She was not, but she knew that Wad was watching her and would help bring out the baby. He had already told her that the child was turned inside her, ready to be born. She had already had slight pains. When the baby came out, Wad would make sure the boy was healthy.

When Prayard arrived, he had men-at-arms with him—the women had told him of the strange man, as well as Bexoi's sudden appearance in the midst of her travail.

"He came because I called for him!" cried Anonoei the moment Prayard came in. "Now come, husband! Help me deliver our child!"

"Frostinch!" Only in that moment did Prayard realize who the intruder was.

"Let this baby be born of cooperation between Gray and Iceway!" shouted Anonoei. "Let me say that my husband and my nephew both helped me bring forth this child of both nations!"

Then Anonoei raised a cry of pitiful agony and, on cue, she felt the baby begin to push down, felt her own muscles contract. Labor was beginning in earnest. Wad was coming through for her. Either that or Bexoi's body was unusually susceptible to suggestion.

Prayard gingerly came and took his place beside Frostinch. "What do I do?" he asked.

"I have no more idea than you," said Frostinch. "She asked me to help brace her legs."

"Then I'll take this leg," said Prayard.

"Yes!" cried Anonoei.

The midwife came in, all a-bustle. "What are men doing inside this place!"

"I command it!" cried Anonoei, and the midwife had no more power to resist her than the two rulers did. "And let the men-at-arms be witnesses, that the king and the jarl both held me as the boy came forth!"

The midwife pushed her way between the men. "If the baby dies, it's not my fault," she muttered to them.

But neither man faltered in his resolution to do what Bexoi—as they thought—demanded.

It was such a swift and easy birth. The boy was healthy and didn't have the scrawny, dwarfish look of one born too soon. The midwife was preparing to tie off the cord, but Anonoei cried out. "No! Prayard will tie the cord, and Frostinch will cut it! Let Gray cut the bondage that Iceway has been held in, and give us our freedom!"

Prayard took the string from the midwife's hand, and carefully followed her nervous directions. Then the midwife turned to Frostinch, holding out the umbilical cord for him to cut between the ties.

"Prayard must hold the cord!" cried Anonoei.

Frostinch was looking about for something to cut with.

Suddenly Anonoei felt the hilt of a dagger under her right hand. She picked it up by the blade and held it out to Frostinch. Of course he recognized it instantly as his own dagger, the one he had tossed on his bed in Graywald. But he took it by the hilt and made the slice.

The baby was crying lustily.

Prayard picked up the boy to try to still him.

Anonoei already had a bit of her outself in the baby, making him cry all the more fervently.

"Both of you hold him," she said. "Both of you bring him to me."

They were so clumsy, it was quite endearing. Terrified of dropping the baby, they sidled along the bed, carrying the baby tenderly between them. She hoped that Wad was ready to catch the child if he slipped out of their awkward grasp.

But they didn't drop the boy, and by the time they put him into Anonoei's arms, he had stopped crying at all—if there was one thing Anonoei knew how to do, it was ease the heart of a crying child.

"My husband of Iceway," she murmured, now allowing herself to show the exhaustion of childbirth. "My nephew of Gray. My baby of both lands." And then she closed her eyes.

The midwife felt a new burst of officious confidence. "Now, all you men, she's asleep," the midwife whispered fiercely. "Get out and tell what you saw, while this great lady has the peace she needs to sleep!"

Frostinch fled the room immediately, handing the dagger to one of the men-at-arms as he passed. It would do him no good to be seen armed in the palace of Nassassa. Prayard paused only to kiss Anonoei's brow very tenderly, and to stroke the baby's head. What a loving man he is, thought Anonoei.

The word quickly spread throughout Kamesham, and people cheered quite sincerely. Except all the representatives of Gray who had thought their duty was to keep Iceway in subjection and prepare to be saboteurs when the invasion began. How had the jarl reached Nassassa without any of them knowing it? What did he want them to do?

It wasn't until late that night, in a conference around her bed while Anonoei nursed the baby, that she helped the two rulers work out the terms of the new arrangement. Frostinch would go home to Gray, accompanied by all his agents. In case he was tempted to cheat a little, Anonoei carefully named every single one of Gray's spies, including a few of his father's old agents that Frostinch hadn't even known about. Both nations would be free to put into each other's ports to buy provisions, and any ship in distress would be well-treated by the people of the other land.

It was all written up and signed before anyone went to bed, and at noon the next day, Frostinch led his thousand men and women down to the docks of Kamesham. King Prayard made sure they were well supplied on their journey, and he made sure that the ships' captains knew that they must deliver this cargo safely to ports in Gray, without any unfortunate incidents on board ship.

There was an hour in the late afternoon of the following day when Anonoei sent everyone out so she could be alone with her new son.

Wad came almost at once. "You did it better than I would have thought possible," he conceded at once. "Though I still don't trust Frostinch as far as I can spit."

"No sane person would," said Anonoei. "But I can promise he won't betray me."

"I see Bexoi's lips move, and her voice make that promise," said Wad. "But she would mean that she meant to kill Frostinch at some opportune moment before he could break his word."

"Naming this boy," said Anonoei, changing the subject before he remembered that Anonoei would still deprive Frostinch of any freedom of choice. "I thought of naming him after the son of yours that Bexoi murdered. It's so unfortunate that you called him 'Trick.' That name just wouldn't sound right to the people of either kingdom."

"It's sweet of you to think of naming him that way," said Wad, his eyes filling with tears even though Anonoei had done nothing to enhance his emotions. "But no child can replace my little boy. I knew him well, and I doubt I'll have much chance to know this lad of yours."

"Well," said Anonoei, "not *mine* . . ."

"Not a child of your original body," said Wad, "but a child of the body you have now and for the rest of your life. And you *will* raise him to be the best man he has it in him to be."

Anonoei nodded. "But what about my own sons? My first two sons? The ones that were really made by King Prayard and me?"

"They're remarkable boys. Very smart and highly talented. When things become clearer, we'll both know whether they should remain in Mittlegard."

"They can't come here," said Anonoei. "They will always be in danger here, because extra sons will always attract would-be rebels."

"Wherever they are, you can go to them from time to time. Now that Hermia has proven that this new kind of gateless movement works between the worlds."

"I didn't think of that."

"Something you didn't think of!" said Wad in feigned amazement. "I hope you saw how loyally I followed your lead. As I moved the baby outward, by tiny relentless fractions of an inch, your body responded magnificently. It was a completely natural childbirth, by the end."

"You've been loyal to me even when you didn't trust me."

"That's what puzzles me," said Wad. "Your plan required my compliance, and not just to retrieve Frostinch's dagger. Yet you never managed me. I still had all my misgivings every step of the way."

"Why should I try to compel a willing friend?" she asked.

It was even mostly true.

15

Danny North took little pleasure in high school anymore. It was a refuge, where he had meant it to be an adventure. After a school year treading its halls, everything was familiar, including the faces of the other students. He didn't feel the disdain of the Families for drowthers; rather it was the disdain of high school students for their fellows. It was the tribe he dwelt with, but could never fully join. How could he? To them, their classes and grades mattered; or if not those, then their position in the social hierarchy of the school, or the college they would go to, or the job they planned to get. To Danny, all these things were the business of children.

"What are you thinking?" asked Pat.

Danny could hardly hear her over the din of the other students milling about at the end of the school day.

"That my life was better when Coach Bleeder was on my case and the worst problem I faced was whether to compete with the track team."

"Oh, well," she said. "Feeling sorry for yourself is always an entertaining train of thought."

"I allow myself a half-hour a day of self-pity," said Danny.

"I was noticing the cloud of unrelated prets that seem to cluster around some students, and not others."

Danny hadn't even been noticing prets. Familiar as the faces were, he had been looking only at the people, not the prets they were composed of, and certainly not unrelated prets dogging them through the halls.

But now that Pat pointed them out, Danny could see that several of the students had dozens, and some hundreds, of prets that didn't seem to belong to anyone or anything. Not even particles of dust. Yet it was no accident they were there, and it took only a moment's thought for Danny to realize.

"Sutahites," he said.

Pat looked at him with that weary look that said, Maybe that meant something to you, but not to me.

Then she remembered. "The slaves of Set."

"Rather his fellow travelers. They don't have his power to take over people's minds or bodies. But they still insinuate themselves, destructively, into people's minds. I wonder what they're whispering to that poor girl—look, the prets are almost a raincloud all around her head."

"I know exactly what they're saying. You're so ugly, nobody really likes you, even your friends would hate you if they knew what you're really like, no boy will ever want you, why are you even alive, if there's a God he's sick of you and your sad little prayers, why do you bother getting out of bed, just get home and sleep, that's the only place where you get relief, sleeping, only why should you wake up? Why not sleep and sleep forever?"

"Stop it," Danny said softly. "You know that monologue all too well."

"Do you suppose I had my own cloud of Sutahites around me all these years?" Then a thought crossed her mind and she said, "Danny, look at me and tell me—do I have one now?"

"No," he said.

"Good," she said. "Because I haven't thought like that in years. Before I met you, when I was still in middle school, I decided to be content with myself. To revel in the things I was good at, like classes and reading and seeing how ridiculous everything is."

"I wonder if they left you alone after you made that decision," said Danny. "Or if they didn't abandon you until you died."

"You really shouldn't say that out loud here," said Pat. "We might be overheard."

"And I'm sure whoever heard us would believe it," said Danny. "Besides, I can barely hear you, so I doubt anybody else can."

"You'd be surprised what you can hear if you're standing in just the right place." And she gestured toward a freshman a little way down the corridor. "For all we know, the lockers are transmitting our voices like a megaphone, right to him."

"Hello, Tillman," said Danny, remembering the boy's name.

Tillman probably didn't hear him. But he did turn and walk away along the corridor right at that moment. So . . . maybe.

"All these Sutahites," said Pat. "How strong are they?"

"They only have the power to bring thoughts into your head," said Danny. "To remind you of desires you already have. So . . . they're only as strong as their victims let them be. How strong were they with you? Back when you still listened?"

"Oh, I never actually *planned* a suicide attempt. Mostly, my despair led me to oversleep and do badly in class and alienate anyone who might have become a friend. Normal middle school things. I wonder what it's like for thirteen-year-olds in Westil."

It took Danny a moment, but then he smiled. "That's right. That was Loki's whole project. To keep the Sutahites out of Westil."

"I get the impression that life there can be perfectly miserable without any help from the Sutahites," said Pat.

"Maybe," said Danny. "The woman who murdered the boys' mother, or tried to, anyway—"

"Her body died," said Pat.

"Murdered her, then. She didn't need any little voices seducing her. Nothing but her own naked ambition."

Pat was silent for a moment. "What about you, Danny? Do you have any ambitions?"

Danny thought about that. "Well, I . . . not specific ones. I don't even know what I want to major in in college."

"By all means, let's go see the school counselor! You're only a year from graduation, it's time to decide where you want to go to college and whether you're premed or, I don't know, aviation? Astrophysics? Maybe you can figure out faster-than-light travel, or interstellar voyages, or maybe just the ability to travel instantly from one place on Earth to any other place."

"Now you're being silly," said Danny. "That's just sci-fi stuff, you can't actually *do* those things."

She clung a little closer to his arm. He was aware of how her body pressed against his.

"I'll tell you my ambition," said Danny. "To be with you, living in the same house, raising the same ugly little children—no, wait, your genes might prevail."

"You can heal their acne for them. I don't think that's cheating. Acne doesn't build character, it prepares you to buy a gun and shoot people."

"I'm even more ambitious than you think," said Danny. "I want to have the kind of job where I can break away when I need to."

"Like Superman," said Pat. "Somebody needs saving, so you duck into a storage closet to change into your cape."

"No," said Danny. "So I can break away and come home when one of the kids needs a doctor's appointment."

"Oh, like that'll happen," said Pat.

"We have to let them get their immunizations and checkups or we'd look like irresponsible parents," said Danny. "And sometimes I'd break away just to come home and have you hold me like this, and to remember, This is why I left my Family, this is why I left Silvermans' . . . to find *you*."

"That may be too extravagant an ambition," said Pat. "It presupposes that they'll ever leave you alone. It seems to include the idea that somehow, someday, you'll get rid of that ugly terrible thing inside you."

"I don't want to be rid of it," said Danny. "Right now I always know where it is. If it leaves me and goes anywhere but Duat, then my real worries begin again."

"So your parents taking over the U.S. military isn't a real worry?"

"They haven't started any *new* wars, just made it so our allies—America's allies—have a better chance of winning."

"So you don't think it meant anything when Hermia took your mother to Westil?"

Danny shook his head. "I don't know what that was, but they're not insane."

"Your mother's not," said Pat. "But Hermia?"

Danny had more confidence in Hermia's sanity than Mother's. "Let me walk you home," said Danny.

"The others will be waiting up on the hill," she said. And then, before he could protest: "Danny, they're afraid you'll lose interest in them."

"When a guy has a girlfriend he's really in love with, he *always* loses interest in his other friends."

"And they all feel abandoned and resentful," said Pat. "I've read the same young-adult novels as you."

"I think this is important—seeing the Sutahites. Seeing where they cluster. Now it's so obvious, I wonder that I didn't see it before."

"You're always walking through dust, tasting it, inhaling it, collecting it on your clothes and skin. But you only notice it when it's caught swirling through a beam of sunlight."

"Well, Thou Beam of Sunlight, thank you for showing me. Wish I could hear what they're saying."

"I already told you," said Pat.

"Every kid the same?"

"Pretty much. Come on, Danny. Adolescence is when you dream of being a superhero and come to understand your own worthlessness, both at once."

"So which belief are the Sutahites pushing on these people?"

"Both at once," said Pat, "and then they follow up on whichever message starts to succeed. At least, if I wanted to destroy teenagers' lives, that's what I'd do."

Danny chuckled mirthlessly. "I guess they're working me with both stories all the time."

Pat stepped away from him and looked him up and down. "No Sutahites that I can see."

"How many that you can't see? Think of it as 'unproven reserves.'"

"I think I can see them all, and you don't have any," said Pat. "And neither do I."

"Maybe they gave up on you because you're too strong," said Danny.

"Or because we both went to Duat and got the ability to see prets and move as prets. Maybe they don't even think of us as people now. Or maybe talking to This One made us immune."

"Or maybe *I* don't get any Sutahites because I have their master inside me, and so they keep clear."

"Let's sneak off and get married," said Pat. "I think all this *not* going home with you is silly."

"I've got the devil himself inside me," said Danny. "Perhaps not the time to start a family."

"But he's not controlling you anymore. Maybe you've got him imprisoned forever."

"Even if he really can't get away, 'forever' means 'until I die,' and that's definitely *not* forever. What if I died and turned him loose on you? Or on one of our children?"

"And what if a satellite falls out of the sky and lands right on top of you, killing you so quickly and completely that you don't have time to jump anywhere and heal the flat, roasted, radioactive paste that your body would instantly be turned into?"

"You're a poet at heart, my love," whispered Danny, and he kissed her.

"*Please,*" said a passing guidance counselor. "Young love is beautiful to feel, but repulsive to look at."

"Thank you," said Pat. "For a moment there I actually felt attractive and lovable." The guidance counselor was already many paces away. Pat called after him, "But you put a stop to that!"

"If they didn't have rules like that, the halls at school would probably be one continuous orgy," said Danny.

"But he was really titillated by it," said Pat. "That's why it made him so uncomfortable."

"He doesn't want to think of students in a sexualized context," said Danny. "I think that's part of his job description."

"I'm glad it wasn't part of yours," said Pat.

"But it was," said Danny. "I'm just bad at my job."

The school was mostly cleared out, because this close to the end of the school year, few clubs or teams had any activities or practices. It was easy to get behind the building and then shift to the clearing on the hill. The others were already there.

"Oh, look, they took a breathing break," said Xena.

"You can breathe while kissing," said Laurette.

"You can also blow down the other person's throat," said Sin, "and it sounds like a backward burp."

"Have we stumbled into Anthropology One?" asked Pat. "Or a horror movie where the teenagers all deserve to die?"

"If they were literate," said Hal, "they would have called it snogging instead of kissing. That's what J. K. Rowling taught Americans who could read."

"Oh no," said Wheeler. "We're muggles."

"You're only just *now* realizing that?" asked Xena.

"What were you talking about before we got here?" asked Danny.

"The usual," said Laurette. "School's almost over and next year is senior year and I'm not going to be valedictorian."

"We were patting her hand and saying 'poor baby,'" said Xena.

"We were gloating," said Hal.

"She never had a realistic chance of it," said Sin, "and she's finally entered the wonderful world of sanity."

"Said the girl with thirty festering piercings," said Wheeler.

"Eighteen," corrected Sin.

"But most of them are festering on both entry points," said Danny, "so I think Wheeler might be close to the truth."

"If they ever get too bad," said Sin, "I go through the gate that leads here and then I'm fine."

"So you *walked* up here?" asked Wheeler. "On *purpose*?"

"Those of us who want to live past forty-five seek opportunities for exercise," said Sin.

"And those of us hoping to reproduce someday don't punch holes in ourselves like spiral notebook paper," said Xena.

"Bitch," muttered Sin.

"So the end of junior year means the end of civility," said Danny. "Duly noted."

"*You* don't have to worry about it," said Wheeler.

"Worry about what?"

"Senior year, graduation, college, what you're going to *do* for a living," said Wheeler.

"There aren't a lot of job openings for gatemages," said Danny. "Especially the ones who've lost their gates."

"You *say* you lost them," said Hal, "but from what I can see, you and Pat *both* gate wherever you want."

"We all took the PSAT this year," said Wheeler, "and they say that's a pretty good indicator of college aptitude. So even though I'm preternaturally intelligent and sexily tech-savvy, I'm probably not going to college."

"That's just dumb," said Danny. "I remember your score and there are thousands of colleges that would take you."

"I have to get into a no-tuition school," said Wheeler, "or one where I can live at home, because no way can my parents *or* me earn enough to cover tuition *and* room and board."

"He rejects Dabney S. Lancaster Community College," said Laurette, "because they don't meet his lofty standards."

"I'm poor," said Wheeler, "but that doesn't mean I should waste my brain going to a school that *anybody* can get into."

"A snob who looks down on everything that he can afford," said Hal. "It's a catch-22."

"It's preventable self-destruction," said Pat. "If you hadn't goofed off you'd have the grades to get a scholarship to UVA. And you probably *could* get into Washington and Lee."

"Bunch of snobs," said Wheeler.

"They have an eighteen percent acceptance rate," said Sin. Apparently she felt a need to explain how she knew. "I had dreams."

"What about you, Danny?" asked Xena. "You could get into *any* college, but why bother?"

"I can *physically* get into any college, but if I want a degree, I don't have anybody prepared to pay my tuition at Harvard."

"Harvard has a six percent acceptance rate," said Xena, "and no, I *never* thought I could go there."

"You have to have, like, a four point oh," said Laurette, "a perfect SAT, and either a Nobel Prize or a letter of recommendation from a President."

"Only if it's a Democratic President," said Wheeler. "A Bush letter will keep you out. Even at Yale."

"Poor Republican Wheeler."

"I'm really a Libertarian," said Wheeler.

"But look at Danny," said Laurette. "When I mentioned a four point oh and a perfect SAT, he didn't blink."

"No, he actually kind of did his maybe-I'll-blush thing," said Xena.

"Straight A's?" asked Hal. "Really?"

"You already took the SAT?" asked Pat.

"I was homeschooled back in Ohio. You have to present proof of achievement after every school year, so I took the SAT every June. Except then they also made me take the ACT to prove that it wasn't a fluke."

"So you got a perfect score," said Hal, sounding depressed about it.

"I knew the answers," said Danny, "or I guessed really well."

"Just the last time you took it, or every time?" asked Wheeler.

Danny didn't want to answer. But his hesitation was all the answer they needed.

"Oh ye gods," said Xena. "When he *came* to Parry McCluer he had already gotten a perfect score on the SAT *and* the ACT."

"Five times," said Wheeler.

"I earned those scores," said Danny. "And it wasn't five times, I only took them twice each. I studied long and hard."

"So, he's a god," said Sin, ticking things off on her fingers, "*and* nondisgusting in appearance—"

"Matter of opinion," said Wheeler.

"A matter of *female* opinion," said Xena, "with considerable corroboration from nonmembers of this group, including the pregnant one."

"And he can go anywhere in the world and send anybody else anywhere, he can get into anything, he can get away from anything, he can gate the clothing right off any woman—"

"We don't need to hear about your erotic dreams, Sin," said Laurette.

"Can he?" Xena asked Pat.

"I wouldn't know," said Pat.

"*And* he has straight A's and perfect college entrance exams," Sin finished.

"But his community service sucks," said Wheeler.

"He's just not a Princeton man," said Hal with fake regret.

"Have any of you thought of going to Southern Virginia?" asked Danny. "It's right here in town."

"It's a religious school," said Laurette, "and we don't go to that church."

"You could get into any Ivy," said Hal. "Or probably MIT or Cal Tech, since you aced the math side."

"I don't have any desire to go to an Ivy," said Danny. "Or MIT or Cal Tech or Stanford or the Sorbonne."

"What I can't figure out," said Wheeler, "is why you had any desire to come here to Parry McCluer."

"He's told you," said Pat. "He used to gate to this hill and spy on the school. So this was the high school he wanted to go to."

"Have we fulfilled your wildest childish dreams?" asked Hal.

"Wildest childish dreams, wildest childish . . . ," Xena intoned rapidly, making a tongue twister out of it.

"What *do* you desire, O thou onliest god of our acquaintance?" asked Laurette.

"What *dost thou* desire," corrected Hal.

"Why are we talking about what happens after senior year?" asked Danny.

"Meaning he's already made his plans and they don't include us," said Xena.

"How could they?" said Sin. "He goes to other planets. He has titanic struggles with dark gods from other worlds."

"He can shit into a gate and not have to wipe his ass," said Wheeler.

To the universal groans and protests, Wheeler held up sheltering hands. "Come on, you know you've all thought of it."

"Toilet paper works fine," said Danny. "The most fastidious gods all use it. What are you guys doing this summer?"

"We were kind of hoping *you'd* tell us," said Sin. "It's not like we have any money, except Laurette and, sort of, Hal. We can't *go* anywhere."

"Unless," said Wheeler.

"No!" the others shouted him down.

"We agreed not!" Laurette said.

"Failure to argue is not agreement," said Wheeler.

"It's all right," said Danny. "Transportation's not a problem. Where do you want to go?"

"Disney World," said Xena.

"The Harry Potter place at Universal Studios," said Sin.

"Wizarding World of Harry Potter," said Xena.

"What about the rides? They cost money," said Wheeler.

"We can't lay hands on enough money to pay for the rides?" asked Danny.

"Well, there's lots of it lying around inside banks," said Wheeler, "which *some* people could get to easily."

"Haven't we learned *anything*?" asked Pat.

"We've never even *tried* robbing banks," said Wheeler.

"I meant about Danny," said Pat. "About what kind of person Danny is. You keep projecting onto him your own childish fantasies about what you'd do if you had a cloak of invisibility or something."

"Cloak of invisibility is nothing," said Wheeler. "You still have to travel all that distance, and on foot, too."

"Wildest childish, wildest childish . . . ," began Xena again.

"Shut up, Xena," Laurette said sweetly. "I'm saving you from yourself."

"I'm willing to get us to any place in the world," said Danny. "But we can't go on rides without tickets. And they probably have some kind of serious ID system and my abilities don't extend to holographic forgery."

"So, really," said Hal, "you're pretty much useless after all."

"It'll be winter in the Andes, so I don't suggest Machu Picchu," said Danny. "The Alps?"

"I've seen pictures," said Hal. "If we went in person, I'd just think, Oh, it looks very much like the pictures."

"You taught Pat," said Wheeler. "Why can't you teach *us*?"

"Because you *would* go inside the bank vaults," said Hal.

"You don't trust us," said Wheeler.

In a word, No, thought Danny. And apparently it showed on his face. Wheeler looked away in disgust.

"I can see you not trusting Wheeler," said Laurette, "because he's, like, the human ambassador to the roaches."

"He's a roach prince who just needs our social security numbers to help him receive his inheritance," said Sin.

"Slug prince," said Xena. "Nematode prince."

"We introverta," said Hal, "are quietly proud to count the nematoda among us."

"Science puns," said Laurette with a shudder.

"May I interrupt this punfest plus envython to point out something to Danny that he may not have noticed and that nobody else can see?" asked Pat.

"That sounds rude," said Laurette. "Like rich people comparing their bank balances in front of homeless people."

"Which they do all the time," said Pat. "Danny, the free prets are clustering around all of them, but Wheeler's are the ones I was noticing. One or two would kind of divebomb his ka, and then he'd pop up with some bit of grossness or envy or, you know, a Wheelerism."

Danny hadn't noticed, but as she spoke, he could see—or sense—the hovering clouds of undifferentiated prets, and saw many of them zip inward toward Wheeler's ka.

Wheeler whirled around and flared at Pat. "Oh, do I have some mark of *Cain* on me? Something that makes me an animal that doesn't understand English, that can't feel the *contempt* you have for me, Pat? You with your windmagery and your gate travel, you with the love of your life who happens to be a god panting along beside you, do you find a lonely guy like me disgusting? Ugly? Horrible?"

"You're inverting cause and effect," said Laurette.

Danny held up a hand, watching how more of the prets moved in close to Wheeler's ka, which seemed to welcome them. They weren't even orbiting, they were practically attached to him.

It occurred to Danny that gates—or any kind of outself, really—consisted of prets that were bonded to somebody's ka. He knew that they came with human kas when they left Duat and were born on Earth. But these unattached prets—they weren't part of anything. Not part of atoms or molecules, not part of any person or animal.

"Sutahites," whispered Pat.

Exactly, thought Danny. The prets that followed Set to Mittlegard when he was thrown out of Duat, permanently bodiless. Set had the ability to take possession of a human, to control his actions one way or another. But the other Sutahites were far weaker. More limited. They could only . . . suggest. Remind.

But if they were like gates that had no gatemage, could he gather them in the way that he had taken all of the Gate Thief's own gates and captive gates back last fall?

No. That gathering motion didn't work, because they weren't used to being part of anything. They didn't respond to any kind of law.

But that didn't mean Danny had to give up.

He could see Pat raising her hand to keep the others from speaking, from interrupting his concentration. And even though Wheeler was seething, Danny could see how he controlled himself and did *not* keep on acting out his anger and hurt. He just waited, as the Sutahites kept trying to entice him to act in a destructive way.

So Wheeler *did* have the power to resist them, when he had a stronger desire for something else. The desire to see what Danny was going to do.

What Danny did was *invite* the Sutahites to come to him. He was afraid that he might be repeating his mistake of inviting Set to come into him, but no. He wasn't asking them to *enter* him, to enter his body. He was asking them to attach themselves to his ka, as if they were becoming his gates.

But not his gates. He couldn't "make" them as gates because they didn't know how. They were lawless. They didn't know how to do anything except move to him, attach to him.

He could feel them coming. It wasn't hard to lure them away from Wheeler. None of them had a very strong will of its own. Danny's own ka was so strong, so . . . charismatic? . . . that they could hardly resist the invitation, if in fact any of them tried.

When they attached to him, he could sense them like a distant clamor of voices, like a crowd moving through a street on the other side of a large building. It wasn't words, really. They had learned how to trigger emotions, and Danny could feel them jostling him that way. Tiny pinpricks of envy, lust, greed, disgust, pride, resentment, ambition, even affection and humor. And the desire to hurt people. That was underlying almost all of them. Not rage, really. Just a desire to cause damage.

But it was all so very faint and weak. And Danny's own will overpowered them. They gave into him. Accepted his rule. Made him their king, became part of his domain.

And when the last of them was gone from Wheeler, he turned back around. "I was such a *jerk*, guys," he said. "I'm sorry."

"Don't tell me," said Xena. "You didn't mean what you said."

"Oh, I meant it," said Wheeler, "because I really am a jerk. But . . . I knew better than to *say* it. Danny's my friend, man. I wouldn't say stuff like that to a friend, I don't know what I was thinking."

"I do," said Pat. "And I know why you're not thinking it now.

Because Danny just took away the tiny *things* that were prompting you to say those things. To *feel* them."

"Oh, get real," said Hal. "Next thing you'll tell me is we really do have a tiny angel on one shoulder and a devil on the other, like in cartoons."

"We do," said Pat, "except . . . no angel."

The others looked to Danny for confirmation. "It's hard to explain it when you can't see it. Sense it. But yes, Pat saw it and I didn't till she pointed it out. That creature I had inside me, when I wasn't acting like me—"

"Set," said Laurette and Xena together. "The Belmage," said Sin at the same time.

"When he was expelled from Duat and came to Earth without a human body, there were millions that came with him. Also without bodies. Smaller than microscopic. More like geometric points. But they joined in Set's cause, which was to make human beings as miserable as possible, to make us destroy each other."

"So the devil made me do it," said Wheeler, halfway between scorn and hope.

"Not *made* you," said Danny. "They would if they could, but no, they can only sort of *trigger* you. Remind you of something you already felt or thought. Every angry word you said to me was something you truly thought of. But it wasn't *all* you thought about me. Just the parts that might destroy our friendship."

"Why would they care if I had you as a friend?" asked Wheeler.

"Any bonds between people—they're real, even if they're insubstantial. We bind ourselves to each other in friendship, in families. And the Sutahites want us all to act in ways that tear that down."

Xena blushed. "So when we tried to, like, seduce you—"

"When we threw ourselves at you like discount whores," said Sin.

"Clearance-table harlots," said Laurette.

"Sutahites were working on us?" asked Xena.

"I don't know," said Danny. "I couldn't see the prets then. But I think, probably so."

"Do we have them now?" asked Laurette.

"When you guys were competing to find the most disgustingly clever way to describe your own behavior," said Pat, "each time you had a couple or three sort of divebomb your ka, your inself."

"Great," said Sin. "So whenever I'm clever, it's really the devil that's clever and I'm just his puppet."

"No," said Danny. "You're never a puppet. They can't *make* you say or do anything. You have no strings to pull. I mean, when you're hungry and you pass the bakery department at Walmart—"

"Nothing there makes me hungry," said Sin.

"Liar," said Xena.

"Is your sudden rush of hunger *forcing* you to stop and pick up something to eat?" asked Danny. "You *can* just walk by, and when you're broke, that's exactly what you do. Your brain doesn't switch off, you can still choose."

"So Wheeler was responsible for every mean thing he said?" Xena asked.

"Just as you're responsible for *that* mean thing," said Pat. "But Danny just gathered up the ones that were hovering around Wheeler."

"So if I say something nasty now, it just came from me," said Wheeler.

"Or from habit," said Danny. "Look, I don't understand this yet, we just saw something and I *tried* something."

"But I'm clean," said Wheeler. "I got none of them anymore?"

"No," said Pat. "Already you've picked up some new ones. Maybe they were strays, maybe they came from somebody else."

"So . . . my pure-thoughts phase was, like, ninety seconds long," said Wheeler.

"Your thoughts were never pure," said Pat. "You still had your full dosage of testosterone."

"He's only got half a dose," said Hal. "I thought you all knew that."

"Not true," said Wheeler, "but funny."

"You mean they didn't know?" asked Hal.

"When you say something mean to a friend," said Pat, "you can pretend you're joking, but you thought of it, you had the mean idea, and then you chose to say it. Laughing doesn't erase that. Not your laughter and not Wheeler's."

"Can you take them away from all of us?" asked Laurette. "Because you have no idea how many bitchy things I've thought of to say in the last three minutes."

"And I'm just dying to say, 'You mean besides the ones you *did* say?'" said Sin.

"Very busy Sutahites," said Pat.

"I don't know that it does any good to take them," said Danny. "More come anyway. I think there are probably millions. Billions maybe. I don't know if I can gather them all. I sort of hear them, they do to me whatever they were doing to you. Probably not as strongly, maybe because they don't know me as well as they got to know you. I'm just saying . . . it won't necessarily do you any long-term good."

"Because they can't become a part of you," said Pat, "people can't take these Sutahites with them when they pass through a gate. Or a Great Gate. They get stripped away and left behind. I think what the Gate Thief fears about Great Gates is that Set will get through, and if *he* gets through, he can bring all the Sutahites with him, and the people of Westil have never had to deal with them. They really might become slaves."

"Not that they haven't been perfectly capable of coming up with horrors and evils on their own," said Danny.

"Seriously," said Hal. "We're supposed to believe that our heads are surrounded by a cloud of gnats that tell us to do bad things."

"Let's see," said Laurette. "We've seen people disappear in one place and appear in another. Injuries healed in an instant. Kids flying up a mile above Buena Vista and coming back down not dead. A girl we've known half our lives suddenly being able to whip up dust devils and tornados. But you're right—clouds of tiny creatures around our heads is *way* too much to swallow."

"It just feels so childish," said Hal.

"Shut up," said Sin. "Not you, Hal, Xena. She was about to start that stupid 'wildest childish' tongue twister again."

"Do you know how it feels to me?" asked Wheeler. "Weirdly quiet. It's not like I heard actual voices or words or anything. But it's like something that used to keep me agitated all the time has taken a vacation."

"Will that make Wheeler less weird?" asked Laurette.

"Doubtful," said Pat.

"This is what makes me so frustrated," said Danny. "We do this banter all the time, everybody does it, insulting each other, mocking each other, only . . . it hurts, doesn't it? We hurt each other. Can't we just stop? Can't we just be kind? Wheeler's not weird, he's just another human trying to figure out how he can belong to a tribe. And in *this* group he doesn't exactly stand out for weirdness, does he? Look at us. The 'popular' kids call us weird, because we don't obey them and dress like them and worship them, but screw them, they're nasty and stupid. We're smart and . . . let's stop treating each other the way *they* treat us. Because we don't deserve it."

They were all silent for a while.

"I didn't know it bothered you," said Laurette.

"It didn't. I didn't even notice it till now. But here's Wheeler telling us that he used to be agitated all the time, and Pat and I are telling you that he was plagued with these *things* from outside himself, trying to make him unhappy and self-destructive, and then you have to call him *weird*?"

"I'm the one who said it," said Laurette, "and I was asking if it would make him *less* weird—"

"I know what you said, Laurette, and it wasn't just you. Everybody laughed. Including me!"

"But not Pat. She never laughs," said Xena.

"Yes, she does," said Danny. "All the time."

"With you," said Sim.

"*At* you," said Hal. "No, erase that, sorry. It's just such a *habit*!"

"It's how we know we're part of the group," said Laurette. "The popular kids, they make fun of people *outside* their group. We tease each other, but we're never mean to people outside."

"Yes, we are," said Sin.

"We're as vicious as the popular kids," said Xena.

"Yes, but we're smarter, so the things we say about them are actually funny."

"I didn't mean to disrupt everything," said Danny. "I'm not mad, and I'm not blaming you or anybody because I do it too. It just felt wrong, right at that moment, for us to mock Wheeler. It's like, we found out he had a hidden wound, a dagger sticking out of his ribs, and I pulled out the dagger and then we started laughing at him for bleeding."

"That was a really bad analogy," said Laurette.

"It was only a little bad," said Danny. "It was also a little accurate. Of course we can tease each other. If we didn't poke each other, yeah, how would we even know that we belonged. I just wish we could stop poking each other right in the bleeding wounds. Let's try to heal the wounds, and poke somewhere else."

"I'll try," said Pat. "But we're high-school kids, you know."

"We haven't all aced the SAT and the ACT," said Hal.

"You know that those tests measure nothing except your ability to take tests," said Danny.

"But since college consists of passing a whole bunch of tests for four years, that's a good skill to have," said Sin.

"I wish we were smarter so we could form a team like Scorpion," said Wheeler.

"Which one are you?" asked Hal. "Sylvester?"

"I wish," said Wheeler. "I'm more like . . . one of the civilians who gets in the way."

"I'm Paige," said Laurette. "I'm the normal one who helps them communicate with humans."

"So Danny is Walter?" asked Wheeler. "The genius?"

"I have no idea what you're talking about," said Danny.

"You *so* need to get cable in that little house of yours," said Xena. "*Scorpion*. It's a TV show about a team of geniuses who don't get along, only they really need each other so they keep almost breaking up but then they can't survive without each other."

"We don't keep almost breaking up," said Danny.

"We also don't have to get ratings every week so we can stay on the air," said Pat. "It's always got all this fake conflict, only I find myself caring even though I know it's just writers manipulating me."

"It's the little boy, Ralph," said Xena. "That's what makes me care."

"Danny isn't Walter," said Hal. "Danny is Cade. The grownup with real power in the real world, who comes in and saves their asses time and again."

"But also he's the one who keeps getting them into danger in the first place," said Laurette. "Sorry, Danny, but . . . kind of true."

"We're discussing a TV show," said Pat.

"Because it applies to us," said Hal. "Come on, Pat, we can't just sit around thinking serious thoughts and discussing Nietzsche and Kierkegaard and the Elder Eddas."

"Where did Kierkegaard come from?" asked Pat. "Who's heard of Kierkegaard?"

Sin had her phone out, trying to remember how to spell Kierkegaard—if she had ever known. Hal started helping her.

"Danny doesn't need cable," said Wheeler. "He needs a tablet."

"But to stream any shows, he'd have to get wi-fi, which he doesn't have unless he gets cable, and then he'd have cable," said Xena.

Sin started reading. " 'Boredom is the root of all evil—the despairing refusal to be oneself.' "

"I have no idea what that means," said Danny.

"Neither do I," said Sin, "but Kierkegaard said it."

Hal started reading off her phone. " 'Adversity draws men together and produces beauty and harmony in life's relationships, just as the cold of winter produces ice-flowers on the windowpanes, which vanish with the warmth.' "

"Sounds like a depressed Dane," said Pat.

"But he's a *great* Dane," said Wheeler.

"Woof," said Xena.

Sin was reading again. "OK, here's one. 'Don't forget to love yourself.' "

"Maybe Danes need to be reminded of that. Especially in winter," said Pat. "But Americans usually need to be reminded to love somebody besides themselves."

" 'The function of prayer is not to influence God, but rather to change the nature of the one who prays,' " said Sin.

"If Danny's a god," said Wheeler, "I wonder if anybody prays to him."

Danny held up his hand, knowing that somebody would start doing it just to be cute. "Please don't. Please be my friends and don't ever call me a god. I don't act like I think I'm a god, do I? I try not to."

"You just, like, cast out Wheeler's devils," said Xena. "You may not be a god but you're *something*."

Danny buried his head in his hands. "I'm Danny North, and I've got way more power than any human being should have, but I still can't figure out what I'm supposed to do with it. A lot of terrible things are happening and worse ones are coming and it's partly my fault, so I think it's my job to stop them but I don't know how and, hell, I don't even know how things are *supposed* to look when I set everything to rights, because the world kind of sucked *before* I found out I was a gatemage, and I know *that* wasn't my fault. So do I scale back the suckage until it only sucks as much as usual? Or am I supposed to fix the whole thing? Or just stop the *worst* suckathons and then crawl in a hole somewhere like Loki did after he closed all the gates?"

"Danny is confused," said Laurette.

"He doesn't like to be confused," said Sin. "He's an organized person. This is not the right planet for him."

"There *is* no right planet for me," said Danny, "and I've been to all three."

"Stay on this one," said Pat. "For me."

"Love is the ultimate aphrodisiac," said Xena brightly. "Don't correct me, Laurette, I wasn't being stupid, I was being ironic."

" 'It is perfectly true, as philosophers say, that life must be understood backwards,' " read Hal. " 'But they forget the other proposition—' "

But he couldn't finish, because the others howled him down. "Forget Kierkegaard," said Sin, taking back her phone.

" 'People demand freedom of speech as a compensation for the freedom of thought, which they seldom use,' " Hal recited quickly.

"Hal's going to major in philosophy," said Xena.

"*Danish* philosophy," said Wheeler.

"The philosophy of danishes," said Xena. "He'll get so fat."

"I think Kierkegaard sounds cool. Paradoxical and stuff. Not as insane as Nietzsche."

"You've read Nietzsche," said Laurette.

"After I met an actual superman, I thought I owed it to myself to read *Man and Superman*," said Hal.

"That's George Bernard Shaw," said Pat.

"I know," said Hal. "But it was Nietzsche who coined the term 'ubermensch,' so I read *Also sprach Zarathustra*—"

"Please tell me you didn't read it in German," said Pat.

"I can't read German," Hal said. "And I can't understand Nietzsche even in English, only he sounds like he thinks he's smarter and better and more dangerous and cool than everybody else, which means he's the opposite of Danny, because Danny keeps apologizing for being what he is, which is dumb."

"Thanks," said Danny.

Hal read off the screen of his own phone, " 'The most common form of despair is not being who you are.' "

" 'Be yourself,' " quoted Xena. " 'Everybody else is taken.' "

"She used to have a T-shirt that said that," said Sin.

"I still have it," said Xena. "But I bought it before I got my boobs, and now I can't get the shirt to go down over them, so nobody could read it anyway."

"Anybody looking at your chest *now*," said Laurette, "is not reading."

"Thank you," said Xena.

" 'The most painful state of being is remembering the future,' " read Hal, " 'particularly the one you'll never have.' "

Danny laughed wryly. "That sounds like it actually means something. If only I were intelligent enough to see how it applies to me. Guys, I learned a lot today, and on top of that, I found out that you're willing to listen to me go on and on about how *hard* my life is, which is ridiculous because if anybody in this world can get whatever he wants, it's me. So thanks."

"I think we should all get college credit for a class in Kierkegaard," said Laurette.

"Just remember that Danny took away *my* devils," said Wheeler, "but you've still all got yours."

"That was kind of inaccurate," said Pat, "since you've already got a bunch of new ones."

"The devil made me say it," said Wheeler.

"I've got to go think about stuff," said Danny. "Meaning I need some sleep."

"If you take Pat with you, you won't sleep," said Laurette.

"Get a life, Laurette, it's not like that," said Pat.

"If I take Pat with me, I'll think better," said Danny.

"With your *brain*?" asked Wheeler.

"Wheeler doesn't need Sutahites to be a jerk," said Pat. Then she turned to Wheeler. "Of course, I meant that in the nicest possible way."

Danny took Pat's hand. "Want to come with me?"

Her answer was to jump to his house—taking him with her. It was strange being her passenger. But also kind of nice. Like he could turn things over to somebody else, even if only for a minute, and it would still come out OK.

16

There have never been dragons," said Lus, the old loremaster. "They're a legend that originated in Mittlegard, but such creatures have never existed anywhere, least of all here in Mitherhame."

Gerd only smiled—which, Hermia knew, was exactly the pose a person needed to strike if she was to be thought powerful. However, Hermia's pose was not one of power; she wasn't CEO of a powerful corporation, she was merely a consultant, and what she had to sell was her wisdom. Or at least her useful data.

"When we call it a dragon," said Hermia, "everyone knows what to expect. It will fly. It will spew out fire and kill from a distance and up close. And it will be impervious to arrows and swords. But no, there has never been a *living* dragon, and that is not what Lady Gerd of the North will demonstrate here today. For instance, everyone knows that the only thing that a dragon cannot penetrate is stone. The city of Y was built here in these craggy hills precisely so that it could be built of local stone, which is very hard. What could a dragon—if there were such a creature—do against these walls?"

"Nothing, of course," said Lus, because he was a lover of logic.

"Your implication," said Queen Genoesswess, "is plain. This 'dragon' of yours *will* harm our walls, or why show it to us? Suppose that your claim is true. To harm our walls would certainly impress us. But then we would have to rebuild the wall."

Hermia glanced at King Sorian, who, as usual, was listening to everything and saying nothing. "Have you no stonemages?" Hermia asked.

The queen smiled. "The walls of this redoubt were built by ancient Stonefathers, from the age when we passed between the worlds. It is all living rock, drawn up from the bowels of these hills and shaped according to their dreams. There's no stonemage in all the world who can do any such thing."

"Then perhaps," said Hermia, "we could choose a different target. What do you think, Lady of the North?"

Gerd turned at the sound of the impressive title they had agreed upon. "I'll see to it that it happens as you said." She pointed to a nearby butte. "Perhaps if we show what the dragon can do to *that*."

"We would consider that a perfect demonstration of its power against walls," said Queen Genoesswess. "It's also living rock, and it's neither weaker nor stronger than these walls."

There came a sound, different from the wind, a kind of juddering beat in the air, like great wings flapping. Hermia knew where to look, of course, because she could sense where the pilot was, but she feigned a search until she could see the dot of the approaching helicopter. Gerd, who was more practiced at spotting

her own air force, was already guiding Sorian, Lus, and Genoesswess to look at the right spot in the southern sky.

"It's either very small or very far," said Lus.

"From the noise, it must be very loud," said the queen.

"It's larger than any horse," said Gerd, "though many ships are
larger. And yes, it's quite noisy, so that when it's near you, you have
to shout to be heard."

Hermia knew that the pilot had already received his change of
orders from Gerd, who had mastered the art of causing the on-
board computer to respond to her course corrections. The pilot
could override her, because he was the one who understood what
wind or birds or updrafts might do to the chopper, and Gerd was
not interested in losing a chopper because it was stupidly obedient to her. But he understood his target and was now flying the
chopper toward the targeted butte.

That was when Hermia felt the making of a gate, and knew that
another human being had just arrived on the terrace. There was
only one gatemage left in either world who had the power to make
gates in the old way, so she was not surprised to see Loki standing against the wall of the castle, far out of earshot.

She excused herself and walked to where he stood. "Came to
see what Danny North's mummy and dad have been doing?"

"I know what they've been doing," said Loki. "I'm here to decide whether to allow this demonstration to take place or not."

Hermia chose not to roll her eyes, though he deserved it.
"They'll fire a rocket and it'll hit the bluff and spray a bit of rock
around and make a lot of noise."

"And then the king and queen will decide that now is a good
time to avenge their ancient injuries. Which neighbor will it be?
Suffyrd? Nefyryd? Or poor little Badys?"

"I don't know what Gerd has in mind. I don't think *she* knows.
Westilian politics is still beyond her."

"But you're an expert?"

"They're not my helicopters and tanks and submarines," said Hermia.

"When you brought them here, you became responsible for them."

"It really wouldn't be sporting of you to take them away," said Hermia. "And I'll only bring more."

"Once I've moved them, you won't know where they are, and the supply isn't infinite," said Loki.

"Why would you meddle? We're gatemages. In the old days, each side allowed the other to gate people as they would, and engines of war as well."

"Within limits," said Loki.

"None that I heard of," said Hermia.

"Apparently your knowledge also has limits. I was there."

"Let them have their demonstration," said Hermia. "Nobody's impressed with this stuff on Mittlegard anymore. They've all seen too many movies with special effects to think real explosions matter—unless they get caught by the shock wave or eat a little shrapnel."

"I suppose I should let the demonstration happen, so *I'll* know what a shock wave and shrapnel are."

"We aren't close enough for you to experience those, and that's a good thing."

"But that's no use," said Loki. "I think we need to see the effect of these devices on a human body."

"Not a good idea," said Hermia. "I'm not sure you can make a gate fast enough to repair your body from the effects of an explosion."

"Thanks for the suggestion," said Loki. And he was gone.

Hermia turned and saw him standing in midair, about twenty

yards out from the face of the butte. She could see that he was continuously falling through a gate that raised him about a millimeter so he would fall through again and again. Since gates would not be affected by the explosion, gravity would pull him through the gate and heal him, even if he was torn to bits.

Unless fragments of him were blown every which way, so they'd miss the gate entirely. She might have warned him about that—part of the shock-wave concept—but he was such a know-it-all he deserved whatever happened.

The chopper was still about two hundred meters out when it loosed a missile. The pilot might have seen Loki in the air near the target zone, but probably not, or if he saw him, he wouldn't have known what he was seeing.

It turned out Loki was far enough away that while his body shuddered with the shock wave, it didn't fly into fragments, and if for a moment it lost coherency, it was instantly reassembled in proper order by its passage through the gate. And now she saw that Loki had a very large gate on the far side of himself from the explosion. If he had been torn to pieces, the pieces would have been caught by a gate. Whether it would still have the power to heal such a torn-up corpse would have been interesting to learn, but . . . not today.

"Why would you send your clant so close to the target?" asked Queen Genoesswess.

Before she had finished her sentence, Loki was standing with them. "I'm not a clant," he said cheerfully. He bowed deeply to the queen—the respectful action of a foreign lord, not the groveling of a servant or tradesman. Hermia admired his savoir faire—it would have been good to have him as her tutor before she came here to try to help Gerd make her way in Westil. Hermia was having the problems that anthropologists and sociologists always faced: It was hard to know which behaviors were general among all cultures, particular to this culture, or a quirk of the individual. But Loki already knew.

"Who are you, then?" asked the queen.

"I'm a close companion to Queen Bexoi of Iceway," said Loki. "You may call me Hull."

"A seafaring land, this Iceway?" asked King Sorian.

"For the past thousand years, yes," said Lus. "They came pouring out of the frozen Icekame and conquered half of Gray, seizing a long coastline and then moving their capital of Kamesham down to a deep inlet of the sea. Their king at the time was a Tidefather—he would have been remarkable if he had been able to pass between the worlds—but he had power enough to destroy the fleet Gray sent against them. Ever since then—"

"We become wiser with every word," said King Sorian. "But I have reached the limit of my wisdom for now." He turned to Gerd. "I want to know why this man has come to join you foreign women. He is *not* the husband of either of you?"

"I do not have that pleasure or honor," said Loki. "I'm here to see what their toys can do. I felt a portion of the power of that device."

"It tore a great gouge in the rock," said Queen Genoesswess. "If that were directed against our castle, it could not stand for long."

"But it will not be," said Hermia.

"Unless it is," said Gerd, who was always ham-handed in negotiation.

"It will not be," said Hermia, "because our sole desire is to serve you and restore Yffyrd to its rightful place as the great nation of the southeast. Once the city of Y ruled from one end to the other of the Cotton Road, and all the ports and islands from Braccuin to File paid tribute. Now, the people of Ny sneer at the accent of Y, while your last coastline is now under the control of the ungrateful merchants of Fyrdhaven."

"I know our history," said Genoesswess.

"But Hermia's afraid that I might not," said Loki. "And she was right. My attention has been mostly to the north for the past year or so. I can see that you have legitimate grievances. But what I can't see is how you plan to use the dragon these women are offering."

"Our enemies have castles," said King Sorian. "Until they meet the dragon."

"And castles are filled with soldiers. How many will die?"

"Men die in war," said Sorian.

"But they die fighting, or standing guard," said Loki. "They have some kind of chance to protect themselves, or defend, or counterattack. How can they stand against this?"

"That's why we're going to ask for ten of these dragons," said Sorian. "So our victory will be swift, and our enemies will surrender rather than resist us."

"And what will you do then, when you win?" asked Loki.

"Aren't we getting ahead of ourselves?" asked Queen Genoesswess. "Though you are clearly a gatemage—a Gatefather, no doubt, or so you will claim—you must surely know that no mage can plan very far into the future. Least of all a gatemage, since the Gate Thief waits for you."

"Only if I make a Great Gate," said Loki, "which I do not intend to do. But I do intend to know what it will mean to the common people of Suy, Ny, Badmardden, Brac, and Fyrdhaven, to have you as overlords instead of the houses that rule them now."

"To the common people, there should be no difference at all," said Queen Genoesswess. "Why should they care to whom they pay their taxes? Their lives may even be better, since there will be no duties to pay at border crossings, once the borders cease to exist."

"A free trade zone," said Hermia. "It boosts every economy."

Loki didn't even look at her. "What about those who resist you?"

The queen looked at him as if he were insane. "Drowthers don't resist mages."

"But mages do," said Loki. "And drowthers sometimes do as well."

"We handle traitors and criminals as each case comes up. What business is it of yours?"

"I wanted to have some idea of who would be wielding this fabulous new weapon, if I allow it to stay," said Loki.

"He thinks he's the protector of the world," said Hermia. "It's a sad delusion."

Hermia abruptly found herself on a lonely, windy mountaintop, as the gate that Loki had used to send her there disappeared. He had to know how useless the gesture was. She took a moment to get her bearings and leapt back to the terrace in Y.

"That," she said to Queen Genoesswess, "is what he plans to do to your dragons if you don't use them in a way he approves of."

The queen looked a little queasy. "I knew what gatemages used to be, back before the Gate Thief. But to see it. Or . . . not see it."

"Dear Queen of Y," said Loki, "you and your husband don't seem to be the most horrible of the powerful people that I've known. Far from it. You are definitely better than Gerd, here, who once tried to kill her own child because he was a gatemage."

Gerd reddened. "You know that I protected him in every way I could."

"But when they came to kill him, there you were," said Loki.

"She behaved as well as she could," said Hermia. "Better than you, if what we hear from Eluik and Enopp is even half true."

Now it was Loki's turn to blush. "And is the traitor bitch now my judge?" he asked.

"I think so," said Hermia, refusing to let his goading irk her. "I did as little harm as possible, while still obeying my very dangerous Family. I never terrorized children by perching them in downsloping caves for years on end."

Loki turned his back on Hermia and faced the king and queen. "We mages are such an imperfect lot," he said. "Yet I repeat: You and your husband are better than most ruling mages."

"You learned this from a few foolish questions here on our terrace?" asked the queen.

"I learned it from walking the streets of Y and several villages in Yffyrd. From listening to the talk in the pubs and the comments among the merchants. Few loved you, but none hated you, either. In fact, they were rather proud of your work as Grass-sister, Queen Genoesswess. The harvests are bountiful and the people of your land have not known want since you came of age. While King Sorian has used his power as Rockbrother to carve out dry caves for many poor families to live in, without paying rent. Such kindness is rare among the mages. Treat your enemies' people as you have treated your own, and I won't take away these terrible toys. But if you start to use them against the common people, I'll turn these weapons on *you* before I destroy them."

"I understand your rules," said King Sorian. "We'll take your concerns into account, until the Gate Thief takes you. But we will always act in the best interests of the dynasty." He took Queen Genoesswess by the hand and they walked toward the door.

"He didn't seem as impressed as I had hoped," said Loki.

"You don't look as fierce as you sound, Loki," said Hermia. "There's more than a hint of the strutting little boy playing at being king." She winked at the loremaster, Lus, who was still there, watching and listening.

"I'm not king of anything," said Loki mildly, still watching the king and queen as they passed through the door.

"If you're not going to gate their helicopters to the bottom of the sea," said Hermia, "why don't we go in search of supper?"

Hermia looked at Gerd, who smiled and nodded slightly.

"I'll return soon, Great Lady, to bring as many dragons as you and Lus agree upon," said Hermia. "For now, though, we gatemages have a few things to discuss."

WAD LED THE girl to an alley outside a tavern in Kamesham, for no better reason than its familiarity. He did not eat there often, but had done so often enough that no one would think of him as unfamiliar. When Hermia followed him, though, Wad realized that her outlandish costume—not of Mittlegard, but of Y—would mark her as a foreigner. Add to that her air of confidence, not to say arrogance, and she would be noticed as an unusual and, be it said, slightly frightening woman.

"We'll enter separately," said Wad.

"I'll enter clinging to your arm like a newlywed," said Hermia, "or I'll simply appear in the middle of the room."

"You have some need to make everyone look at you?"

"They'll look at me no matter what I do. I only want them to look at you as well. But think, Loki. If we look like young lovers, who will come up and bother us, or even try to listen in? Nobody wants to hear the sweet stupidities of young lovers. Married couples don't become interesting till they've wished each other dead a few times."

"I'm fairly sure I never married back in my previous life," said Wad. "I wonder if that way of thinking formed part of my reasoning. I hope not."

"You mean your memories are still foggy?"

"Living inside a tree for a millennium and a half does odd things to your mind," said Wad.

"If you know you're mentally defective, I wonder why you've appointed yourself the policeman of Westil," said Hermia.

"I'm not so unambitious," said Wad. "Fifteen centuries ago, I appointed myself the policeman of Westil *and* Mittlegard."

"Declared everyone guilty and sentenced them to perpetual imprisonment on their home world."

"Weakening the mages was good for everybody, mage *and* drowther."

"Birds are always happier with their wings broken."

"It wasn't *their* wings," said Wad.

"Nor yours," said Hermia. "But I know the real reason for keeping the worlds apart, and I wonder if you're even right."

"Confining Set to one world instead of two was a great improvement."

"I'm sure you're right," said Hermia. "But the two worlds are far from equal. Mittlegard has billions of people. I doubt there's been a census, but I get the impression that the low population density brings Westil to, at most, two hundred million."

"Possibly twice that," said Wad. "There are places with far larger populations than Y or Ny."

"But either way, it amounts to a small percentage of the population of Mittlegard, where agriculture has been mechanized and fertilized, with enhanced seeds and plants that bear far more fruit, and an atmosphere lush with carbon dioxide so the plants will grow. Six billion."

"I have visited Mittlegard," said Wad. "Even before the closing of the gates, Mittlegard was more prosperous and sustained a larger population. We didn't have the science to measure, but I think our habitable land mass is markedly smaller."

"So my question, Loki," said Hermia, "is a simple one. Why is it that the world with Set in it is far richer, larger, more populous, more advanced, more *powerful* than the world that you have kept pure."

"You tell *me*," said Wad. "You know the history of your world. How much death and suffering have the people endured?"

Hermia nodded to concede the point. "When you have a larger population, then cruelty can touch larger numbers of people. Thirty million die in one country, because the ruler wants to rid himself of troublesomely independent kulaks. Six million die in another, because the ruler has conceived a mad hatred for people he thinks pernicious and dangerous. Three million in a much smaller country, to eliminate all those who know how to make money from trade instead of agriculture. And then the wars. But I know that Westil also has wars, and if fewer people suffer and die, isn't that only because nations have fewer people to begin with?"

"That's what I think you don't understand," said Wad. "There have been devastating wars. The vast desert of Dapnu Dap was created by the sandmages who finally defeated the manmages of Ethue Dappa. It was a terrible price to pay, but since then, warfare has been rare, and mostly between mages."

"You can't tell me that soldiers and sailors don't die in these wars."

"They do," said Wad. "But such losses are rare and relatively few. That isn't all, though. Slavery is unknown here, partly because owning another person smacks of manmagery, and partly because when there are gatemages, it's hard to keep slaves confined to one place. It is almost unheard of for anyone to mistreat a child, and when it happens, the punishment from the neighbors is swift and sure."

"Really?" asked Hermia. "Death?"

"No," said Wad. "For the first offense, a Wingbrother might bring his heartbound to peck out an eye. For the second offense, the person loses his children, his wife, his place in the village. He goes one-eyed out into the world to make his way, where he'll have no children within his power. But Hermia, you won't conceive of how rare this is. Because in Westil, even though people have all the same weaknesses and harmful impulses as in Mittlegard, they don't have the Sutahites constantly prodding them, making them think obsessively of their dark desires. Whatever evil they do comes from *them*, not the servants of Set working to undo all the ties that hold people together as friends and neighbors."

"But how do you know that the Sutahites are the cause, or that bringing Set to Westil would be so terrible? Think what the lack of gates has done to all the mages of both worlds, all because you fear something that may not be all that terrible."

"I saw the difference between the worlds back when their levels of technology were more nearly the same," said Wad. "I had a century and more to study the situation, to see how the Semitic religions brought Sutahites to ever greater power and influence. They might call Set the devil, or Satan, or Lucifer, but it was the Sutahites who most readily answered their prayers, prompting them to do this or that terrible thing. I knew what I was doing when I did it."

"But you Westilian mages, you Indo-European gods," said Hermia, "look at the terrible things *you* did."

Wad knew he could not relieve her ignorance in the little time they would have together. But still he had to try. "Hermia," he said, "the Eddas, the Upanishads, the Iliad, all the writings about the deeds of the Mithermages—they weren't written by *us*. They were written by drowthers who thought we were immortal, who thought we had far more control over the natural world than we really do. They thought we cared what happened to drowthers, that some ignorant 'mortal' could provoke a war among the gods. We *could* have meddled far more than we did, and we would have, *if we had cared*."

Hermia looked thoughtful. "Well, you have a point. Those writings all seem to assume that the Families cared what the drowthers did to each other. Or they consist of drowther fantasies about how we interact with each other."

"There was savagery in Mittlegard before I closed the gates," said Wad. "But what I saw was that as Set gained power and experience, the Sutahites became far more effective at goading drowthers *and mages* into doing unspeakable things. And then came the day when I learned that Set could not be expelled from a person by passing him through a gate. That meant that if Set possessed someone who knew where a Great Gate was, he could pass over to Westil, bringing millions of Sutahites with him. The people of Mittlegard had hundreds of generations of experience, learning how to ignore the Sutahites, resist them, defy them. But the Westilians had no such experience."

"So you closed the gates."

"No, I *ate* the gates," said Wad. "I gathered them into myself and held them, and if anyone on either world even tried to make a Great Gate, I stripped them of their gates, because Westil is not capable of coping with an onslaught of Sutahites."

"So the real danger is the Sutahites, not Set himself," said Hermia.

"Set, by himself, can only rule one person. Now, that person might do terrible things. But think of the worst tyrant in Mittlegard history, and ask yourself—how much evil could he have accomplished if there weren't hundreds or thousands of people eager to obey his evil commands? And why did they do such terrible things? Because Sutahites were goading them, convincing them to follow their darkest desires, to take pleasure in following orders that they *knew* were immoral. Unspeakable. Isn't that so?"

"If you say," said Hermia. "I don't know how you can pretend to *know* any of this. Danny and Pat think they can *see* the Sutahites now."

"See?"

"Well, *sense* them. Somehow."

"Can they sense Set himself?" asked Wad.

"Danny obviously thinks he can, because he's sure he's got the old devil locked up inside him, the way you locked up all those gates."

"If he thinks he can do that, he's a fool," said Wad. "Or maybe I'm the fool. Who knows what Danny North became when he went to Duat? His powers increased to such a degree that he doesn't even *want* his gates back. And the effect has spilled over to you and Pat and . . . anybody else I should know about?"

"I think you know who the others are," said Hermia. "Because they're from *your* world. The boys and their mother. They know how to leap from place to place the way I do. Sooner or later they'll realize, as I did, that they can go from world to world."

"And so every one of you has become exactly the person Set has been waiting for. If he can possess you, he'll have your power to gate from world to world, only without having to make actual gates, so that I can't prevent it by eating those gates."

"So you've lost," said Hermia.

"I had my fifteen hundred years," said Wad. "And so far, Danny *has* kept Set in his place. But Set is intelligent. He learns. He experiments. He learned how to attach himself to people so he isn't expelled when they pass through gates. What is he learning right now? Because I think that's what's really happening—he's not under Danny's control, he's just trying to learn to do what Danny *does*. What *you* do."

"What if he's learning that he wants to be more like Danny? Not just to have Danny's power, but his genuine kindness, his desire to do no harm?"

"You'll have to discuss that with Danny," said Wad. "I've never been possessed by Set, I've only seen the effect on others. They all became completely despicable and dangerous, so it seemed to me that Set was toxic. Incorrigible. He's not a person. He was never a child, he didn't grow up with human connections. He doesn't have any maternal or paternal feelings, no sense of brotherhood or belonging, none of the impulses built into our minds and bodies that help us live together in peace. It isn't in his nature to do *anything* that would help somebody else at his own expense. But maybe Danny thinks that Set is learning virtue."

Hermia studied Wad. "No, you don't believe that," she finally said. "In fact, I think you're afraid that Danny might *think* that, but you're so sure he's wrong that . . . are you planning to kill Danny North?"

Wad shook his head. "I'm not planning anything. This is out of my control."

"Really? Then why did you show up in Y, deciding in your infinite wisdom whether Gerd and I should be allowed to bring dragons into Westil?"

"Because Gerd is a typical Mittlegard mage—the Families think they're entitled to do anything."

"But I'm not," said Hermia.

"You're as much a product of a Family as she is," said Wad. "You show it in everything you say and everything you do."

"And you're not?"

"Drowthers need protection from people like you," said Wad.

"So you would never make an arbitrary decision that damages everybody in the world, without consulting with anybody else?" asked Hermia.

"Damages a few people," said Wad. "Damages them slightly, and saves far more people from invasion by these invisible monsters. And also from having the Families run roughshod over them."

"The hero of the drowthers. Robin Hood. The champion of the people."

"You say it scornfully," said Wad, "because you're so arrogant you think that you have the right to be a god."

"I'm not the one who set up a flaming sword to keep Adam and Eve out of the garden," said Hermia.

"I'm trying to keep the serpent confined to the place where he already is," said Wad.

"To the place where, if you're right, he and the Sutahites have already brought suffering and death to hundreds of millions of people, in order to protect *your* little village-sized world."

"This?" asked Wad, indicating the tavern, the city, the world of Westil. "This isn't my world. I wasn't born here, I didn't grow up here."

Apparently that had never crossed Hermia's mind.

"I grew up among the Norse. Before the Sutahites prompted them to rage through the world, burning and ravaging and ravishing. I grew up among farmers and fishermen of Mittlegard."

"And played tricks on them," said Hermia.

"Mercilessly," said Wad. "I *am* a gatemage."

"But in Westil, you never did that?"

"I wanted to end the warfare between Families," said Wad. "So, as the most powerful gatemage in the world, I created Great Gates in a dozen different places. I made sure that no Family would have an advantage over any other because of superior access to the other world. And it worked. Except that then all the Families exploited the drowthers, practically enslaved them. All the worst mages from Westil came to Mittlegard because it was a bigger, richer place, and there were more drowthers to use and control. So yes, even before I realized that Set could pass through a gate, I realized that it was a mistake to let the Families have easy access to Great Gates. Because they do things like . . . you know . . ."

"What Gerd and I are doing," said Hermia.

"Well, you *are* a fine example of the Families at their worst."

Her response surprised him. She looked stricken. Tears came into her eyes. Wad had thought she was heartless, calculating. But apparently *this*, out of all the rude things he'd said to her, was the one that hurt her feelings.

Or else she was faking the emotional response in order to trick him.

"I don't want to make things worse for the drowthers," said Hermia. "I don't want to make things worse for anybody."

"Then take your helicopters back to Mittlegard," said Wad.

"No," said Hermia.

"Why not?"

"You want to keep Set and the Sutahites out of Westil," said Hermia. "I want to get the really dangerous mages out of Mittlegard."

And with those words she disappeared. Because there was no gate, Wad couldn't tell where she had gone. But wherever it was, she'd be causing more and more trouble, for him and everyone else.

So if he couldn't steal her gates, Wad had to try to think of a way to kill a gatemage.

17

Danny wasn't surprised when it turned out that Wheeler hadn't even asked his parents for a little money. "I couldn't tell them I was going to Busch Gardens," he said. "They would have had so many questions!"

"Like what?" asked Hal, disgusted.

"Like how am I going to get there!"

" 'I'm going with my friends,' " suggested Laurette. " 'Danny North's aunt is taking him and he invited all of us to go along.' "

Hal joined in. " 'Danny North is a gatemage and he's going to magically transport us to Williamsburg.' "

" 'But he won't take us through the damn gates,' " said Wheeler. "Sure, I could have told them that."

"I told you from the start that I wasn't going to get us in illegally," said Danny.

"There's no law against *magically* entering an amusement park. Why do they call it the Magic Kingdom?"

"That's Disneyland," Sin said with disgust. "And there *are* laws against it."

"If we don't break anything," said Wheeler, "then it isn't breaking and entering."

"Still trespassing," said Hal. "And in your case, the added charge of 'trespassing while stupid.'"

"I'm not stupid!" said Wheeler. "Danny refusing to get us inside is stupid!"

"You have to show your ticket *everywhere*," said Laurette. "Being inside is useless if you don't have a ticket."

"And Danny told us," said Xena, "anybody who can't come up with the seventy-five bucks, tell him and he'll help."

"I thought I *could*," said Wheeler.

"No, you mean you thought you could force him to gate you in," said Hal, "and you were wrong."

"The whole point of going to Busch Gardens instead of Disney or Harry Potter or anything else was that Williamsburg is in Virginia," said Laurette. "So our parents would actually *believe* we could make a quick trip here and back. As I recall, we made that switch because *your* parents were the ones who wouldn't let you go to Florida."

"So my parents are worse than I thought," said Wheeler. He turned to Danny. "I need help after all. Can't you get the money now?"

"So I should go to Veevee," said Danny, "and then we go to an ATM and she withdraws the money, and then I come back here, all because . . ." The truth was that Danny could do this all quite easily. It wouldn't take five minutes, and Veevee would think it was hilarious. Why was he so annoyed?

"I think Danny's getting pretty fed up with you, Wheeler," said Laurette. "I know *I* am."

"Fine, I'll wait out here while you all go in and have fun," said Wheeler. "But I'll tell you, if *I* were a gatemage, there wouldn't be an ATM in Williamsburg with any money left in it."

"Such a genius," said Hal. "So you stand in front of each ATM, *on camera*, make a little gate and reach inside the machinery, fumble around till you find all the twenties, and then wait for them to identify you and come to your house and find stacks of stolen twenties, and *then* you get to explain how you got the money out of the machines."

"They couldn't hold me in prison cause I'd be a gatemage," said Wheeler.

"A one-man crime wave," said Hal. "The anti-Batman."

"I can't even reach inside ATMs anymore, Wheeler," said Danny. "That was something that was only possible when I had gates. I can go places, I can take people with me, but I can't make little gates and reach into things, or listen to something without being there myself." Well, that wasn't strictly true, Danny thought. I can make a clant, which I never could before. But the *clant* would be there, so it's pretty much the same thing.

"Why didn't Pat come?" asked Xena.

"She doesn't like rides," said Laurette.

"She doesn't like *Wheeler*," said Sin.

"None of us like Wheeler," said Xena, "but we all came."

"She's coming," said Danny. "When she finishes her chores."

"Her parents treat her like a *child*," said Xena.

"Her parents treat her like an adult who has to do her share of the work," said Danny. "It's the whining that turns it into something only children do."

"That means you've got the money for Pat's ticket," said

Wheeler. "Pay for me to get in, and then you and Pat can go get more money from your aunt."

"You're so clever when you're spending other people's money," said Laurette.

"No he's not," said Hal.

"Come on," said Wheeler.

Danny counted out the cash.

"Why didn't your aunt just give you a credit card?" asked Wheeler.

Danny handed the money to Hal. "Spend it all in one place," he said.

"Hal gets to carry the cash because, like, he's our *daddy* now?" said Sin.

Hal handed the money to Laurette.

"What does this make me, the mommy?" asked Laurette.

"How can you stand being with these repulsive drowthers?"

Danny had felt Hermia arrive, but the others were visibly startled.

"Oh, the traitor bitch expects to come with us now?" said Sin.

"Why aren't you *dead*?" asked Laurette.

Hermia ignored them. "Danny, we need to talk."

"Talk," said Danny.

"Without the children," said Hermia.

Danny wasn't going to play along. It was dangerous to be alone with Hermia.

"I could send them away," said Hermia.

"No, you could only *take* them away and come back without them," said Danny, "and they'd have to hold your hands, which I doubt they'd do."

"How do you know I haven't learned to send people without touching them?" asked Hermia.

"Have you?" asked Danny.

"No," said Hermia. "But it's stupid of you to underestimate me the way you always do."

"I never underestimated you," said Danny. "I trusted you."

"See?" said Wheeler. "I'm not the only stupid one."

"I always acted in your best interests," said Hermia, "even if you were too ignorant to know what your best interest actually was."

"Which is more dangerous," Danny asked his friends, "the man who swears to kill me, or the friend who knows better than me?"

"The most dangerous is Set, the one who made your own hands kill your lady love," said Hermia.

In the moment, Pat appeared. But she said nothing.

"Of course your lady love knew the moment I showed up," said Hermia. "What took you so long, O thou omniscient lover?"

"I knew you'd have to talk for a while before you did anything," said Pat mildly. "So I had time to wash my hands before I came."

"Outnumbering a gatemage is pointless," said Hermia.

Pat said nothing. Danny said nothing. Danny's silence came from his fear of what Hermia intended to do next. He had heard her claim to serve his interests, and her assertion that Set was his most dangerous enemy. She could not possibly be so stupid as to try to take on Set directly . . . could she? Danny had been able to sense prets for long enough now that he not only knew where and how many they were, but also the nature of individual prets. They weren't complicated. Either they were weak or strong. The strong ones were able to become human beings, because they could rein in the instinctive behaviors of the beast, and the most powerful also carried with them an entourage of lesser prets, which formed their outself.

The outself prets were not weak. Only strong prets could bind themselves to a human, either as inself or outself. And strength was not the only attribute that Danny could sense in them. He also knew which ones were bold, and which were fearful. That was what he always sensed in the Sutahites—fearfulness. At first this had struck him as odd. The Sutahites had nothing, so they had nothing to lose. What would they be putting at risk?

But then he had realized that their timidity was not situational, it was inherent, it was part of who they were. They were not timid because they had anything to lose; they had followed Set because they were timid, and he had promised to take care of them, tell them what to do, keep them safe.

Were they safe? Or were they nothing? They were not part of anything except Set himself, and *he* was nothing, except whatever human he could dominate. And now he wasn't even dominating the human that he occupied. Danny had taken such firm control of his body that there was nothing now for Set to play with in order to manipulate him. What did the Sutahites think of that?

And there was another attribute of prets: the will to power. They all had some of it, or at least all of them that composed a part of a human being, ka or ba. But Set had a will to power that was insatiable. Perhaps it was this bright flame of ambition and pride that the Sutahites attached to.

Not for the first time, Danny wished he could sense his own pret, and see himself truly. But that was beyond his power, and Pat had told him that it was beyond hers as well. This meant that Hermia, too, could not see her own attributes. But Danny and Pat could. Hermia was very ambitious, and so bold as to have no inhibitions at all. Strength, though—she had little. Not enough to control her impulses, not enough strength to wait before acting.

This was not a promising combination: vast ambition, utter fearlessness, and a nearly complete lack of self-control. Pat and Danny had discussed this more than once. Danny refused to believe that human character could really be reduced to these three attributes, and Pat was inclined to agree—"too reductionist," she said—and yet neither of them could detect any other attributes in the pret of any person's inself or outself. "Just because we can't see more doesn't mean they aren't there," said Danny.

"And surely the experiences we have in life can shape our character and change it," said Pat.

"Or maybe not," said Danny. "People think that heredity is everything, but we see people overcome both heredity and environment all the time, while others with every advantage collapse into a puddle of ruin at the first challenge. We haven't been able to see and judge prets for long enough to know if *they* can change."

"Maybe when we have children," said Pat.

But Danny didn't know if they even *should* have children. They couldn't pretend not to know what they would know about their children's prets. About their deep inner character. About the part of them that quite possibly could not change.

Hermia, however, was not their child. She was an erstwhile friend who had proven herself utterly unreliable. Not for the first time Danny wished that he could have discussed Hermia with the Gate Thief, especially now that they had conversed together for a while. But Danny could not go to Westil to talk to Wad without bringing Set there, or exhausting himself by making another clant. And Wad could not come to Mittlegard without making a Great Gate, which he *would* not do—especially because Hermia would know he had done it, and then could not be stopped from taking people to the Great Gate and passing them through it.

The Greek girl has us both stymied. So I have to deal with her on my own. I just don't know how I *can* deal with her, or what "dealing with her" would even look like.

"You're not going to forestall me?" asked Hermia. "Gate me somewhere?"

"You'd just come back," said Danny.

"You're learning," said Hermia.

"No," said Pat. "*You* learned this from *us*."

"It's not as if you invented it," said Hermia. "I'm not violating some patent. You died and came back knowing stuff, and I learned it because I'm a gatemage and I could tell more about what was and wasn't happening. Give me credit here, Pa-*tree*-cee-ah. I *took* this from you, you didn't give it."

Danny didn't even bother looking at Pat, and his peripheral vision told him that Pat didn't look away from Hermia, either.

"Whatever you're going to do," said Danny, "just do it."

"No, *don't!*" cried Xena. "I mean, for pete's sake, how inconsiderate *are* you! We don't want any wizard war while we're *right here*."

"*I* do," said Wheeler.

"No you don't," said Hal.

"Buy the tickets for all of you," said Danny, "and hang on to the change or use it to buy food. Pat and I will be in when we can."

"If," said Xena.

"Move," said Pat, giving Xena a little push.

Hermia was laughing, and not nicely, as Danny's friends walked briskly away.

"Glad to provide you with amusement," said Danny.

"You should have let them stay. Remember, I'm the one who told them what you are and explained everything. I'm part of your group whether you like it or not."

"Not," said Pat softly.

"Maybe you'll like me better when we're done here," said Hermia. "Because I'm here to relieve you of a burden you aren't really qualified to bear."

"Me?" asked Pat.

"You?" asked Hermia, looking annoyed. "What, are you pregnant? If you are, then I'm not relieving anything. No, I'm talking about what Danny's got inside *him*."

"No," said Danny. "Don't do it. I don't think you *can*, but don't even try, because believe me, *you're* the one who isn't ready."

"*I'm* qualified because I'm the only one who's got any perspective. You've picked up Loki's absolute horror of letting Set get to Westil, but—"

"Look at her Sutahites," said Pat. "Not a cloud outside of her, they're riding inside, as if they were her gates."

"I don't have gates," said Hermia. "You took them."

"Inside her hoard," said Danny. "So many."

"Do you think they've possessed her?" asked Pat. "Do you think she's making her own choices?"

"I know she is," said Danny. "Her mind is made up. She has no idea of what she's doing, but she also doesn't care about the consequences, because all that matters to Hermia is that she's hungry to prove that she's greater than I am."

"I don't have to *prove* that," said Hermia. "The real question is, am I greater than Loki?"

"The one thing you don't understand," said Danny, "is that you're not greater than Set."

"Gate away, Danny," said Pat.

"She can follow me anywhere," said Danny. "I can't hide from her."

"Exactly," said Hermia.

"So do the insane thing you came here to do," said Danny, "and *then* I'll decide how to respond."

Hermia smiled. "I didn't come here for you, so I don't care how you respond, Danny North. Once you were the most important thing that ever happened in my life. But now that place has been taken by someone else."

Danny said nothing.

"Set," Hermia said, her voice turning oddly seductive. Who feels the need to seduce Satan? "I invite you into *me*. I can do anything Danny North can do. You can leave him behind and really accomplish something with me. Come into me, Set."

What Hermia didn't realize was that Set made the jump the moment she first invited him. But Danny could see that it took Set awhile to find his way into Hermia's body. He had learned something from the new skills Danny had acquired in Duat. Set rooted more deeply in her than he ever had in Danny.

Hermia fell silent, her face looking a little surprised, then vacant, then exultant.

"Should I kill your little friend again?" asked Hermia—but Danny knew it was Set speaking now.

"You can't," said Danny.

"Why can't I?" asked Hermia.

"Because I forbid it."

Hermia's hand flashed out, holding a handgun that Danny had not realized she carried in her purse.

And then the handgun was gone. Pat must have moved it.

"Really," said Pat. "Is that all you've got?"

Hermia looked at her savagely, then at Danny with complete loathing. "Do you want to know what hell is? Being trapped inside somebody as weak and stupid and . . . *nice* as you."

"Thanks," said Danny. "I won't say I'll miss you."

"Oh, you will," said Hermia. "Why haven't you tried to kill me yet? Gate me inside the sun? Loki tried that. An inconvenience, a delay."

"It's all right for you to kill Hermia," said Pat. "She asked for it."

"I don't kill people just because they ask for it," said Danny. "And it wouldn't work."

"Do you know what else won't work?" asked Hermia. "Trying to keep me from going to Westil."

"Nobody's keeping you from anything," said Pat.

But Danny *was* doing something. It was what Pat said, about the Sutahites being inside Hermia like gates. Danny reached out, the way he had when the Gate Thief first tried to take his gates, and ate Hermia's Sutahites.

And just like that, he had them locked inside himself.

But the Sutahites were not Hermia's, never *hers*. They always belonged to Set. They had followed him out of Duat, the way that near-human prets followed the strongest prets, becoming their ba, giving them the powers that would turn into magery.

So when Danny ate Hermia's Sutahites, it was Set who reeled at the sensation. Nobody had ever done anything like that to him, Danny knew.

In his alarm, Set did something by reflex: He polled his ba. He enumerated his Sutahites, called to them, kindled them, woke them.

Even though they were scattered over the surface of the Earth, accompanying billions of people, every one of them became clear to Danny North, not by number, but by location.

And he ate them all.

It felt strangely familiar, to have tens of billions of Sutahites inside him, completely contained in his hearthoard. It took Danny a moment, but he realized: Ever since he had given all his gates to Wad, and then returned all the imprisoned gates to themselves, Danny had felt empty. And now he was full again.

Well, half full.

I had more gates in me than Set has Sutahites, thought Danny. How is that even possible?

Or his Sutahites are somehow smaller than my gates were, so they take up less space.

These were fleeting thoughts, and Danny had no time to pursue the answers because Hermia's face now wore a look of complete panic. "What have you done?" she asked.

"Played a little Hungry Hungry Hippos with you," said Danny. "I win."

"You won *nothing*!" shouted Hermia. "Nothing!" And then, very quietly: "Nothing."

It seemed to Danny that the last "nothing" referred to what Set had left. Instead of possessing the body of a gatemage and using it to carry half his Sutahites to Westil, he had no Sutahites. They were gone.

They were his kingdom. His body, his *self*. He could reach out with them, influence people, and he did. They were his wings, his eyes, his ears, his voice whispering into the ears of everybody all at once, and now he's blind, deaf, mute, wing-broken. He has Hermia. And nothing else.

Hermia's hands lashed out, but whatever Set meant to do— jab his eyes out? slash his cheeks? throttle him?—Danny would never know, because he was suddenly thirty feet away. He hadn't done it—Pat had.

"Really, Danny," she said, "letting her slash you was just *too* nice."

Hermia knew where they were, of course, and a moment later she had gated in front of them. "I think I'll go to Westil," she said.

"Go," said Pat. "You'll be the only passenger."

Danny waited until Hermia disappeared. "Please stay here and get the others home," he said to Pat. Then he leapt directly to Loki. The Gate Thief needed to be warned what was happening.

He also needed to help Danny figure out what to do.

18

Wad was with Queen Bexoi when Danny came to tell him the news.

"So you didn't have him under control after all," said Wad.

"I never claimed that I did," said Danny mildly. "I invited him to stay, and he stayed. She invited him to go, and he went."

"I already thought she was dangerous," said Wad.

"My question is, how dangerous is Set?" asked Danny. "No matter how evil somebody is, how much damage can they do without a lot of followers doing what they command?"

"He'll have no trouble gathering followers," said Wad, thinking about Queen Bexoi, who had managed to find minions to do her work. Including Wad himself, when he was besotted with love and admiration for her, when he had put his gatemaking abilities at her disposal.

Then Danny explained what he had done to the Sutahites.

Wad looked at Danny and shook his head. "You still don't have any gates."

"I said it was *like* eating gates," said Danny. "That doesn't turn them into gates."

"I can't see anything like that," said Wad.

"You couldn't see Set himself, either," said Danny.

"And you can."

"More easily and clearly now that he's inside Hermia," said Danny.

"Not shaped like a man. More like a flyspeck."

"Less than a flyspeck. A geometric point. No dimension to him. Just location, persistence across time, the ability to move."

Wad watched as Danny got a momentary faraway look.

"He's never been human, so it's hard to evaluate his character. But he seems to be a creature of pure ambition. Fearless and strong, without a scrap of empathy."

"Sounds like a gatemage," said Wad ruefully.

"But we're funny," said Danny.

"Not very," said Wad. "Not lately."

"I think Hermia poses less danger than she would have, before I took the Sutahites."

"How long will you live?" asked Wad. The boy was still so young; he didn't think things through.

"Oh," said Danny. "Of course. When I die, the Sutahites will be released. So even if Set doesn't have them now, he will."

"And don't imagine that it will help if you climb inside a tree," said Wad. "That only postpones the day."

"A lot can happen in fifteen hundred years," said Danny. "More to the point, a lot can *not* happen."

"We need a permanent solution."

"Set and the Sutahites have never been alive," said Danny. "So they can't exactly die."

"They don't have bodies that can die," said Wad. "But that doesn't mean they can't be destroyed."

"Prets can't be extinguished," said Danny.

"And you know that because?"

"Because that's what I was told in Duat," said Danny.

"And everything you learned there is absolute truth," said Wad.

"If you had been there," said Danny.

"I'd believe everything?" said Wad. "Quite probably. All that means is that liars can do a better job of deceiving people when they're physically present."

"There was no lying in Duat," said Danny. "There was no *language*."

Wad didn't answer.

"All right," said Danny, "I know you can deceive without language, but what I got there, it was pure knowledge. It wasn't *told*, it just *was*."

There was no way for Wad to dispute the point. And it might even be true. "There's plenty of lying *here*," said Wad.

"You have to pick something to believe or you could never *do* anything," said Danny.

Wad could only agree, though he remembered how he had loved Bexoi and trusted her, doing her will in everything. Well, up to a point. When Bexoi commanded him to kill Anonoei and her sons, Wad had kept them alive and lied to her about it. *That* was when he stopped loving her. When she murdered Wad's son Trick, that was when he began to hate her.

"Maybe it's time for you to go back to Duat and find out how to solve this," said Wad. "With all that pure knowledge lying about, maybe you could pick up something we can use to keep the Sutahites imprisoned even after you die. Or, you know, oblit-erate Set from the universe."

"I've thought about this a lot," said Danny. "How much of the evil in the world comes from Set, and how much comes from human nature. I mean, chimps are violent. Alpha males *own* the females. The other males kidnap females and carry them off and rape them repeatedly. They make war, they commit genocide. They can't hack into computer systems or build nuclear weapons, but they do a lot of really terrible things, without Set or the Suta-hites goading them."

Wad had to think hard to imagine what a "chimp" might be.

It was as if Danny were reading his mind. "Chimpanzees. A kind of ape. The one that's genetically closest to human beings. Next time you're in Mittlegard, visit a zoo."

"Or I'll read a book," said Wad. "Great invention, books. Paper—amazing stuff. Why couldn't Hermia have brought *paper-making* to Westil?"

"Maybe she will. Dangerous and terrible ideas spread better with widespread literacy," said Danny. "Along with the good ones, of course."

"I think your original point was that people are terrible whether Set's around or not."

"They *can* be terrible," said Danny. "They can also be good."

"Does Set stop them from being good?"

"Only the person he's possessing."

"When Set was first inside you, he completely controlled your body, right?" asked Wad.

"That's how it felt. I felt like I couldn't do anything. *Now* I know that I had the power to take back control at any time. But it took a level of self-awareness—*physical* self-awareness—that I had never had."

"Is this part of your ability to sense prets and Sutahites?"

"Sort of," said Danny. "I'm still finding out what I can actually sense, what I can do, what any of it means."

"But you were able to regain control of your body with Set still inside you. Can Hermia?"

Danny shook his head. "She didn't try to learn anything from Pat and me except how to travel instantly without gates."

"How's she doing with that?" asked Wad. "What are her limitations?"

"She can go, she can return, and she can carry whatever she's touching that she wants to bring along."

"So, people and those dragon things," said Wad, "but only if she's touching them."

"So far," said Danny. "Trying to figure out how much damage Set can do?"

"I need to know the limitations on what he can get Hermia to do," said Wad. "And the limitations on what I can do to Hermia."

"Killing her wouldn't kill Set," said Danny.

"But killing her would deprive him of her set of abilities," said Wad. "Who else can do these things?"

"When Pat separated the boys, they both saw and understood. I think they can do it. And when I helped Anonoei get possession of Bexoi's body—she can do it."

"I know," said Wad. "Not sure how dangerous that makes her—I don't trust my ability to judge people anymore. Least of all women. But the boys. They're young. They're vulnerable."

"Enopp seems to be the one who learned the most," said Danny. "But maybe I only think that because he's also the talker. Who can guess what Eluik knows and what he can do?"

"So if Hermia dies," said Wad, "Set will want to jump to you, to Pat, to Anonoei, Enopp, or Eluik."

"Or you," said Danny.

"Who, me?" Wad chuckled. "I'm just an ordinary Gatefather."

"He won't jump to *me*," said Danny. "I proved I could shut him down."

That was the pertinent skill. "Can you teach me how to do that?"

"I can try," said Danny. He seemed hesitant.

"But . . . do you want to?" asked Wad, amused. "After all, I'm the terrible Gate Thief. How can you trust me with so much power?"

"It's not that," said Danny. "It's . . . When I taught Anonoei, I had to take possession of Bexoi's body first, to get rid of Bexoi's ka and to show Anonoei how to go deep."

"You don't want to take possession of me?"

"It wasn't Anonoei's original body," said Danny. "She knew how to ride inside someone else. She's a manmage. But you—what if I go deep and it drives you out like it did with Bexoi, only you can't come back? What if it kills you?"

"Sweet of you to care," said Wad. "But I don't expect to live forever."

"You've come closer than most," said Danny.

"Only a few centuries from two thousand years," said Wad. "That's still a long way from forever."

"Like I said, closer than most."

Wad shook his head. "I would risk my life to learn it, but you won't risk killing me to teach it. I understand the choice. For now. And I thank you for warning me."

"I'd rather not kill Hermia," said Danny.

"We differ on that," said Wad. "But since neither of us knows how to kill her, and neither of us wants to see what Set would do after she died, we will both do nothing for now. Am I right?"

"Not nothing," said Danny. "Just . . . nothing about Hermia."

"And I won't do *nothing*, either," said Wad. "I'm going to make sure Hermia can't bring her dragons to Westil."

"Helicopters. My parents' augmented versions. In Mittlegard, they give one side an advantage. Not an overwhelming one, but not trivial. Here, though, they're unstoppable."

"I'm not sure," said Wad. "The explosions are impressive. And dangerous. But how well could a flying ship do against a tornado raised by a Galebreath?"

"Is that what Ced turned out to be?"

"Maybe a Tempester. His teacher isn't sure, and I'm not surprised, since he's a treemage."

"Whatever you do to the helicopters and tanks and whatever else Hermia and my parents decide to bring, please remember that the pilots and crews are drowthers who volunteered for a war to defend an ally from attack. They don't know anything about what's happening here. They *do* know that my parents have terrifying power. So they obey. But they don't deserve to be killed for it."

"They're soldiers," said Wad. "I'm trying to decipher your moral quibble."

"They didn't choose to fire their weapons against Westilians armed with spears or arrows," said Danny.

"Nor against mages armed with wind or sand or whatever else I'm able to raise against them?"

"All I'm asking is that you gate them back to Mittlegard, or gate the men out of the choppers before you put them into a mountain or deep in the ocean."

"I hear your request," said Wad, "and I admire your virtue. But I'm not going to make a Great Gate, so I can't send them back to Mittlegard."

"Then put them somewhere harmless here, and I'll come fetch them back," said Danny.

"I will if I can. But wherever I put them, Hermia will find them."

"Put them in the middle of a windstorm so severe that even

my parents can't make them fly. Or a sandstorm that disables the tanks. Or whatever."

"So much trouble to protect the lives of soldiers who signed on to risk their lives."

"Soldiers being coerced into the wrong war," said Danny. "This isn't a quibble. Don't make me go to war on their side."

Wad shook his head. "Danny. Can't you tell when someone is agreeing with you?"

"Can't you stop playing devil's advocate long enough to simply say, 'Yes, Danny, I'll do my best not to let any of these men from Mittlegard die'? "

"I did say that," said Wad. "Now go away, so I can find Hermia and see what she and Set are doing."

"How will you find her?" asked Danny. "You can't sense her ka the way I can."

"But I don't find her the way you do," said Wad. "I find her because she's a gatemage and I have her gates. Only a few, but I found them in the hearthoard you gave to me. So whenever she comes to Westil, those gates reach for her, and I know where she is."

"She knows where you are, too," said Danny, "and not through her gates."

"Come back and teach me to do what you do," said Wad.

"Let's see," said Danny. "You have all my gates, and even though you know Set can't get anything from me, you haven't returned them to me."

"I like having so many billions of gates in my hoard," said Wad. "Why should you have all the glory?"

"I'm only wondering why I should teach you anything, when you still hold my gates as hostages."

"If I give them back," said Wad, "you'll make a Great Gate again."

"I might," said Danny, "but so what? I'd do it to help the mages of Westil strike some kind of balance with the augmented mages of Mittlegard. To restore balance."

"There's never any balance," said Wad.

"Set is already on Westil," said Danny, "and I have the Suta-hites. One of the things you were trying to prevent has happened. The other can't happen while I'm alive. But go ahead, Gate Thief, keep my gates. You can't possibly trust me to use my own gates wisely."

Wad hated it when his opponent had logic and fairness on his side, and all Wad had was a deep reluctance to comply. "Don't be snippy with me, boy," said Wad. "I'm probably your ancestor."

"Statistically speaking, after fifteen hundred years you're probably everybody's ancestor."

Then Danny was gone. Back on Mittlegard.

What if he's right? Is there really any point in keeping the worlds separate now? Why not break down all the barriers?

Would that make Westil a colony of Mittlegard, with its huge business empires and amazing machines? Or would Mittlegard be divided into the fiefdoms of a thousand godlike Mithermages, passing back and forth through Great Gates?

Probably both, thought Wad. Whatever happened, it would destroy whatever they now were. There were plenty of evils among the drowthers and mages of both worlds. But also much good, especially in the lives of the drowthers—good that would never survive easy passage between the worlds. Nobody would really gain anything worth having, while the drowthers everywhere would lose.

That's why I put myself into a tree, thought Wad. The war isn't over, just because we lost. Because Danny North ate the Suta-hites somehow. And maybe we can find a way to extinguish the Belgod Set.

19

With everyone calling her by Bexoi's titles instead of her name, Anonoei was beginning to believe that she really was King Prayard's consort, and not an interloper. It only became painful when she and Prayard were alone, because he always called her Bexoi, the name of her supplanter, the name of her murderer.

Eventually I'll get used to that, too. Eventually I'll stop wishing that Prayard could be with me now as he used to be—playful, tender, not so *respectful*. Doesn't he ever miss the way *we* were together? Is he really happier being the man he is with her?

But not *her*, not anymore. Bexoi is *me* now.

So why does it feel as if he is being unfaithful to me by being with . . . me?

Give it time, Anonoei.

Or rather, give it time, *Bexoi*. Because the real difference will come when you stop thinking of yourself as Anonoei and really believe that you *are* Bexoi. Not the vile monster that she was, but the Bexoi of today.

Anonoei was sitting in the nursery, letting baby Jib suck his little brains out. Greedy child, far more than Eluik or Enopp, who both seemed so eager to be weaned. Though that was later, not at the start. Yet they grew impatient with the breast long before they had upper and lower teeth. Fitful, rooting for something better, but finding nothing else.

What would the boys have become, if I had been Prayard's wife all along, if they had been raised as princes, as heirs? Their insatiable curiosity, their searching . . .

No. I'm thinking of them as if they were both the *same*, and they never were. Those months in prison, unable to see them. And then the way they were locked together—of course I thought of them as one boy, because only Enopp's voice could be heard, only Enopp's personality could be expressed.

And then, as if her thoughts of the boys had drawn them, there they were, standing near the window. Not a dream, not a wish— these were the real boys. Anonoei's first thought was that Wad had gated them here. But no, they had learned how to move by themselves, when Danny North's girlfriend—Pat?—had helped them separate.

She couldn't converse with them here, in front of the women. They mustn't even be noticed. Anonoei gated into one of the cul-de-sac rooms that Wad had shown her, accidental spaces created by the architects when interior rooms couldn't be reconciled with exterior walls. In moments, the boys were with her, and now they were completely alone.

"Let me go back and dismiss the women before they notice that I'm gone," said Anonoei.

"Glad to see you, too, Mother," said Enopp.

"Mittlegard television has made you disrespectful," said Anonoei.

"I think the word you're searching for is 'snotty,' " said Eluik. "And he's always been that way."

Anonoei smiled and shook her head. It took only a moment to reappear where she had been nursing moments before. The women attending her hadn't even noticed she was gone. "Ladies, I need to be alone for a while. Please go."

The women graciously arose and left the room. Then Anonoei gated back to the doorless room where her sons were waiting.

"I'm glad to see you," said Anonoei. "Always. And this is your brother, Jib. That's just his temporary name, until we can work out something dynastic."

Enopp gave the baby a tiny wave. Enopp's eyes never left Anonoei's face.

"I'm assuming," said Anonoei, "that something is wrong."

"The monster has left Danny North and now it's in Hermia," said Enopp. "She can't control it at all, so it's controlling *her*. What are you going to do about it?"

Anonoei had no answer. She realized that the baby was getting frustrated because her left breast was apparently near empty. Anonoei changed sides as she thought about Enopp's question. "I'm trying to think why *you* think I'm going to do anything at all. Do you think Set is susceptible to my poor powers as a manmage?"

"The way Pat separated us," said Eluik. "Can't you get Set out of Hermia?"

"I suppose I might—exactly the way Hermia got Set out of Danny."

"No, don't let him into *you*," said Enopp.

"Nobody *expels* Set, you just offer him a new place to live," said Anonoei. "And the less I see of Hermia, the better."

"You lived inside somebody," said Eluik. "Helpless to make the body do what you wanted."

"And Enopp was inside *you*, Eluik, and neither of you realized that was what was happening. So why aren't *you* the experts?"

Eluik shook his head. "We're *children*. We don't just *solve* problems that have adults stymied."

"We know that killing Hermia won't do any good," said Enopp. "Set would only jump to somebody else."

"That's the advantage I had," said Anonoei. *I was the man-mage, the visitor. But Hermia's the host, and she can't leave her own flesh. Set's got control. So help* her *get control. You did it, help* her *do it.* "Bexoi was ready to die," said Anonoei aloud. "And still, expelling her was something I couldn't do on my own."

"You can still help Hermia get control of her body," said Eluik. "Can't you? Show her how?"

"It's not that easy," said Anonoei.

"But it is," said Enopp. "Pat showed us what to do, and now we know how."

"Then you show Hermia."

"Earlier point again," said Enopp. "I'm a child."

"Showing Hermia is the same as showing Set," said Eluik.

"Yes—one is as useless as the other," said Anonoei. "You saw and you learned because it was being done to you. Inside your own bodies. But Wad watched Danny North liberate me, he saw as much as Hermia ever did, and he learned nothing. He still needs to make gates in order to go anywhere."

"Or that's what he lets you think," said Eluik.

"You two and I were able to learn much, because we *had* to cooperate for Danny or Pat to set us free. And Pat and Danny learned what they learned because they were *dead*, an option that I don't think is available to us, because I don't think Hell will let us come back again."

"They call it Duat," said Enopp.

"And I call it Hell," said Anonoei, "because that's what it would be for *us*."

"You don't think we should do anything," said Eluik.

"I think you should return to Mittlegard and never come back here. Just because you *can* do a thing doesn't mean it's wise to do it."

"Maybe between the two of us," said Enopp, "we could control Set."

"Get that stupid thought out of your head," said Anonoei. "Hermia had ten times the experience and training that you've had, and is she free?"

"We don't know," said Eluik. "Because we don't know to what degree she consents to the things Set is making her do."

The boy was subtle beyond his years, Anonoei was pleased to see. He must get that from me, she thought. I've never seen much subtlety in Prayard. Though that may mean that he's *so* subtle I never detected it.

"If she has become Set's willing partner," said Anonoei, "that's all the more reason he won't come out of her to dwell in you. And which of you would he choose, do you think? The one who spent years being inhabited by another boy's inself?"

"Seems likely," said Eluik.

"Or the one evil and stupid enough to do it?" asked Enopp.

"Neither evil nor stupid," said Anonoei. "Naive and inexperienced, that's what you were, Enopp, and you had no idea what was actually going on."

"I could sense all of Eluik's thoughts. I believed that meant he was inside me."

"Go back to that farmhouse in . . . Ohio, was it?"

"Kentucky, now," said Enopp. "It's another state."

"We're not supposed to say it aloud," said Eluik.

"Mother already knows," said Enopp.

"We're never to call her 'mother,' " said Eluik.

"Nobody can hear me but Mother and you," said Enopp.

"As far as you know," said Eluik. "Are you sure you can always tell when a gatemage is listening in?"

This had gone on long enough. "Boys, I miss you terribly and I'm glad to see you're well. But you must go home."

"It won't be home till you're there," said Eluik.

"I can't," said Anonoei. "I'm the queen here now."

"So what?" said Enopp. "If you went back to Mittlegard, it's not like they could send bloodhounds to track you down and bring you back."

"Are you sure you want me like this?" Anonoei gestured to include Bexoi's face and body.

"Oh, definitely," said Enopp. "Women in America pay a fortune to get a face and body like that."

"So you think I'm prettier in this body than I was in mine?"

"It's a trap," said Eluik to Enopp. "Don't answer."

"We want you with us, Mother," said Enopp. "I'm not done growing up yet."

"I am," said Eluik. "Childhood was brutal. I'm glad it's over."

Anonoei had to laugh. "Perhaps it is. Go back and wait for me. When I can, I'll come to you."

Jib gave a cough, and Anonoei looked down to see if the baby was throwing up or simply hungry. When she looked up again a moment later, the boys were gone.

Were those the only choices? Either kill the person possessed by Set in a way that wouldn't allow him to escape, or simply accept that Set could not be stopped?

And there *was* no way that wouldn't allow Set a chance to jump to someone else's body. Especially not now, when he had had multiple chances to see this new kind of travel in action.

Why do I care? Anonoei asked herself. Set has nothing to do with me. My monster was Bexoi and she's gone. I'm now married to a man I love. I still have both my sons, and a decent hope of being able to spend time with them once all these struggles are over. I'm in the midst of my own happy ending, even if it is a little complicated. Let the gatemages sort out the messes they made. I'm busy cleaning up my own messes, thanks.

Yet even as she reached this conclusion, she despised herself for thinking that way. I owe everything to Danny North, she admitted. And what if I, having pushed one person out of her own body, am the only one who can push Set out of Hermia's meat puppet?

We'll see. No need for panic yet.

20

Danny sat on the bench that the Diamonds had placed near a shingle oak—a species that Colonel Diamond explained "has such small acorns most people don't realize it's an oak at all. We've got the only two known examples in this part of Kentucky."

They named almost every spot on the whole farm by the tree or trees that mattered to them. Their favorite was a chinkapin oak that dominated one hillside, but here on the shingle oak bench he and Pat had a good chance of not being interrupted.

"I don't think This One sent us back to Mittlegard so that you could die," said Pat.

"I'm already cheating death by being here, so . . . if I die, I die."

"Easy for you to say," said Pat.

"Why do you think it's easy?"

"Because you're an idiot," she said. "*I* was the one who was murdered, remember? I was the one who died. You just bound yourself to me and followed. You were my passenger. *I'm* the one who cheated death, and guess what, if *I* die, I think that sucks. Because I want to live a *life*, complete with husband, babies, grand-children, the whole shebang. And since you got sent back here with me, I think we're supposed to do that together. We've done death, so now let's do life."

"And when it's over, I release these Sutahites back into the world."

"Danny, have you noticed a sudden blossoming of kindness and goodness in the world since you gathered them in? Have wars stopped? No more terrorism? No more slaughtering people who have a different religion? No more hating?"

"It takes time for people to overcome longtime habits of thought," said Danny.

"The Sutahites prompted people to act, but some people don't need prompting," said Pat. "It will take time for the decrease in bad actions to show up as some kind of statistical blip. Maybe it'll be big. What if it cuts crime in half? There's a shitload of crime, Danny. What's half a shitload?"

"Not sure it's a unit of measure."

"It's good to keep the Sutahites locked up. But Danny . . . they're still bound to Set. They're still *his*, the way your gates are still yours, even though you gave them to Loki. They don't fight him, they obey him, but only because *you* commanded them to. They're yours. And the Sutahites are Set's."

Danny thought about that. "Are they?" he asked.

"He commanded them, they supported him. Danny, I'm sure they got Laurette and Sin and Xena to act on their insane lust for you. That was a coordinated assault. Yes, they're tied to Set."

"Oh, yes, you're right, but I'm just . . . thinking here. Our ba gets tied to us when our ka goes into the body and bonds with it.

When we leave Duat to be born, the prets of our ba, they're the clouds of glory that we're trailing when we come."

"I should never have gotten you to read Wordsworth."

"*Re*read. I had already read 'Intimations of Immortality' during my home schooling."

Danny quoted:

> *Waters on a starry night*
> *Are beautiful and fair;*
> *The sunshine is a glorious birth;*
> *But yet I know, where'er I go,*
> *That there hath pass'd away a glory from the earth.*

"I thought when we read it together," said Pat, "it was the first time."

"It was the first time I read it when I was in love," said Danny. "The first time I read it with you. The first time I had some inkling of why it mattered."

She nestled against him. Danny noticed how uncomfortable the bench was, and yet he didn't want to leave it. Ever.

"Set wasn't born," said Danny. "He wasn't trailing clouds of glory. He was thrown out. Evicted. Ejected. And the Sutahites went with him. Or maybe they were also tossed. But none of them ever formed the kind of bond that we have. With a body. Between inself and outself. Are the Sutahites really part of Set's *self*? I don't think there's room in his ego to include anybody else. They obey him, because what else is there to do? But does that mean they're *bound* to him?"

"What are you thinking?" said Pat. "That you can uncouple them from him? Like peeling cars from a locomotive in a train-yard? They've been together for thousands of years, Danny."

"Some people become friends because there's nobody else.

They go along just so they can feel like they're part of something larger than themselves."

"Wheeler," said Pat.

"Yes," said Danny. "I think there's more to him than meets the eye, but yes. The group tolerates him because you all know he's got nowhere else to go, nobody else to eat lunch with or hang out with."

"Pity?"

"He's useful," said Danny. "He may complain and slow everybody down, but it's more fun because he's there."

"I'm not sure that idea would survive a poll of the group," said Pat.

"I don't care what everybody *thinks* they think of Wheeler. He's part of the group. The bond is real. But it's also breakable. Even if the group has been together a thousand years, it's not like the bond between ka and ba. He can walk away. He can join another group."

"So you think you can get the Sutahites to . . . change teams?"

"I've done that, or at least I've taken them off Set's team. For a while. No, I'm talking about something more. They followed Set because they had nowhere else to go. They weren't *tied* to anything. They weren't part of anything, not even a molecule, an atom. Nothing. Alone. But what if I offered them a place? A bond?"

"How could you trust them?" asked Pat. "They've spent thousands of years trying to disrupt people's lives, make everything worse and everybody unhappy. And you want to invite them *in*?"

"Exactly," said Danny. "Instead of holding them as captives, offer them what Set never could: a bond with a living person. And not just a bond like the cells of my skin are bonded to me. They'd be important, part of my power, my magery. They'd become part of my ba."

"You realize that means they'd become *gates*?"

"I'm a gatemage. That's what the prets of my ba *do*."

"You've already made a Wild Gate."

"It was wild because they were part of the ba of another mage, a dead one. They were lost, angry, frustrated. They'd been captives for centuries."

"And they weren't part of your actual ba," said Pat.

"I don't know if this *can* happen," said Danny. "In the natural order of things, this is a bond that happens when a pret leaves Duat to be born. That was a long time ago for me."

"Seventeen years," said Pat.

"That could be a quarter of my life. No less than a fifth. That's late in the process. I already walk and talk and feed myself. So maybe Thoth will allow it, and maybe he won't."

"Thoth?" asked Pat.

"I can't just keep calling him 'This One,'" said Danny. "We got the name of Duat from Egyptian lore, along with 'ka' and 'ba.' And Thoth is the Egyptian god who best fits what This One seems to do."

Pat was already reading from the Wikipedia listing on her phone. "'Thoth played many vital and prominent roles in Egyptian mythology, such as *maintaining the universe*'—OK, that fits— stuff about Ra's boat, yadda yadda, 'the arbitration of godly disputes, the arts of magic, the system of writing, the development of science, and the judgment of the dead.' OK, yes, if the name fits . . ."

"The Sutahites aren't dead, because they never lived. They're still unborn. *Pre*born. So while Thoth is busy maintaining the universe, maybe he'll allow a late birth-bonding between the Sutahites and a living human ka."

"You," said Pat.

"If they're attracted to strength," said Danny, "I must have been strong because I came here with a lot of gates."

"Big-time clouds of glory," said Pat.

"But why should they only have one choice? My way or the highway? Why not you, if they feel like it? Or . . . Veevee. Or Eluik and Enopp. Anonoei."

"The people who are aware of their prets."

"Loki too," said Danny. "He saw what I did with Anonoei and Bexoi. He knows, he just hasn't tried to do it."

"Do what?"

"Live as a pret. Move from place to place, and trust our body and anything attached to us to come along. That's not the only power we have."

"Maybe we have the power to invite free prets and bond with them."

"Yes," said Danny. "Except . . . I think it's wrong to call the Sutahites 'free prets.' Because that suggests the others, the ones that are already in our ba, or in our bodies, or in the natural universe—that *they* aren't free."

"They're bound. Bond and free—always treated as opposites," said Pat.

"But that's about slavery. About people, not prets. Look, a pret that's part of the natural universe—a blade of grass. Part of a rock. Those prets have a place, they have a *job*. They're *something*. The Sutahites aren't part of anything. As far as the universe is concerned, they're nothing. Utterly powerless to *act*."

"It's not like a pret that's part of a rock is particularly powerful," said Pat.

"Yes, it is," said Danny. "It has work to do. When gravity calls, and nothing blocks it, it rushes toward the center of the Earth. Joined with all the other prets in the rock. They move together. Somebody throws the rock, it hits a jackal, and the prets of the rock all interact with the prets of the jackal's skin and skull and brain according to the rules. Together, the prets of that rock can be powerful. They can kill a jackal."

"If somebody throws the rock," said Pat.

"Right. And the prets in my ba can become gates, taking people from one place to another, from one world to another— but somebody has to make them into a gate. Me. They only do it when I command it. The way my hand only touches yours when I want it to." He demonstrated.

She kissed his hand.

"So you're thinking, they'd rather be a part of your ba than continue to be unattached. And that will make them nice."

"The only thing *like* a bond that gave them any purpose in life was obeying Set. Were they evil? I don't think so. Maybe they were, but what would the second most evil pret in Duat have done when Set was expelled? Does he *follow* Set into exile? Or does he figure, OK, Set just proved that rebellion doesn't work. So I'll play along, I'll be born, I'll have a body, I'll have whatever powers come with it. Maybe the second most evil was, like, Hitler. Or Stalin. Or Tamerlane. Or just some hideous child-abusing mother or father. But all the strong, ambitious, fearless ones like Set—they wouldn't follow *him*. They'd come to Mittlegard and get themselves born."

"So the Sutahites aren't ambitious enough to be evil—"

"They're the ones who saw Set as powerful, a protector, a leader. They attached to him and then found out that it didn't get them anywhere. He let them down. Thousands of years of disap-pointment. Some of them might be pissed off. But Pat, they aren't people, they aren't *part* of anybody. They're not even part of Set. They're lonely, unattached. They don't have to attach to somebody evil. They just have to attach to somebody *strong*."

"I'm not all that strong," said Pat.

"You can't see your own pret," said Danny. "You're strong enough. But different from me. Strong in a different way. So are the others. If we *all* invite Sutahites to join us, and *if* Thoth allows bonds to form, then they become part of the ba of a Mithermage, and *we* get stronger. For all I know, that's exactly what happens when a mage passes through a Great Gate—maybe as we leap from one spot in the universe to another, we pass through the unorganized place where prets come from. Maybe prets attach themselves to our ba as we go."

"And maybe not."

"Somehow we get stronger," said Danny. "But I don't think we can invite them to join us so *we* can gather more power. I think we have to offer them a place. A promise that we'll use them wisely and well. Remember how Bexoi's body rejected her? The prets of her body hated what she had used them to do."

"And when Enopp's ka left Eluik, and Enopp was going to leave his body behind and *die*," said Pat, "Eluik's body called to him. Not with a voice or anything, but it was a call. A hunger. An invitation. That's what you want us to do. Give that invitation to the Sutahites."

"And maybe none of them come," said Danny. "Or they want to, but the bond can't form. Or maybe it *can* form, but only five or six out of all these billions actually do it."

"We'd be no worse off than we are," said Pat.

"Maybe they come and maybe they bond, only they're not completely reliable. Maybe they still want to subvert the organized universe," said Danny. "Maybe they really are as evil as Set."

"If that's what they want, I'll bet that Thoth won't let them bond to us. Because they wouldn't actually mean it, and Thoth would know."

"We're putting a lot of trust in Thoth, considering he didn't actually tell us to do this."

"We've got to do something," said Pat. "And this is better than taking Set inside yourself and then relocating to the center of the sun."

"Prets can't be destroyed by fusion and they can't be trapped by gravity. I'd die, but my pret would return to Duat. And Set is already nothing but a naked pret. So he'd just relocate back to Earth. Nothing accomplished."

"Even if we can gather up all the Sutahites," said Pat, "there's no chance *Set* would join with somebody else in a subservient role."

"Which is why I'm not inviting Hermia," said Danny.

"She'll see that we've gathered," said Pat, "and she'll show up."

"I'll deal with that when it happens," said Danny.

"Or I should say, *Set* will see that we've gathered, and *he'll* show up, wearing Hermia."

"Let's get this started and see what happens."

"You mean now? This second?"

"What will we gain by delaying?" Even as he spoke, Danny had already begun. He knew where all the others were, the ones who had become aware of the prets. He didn't use words, he just . . . wanted them to come to him. Invited them.

It'll be like this with the Sutahites, he thought. And as they each winked into existence around the bench by the shingle oak, he showed them what he meant to do. As I invited you, you can invite the Sutahites. Only not just to come near you. To come into you. To become part of you. To become part of your outself. Instruments of your will. A permanent place, as part of the power of a mage.

"Let them see what kinds of magery you do, if you know," said Danny. "Let them see what they'd be a part of."

Loki was the last to arrive. "You already *have* them," he said. "Why are you weakening your hold on them?"

"I don't have them," said Danny. "They don't have anything, and nothing has them. Unless they come to us. Look at how bright and powerful you are, Loki. See how they long to be part of you."

Then Danny realized that as he freed the Sutahites to make

their choice, he was also freeing his own ba. It only existed in Loki's hearthoard, because he had given his gates to Loki. But now some of them chose to be, not on loan to Loki, but truly part of him. Truly his.

Danny felt a stab of regret, but then he remembered what he had learned on Duat. These prets came with me freely. Not as slaves, but because they wanted to share my life forever. The prets of the ba are the highest and strongest, only just short of being human. Now I'm setting these prets free, and some of them have come to love and admire Loki. Of course they choose to stay.

Then, in a rush, all the rest of them streamed back to Danny. To his hearthoard. He hadn't taken them back from Loki. He had only given them their freedom, and they respected and affirmed their bond to Danny. They came home.

But these were the prets that had already been attuned to Danny all his life. Of course they understood his invitation and of course most of them heeded it. What were the Sutahites seeing? What sense could they make of his invitation?

He felt the first one after only a few minutes. But those minutes were long, and it was only one.

Then another. And one of the Sutahites went to Loki. And three to Pat. And five to Veevee. And ten to Anonoei and a hundred to Enopp and ten thousand to Eluik and a million to Loki this time and now ten million to Pat and billions to Danny North. He felt them gathering in his hearthoard, settling among the prets that had served him, had been a part of him since birth. Perhaps learning their work, understanding their lives by sharing memory with Danny's longtime prets.

All the Sutahites were gone. Yet none were loose in the world, and none had returned to Set. They had all been incorporated into someone's outself. And every one of the Mithermages gathered at the shingle oak was now far more powerful than if they had passed through ten Great Gates.

Is the bond real? Danny had no way of knowing, except to see what would happen.

He made a gate. Veevee opened it. Closed it. Moved it. Locked and unlocked it.

Then Veevee made a gate. For the first time in her life, she was a full-fledged Pathsister, at least, if not a Gatemother. She could make gates and make them public and they would persist in time and space. She wept.

Danny felt a momentary pang at not having included the Silvermans in this, or Stone. But then he thought of his parents and aunts and uncles, and imagined what this vast increase in power would have changed them into, and he was content that it was only this group.

"So now you have to decide how you're going to use this new part of yourself," said Danny aloud. "Because it matters to the prets how you use them. Let it be a joy to them, to be part of your life and all your actions. Not a burden or a shame."

"Thanks for saying that," said Loki. "I've now changed completely from bad to good."

"Don't be such a brat," said Anonoei. "You've always been good."

"I had odd ways of showing it," said Loki.

"Time for self-analysis later," said Danny. "All of you should go back where you were, please. Because Hermia's coming."

"How do you know?" asked Pat.

"Because I've been sending her away the instant she appeared."

"How long has that been going on?" asked Loki.

"Since I first started calling you to come to me," said Danny. "But now it's time to see what Set has to say."

"Then let us stay," said Pat.

"And give him more options of people to jump into?" asked Danny.

"We're so much stronger now," said Enopp.

"Stronger than Set?" asked Danny.

Enopp shrugged.

"Are you stronger than me?" asked Danny. "Because he *was* stronger than me. And stronger than Hermia. Please go, all of you."

"But Hermia can follow any of us."

"Set won't follow anyone but me," said Danny, "because I have nine-tenths of his kingdom inside me now, as part of myself. I'm not going to give it back. Nor are you going to give back your share. Go, please."

They all left, except Pat and Loki.

"So you think you're immune?" asked Danny.

"No," said Pat. "I just don't mind dying, if I might help you somehow."

"I do mind dying," said Loki, "but if I don't watch, I'm not sure I'll know what actually happened."

21

Hermia appeared in front of the bench almost at once. She glanced from Danny to Pat and smiled. "How judicial. The judges sit on the bench."

Danny didn't bother answering, and Pat was already skilled in saying less than she was thinking.

"I'm not causing any harm, you notice," said Hermia. "Having Set inside me hasn't changed my character at all."

Pat laughed a little.

"Set, we're not interested in hearing your lies," said Danny. "I brought you here to talk to Hermia."

"It's really just a means of transportation. Like owning a new car." Hermia sniffed. "Still has the new-car smell."

"Hermia's not struggling," said Pat. "Maybe this really is her talking."

"It isn't," said Danny. "Because I can hear her inward screaming."

"Then maybe Set sounds so much like her because he's found a compatible host," said Pat.

"Hermia was wrong and she was arrogant and she was ignorant. Now the only way to set her free is to get Set to jump to someone else."

"Is either of you volunteering?" said Hermia.

"Been there, done that," said Danny.

Hermia turned to Pat and grinned. "I really like being female better."

"You've never *been* anything at all," said Pat.

"Hermia," said Danny, "I know you can hear me, because when he ruled over me, I heard and saw everything."

"Of course I can hear you," said Hermia. "Just because you and Set didn't get along doesn't mean he and I can't hit it off."

"So I'm going to strike a bargain with you. Of course, you have no way to signal agreement in advance. You'll simply do what I suggest, or not. I'm simply going to tell you. Duat is actually a good place. It's a place of justice and mercy. It's also a place without bodies, and I won't lie to you. I missed my body when I was there. You miss hearing and speaking and seeing and touching and smelling. All the bodily functions are beautiful and precious as soon as you don't have them. Yet it's still better there than being a slave to Set."

"You know that killing me will only cause him to jump to someone else," said Hermia.

"As long as Set remains unconnected to a human body, then he hasn't yet lived, and so he can't die and return to Duat. I spent a couple of months with him in control of my body. I know exactly how boring it can be."

"Set isn't in the body of a boring teenage boy," said Hermia. "He's in *me*. He is not bored."

"*So* bored," said Danny. "Every person you've taken over, Set, is too much like all the ones before. You've committed all the crimes, you've achieved vast power and infinite fame and made millions of people miserable. What is there left for you to do in Hermia's corpse?"

Suddenly Hermia was beside Pat, reaching toward her. Just as abruptly, Danny moved her back to where he wanted her. "You've murdered before, Set."

"But never so efficiently. I really do come out of nowhere now," said Hermia.

"Hermia, you made your choice," said Danny. "I can't save you now. But you can save yourself. Not the way you hope, though it will seem that way for a moment or two. The only way to save yourself now is to save everybody."

"Oh, you think you have tricks up your sleeve, Danny," said Hermia. "But I was inside you too long. I *know* you. You can't surprise me."

"You really did help me, Hermia," said Danny. "Your help outweighs your betrayal, in my mind and heart. I think of you as my teacher and my friend. I'm truly sorry that I've lost you. If there's anything you regret, in our friendship, I forgive you and I ask your forgiveness."

"Oooh, now you're *scaring* me," said Hermia, chuckling.

Danny said no more words. He simply plunged his inself into Hermia's body and began to guide Set's ka into the flesh. Danny could feel Pat grow more alert beside him, and then her ka was with his, leading Set, pushing him.

Each deeper penetration of Set into Hermia's body displaced Hermia's own ka, and yes, there was the momentary flash of hope, as she misunderstood what Danny and Pat were doing. And then she understood.

"Hermia, I'll tell you when," murmured Danny.

Hermia shuddered. But Danny knew that it was Set shuddering, as, for the first time in his sojourn in Mittlegard, he was actually feeling something of what the body felt. Hearing with ears, breathing with lungs, seeing with eyes.

"Oh God," Hermia's voice murmured. "Oh, God, so much, all at once."

And then it was complete. Set was attached to this body as if it were his own, and Hermia was almost separated from it.

Almost, but not quite. "It will still go with you," said Danny, "even though it belongs to Set now, because whatever you're attached to travels with you."

Danny sensed the grim determination in Hermia now. And something else. Yes, he knew that aspect of the ka. Hermia was filled with love.

Then she was gone.

But Danny knew where she was. Danny was still with her, and Pat too, not possessing the body, but observing. They were at the bottom of the ocean—a few hundred miles out into the Atlantic. Instantly Hermia's body was crushed by the pressure. Drowning was out of the question; her lungs couldn't draw breath. Life functions stopped almost immediately.

Too late Set realized the trap. They had bonded him to the body, making it his own. He had consented to it, and the flood of sensations had confused and distracted him. Too late, he tried to pull away from Hermia's body, the way that Enopp had withdrawn his ka from Eluik. But by then he was too deeply connected to jump free as easily as he always had before. For a few seconds, Set had actually been alive in that body, and now it was crushed and he was dead. He had no power to jump to another body. There was only one destination he could leap to.

Hermia, too, was dead, but her ka had already been withdrawing from her body as Danny and Pat guided Set in displacing her. The choice Danny had offered her was to lose herself in order to save the world from any further interference by the monster she had so recently invited to dwell within her. Now she knew that she was not strong enough to master him. Nor could she have tricked him; that was Danny's and Pat's work. The only choice she had was to allow the death of her own body, after first surrendering it to Set. She had lost all, yet had one more act she could perform to change the world, and she did it. Instead of transporting her crushed body to a place with normal atmospheric pressure, thereby healing it, she let go of her body.

She had a choice that was not under Set's influence or control, and now she had chosen. She let her body die, and, with it, Set.

Danny had known no death but Pat's, and when she went to Duat, only he accompanied her. But Danny was not surprised that Duat sent a pret to greet Hermia. Not Thoth, the one they had thought of as This One. Yet the one who met her and traveled with her, he seemed to Danny to have the same kind of vividness and brightness that This One had possessed. Hermia responded as if she knew him at once, and for all Danny knew, they *had* known each other from some time before her birth. But now she was gone.

And so was Set. He, too, was accompanied on his journey by a bright pret, a ka sent from Duat. Yet it was clear that Set shrank from the one who greeted him. It seemed more like a prisoner being guarded than an honored traveler being welcomed home.

However they traveled, and whoever their companions were, Danny knew that the voyage would take only moments, and from

Duat there would be no return. After all these thousands of years, Set was finally dead.

Danny could feel it inside himself, not because Set had been there, but because the Sutahites who had chosen him felt their last connection with Set dissolve. He was gone from Mittlegard, and now Danny's Sutahites were Sutahites no longer. They were part of Danny, completely in his ba. They were *him*.

Pat sighed. "Oh, Danny," she whispered. "Who would have thought that the only way to end his life was to begin it."

"Now that it worked," said Danny, "it feels obvious."

"They're truly mine now," said Pat. "The prets that chose me."

"You chose them back," said Danny. "Till death do you part."

Danny called the others, and they came, and they touched each other or held each other or, in the case of Anonoei and her sons, clung and wept together.

"Now it's official," said Loki. "I'm the worst human being alive."

"Maybe," said Danny North. "But I doubt it. You haven't met Grandpa Gyish or Uncle Zog."

"Should we tell Hermia's family?" asked Pat. "She died well."

"They won't understand what she did," said Loki.

"But they'll know we honor her for it," said Pat. "That's something. And if anyone in her Family loved her, they'll want to know."

So Danny took Pat by the hand, and led her off to tell the Greeks.

22

The world should have changed. There should have been headlines, like, "People aren't thinking of doing so many rotten things." "Chances of another Hitler dropped by 40 percent." "Fewer traffic accidents caused by driver aggressiveness and road rage."

It was kind of a disappointment. "We went to a lot of trouble to save the world, and it doesn't feel saved," said Pat one day.

"Hermia died for it," said Danny.

"Hermia put herself in that situation all on her own," said Pat. "I don't miss her."

Danny already knew better than to suggest that some of Pat's hostility toward Hermia, even after her death, was misplaced jealousy. He could imagine her saying, "Oh, if not Hermia, then who is it I *should* be jealous of?" It was one of the problems with sharing his life with a really smart person. She had at least as many quick, devastating comebacks as he did.

The report to their friends at Parry McCluer was simple enough. "That entity who possessed Danny?" said Pat. "He's dead."

"Hit by a bus?" asked Sin.

"Plane crash?" asked Wheeler.

"Bored to death by possessing one of you two?" asked Hal.

"Hermia did it," said Danny.

"She was so good-looking," said Wheeler.

"Also, completely out of your league," said Laurette.

"Everybody's out of Wheeler's league," said Xena.

"Maybe, but in which direction?" said Wheeler.

"You think there are girls who are, like, *beneath* you?" asked Xena.

"Like, yes," said Wheeler, with a Groucho-like leer. "And don't ask who, or I might have to break your heart."

And that was it. Done with. Back to planning how to be bored together all summer. The Busch Gardens trip was judged to be a bust because Danny bailed. Nobody wanted to do any of the free things Danny could get them into. "The International Peace Garden in North Dakota is a really cool place," Danny assured them.

"It's in North Dakota," said Hal. "Therefore, not cool."

"North Dakota's having a huge economic boom because of the Parshall Oil Field," said Danny. "Lowest unemployment in the U.S., per capita gross domestic product a third higher than the rest of the country."

"What Danny's saying," said Laurette, "is that when we graduate, anybody who isn't going to college should head to North Dakota."

"They have colleges in North Dakota," said Wheeler. And then, "Don't they?"

"Missing the point, Wheeler," said Laurette.

"It's fine for you smart people who get good grades," said Xena. "All I have is hair and cleavage."

"Plenty of employment opportunities," said Hal. "In fact, *infinite* employment opportunities."

"Not funny," said Sin.

And it finally dawned on Danny that maybe high school friendships weren't necessarily a lifetime choice. "Can't we both take the GED?" asked Pat. "I don't know if I'm going to care about high school this year."

"Let's decide after a few more weeks," said Danny. "We just did some really important things. But we're human—it will stop feeling all that important and then we'll go back to caring about stupid stuff."

"That's so . . . encouraging," said Pat. "What about getting married?"

"Eventually," said Danny. "Maybe soon. But this isn't the week to decide, because marriage and having kids, that's the only thing that feels as important as killing Set and liberating the Sutahites."

"I hate it when you're sensible," said Pat. "I want to always be the sensible one."

"That means you always have to be sensible," said Danny.

"No, it just means I always have to be more sensible than you."

The visits to the Families went reasonably well, meaning that none of them had any idea about Set or the Sutahites, and all they cared about was Great Gates and what the Norths were going to do now that they had control of America's whole war machine. "We have no choice but to go for China," several of them insisted.

Danny didn't bother arguing with them. As he told Pat, "They don't speak Chinese *and* they're idiots."

"So you're saying they should only try to take power in a democracy, where those are regarded as qualifications."

Stone and the Silvermans *did* understand what they had accomplished, but they refused to offer any advice. "We can't undo the fact that all the Families and all the Orphans that we know about went through a Great Gate," said Stone. "Most people aren't aware yet that there's been a massive power shift, but the stories of great mages are spreading."

"Nothing in the grocery store tabloids," said Leslie.

"Which means that they actually *do* have standards of credibility," said Marion. "Who knew?"

"Maybe if we leaked it to them that we Mithermages are all aliens from another world," said Leslie.

"That would do it," said Stone. "So please don't."

Finally, it came down to a summit meeting of all the mages who could go anywhere, with or without gates. The same group that had gathered by the oak at Persimmon Knob. Only this time, they met in a clearing in Westil, with Ced and a half-dozen treemages watching and listening.

And it was Ced who offered the first serious proposal. "Look, I'm the one who screwed up big time when I first got here," he said. "But here's the thing. Everywhere I went, trying to make up for the destruction my tornados caused, everybody already understood that a windmage had done it. They couldn't *prevent* what I did, and it shocked them that I would come and try to help clean up the damage. But they knew about magery. They knew about affinities, they watch their children to see if they have some kind of potential."

"Doesn't work that way in Mittlegard," said Danny. "They believe it if and only if they see it, like what my parents did with choppers and tanks. But then they treat them like irresistible . . . superheroes. Or supervillains. Like Zod in *Superman*."

"*Superman Two*," said Pat. Then she waved her hand to erase the comment. Nobody cared about a movie from 1980. Nobody had *seen* the movie except her and Danny, and he watched it only because Hal and Wheeler made them all watch every superhero movie.

"Marion and I don't watch comic book movies, dear," said Leslie. "But we get the point. Having really powerful mages pop up all over Mittlegard is extremely disruptive, but everybody in Westil knows what's going on."

"We already know that we've got to keep American military hardware out of Westil," said Danny. "But Ced, I think you're right. The Mithermages have to come home to Westil."

"It isn't home," said Stone. "We've lived on Earth for fifteen centuries."

"More to the point, we're used to indoor plumbing," said Marion.

"Drowther inventions," said Danny. "I'm sure Gyish and Zog will *prefer* whatever they do with pee and poo here."

"Gyish and Zog think people should worship their pee and poo," said Marion. "And there are bound to be mages just as arrogant in all the other Families."

"With the power they have, they'll all become arrogant," said Danny. "It's like doctors. They don't have any magic, of course, but people believe they have powers. Healing powers. So people treat them like gods, and a lot of doctors get sucked into the mystique and start *acting* like gods. It makes them bad doctors and it makes them bad people. Same with politicians. Bureaucrats. Rich people. It's human nature. If people treat you like an alpha, you think you *are* an alpha, and other people's feelings and choices don't matter."

"So let me see if I get what you're suggesting," said Loki. "You want to protect Mittlegard from arrogant people who think their power gives them the right to decide for other people, without consulting them."

"Irony noted," said Danny. "But we're gathered here because this is the group that controls access between the worlds, and because we have the power to move people from one world to the other and make them stay there."

"And therefore we have the *right* to choose."

"No," said Danny. "We got manipulated into letting them all go through Great Gates. It was a mistake, and we knew it. What we're deciding is how to undo it. How to protect drowthers from people who have way too much power."

"Like us," said Loki.

"You can go back to stealing gates from every gatemage who's ever born," said Danny. "Once we've sorted things out."

"I'm not going back into the tree," said Loki.

"Look," said Pat, "it's not our job to sort this out for all time. We're only responsible for the time we live in, which is now. And here's the thing. If we decide to move all the Families, all the Great Gate mages, to Westil, and then we realize it was a terrible mistake, we can put them back where they were."

"Where do *we* go?" asked Enopp.

Anonoei laughed. "Darling, we can go anywhere we want."

"That's the big hole in all these plans," said Danny. "We're like Congress. We make huge decisions that wreck things for everybody else, but then we exempt ourselves."

"Nobody can force us to go anywhere or stay anywhere," said Eluik. "But apart from that, and healing people, we don't have all that much power. We do transportation and healing."

"We're like emergency medical technicians," said Enopp.

"We can do harm," said Pat.

"But *this* group," said Danny, "I think we're all decent people. Anonoei, Eluik, Enopp, you *know* just how terrible a gatemage's powers can be. Will you ever do something like that to somebody else?"

"We *can't* do it," said Anonoei. "We don't make gates, we just *go*."

"I'm going to be a gatemage," said Enopp. "I think I already am one."

"So here's how it works," said Danny. "We use our own power to visit back and forth between worlds as often as we like. But we don't hurt anybody, and we don't show off. Nobody knows there are still gatemages on either world. And if Enopp grows up to be an asshole, the Gate Thief takes away his gates."

"Not if I take his first," said Enopp.

"Not if I take yours *now*," said Loki.

"Whatever kind of mage you grow up to be," said Pat, "there's nobody here with even a visible fraction of Danny's outself. And Danny won't tolerate anyone using their powers to hurt . . . regular people."

Danny buried his face in his hands. "I don't want to be boss of the world."

"Too late," said Anonoei. "But you're doing fine, and nobody here wants you to stop."

"Except me," said Danny.

"Let's meet here every year or so," said Anonoei. "So we can size each other up. See how things are going."

"There's another danger," said Pat. "I'm not a gatemage, and neither are Anonoei and Eluik, but we learned how to do this direct movement of our ka. I learned it in Duat, without even realizing it, and Anonoei learned it from Danny getting Bexoi out of her body, and Eluik learned it when I helped him and Enopp disentangle. But Hermia and Veevee learned it just by watching."

"We were already gatemages," said Veevee.

"But Eluik wasn't, and I wasn't, and Anonoei wasn't."

"You're saying that there's a danger of this kind of magery propagating," said Danny.

"We don't teach it just by *using* it," said Eluik. "And if we use it when nobody else is watching, then it *can't* spread."

"We have to promise to be careful," said Anonoei. "Beyond that, what can we do?"

"So we'll remain in both worlds," said Loki. "Watching to see what happens. But all the other mages get moved to Westil."

"With or without giving them time to pack?" asked Pat.

"Can't give them any kind of notice," said Veevee, "or they'll go into hiding, some of them, anyway."

"Huge imbalance," Ced commented, raising his hands to get them to stop. "All the mages from Mittlegard will have passed through a Great Gate several times, and *none* of the mages from Westil."

That left them silent for a while.

"If we just plunk them down here in Westil," said Pat, finally, "they have to have superior power just to survive. People will have to treat them with respect for a while. Make a place for them."

"I'll be here," said Loki. "If it turns out the Mittlegardians are too powerful, I can select a few Westilian mages to pass through a Great Gate, as a counterbalance."

"You?" asked Danny. "The Gate Thief, making a Great Gate?"

"A tightly locked Great Gate, which nobody else can find except another gatemage," said Loki.

"So how do we do it?" asked Pat. "We don't know where every member of every one of the Families is."

"We invite them all to pass through a gate," said Anonoei. "Children included. *Babies* included. Everybody. We just don't mention that we won't be bringing them back."

"And if somebody hides out," said Danny, "then the moment they surface and start maging around in Mittlegard, I gate them here."

"Permanent policeman of the world," said Veevee.

"Somebody's got to do it," said Danny.

"Oh, I wasn't arguing against it. It just occurred to me that all those years I *wished* for gatemagery, I never thought it would turn me into a cop."

"Think of yourself as the angel with a fiery sword," said Danny. "Standing outside the garden of Eden, telling Adam and Eve not to even *try* to get back in."

"I'm not sure which I like most," said Veevee. "Angel or fiery sword."

"When do we do this?" asked Pat.

"It's morning here," said Loki, "so I'm ready to put in a full day."

"Nobody knows you," said Eluik. "I mean, in Mittlegard."

"Nobody knows me anywhere but in Iceway," said Loki. "But when I magically appear in front of them, they'll recognize my authority."

"It's early afternoon for Pat and me," said Danny, "but we can put in the rest of the day doing this."

It ended up taking a couple of weeks, because the Families were pretty spread out, looking out for their business interests. The only ones who suspected anything were Danny's own parents.

"We knew Loki was against our taking armaments to Westil," said Mother. "But I think it was you that brought our tanks and chopper back."

"And all their crews and pilots," said Danny. "When they invent explosives on their own, *then* they can fire projectile weapons at each other."

Mother and Father looked at each other. "You're going to send us there, aren't you," said Father.

"I am," said Danny. "And I'll do it right this second, unless you can convince me that you won't tip my hand to the rest of the Family."

"You'd just gather us all up anyway," said Mother. "All we'd accomplish is making it take longer."

Danny shrugged. "I might miss somebody. I don't carry a perfect census of the Family in my head. And Thor had roamers, didn't he? Family members who never came home."

"We can ask him," said Father.

"I've had a chance to see a lot more of Westil than a grassy hill with standing stones," said Mother. "You aren't exactly punishing us."

"No running water. No airplanes. No sewers."

"But you forget," said Father. "We specialized in drowther machines. I don't know how long we'll have to be without the modern amenities."

"Better plumbing than tanks," said Danny. "But don't count on finding fossil fuels. I have no idea if Westil had a carboniferous period."

"I guess we'll find out," said Father. "But I think we proved that we're not reliant on fossil fuels."

"I hope," said Danny, "that you give the drowthers a better life, the way their scientists and engineers and doctors gave a better life to *us*."

"And you don't want us to improve their weapons," said Mother.

"Arrows and swords cause plenty of damage," said Danny.

"Especially without a gatemage to heal them," said Father. "That choice was *yours*."

Danny listened to that. When he left the Families stranded in different parts of Westil, he gave each Family a half-dozen healing tokens—gates that would move a person a fraction of an inch whenever they were touched by the face of the amulet. He also gave Loki dozens of them to pass out among the Westilians—mages and drowthers alike.

"I think I need to learn how to make more like this," said Loki.

"Knock yourself out," said Danny.

Anonoei brought her sons home, but they returned to Ohio and Kentucky whenever they wanted, because nobody could stop them anyway. As Leslie joked, "It's not like we can send them to their rooms for a timeout when they're naughty."

"Then again," said Marion, "they're never naughty."

"And that's what should worry you the most," said Veevee.

By the time all the mages were transferred to Westil, it was time for school to start in Buena Vista, Virginia.

"You were right," said Pat. "I still want to marry you. But maybe we finish high school first. Do it at a more regular time."

"I don't know if I can keep my hands off you that long," said Danny.

"Why should you be the only boyfriend in an American high school who keeps his hands to himself?" asked Pat.

"Because I already have one son," he said.

Danny hadn't admitted paternity to anyone, but he kept a gate attached to the boy, so he could see everything he was doing, everything that happened around him. He called it his baby monitor. Nicki Lieder didn't know it, but she wouldn't have to worry about childhood diseases or accidents. Nothing was going to go wrong in her baby's life.

And Coach Lieder was so glad that his daughter was alive that he got over his fury that she got pregnant; and Lieder naturally fell in love with the little boy, whom she named after him. "Because you're the only grandfather he'll ever know," Nicki told him, and there was a definite opinion at Parry McCluer that Coach Lieder had somehow become a human being since his grandson was born.

Danny ran track. He won a lot. He also lost sometimes.

Pat and Danny did well in school, but they did it by studying, not by using gates to pass information to each other. "What's the point of cheating on a test?" Pat asked, when Xena suggested it. "If you learn it, then you know it, and you pass the test. If you pass the test without knowing the stuff, then the only person you've cheated is yourself." Xena wanted to call Pat a complete selfish bitch for that policy—in fact, she *did* call her that, one time, but Laurette and Sin sided with Pat and then Pat helped Xena study.

Danny's studying consisted of brushing up on things he had learned during his homeschool days. He also became very good at *Super Smash Bros.* on Sin's Wii and *League of Legends* with anybody who would let him on their team, provoking both despair and admiration among the geek elite at Parry McCluer. But, as with running, he didn't win *every* time.

Stone kept discovering Orphans from time to time, but because they weren't receiving any training, only a couple of them reached a level of power where they needed to be given a choice: Play nice with the drowthers, or find yourself on Westil. Everybody decided to play nice, so far.

Danny and Pat went to all the proms, wearing clothing Vee-vee chose for them. They walked at graduation, and they were both happy that Danny got a huge ovation from the other students, and Pat got far less—but heard some heartfelt whoops from her real friends.

And a week after graduation, Pat's parents put on an affordable wedding for them at St. John's United Methodist in Buena Vista—Pat, determined not to be a bridezilla, put her foot down whenever anyone proposed something extravagant. But she couldn't prevent Danny from giving her an absolutely amazing, yet perfectly tasteful, ring.

"You didn't *borrow* this from some jewelry store, right?" she asked.

"I understand that you had to ask," said Danny, "but no. I had it made for you by a metalmage in Westil. He was very proud of his work, and it's not like he needed a lot of money for it, since he can draw gold up out of the earth whenever he wants."

"So how *did* you pay him?" she asked.

"A couple of amulets of healing," said Danny. "The ring was easy for him, the amulet was easy for me. But a fair exchange, for a man still raising stupid, reckless children."

"You got to know his kids?"

"All children are stupid and reckless. Just . . . some more than others."

And then they set about producing some stupid, reckless children of their own, while keeping track of their friends and making new ones and then doing a fairly lazy job of working their way through college while pursuing their real career, which was to try and make each other and their children amazingly happy every day of their lives.

10 – 15